# MASKS OF THE OUTCASTS

## BAEN BOOKS by ANDRE NORTON

# MASKS OF THE OUTCASTS

# ANDRE NORTON

# Masks of the Outcasts

A Baen Books Original

Baen Publishing Enterprises
P.O. Box 1403
Riverdale, NY 10471


ISBN 13: 978-1-4165-0901-1
ISBN 10: 1-4165-0901-1

Cover art by Bob Eggleton

Distributed by Simon & Schuster
1230 Avenue of the Americas
New York, NY 10020


Production & design by Windhaven Press, Auburn, NH
Printed in the United States of America

# CONTENTS

# Catseye

# ONE

Tikil was really three cities loosely bound together, two properly recognized on the maps of Korwar's northern continent, the third a sore—rather than a scar—of war, still unhealed. To the north and west Tikil was an exotic bloom on a planet that had harbored wealth almost from the year of its first settlement. To the east, fronting on the spaceport, was the part of Tikil in which lay the warehouses, shops, and establishments of the thousands of businesses necessary for the smooth running of a pleasure city, this exotic bloom where three-quarters of the elite of a galactic sector gathered to indulge their whims and play.

To the south was the Dipple, a collection of utilitarian, stark, unattractive housing. To live there was a badge of inferiority. A man from the Dipple had three choices for a cloudy future. He could try to exist without subcitizenship and a work permit, haunting the Casual Labor Center to compete with too many of his fellows for the very limited crumbs of employment; he could somehow raise the stiff entrance fee and buy his way into the strictly illegal but flourishing and perilous Thieves' Guild; or he could sign on as contract labor and be shipped off world in deep freeze with no beforehand knowledge of his destination or work.

The War of the Two Sectors had been fought to a stalemate

five years ago. Afterwards, the two leading powers had shared out
the spoils—"spheres of influence." Several major and once richer
planets had to be written off entirely, since worlds reduced to
cinders on which no human being dared land were not attractive property. But a fringe of frontier worlds had passed into the
grasp of one or the other of the major powers—the Confederation
or the Council. As a result, the citizens of several small nations
suddenly found themselves homeless.

At the outbreak of the war ten years earlier, there had been
forced evacuations from such frontier worlds; pioneers had been
removed from their lands so that military outposts and masked
solar batteries could be placed in their stead. In this fashion, the
Dipple had been set up on Korwar, far back from the fighting
line. During the first fervor of patriotism the Dipple dwellers met
with good will. But later, when their home worlds were ruined or
traded away across the conference tables, there was resentment,
and on some planets there were organized moves to get rid of
these rootless inhabitants.

Now, before dawn in Tikil, men from the Dipple leaned their
bowed shoulders against the outer wall of the Casual Labor Center or squatted on their heels before the door that marked the
meeting place between the haves and the havenots.

Troy Horan watched the pale gold in the morning sky deepen.
Too late to mark stars now. He tried to remember the sky over
Norden—and had again one of those sharp picture flashes of
recollection.

A silver bowl arching above a waving plain of grass, grass
that was pale green, mauve, and silver all at once, changing as
the wind rippled it. He knew the warmth of a sun always half
veiled in rainbow haze, felt the play of muscles as the animal he
perched upon as a small boy, rather than bestrode, broke into
a rocking canter. That was one of his last memories of Norden.
They had been out "riding track," cutting a wide circle about the
grazing herd of tupan to check that none of the animals had
drifted toward the quicksands near the river.

It had been that same morning that the Council ships had cut
out of the sky, burning portions of the plain to charred earth and
slag with their tailbursts. Within three days Troy and his people

had left Norden for Korwar—three Horans, a small clan among all the others. But not three for long. His father—big body, laughing voice, quiet steady eyes, a pair of hands that did everything well, a man who was able to establish a strange bond of sympathy with any animal—had put on a trooper's tunic and vanished into the maw of a transport. Lang Horan had not returned.

After that the Big Cough had hit the Dipple, leaving only Troy Horan, a lanky adolescent who inherited skills and desires for which there was no need on Korwar. He also possessed a stubborn, almost fierce independence, which had so far kept him either from signing on as contract labor or from the temptation offered by the Guild. Troy Horan was a loner; he did not take orders well. And since his mother's death, he had no close attachments in the Dipple. There were few left there now who had come from Norden. The men had volunteered as troopers, and, for some reason, their families had been particularly susceptible to the Cough.

The door that was their gate to the day's future slid back. Men stood away from the wall, got up. Mechanically Troy made a brushing gesture down the length of his thin torso, though nothing would restore a vestige of trimness to his clothing.

Spacer's breeches, fifth-hand, clean enough but with their sky blue now a neutral, dusty gray; spacer's boots, a little wide for his narrow feet, the magnetic insets clicking as he walked; an upper tunic that was hardly more than a sleeveless jerkin, all in contrast to the single piece of his old life that he wore pulled tight about his flat middle. That wide belt of a Norden rider was well oiled, every one of its silver studs polished and free of tarnish. Those studs formed a design that was Troy's only heritage. If he ever rode the grass plains again, with tupan galloping ahead—well, those tupan might bear that same pattern on their cream-white hides. Lang Horan had been Range Master and Brand Owner.

Because he was young, tough, and stubborn, Troy was well to the fore of the line at the mechanical assigner. He watched with alert jealousy as three men ahead ran toward the stamper, assured of work—the mark on their wrists giving them the freedom of the city, if only for a day. Then he was facing that featureless, impersonal mike himself.

"Horan, class two, Norden, lawful work—" The same old formula he uttered there day after day. He stood, his feet a little apart, balancing as if the machine were an opponent ready for battle. Under his breath he counted five quickly, and a tiny hope was born. Since he had not been rejected at once, the assigner *did* have some request that might be matched by his meager qualifications.

The five he had counted doubled into ten before the assignor asked a question: "Knowledge of animals?"

"That of a Norden herd rider—" Troy stretched the truth to a very thin band, but his small hope was growing fast.

The assigner meditated. Troy, through his excitement, felt the impatience of the men behind him. Yet the length of time the machine was taking was so promising—

"Employed." Troy gave a small gasp of relief. "Time of employment—indefinite. Employer—Kossi Kyger, first level, Sixth Square. Report there at once."

The plates in his boot soles beat a rhythm as he hurried to the stamper, thrust his hand into the slot, and felt that instant of heat that set the work mark on his tanned wrist.

"First level, Sixth Square," he repeated aloud, not because it was so necessary to impress his memory, but for the pure pleasure of being able to claim a work address.

Sixth Square lay on the outer fringe of the business district, which meant that Kyger was engaged in one of the upper-bracket luxury trades. Rather surprising that such a merchant would have need for a C.L.C. hireling. The maintenance force and highly trained salesmen of those shops were usually of the full-citizen class. And why animals? Horan swung on one of the fast-moving roll walks, his temporarily tattooed wrist held in plain sight across his wide belt to prevent questions from any patroller.

Because it was early, the roll walks were not crowded, and few private flitters held the air lanes overhead. Most of the shutters were still in place across the display fronts of the shops. It would be midday before the tourists from the pleasure hotels and the shoppers from the villas would move into town. On Korwar, shopping was a fashionable form of amusement, and the treasures of half the galaxy were pouring into Tikil, the result of stepped-up production after the war.

Troy changed to another roll walk. The farther westward he went, the more conspicuous he became. Not that clothing was standardized here, but the material, no matter how fantastically cut and pieced together, was always rich. And the elaborate hair arrangements of the men who shared the roller with Troy, their jeweled wristbands, neck chains, and citizens' belt knives, took on a uniformity in which his own close-cropped yellow hair, his weaponless belt, his too-thin, fine-boned face were very noticeable. Twice a patroller stirred at a check point and then relaxed again at the sight of the stamp on the boy's bony wrist.

Sixth Square was one of the areas of carefully tended vegetation intended by the city planners to break the structure pattern of the district. Troy jumped from the roller and went to the map on a side pillar.

"Kyger," he said into the mike.

"Kyger's," the finder announced. "Gentle Homos, Gentle Fems—visit Kyger's, where the living treasures of a thousand worlds are paraded before you! See and hear the Lumian talking fish, the dofuld, the priceless Phaxian change-coat—the only one of its kind known to be in captivity alive. Follow the light, Gentle Homo, Gentle Fem, to Kyger's—merchant dealer in extraordinary pets!"

A small spark, which had glowed into life on the wall below the map, loosed itself and now danced through the air ahead, blinking with a gem flash. A pet shop! The inquiry about animal knowledge was now explained. But Troy lost some of his zest. The thin story he had told the assigner was now thinner, to the point of being full of holes. He was ten years out of Norden, ten years away from any contact with animals at all. Yet Troy clung to one hope. The assigner had sent him, and the machine was supposed to be always right in its selection.

He looked about him. The massed foliage of the center square was a riot of luxuriant vegetation, which combined plants and shrubs from half-a-dozen worlds into a pattern of growing—red-green, yellow-green, blue-green, silver—And he began to long with every fiber of his semistarved body that he would be the one Kyger wanted, even for just one day.

His spark guide danced up and down, as if to center his attention on the doorway before which it had paused, and then snuffed out. Troy faced Kyger's display and drew a deep breath of wonder, for he seemed to be staring at four different landscapes, each occupying one-quarter of the space. And each landscape was skillfully contrived so that a section of an outlandish planet had been transported in miniature. In each, small creatures moved about the business of living and dying. It was all art tri-dee, of course, but the workmanship was superb and would completely enthrall any prospective customer.

Reluctantly Troy approached the door itself, a barrier where plexaglass had been impressed with a startling and vivid pattern of weird and colorful insects, none of which he recognized. There was no sign that the establishment was open for business, and he had no guide to lead him behind the mass of buildings to a rear entrance. Troy hesitated uncertainly before the closed door until, among the imprisoned creatures of the center panel, a portion of face with reasonable human features appeared. Round dark eyes set in yellow skin regarded him with no trace of interest or emotion.

Troy held up his wrist so that the employment mark might be fully visible to those eyes. Unblinkingly they centered upon it. Then the stretch of yellow cheek, the broad nose, vanished. The creatures in the panel seemed to flutter as that barrier arose. And a flow of warm air, redolent with many strange smells, engulfed Troy. As if drawn by an invisible cord, he entered Kyger's.

He was given no time to look about the outer reception lounge with its wall cabinets of more miniature other-world scenes, for the owner of the eyes was awaiting him impatiently. Used as he was to oddities, human, humanoid, and nonhuman, Troy still found the small man strange enough to study covertly. He could have walked under Koran's out-stretched arm but his small, wiry body was well proportioned and not that of a dwarf. What hair he had was black and grew in small tufted knobs tight to the rounded bowl of the skull. In addition, there was a rough brush of the same black on his upper lip and two tufts or knots on his chin, one just below the center of his lower lip and the other on the point of the jaw beneath.

His clothing was the conventional one-piece suit of an employed subcitizen, with the striking addition of a pair of boots clinging tightly to his thin legs and extending knee-high, fashioned of reptile skin as soft as glove leather, giving off tiny prismatic sparks with every movement of their wearer. About a slight pot-belly he had a belt of the same hide, and the knife that swung from it was not only longer but also wider than those usually worn in Tikil.

"Come—" His voice was guttural. A crook of finger pointed the way, and Troy followed him through two more showrooms into a passage from which opened a number of screened doors. Now the effluvium of animal—a great many animals—was strong, and sounds from each of the screened doors they passed testified to the stock Kyger kept on hand. Troy's guide continued to the end of the hall, set his small hand into the larger impression of a palm lock, and then stood aside for Horan to enter.

If the yellow man was an oddity, the man who sat waiting for Troy to cross his office was almost as great a surprise. Horan had seen many of the merchants of Tikil, and all of them had been glittering objects indeed. Their jewels, their ultrafashion-able dress, their eyecatching coiffures had all been designed as advertisements to attract general attention.

But Kyger, if this was Kyger, was no such starburst. His muscular body was covered with a hora-silk half tunic and kilt, but the color was a dark and sober blue, and he wore no jewels at all. On his right wrist was the broad service bracelet of a veteran spacer with at least two constellations starring its sweep, while his skull was completely shaven as if to accommodate the helmet of a scout-ship man. The bareness of that deeply tanned stretch of skin made the red, puckered scar down along his right ear the more noticeable. Troy wondered fleetingly why he chose to keep that disfiguring brand; plastic surgery could have erased it completely.

The other regarded Troy for a long moment, his stare both as aloof and as searching as that the yellow man had used through the door panel.

"The assigner reported you as Norden," he remarked, but gave the planet name a slight accent new to Troy. "I would rather have thought Midgard—"

Troy met him eye to eye. This man had a spacer's knowledge of racial types and other worlds right enough.

"I was born on Norden—"

The other might not have heard him. "Midgard—or even Terra—"

Troy flushed. "Norden," he repeated firmly. Lang Horan's father had been from Midgard, right enough. Before that—well, who traced any planet-pioneering family back through generations and star systems to the first hop?

"Norden. And you think that you know something about animals." Those gray eyes, cold as space between far-flung suns, dropped from Troy's face to the belt with its lovingly polished silver studs. "Range Master, eh?"

Troy refused to be drawn. He shrugged, not knowing why the other was trying to bait him. Everyone knew that Norden had been handed over to the Confederation, that none of her former inhabitants could hope to return to her plains.

"All right. If the assigner sent you, you're the best it could find." Kyger arose from the enveloping embrace of his eazi-rest. The yellow man slipped to his side. "Zul will give you your orders. We are expecting a shipment in on the Chasgar. You'll go to the dock with Zul and do just as he tells you—no more, certainly no less. Understand?" There was a flick of razor-sharp whip in that. Troy nodded.

Zul was certainly not a talkative companion. He merely beckoned Troy out through another door into a courtyard. This, too, was sided with pens and cages, but Troy was given no time to inspect their inhabitants. Zul waved him to a waiting flitter. As Troy took his place in the foreseat, the small man reached for the controls and they lifted with practiced ease to the air lanes. Zul circled, then headed them toward the west and the spaceport.

There was more traffic aloft now, personal flitters, heavier vans, and small flyers such as their own. Zul slipped through the lanes with a maximum of speed and a minimum of effort, bringing them down without a jar on the landing strip behind the receiver station. Again a jerk of thumb served to bring Troy, trailing his guide, into one of the many entrances of the clearance section.

His small companion was well known here, for he bypassed two barriers without explanation, their guardians waving him on.

"Kyger's." Zul spoke at last, putting a claim disk down before the man in charge of the third grill.

"Right section, third block—"

Now they were in a corridor with a wall on one side, a series of bins, room size, on the other, each well filled with shipping crates, bales, and containers. There were men hauling these in and out, which testified that the contents of the packages in this particular section were too precious to be left to the mechanical transportation of the port robots.

Zul located the proper bin room and dropped his disk into the release frame at the door. The protecting mesh rolled up, and a light flashed on above two crates and a large, well-padded travel cage. All three packages were bulky, and Zul, fists on hips, eyed them closely before he said over his shoulder, "Get a truck."

Troy went back up the corridor to claim one of the motored platforms. He was wriggling that out of a line of its fellows when he caught a half glimpse of a face, a familiar face. As he jumped on the platform, dug his boot toe into the activating button, and headed the vehicle down the line, he wondered just what would happen if he shouted out that a newly accepted member of the Thieves' Guild was working here, in the very center of the supposedly best-protected treasure-transhipping center on Korwar. Every man who entered this building had been scanned by the psycho-check at the door, and everyone not on legitimate business would have been unmasked by that latest weapon in the armory of the patrollers. Yet Troy was certain he had seen Julnuk Varms shifting a crate, and he knew for a fact that Varms had crossed the line into the apprenticeship ranks of the Guild.

The platform rolled to a stop before Zul, and they went to work shifting their cargo to its surface. Each piece was heavy enough to require the combined efforts of the mismatched workers, and Troy wiped his hand across his face as the second settled into place. He eyed the curtains covering the sides of the cage, wondering just what kind of exotic creature cowered within.

Cowered? That was the wrong word. The inmate of that cage

was curious, interested, alertly eager—not in any way cowed. Inmate? Inmates—two of them—

Troy stood very still, staring at the closely curtained transport cage. How did he know that?

Interest—now increasing—Something touched him, not physically, but as if a very soft, inquiring paw had been drawn lightly along his arm to test the quality of his skin, the strength of his muscles, the toughness of the bone beneath that covering. Just so did he feel that something had very lightly touched what was his inner self in exploration. Touched—and flashed instantly away—so that the sensation was cut off almost the same moment that he was aware of it. Troy helped Zul boost the cage onto the platform. There was no feeling of movement from within—nothing at all. Had there ever been?

# TWO

The cage was stowed with extra care just behind the driver's seat in the flitter, and during the transfer from warehouse to flyer there had been not the slightest sound from its interior. Yet twice more Troy had been aware of those paw taps of exploration, touches that were gone the instant he was alert to them. He was thinking hard as he left Zul in the flitter and went to return the platform. The other had shown no signs of surprise or interest in the cage. Did Zul find those subtle inquiries ordinary—or did he not feel them at all? What kind or species of animal traveled in that container?

Native life on a thousand worlds was now known to spacers, explorer scouts, pioneers. And Troy had heard tales told in the Dipple by men gathered from planets in a wide sector of the galaxy. Yet never before had there been any suggestion that a form of life existed that was able to contact men mentally. Mentally!

Troy paused. Mentally! So—that was it! He had put a name to that elusive touch. But—

He did not know that his eyes had narrowed, that his fingers were drumming a faint tattoo on his belt. This was something to consider by himself. Out of the far past an emotion other than surprise awoke, sent a warning through him. Look, listen, and keep one's thoughts to oneself—the law of survival.

Troy swung around so suddenly that he caught the slight movement of a man he must have startled into that tiny betrayal. Varms stood just outside, his elbow resting on a pile of boxes, obviously waiting for orders. Yet he had been watching Troy, just as he was so patently not watching him now. Did Varms expect Horan to spark a patroller? He knew the inner laws of the Dipple better than that. As long as Varms made no move toward looting Kyger's, where Troy's loyalty was temporarily pledged, Horan would not reveal any knowledge of him.

He walked past Varms without a sign, heading toward the flitter. It was only chance that dictated the next warning. A porter was wrangling with one of the bin attendants, and they now carried their quarrel to the section manager. Since the object of their dispute was large, they were hot-tonguing it, not in the inner office but outside in the corridor. A length of crystal mirror, bright and backed with red-gold, bore a disfiguring crack down its side.

That crack might distort a reflection, but it could not conceal it. And in that patch of mirror Troy caught a glimpse of a tailer—Varms! The interest a new recruit of the Guild might have in a C.L. from the Dipple was negligible, but in a cargo—that was a different matter. And Varms, clumsy and inept as he was, might well be after the contents of the cage—or of the two crates that accompanied it.

Troy came out into the brightness of the flitter park. There were rows of waiting vans, very few passenger flyers. A series of two-story patroller towers quartered the whole area. There must be spy rays throughout every lane here. No one had ever dared a highjacking job in this place. And he did not see how he and Zul could be tackled once they were in the air—If they had been on wheel lock, now—

But he discovered that surface travel was just what Zul was intending. The wheels were extended from the body flaps, and the little man edged the vehicle out on ground level.

"What's the idea?" Troy folded his long legs into the cramped quarters beside Zul. "Don't we lift back?"

For the first time those wide lips split in something approaching a grin.

"No, no lift back." The other mimicked his tone. "We carry those who must ride easy."

Not much of an explanation, Troy thought. If the occupants of the cage had managed to survive passage in a space freighter, they certainly could take very easily a short air flight back to Sixth Square. He had something other to chew on also—that move by Varms. Taken together with this action of Zul's, it began to make sense. Could the yellow man and the novice thief have rigged a highjack between them, with himself set up to pin the blame upon?

Troy dismissed that thought. Too many loose ends. He was not driving; Zul was. He could prove that he had had no connection with Kyger's before this morning, knew nothing of any cargo that was coming in for the shop. And somehow he was certain Zul was not planning any double cross of his employer—in spite of Varms. But there had to be a reason, other than the one he had been given, for this ground-level progress.

It was not a straight-line progress either, he noted. Troy knew the warehouse section of Tikil well enough to be certain with every block they passed that Zul was taking a round-about way. Why? A sidelong glance at the other's closed face argued that this was another question Zul was not going to answer.

Troy settled back as far as he could in a seat adjusted to Zul's comfort, not his own, and waited for further enlightenment. Once more he was conscious of activity in the cage, mental activity. It was no longer directed toward him, but at their surroundings. Troy's breath caught in a tiny gasp as he realized—picking impressions and hints out of those vague, strange currents—that the occupants of the cage were engrossed in studying their new surroundings. Yet how could they see through the thickly padded covering of the cage—unless that covering was not what it seemed to superficial examination?

He would have given a great deal at that moment to be able to turn and sweep the covering to the floor of the flitter, to see the unseen. A great deal, but not today's employment. Troy was very sure that such a move on his part would see Zul's summoning of the nearest patroller, his own ignominious and disastrous return to the Dipple. Curiosity was not spur enough to risk that.

They made two more unnecessary turns. There were other flitters wheeling—usually private jobs delivering passengers to the buildings, so Zul's method of progress was in no way extraordinary. But Troy's attention went now to the visa-screen above the controls. He watched for Varms—was the other still trailing?

He could pick out no following flitter that seemed suspicious. But Troy would be the first to admit that he could not match skills with any of the Guild. For all he knew, every one of those flyers and the men and women in them could be part of some fantastic scheme to loot the one in which he was traveling. Should he warn Zul?

The latter was driving at a rate well within the safety regulations of ground level. A portion of vulnerable skin and muscles between Troy's shoulders began to itch as the feeling of expectancy built up inside him. And his growing distrust was shared by those in the cage. Their interest had changed to a desire to warn—or alert—

Troy opened his mouth to speak. A yowling wail burst from the cage, loud enough to drown out any spoken word. Zul's head jerked up. The yowl sank into silence but Troy caught the message—danger was coming, and fast. His hand shot out, fingers fumbling with the catch of the arms locker. But his thumb pressure could not unlock it.

Zul sent the flitter into a burst of speed, which tore them out of the mouth of an avenue into one of the circles of space surrounded by the first ring of shops. With an expert's skill the small man wove a devious pattern among the other flitters there. Troy, tense, kept his attention divided between the path ahead and the near misses Zul guided them through. There had been no further outburst from the cage. But he did not need the wave of expectation issuing from there to warn him of trouble yet to come.

They might have made it free and clear had not Zul miscalculated, or been outplayed, by inches. Troy was slammed against the arms locker, his raised arm protecting his head, as the flitter smashed into an ornamental standard, edged into that to avoid the forward ram of another flyer.

The shock of his impact must have sprung the lock on the

arms compartment. As Troy pushed back from it, the panel gaped and he grabbed the butt of a stunner inside. The arm that had taken the shock of his weight was numb, hanging heavy from his shoulder, but the other was all right and his fingers curled hungrily about the weapon.

On Zul's left the door had burst open, spilling the little man into the street. He was already dragging himself up, blood pouring from a cut over one eye. When he tried to stand, he gave a grunt and reeled back against the flitter, apparently unable to rest his weight on his right ankle.

Troy sent his shoulder against the door on his own side, went out and down in a roll, the stunner in his hand and ready. He was sure he was going to face some aggressor more dangerous than any indignant flitter owner Zul might have scraped. As he brought up against the twin of the pillar they had crashed, he saw Zul draw his knife and a man leap with the ease of a trained street fighter from between two parked flitters.

There were pedestrians, a crowd of them, gathering. But until they knew that this was not some private challenge-fight, none would call a patroller. By drawing his belt knife instead of trying for a stunner, Zul had labeled this a meeting-of-honor, unorthodox as its setting might be. And had not Troy been warned, he might have hesitated to come to the other's assistance.

His numbed arm bothered him, and he rested the barrel of the stunner on his knees to take aim against the attacker. Knife blades flashed in the sunlight. Zul, his back braced against the wrecked flitter, was seemingly cornered and on the defensive from the first.

Troy pressed the firing stud of his weapon, remembering the long-ago training by Lang: "Point your barrel as you would your finger, boy. Aim means more than speed."

There was the faint "pssst" from the stunner. The man fronting Zul wavered, slewed partly around, and staggered back, bringing up against one of the parked vehicles, shaking his head dazedly. But the small man he had attacked did not try to follow up the advantage. Troy tapped with his thumb, sending another charge into the stunner.

He was just in time, for again that ear-torturing wail sounded from the interior of the flitter, and the impact of warning reached him full blast. Instinctively he hurled himself to the right. A knife struck the pillar and clattered to the ground.

The man who had hurled it was holding back, but his companion came on, ready for another try, his eyes narrow and calculating. Troy aimed at the other's head, praying he would not be wearing a force screen. The determination of the attack, and the time and place it had been delivered, argued that the Guild men either were after some fabulous loot or had been hired at the high rate, which in turn suggested they would have top equipment.

But Troy never had a chance to discover if his fears were correct. A white coil materialized out of thin air only a foot or so above the head of the advancing knifeman. It whirled in a circle, throwing off, with almost dizzying speed, a web of white filaments that fell about the attacker, touching and then clinging to shoulders, arms, body, and, finally, legs. The man struggled against the enwebment fruitlessly. Within a matter of moments he was down, as well packaged as a spider's prey. And a second web had taken care of his companion.

Troy straightened up, dropped the stunner to the ground well out in view, not having any wish for the patrollers to start in on him. Leaving the weapon where it lay, he went to Zul.

Blood made a gory and devilish mask of the small man's face, and he clung to the swinging door of the wrecked flitter with one hand, as if he needed that support badly. As Troy came to him, the younger man was suddenly aware of the fact that the warnings that had flowed from the cage were at an end; there was no contact with its inhabitants now.

The first patroller took charge. Troy answered questions with the strict truth concerning what he had seen—but he did not mention the unheard warnings. And Zul either could not or would not elaborate on that report. Somewhat to Troy's surprise, Kyger himself stepped out of the second patrol flitter. And his efficiency matched that of the law. Zul was sent off to have his hurts tended before Kyger examined the cage. When Troy helped him swing it out to the pavement, he was brisk.

"No harm done, officer," he informed the patroller. "Apparently it was just an attempted highjack—not that such a theft would have done them any good."

"Why not?" The patroller was a Swatzerkan, his green-tinged skin showing a faint lacing of scales across the backs of his hands as he held a small recorder to catch their answers.

"Because these animals cannot live long without their own imported food and trained care, officer. They are a special order—for the Gentle Fem San duk Var—"

The Swatzerkan did not exactly blink, but perhaps there was a shade more deference in his voice when he replied, "You have indeed been favored by fortune, Merchant, in that your shipment did not fall into the hands of these worms' castings." His eyes touched briefly on the bound, or webbed, prisoners. "It will be your wishing to take these precious creatures to your shop. But one fears that your flitter is beyond the power of rising—"

"An accommodation will serve."

"Ah—so. Mulat, an accommodation for the merchant!"

One of the other patrollers went to the com unit of the official flitter. And for the first time Kyger appeared to really notice Troy.

"You used that?" He nodded toward the stunner still lying by the knife-scored pillar.

"Yes."

"Good enough." Kyger crossed to retrieve the weapon and hand it to the Swatzerkan. "I witness my man used this in defense of my goods," he said, using the formal, responsibility-assuming phrase.

"It is so noted, Merchant."

Troy stared at Kyger. Such a move was made on the behalf of a full-time employee, a subcitizen, not for a day laborer out of the Dipple. Did Kyger mean—?

But this was no time to ask questions. An accommodation flitter set down on the clear oval beyond the pillars, and Troy helped Kyger move the cage and the two crates into it. There was still nothing from the transport box. One could almost imagine that he had dreamed that questing thought process. But Troy's curiosity pricked the more fiercely after the events of the past half hour.

Any pets offered to the wife of Var suk Sark would indeed be the most exotic as well as the most expensive obtainable. Suk Sark was of one of the Fifty Noble Families on Wolf Three. But the Gentle Fem San duk Var was not accepted in that lineage-conscious assemblage. Gossip was undoubtedly correct in ascribing the present residence of the Var household on Korwar to that fact. One could not buy one's way into the Fifty, no matter how limitless was the pile of credits one could dip into. But there were other circles one could impress with one's importance—many such on Korwar.

Troy wondered how suk Sark enjoyed running his autocratic government of the Sweepers from so far away. The Sweepers in the galaxy as a whole were small fry, a collection of six minor solar systems, and they never ventured too far into the conflicts between the real lords of space. But sometimes even such small organizations had moments when their allegiance or enmity could tip the scales of an uneasy balance of power. Suk Sark was only one of the "powers" who, for one reason or another, made Korwar their residence, apart from their official headquarters.

"You have a family in the Dipple?" Kyger's abrupt question broke Troy's line of thought.

"No, Merchant."

"Would you take contract, for a limit of time?"

"With you, Merchant?"

"With me. Zul will be of little use for a while. I will need an extra pair of hands in his place. Who knows?" Kyger glanced at him and then away. "It may lead to something better, Dipple-man."

"I will take contract, Merchant." Troy schooled his voice, hoping his elation was not too apparent. Somehow he did not wish this spacer-turned-merchant to know just how much that offer meant to him.

They lifted from the square of the crash and took the straightest line to the court at the rear of the shop. Troy was told to load the two crates on a runner and put them in the storeroom. Kyger himself remained by the curtained cage once he had returned the accommodation flitter on auto-control to the rental station. So far he made no move to open the cage, and Troy's desire to see what was inside grew.

"Shall I take this also, Merchant?" Troy asked as he returned and brought the runner to a halt beside the cage.

Kyger turned on him once more the searching stare with which he had measured him at their first meeting that morning. Then the shop owner pulled at some hidden fastening. The padded curtains fell away and Troy looked into a very well-appointed traveling box. The flooring, sides, and roof were padded with plastafoam, a precaution against the pressure of ship acceleration, and there were two inset feeding and watering niches. But the occupants were close to the mesh front, sitting on their haunches, their front paws placed neatly together, the tips of their tails folded over those paws.

One was black, a black so deep as to have, in the sunlight, a bluish tinge—or perhaps that was a reflection from its companion's coat, for the second and slightly smaller animal *was* blue—or parts of its close, thick fur coat held that shade, muting into a gray that was very dark on head, legs, and tail. And the four eyes of the pair, regarding both men impartially, were as vividly blue-green as aquamarines.

"Terran," Kyger announced with a note of pride plain in his voice. "Terran cats!"

# THREE

Troy studied the animals. Although those blue eyes regarded him squarely, there was no other contact. Yet he was sure it had not been only his imagination that had stirred him earlier.

Kyger opened the cage. The black cat arose, arched its satin-smooth back, extended forelegs in a luxurious stretch, and then padded out into the courtyard, its blue companion remaining behind while the black scouted with eyes and nose.

"Sooooo—" Kyger subdued his usual authoritative tone into a coaxing murmur and held out his hand for the black to sniff.

Cats were part of the crew of every spaceship. Troy had seen them about the docks. But centuries of such star voyaging must have radically mutated the strain if these were the parent stock. None of those possessed such sleek length of limb, or the sharply pointed muzzle, large, delicately shaped ears, color and rich beauty of fur. He might have compared his own bony, work-scarred hand to the well-kept fingers of a Korwarian villa dweller.

The black leaped, effortlessly, to the top of the cage, and its smaller mate emerged. From that mouth ringed in dark gray came no soft appeal but a sound closer to the ear-shattering wail that had screeched through the flitter before the crash. Kyger laughed.

"Hungry, eh?" He spoke to one of the yardmen. "Bring me a food packet."

Troy watched the merchant break open the sealed container and shake a portion of its contents into the bowls he had loosed from the interior of the cage. The stuff—tough, dry-looking as it sifted down—turned moist and puffy in the dishes. The cats sniffed and then ate decorously.

They were to be Kyger's own charges, Troy discovered, though the shop had a resident staff—two yardmen to tend the cages in the courtyard and some for interior work. Oddly enough, Troy was set to work inside, perhaps taking over some of Zul's tasks.

His shoulder still ached from the bruising impact of the crash, but he tried to satisfy Kyger as the other guided him around, issuing a stream of orders, which at least were concise and easy to obey.

Of the four cage rooms along the corridor between office and show lounges, the first two were for birds, or flying things that might be roughly classed under that heading. Troy had to snatch observations between filling water containers, spreading out a wealth of seeds, exotic fruits, and even bits of meat and fish. The next two chambers were dissimilar. One was filled with tanks and aquariums holding marine dwellers; Troy merely glanced into that since there was a trained tankman on duty. The other was for small animals.

The cats disappeared into Kyger's own office and Troy did not see them again. Nor, as he worked about the cages in the animal room, did he again experience that odd, somewhat disturbing sense of invisible contact. All the creatures were friendly enough, many of them clamoring for his attention, reaching out to him with paws, calling in a whole range of sounds. He was amused, intrigued, attracted—but this was not the same.

He ate his noon rations in the courtyard, apart from Kyger's other employees. C.L. men and subcitizens were never too friendly. And in the midafternoon he witnessed the departure of the Terran cats.

A service robot carried the traveling cage and a food crate at the head of the small procession. Then came a jeweled vision of the hired-companion class, for she swung several small bags on their cords. Next, trailed diffidently by Kyger—if that ex-spacer could ever act a merchant's deference—was a second woman, her features hard to distinguish under the modish painted design of glitter stars on cheek and forehead, the now ultrafashionable "modesty veil" enwrapping mouth, chin, and the rest of her head. Her long coat and tight undertrousers were smartly severe and as unadorned as her companion's were ornately embellished.

As she spoke, her voice held the irremediable lisp of the Lydian-born. And it was plain she was delighted with her new pets. Troy ducked into the door of the fish room to let them pass.

He did not understand why he felt that strange prick of irritation. The Gentle Fem San duk Var was almost the wealthiest consort on Korwar, and the cats had been specially ordered to satisfy her whim. Why did he resent their going? Why? He had had his own piece of luck out of this transaction—the chance that Kyger might keep him on the staff, at least until Zul returned.

Kyger, having seen the party off, called Troy to his office. The com plate on the wall was already activated, and on it was the palm-sized length of white Troy had hardly dared to hope he would ever see.

"Contract"—Kyger was clearly in a hurry to have this done—"to hold a seven-day term. No off-world clause. Suit you, Horan?"

Troy nodded. Even a seven-day contract was to be cherished. He asked only one question. "Renewal for kind?"

"Renewal for kind," the other agreed without hesitation, and Troy's confidence soared. He crossed the small room, set his right hand flat against that glowing plate. "Troy Horan, Norden, class two, accepts contract for seven days, not off-world, from Kyger's," he recited, allowing his hand to remain tight against the heated panel for a full moment before he gave way to Kyger.

The other's hand, wider, the fingers thicker and blunter at the tips, smacked against the white oblong in turn.

"Kossi Kyger, registered merchant, accepts contract for seven days from Troy Horan, laborer. Record it so."

The metallic voice of the recorder chattered back at them. "It is so sealed and noted."

Kyger returned to his eazi-rest. "Shop uniform in the storehouse. Any reason for you to go back to the Dipple tonight?"

Troy paused to shake his head. His few possessions of any value had been thumb-locked into a Dipple safe pocket that morning. And the lock would hold against any touch but his own for ten days. He could pick up the contents of that very small locker any time. Was it imagination again, or did Kyger seem to be relieved?

"Zul furnished night watch inside here. One man inside, a yardman out, a patroller on alarm call. Some of the stock are delicate. You'll make two rounds—"

He was interrupted by the showroom gong and pulled himself to his feet. "Change and get to work," he ordered as he left the office.

Troy sealed the fore seam of the shop coveralls and strapped on again his rider's belt. The Kyger livery was of the same dark blue that Kyger affected in his own garments, and it did not include the reptileskin boots Zul had worn—nor was there any knife for the belt. He had risen one short step above the Dipple, but that was all.

Shopping hours ran on into the late evening, and twice Troy was summoned to the display rooms to carry in some animate treasure for inspection. He had just returned a squirming cub, listed as an animal but with fluffy feathers instead of fur and six legs waving wildly in the air, a big-eared head digging chin point into Troy's shoulder as it looked with avid interest at the world, to a cage, where three more of its kind immediately fell upon it in mock attack, when Kyger came to the door.

"That closes us for tonight. Guard quarters are next to the storeroom. I'm aloft—over there." He jerked a thumb at the back wall of the courtyard and the line of windows looking out from a second level. "Here—" His hand cupped over a knob of brilliant scarlet just inside the door and now glowing in the subdued light of the cage room. "Need help, hit one of these. There's one in each room. You'll make rounds at three, again at six. Meanwhile"—below the knob was a lever he pushed up—"you'll be able to hear them through the com if there's any disturbance. The yard cages are not your concern."

"Yes, Merchant," Troy assented.

Kyger went on down the corridor, stopping to thumb-seal the

door of his office—almost ostentatiously, as if he wanted his most recent employee to witness that act.

Then, without any good night, he was gone. Troy felt the nudge of responsibility. He stepped inside each bird room. The light was dimmed; many of the inhabitants were now asleep. In every room the lever was up, the com safely on. Then he went to the padded wall shelf in the cubby off the storeroom, still a little too excited to sleep.

Within a matter of three days the pattern of Kyger's had become a routine into which Troy fitted easily. He had been successful in caring for a delicate and rare fussel hawk, which Kyger himself had been unable to handle, and had begun to hope that perhaps his week's contract might indeed be renewed. He also discovered that Kyger's not only sold—but bought.

There was a second entrance to the shop through the courtyard, an inconspicuous covered way through which men, mostly wearing spacer uniform, found their way, with either carrying cages or other wild-life containers. All of these, he had his orders, were to be shown directly to Kyger's private office. And should the merchant be busied with customers, a certain signal of gong notes was to be sounded.

At the conclusion of one of these visits Troy, or a yardman, would be summoned to take away a purchase. But the majority of these were sheltered in the yard, not among the rarities of the inner shop. And it appeared to Troy that the number of such sellers did not match the number of visitors—as if some of those unobtrusive men might have visited the ex-spacer for another reason. But that too might have an easy explanation; shipmates from old runs could well drop in while in port. Or there might be still a third reason—one that fitted the attack made upon Zul himself with the interest Varms had shown.

Tikil was a luxury port. And the luxuries were not always within the bands of legal imports. Troy could name four forbidden drugs, a banned liquor, and several other items that would never arrive openly on the planet but would promise high returns for the men or man reckless enough to run them through port scanners. If Kyger had activities outside the port laws, however, that was none of his cage cleaner's concern.

On the fourth afternoon after he had taken contract, Troy was called to the showrooms. Two customers were present, and Kyger's attention had been claimed by the one who, with her party, was in the outer lounge. He waved Horan to the man waiting.

"Show this Gentle Homo the box of tri-dees from Hathor. Yes. Gentle Fem"—the merchant turned back to the glittering party he was serving—"there are many other Terran beasts which one might consider, fully equal in beauty and intelligence to cats. Let me show you—"

When Troy would have led the way to the next lounge, the man he was to assist stopped him with a shake of the head. It appeared that he also wanted to see the wonder Kyger was about to reveal.

The merchant pressed a button. A small viewing screen moved outward from the wall at a comfortable eye level for the woman in the foreseat of the party. She was older than Var's consort, and far more elaborately dressed, affecting the semitransparent robes of Cynus, though they were not in the least flattering to her emaciated figure. Her voice was a shrill caw, but as Troy caught sight of her sharp-featured profile, he knew her for the Grand Leader One from Sidona. That was a matriarchate in name only now, a cluster of three small planets about a dying sun. But it still occupied a strategic point on an important star lane, and what power the Grand Leader Ones might have lost in battle they still possessed in alliances.

"This, Gentle Fem"—Kyger clicked thumb and finger together and was answered by the instant appearance on the screen of a tri-dee—"is a fox. I have already a pair in transit so I can promise an early delivery."

"So?" The Grand Leader One leaned forward a little, the corners of her pinched mouth drawing down to deepen lines from a beak nose. "And how many credits will the coming of such take from my purse, Merchant?"

Kyger named a sum that five days earlier would have made Troy incredulous. Now he merely wondered how long the bargaining would continue.

"A fox, now," the man standing beside him said very softly, his observation hardly above a whisper, as if he were thinking aloud.

The animal in the tri-dee was clearly depicted life-size, the usual procedure for smaller beasts. It had a thick coat of orange-red, black legs and feet, a white tip on its brush of tail. The head was almost triangular with sharp-pointed ears and muzzle, and greenish eyes slanted in that alert and mischievous mask. It was larger than the cats, but its expression of sly intelligence was most marked.

But something in the way his own waiting customer had said "fox" suggested to Troy that the other was not unacquainted with the Terran exotic. However, he did not linger now but stepped into the second lounge, and Horan had to accompany him.

"I understand you have a fussel hawk."

"That is so, Gentle Homo."

"Have you flown it yet?"

"No, Gentle Homo. The ship passage left it fretful—we have allowed it cage rest."

Those strangely golden eyes flickered to Troy's middle and the wide belt there.

"You are of Norden?"

"I was born there," Troy replied shortly.

"Then you have perhaps already hunted with a fussel."

Troy's lips twitched. "I have seen such hunting. But Norden is many years behind me, Gentle Homo. There was a war." He kept his tone respectful; in fact, he was a little surprised. The stranger had no signs, such as Kyger carried, of being an ex-spacer. Yet not one Korwarian in ten thousand would have recognized Troy's belt, or would have known that the riders of the Norden-that-was had hunted with fussel hawks in the mountain valleys. He studied the other covertly as he made ready the viewing screen.

They were nearly the same height, but the Korwarian was perhaps ten planet years older. He did not have the look of a villa aristocrat, not even of one who played hard and kept his body in top condition. Since he wore no official uniform, he was not a member of any of the three services. Yet plainly he was a man who knew action and the outdoors. His skin must be as fair as Troy's under the even tan of much exposure. In a concession to fashion he had a braided topknot of hair, banded with two golden hold rings, and that hair was a dull red-gold, not far removed in shade from the metal. His loose tunic and kilt were of a creamy-brown nubb-metalla in which a small golden spark flashed here and there as he moved. There were yellow gems in the hilt of his belt knife and ringing his wrist bracelets, so that the whole effect was that of a golden man, yet did not in any way suggest a villa fop.

"I have not seen you here before. Where is Zul?" There was no arrogance in the question. The stranger asked as if he had a real interest in who might serve him.

"He was injured—there was a flitter smash," Troy replied somewhat evasively, and then added with the strict truth, "I am C.L., on a fill-time contract."

"From the Dipple?" The other gave the name none of the accent that had made that place of abode a fighting word in Tikil. "Well, and what has Kyger got to offer in his Hathor tri-dees?"

He seated himself at last, waving aside the selection of smoke sticks and drinks Troy offered. Horan snapped the button and the first of the views flashed on the screen. It was apparent from the series that this would-be customer was interested only in birds of prey that could be trained for the hunt. But when Troy had run through the entire Hathor collection, the man shook his head.

"When one knows there is a fine weapon within reach, one does not pick up the second best. If Kyger has a fussel worth training, I shall not order from these." Now he did pick a smoke stick, struck it against his fingernail to set it burning with its herb-scented smoke. "Ah, Kyger!" He looked up as the merchant entered. "And did you make that stellar sale? How long will the august mother of three worlds have to wait for her new toy?"

There was something in the lounge, as invisible as the touch from the cats' cage. This was a tenseness, the faintest possible suggestion of strain. Yet both men were outwardly at ease. Kyger seated himself in another chair as if there were no barriers of rank between them.

"Not too long. I have a pair arriving on the Shammor."

"So? Gambling in Terran imports now, Kyger?"

The ex-spacer shrugged. "They want to build up their export trade—and they are willing to pare prices to open a new market. My friends on the ships pass the word—"

His customer nodded. "Yes. Well, trade makes ties to defeat war. And if you can get the Terrans well tied up, you'll have the smiles of the Council, Kyger."

Again that flash of feeling. Troy could not be sure which man was involved. The golden man stubbed out his smoke stick.

"You have a fussel—"

Kyger picked up a refreshment bulb, squeezed its contents into his mouth. "I have. It'll have to prove itself in flight, though, before I market it."

"Just so. I am due to make an inspection trip through the Wild. Trust me with that testing—send along your man here."

Kyger glanced at Horan. "All right. He knows how to handle the bird, uncrated it when the rest of us couldn't get near. Very well, Hunter. When do you wish to leave, and for how long?"

"Three days to be gone. I must swing up as far as the Marches. As to when—well, shall we say in two days? That will give your bird that much longer to rest before we take him out."

Kyger crushed the beverage bulb in one hand. "Agreed. You," he said to Troy, "will hold yourself ready for the Hunter Rerne's orders."

The golden man left, walking with an almost soundless tread that Troy did not now find surprising. Kyger continued to sit for a long moment, his eyes still on the door through which the other had gone.

"Rerne." He repeated that name very softly. If there was any expression in his tone, Troy failed to read it.

The Hunters, the rangers of the Wild, were conservation experts. Guardians of the vast sections of carefully preserved forest and unsettled lands, into which parties of visitors or the villa dwellers of Korwar might be guided to enjoy the thrills of primitive living while still in flyer touch with the safety and luxury of civilization. They were almost legendary in Tikil. And the office had become, through two centuries, hereditary, going to the members of some ten or twelve families, all of them First-Ship pioneers on Korwar.

Rerne's Clan lived to the north. And this man, because of his youth, must be one of the two brothers whose discovery of the ill-fated Fauklow expedition was still something of a saga in the port city. Troy fingered the belt from which no knife hung. Even a subcitizen could seldom hope for a chance to penetrate the Wild. The trackers, foresters, woodsmen themselves all came of lesser families allied by old ties to the Clans. Yet he was going with Rerne in two days' time!

# FOUR

The news flash came during the slack time at the shop. Those visitors who favored the afternoon had gone, and the evening strollers were not yet abroad. Kyger had retreated to his office; his employees gathered for their evening meal. Troy balanced a plate on his knee in the courtyard. Through the window vent over his head he could hear the mechanical recitation of the day's events over Kyger's com.

"—the so-far unexplainable and sudden death of Sattor Commander Varan Di."

Troy stopped chewing. Two feet away stood the flitter, and right now there was a box resting in it intended for the hillside villa of Sattor Commander Varan Di, a special shipment of food for the Commander's pet.

"—resigned from the overlordship of the Council during the previous year," continued the drone from within. "But his years of experience led him to agree to continue as consultant on special problems. It is rumored that he was acting at present as adviser on the terms of the Treaty of Panarc Five. This has been neither confirmed nor denied by government spokesmen. Statement issued by the Council: 'It is with deep regret—'"

The monotone of the com snapped into a silence, the more noticeable because of that sudden break. Troy went on eating.

The death, "unexplainable and sudden" as the com had it, of a retired military leader and former Council lord now had very little to do with Troy Horan. Ten years ago—again Troy's hand paused on its way to his mouth—ten years ago matters might have been different. It had been Varan Di who had arbitrarily decided to make a military depot for Sattor-class ships out of Norden. Not that that made any difference now.

"Horan!" Kyger came to the courtyard entrance. Troy put down his plate, noting small signs of irritation in his employer. "Take the flitter up to the Di villa and deliver that package."

Well, Troy supposed, eating, even for a pet, went on when the master was dead. But why the rush to send him now—and why him at all? The yardman usually took the flitter out on such errands. But this was no time to ask questions. He folded his long legs into the driver's seat, made a creditable lift from the courtyard.

The journey tape had already been set for the trip; he had nothing to do but take off and land, and be ready to assume manual control if any remote emergency arose. In the meantime he settled back in the cramped seat to enjoy this small time of privacy and ease.

The golden haze, which was Korwar's fair-weather sky, somehow reminded him of Rerne and the promised trip into the Wild. Troy had taken time twice that afternoon, after the Hunter had left, to visit the fussel. And on the second inspection the big bird had stirred on his perch and stretched his wings, which was a very encouraging sign. The fussel was male, perhaps two years old, so just entering the best training age. Wild as he had been when loosed from the traveling cage, he had not struck at Troy, as he had attempted to do at both Kyger and the assisting yardman, which could—or might—mean that the bird would be willing to ride with Horan.

"Lane warning—lane warning!" The words spat from the mike on the control board, a light flashing in additional emphasis.

Troy looked up. A patroller hung poised, as the fussel might poise, over the flitter, ready to swoop for the kill.

"Identify yourself!" came the order Troy expected.

He pushed the button that would report to the law the destination and reason for the errand as it appeared on his journey tape, expecting instructions to take manuals and sheer off. If the patrollers were investigating a suspicious death, they would not allow him to set down at the Di villa.

But surprisingly enough he was told to proceed. Nor was he challenged again as the flitter settled before the service quarters of the late Sattor Commander's mountainside retreat.

Like all Korwar aristocrats, Varan Di had constructed a dwelling on a plan native to another world, choosing for a model the stark simplicity of the Pa-ta-du of the sea mountains of Qwan. Even a growth of pink-gray lace bushes could not disguise the rugged wall posts, though their softening color was reflected by the sheets of barmush shell that formed the wall surfaces between those posts. Troy tried to estimate the number of credits that must have been spent to import posts, shell sheets, and doubtless all the rest from across stellar space. And he doubted if it all could have been done on the legal pay of either a sattor commander or a Council lord's post.

He pulled the case of food out of the flitter, shouldered it, and turned toward the delivery port of the villa. Men were moving in the garden, patrollers' uniforms very much in evidence. Their attention appeared to be centered on a small structure half hidden by an artificial grouping of plume trees, a structure as architecturally different from the villa it accompanied as the fussel was from a bob-chit. In place of shell-post walls, translucent, this was a solid block of stone, cut and set with precision, but also giving the impression of a primitive structure from some prespace-flight civilization thousands of years removed in time from the larger house.

A man came out of its doorway, and Troy stopped short. Just as the invisible touch of exploration had alerted him in the warehouse, so now did a feeling within him answer a new, voiceless cry for help. The sensation of terror and, beyond that terror, the breathless need to convey some vital information struck into his mind almost as a physical blow. And without conscious thinking he answered that plea with an unvoiced query in return: "What—where—how—?"

The man who had come from the stone-walled garden house twisted and made a grab into the air as something wriggled from his clutch and sprang into the nearest plume tree. Only an agitation of foliage marked its path from there to the villa—or was it toward Troy? A tree branch bobbed and from it a small body flung itself in a crazy leap through the air.

Troy put down the box just in time to take the shock of that weight landing on his shoulder. A prehensile tail curled about his neck, small legs clutched him frenziedly, and he put up an arm to enfold a small, trembling, softly furred animal. A round, broad head butted against him, as if the creature were trying to ball into a refuge. Troy stroked the thick yellow-brown fur soothingly.

"Kill—" No one had spoken that word aloud; it flashed into his mind, and with it a wavering, oddly shaped picture of a man crumpled in a chair. Troy shook his head and the picture was gone. But the fear in the animal in his arms remained alive and strong.

"Danger—" Yes, that got across. Danger not only for the creature he held, but for others—men—

The man who had lost this animal was hurrying forward, and two of the patrollers also made their way purposefully toward Troy. In that same moment he knew that he intended to protect the thing he held, even against the weight of Korwar's law.

"Sooooo—" He made the same soothing sound Kyger had used with the cats, stroking the furred back gently. The butting of the head against his chest was now not so violent. And Troy tried to establish a contact promising protection and aid. What he was doing, or why and how he could do it, did not matter now—that he was able to establish the contact did.

"Who are you?"

Troy settled the still-shivering animal more firmly into the hollow between shoulder and arm and looked with very little favor at his questioner. "Horan." He pointed with his chin at the flitter, with the shop name clearly lettered on its body. "From Kyger's."

One of the patrollers cleared his throat and then spoke with a deferential note that suggested the importance of the civilian interrogating Troy. "That's the animal and bird importer, Gentle Homo. I believe that the Sattor Commander purchased this thing there—"

The man he addressed was harsh-faced, flat-eyed. He stared at Troy as if he presented some very elemental problem that could be speedily solved—not particularly to the problem's advantage.

"What are you doing here?"

Troy touched with the toe of his boot the box he had just set down. "Delivery, Gentle Homo. Special food for the Commander's pet."

The flat-eyed man looked to the second patroller and that individual nodded. "It was referenced for today, Gentle Homo. Special imported food for the—the—" He hesitated over the unfamiliar name before he offered it. "The kinkajou."

"The what?" his superior demanded. "What kind of an outlandish, other-sun thing—?"

"It is Terran, Gentle Homo," his second underling answered with a small flash of importance. "Very rare. The Sattor Commander was quite excited about it."

"Kinkajou—Terran—" The officer advanced a step or two as he tried to see more of the animal clinging to Troy. "But what was it doing rummaging through the Sattor Commander's desk if it is just an animal? Do you have an answer for that?"

"Danger!" Troy did not need that flash of warning from the creature in his arms. It was plain to read in the whole stance of the man before him.

"Many animals are very curious, Gentle Homo." Troy sought to divert the officer. "Do not Korwarian kattans open any package they can lay claws upon?"

The voluble patroller was nodding assent to that. And Troy pushed a little further. "Animals also imitate the actions of men with whom they are closely associated, Gentle Homo. The kinkajou may have been following the routine of the Sattor Commander. What else could it be? Surely it would not be doing so for a purpose—" But, Troy guessed now, that must have been what the creature was doing when caught. Did this officer have more exact knowledge of that fact?

"Possible," the other conceded. "Just to make sure that there shall be no more such mischief, you will take this kinkajou with you and return it to Kyger. He shall be responsible for it until the investigation into the Sattor Commander's death is completed. Tell him the Commandant of the West Sector orders it."

"It is done, Gentle Homo."

Troy tried to put the kinkajou into the flitter first, before he replaced the box. But the animal refused to loose its hold upon him. In addition, rising above the fear it conveyed to him, there was again that urgency, an urgency that was clearly connected with the stone house in the garden. The kinkajou wanted him to return it to that building until it finished some task, protecting it meanwhile from his own kind. But to that he dared not agree. For the first time the animal gave tongue, uttering sharp, chittering cries, as if so it could enforce the volume of their silent communication.

"Get aloft!"

The Commandant had gone back to the garden house, and the patrollers moved in on Troy. He had no wish to have them turn ugly. Somehow he managed to tip the box back into the flitter, the kinkajou protesting the retreat bitterly—though Troy noted it made no attempt to leave him.

Once they were aloft again, the animal quieted down, apparently accepting defeat. Seated in Troy's lap, its tail curled about one of his arms as if for reassurance and support, it surveyed the world of the sky through which they flew with what might have been taken for intelligent interest. But it made no more attempts to reason with him.

When the flitter set down in the court of Kyger's establishment, the kinkajou moved to the cabin door, patted it with front paws, and looked to Troy entreatingly, every line of its rounded body expressing eagerness to be free. He caught at the prehensile tail, having no wish to see the creature escape by one of its spectacular leaps. Leaving the flyer and grasping his indignant captive firmly, Troy went toward his employer's office.

Kyger appeared at the corridor door, and when he saw the squirming animal in Troy's hold, he halted nearly in midstep. Again Troy caught that spark of unease which he had detected in the meeting between the ex-spacer and Rerne.

"What happened?" Kyger's tone was as usual. He stepped back into his office and Troy accepted the tacit invitation to enter. The

escape attempts of the kinkajou were at an end again. Once more
the animal pushed against Koran's chest as if in mute plea for
protection. But the mental contact had utterly ceased.

Swiftly and tersely, as a serviceman giving a report to a superior
officer, Troy outlined what had happened at the Di villa. But he
made no mention of the odd contact with the kinkajou. He had
early learned in the hard school of the Dipple that knowledge
could be both a weapon and a defense, and something as nebulous
and beyond reason as his odd mental meeting with two different
species of Terran life he preferred to keep to himself—at least
until he knew Kyger better.

Kyger made no move to separate the clinging animal from
Horan but sat down in the eazi-rest. His fingers rubbed up and
down the scar seam from his ear.

"That's a valuable specimen," he remarked mildly when Troy
had done. "You were right to bring it back here. Curious as a
ffolth sand borer. There was no reason for the law to upset it
to the point of hysteria! Put it in the empty end cage in the
animal room, give it some water and a few quagger nuts, and
leave it alone."

Troy followed orders, but once at the cage he had some difficulty in detaching the kinkajou. The animal appeared to accept
Horan as a refuge in the midst of a chancy world, and he had
to pry paws and tail loose from their hold on him. As he closed
the cage door, the captive rolled itself into a tight ball in the
corner farthest from the light, presenting only a stubborn hump
of furred back to the world.

During the few days he had been at Kyger's, Troy had come
to look forward to the early hours of the night when he was
left alone in the interior of the main buildings. He made two
watch rounds according to his orders. But each night before
he napped, he had his own visiting pattern. The fussel hawk,
the blue-feathered cubs that always greeted him with reaching
paws and joyous squeaks, and several other favorites were then
his alone. Tonight he came also to the kinkajou cage. From the
appearance of that furred ball still wedged into the corner, the
creature had not moved from the position it had assumed when
he first put it there.

Deliberately Troy tried mental contact, suggesting friendship, a desire for better understanding. But if the kinkajou received those suggestions, it neither acknowledged nor reacted to them. Disappointed, Troy left the room after setting the com broadcaster.

When he stretched out on his bunk, he tried to fit one event of the day to another. But when he remembered Rerne and the other's request for his services in testing the fussel in the Wild, Troy drifted into a daydream, which, in a very short interval, became a real dream.

Troy rolled over, his shoulder bringing up against the wall with a smart rap, his head turning fretfully. There was a thickness behind his eyes, which was not quite a pressure of pain, only a dull throb. He opened his eyes. The dial of the timekeeper faced him, and the hour marked there was well past the middle of the night—though not quite time for his round. But as long as he was now thoroughly awake, he might as well make it.

He sat up, pulled on his half boots. Then he pressed his fingertips gently to his temples. The dull feeling in his head persisted, and it was not normal. In fact—

Troy's hand flashed to the niche above the head of his bunk, scooping up the weapon that lay waiting there.

Though he had never experienced that particular form of attack before, his wits were now alert enough to supply him with one possible explanation. With the stunner in his hand, he walked as noiselessly as he could to the doorway, peered out into the subdued lighting of the corridor.

To his right was Kyger's office, thumb-sealed as usual. And there had been no betraying sound from the com. No betraying *sound*! But a lack of normal sounds can be as enlightening. Troy had become accustomed to the small twitters, clicks, chattering subcomplaints of the night hours—a myriad of sounds, that issued normally from the cage rooms.

The dull pressure in his own head, together with the absence of those same twitters, clicks, chatters, spelled only one thing. There was a "sleeper" in operation somewhere on the premises—the illegal gadget that could lull into unconsciousness living things not shielded from its effect on the middle ear. And a sleeper was not the tool of a man who had any legitimate business here. It must be turned low enough to handle the animals but not to stun Horan himself into unconsciousness—why?

Troy tested Kyger's sealed office doorway with one hand, the stunner ready in the other. The panel refused to move, so at least that lock had not been forced. He slipped along the wall, paused by the tank room. The gurgle of flowing water, the plop of an aquarium inhabitant—nothing else. The marine things appeared not to have succumbed to the sleeper either.

Horan crossed to the animal room. Again no sound at all— which was doubly suspicious. Inside that door was the alert signal, which would arouse the yardmen and ring straight through to Kyger's quarters. Troy edged about the mesh door, his back against the wall, his free hand going to that knob, ready to push it flat.

"Danger!"

Again that word burst in his brain with the force of a full-lunged scream in his ear. He half turned, and a blast of pure, flaming energy cut so close that he cried out involuntarily at the searing bite of its edge against the line of his chin. Half blinded by the recent glare, Troy snapped the stunner beam at the dark shape arising from the floor and threw himself in a roll halfway across the room.

Troy shot another beam at a black blot in the doorway. But the paralyzing ray seemed to have no effect in even slowing up his attacker. Before Troy could find his feet, the other had made the corridor, and Troy heard the metallic clang of the outer door. Horan stumbled across the room, slammed his hand upon the alarm signal, heard the clamor tear the unnatural silence of the cage room to shreds. Perhaps the aroused yard guard would be able to catch the fugitive now in the open.

# FIVE

The fact that there was no corresponding uproar from the cage rooms confirmed Troy's belief that a sleeper had been set within the shop walls. He turned up the light power to full strength and began a careful search of the room. This was where the intruder had been occupied; what he had sought must lie here.

In the cages the occupants were balled, or sprawled, in deep, beam-induced slumber, save for that corner cage where the kinkajou had been put. Bright beads of eyes peered out at Troy, small paws rested against the netting. Troy gained an impression of excitement rather than fear. The signal of danger had been meant as a warning to him, not a cry for assistance such as the animal had made in the villa garden.

Troy ran his finger down the netting, looked into those round eyes. "If you could just tell me what is behind all this," he half whispered.

"Someone comes—"

The kinkajou retreated. Before Troy's eyes it rolled quickly into its chosen ball-in-the-corner position once again. Troy's boot struck against some object on the floor, sent it to rebound from the wall with a metallic "ping." He wriggled halfway under the rack of cages and picked up a dull-green cube—the sleeper.

He glanced once more at the kinkajou. To all appearances that animal was now as deeply under the influence of the gadget he held as all the other beasts in the room.

But if the stock of Kyger's establishment had been so subdued, the human inhabitants of the building were not. Two yardmen, stunners in fist, came through into the corridor. And Kyger ran in their wake, his chosen weapon a far more deadly hand blaster, which must be a relic of his service days.

Troy held out the sleeper cube, told his story of the assailant who had appeared so totally immune to the direct fire of a stunner.

"Wearing a person-protect, probably," Kyger snapped impatiently. "Anything gone here—or disturbed—?"

He passed down the line of cages, but as he reached the end one, he paused and gave a searching glance at the ball of sleeping kinkajou. Troy made no mention of the fact that the animal had been able to defy the wave of the sleeper, had saved his own life by its warning. In spite of Kyger's treatment of him, some deep-buried and undefinable emotion kept him from warming to the merchant as he had to Rerne. He had no idea what could lie behind the invasion of the shop, but he wanted to know more of what was going on here.

"I could not see anything wrong," he reported.

Kyger had turned, was walking back along the cages, and his fingers rasped across the netting of the one that held the kinkajou. The ball of fur remained unstirring. As the merchant joined Troy once more, he caught the younger man's chin, turning his head directly to the light.

"You have a flash burn there." His tone was almost accusing.

"He was armed with a blaster," Troy explained.

"What is going on here?"

The yardmen in the doorway were elbowed aside; a patroller came in, blaster ready. Kyger answered with a bite in his voice.

"We had a visitor, who brought this—" He nodded to the sleeper cube on the top of a cage. The patroller scooped it up, his eyes cold.

"What is the damage?"

Kyger's hand fell from Troy's chin to his shoulder. He held

that grip, propelling the younger man before him down the corridor.

"So far none, except a flash burn—too close for comfort. Mangy! Tansvel!" The yardmen snapped to attention. "Check out the rest of the rooms; report to me in the office. This officer"—Kyger nodded to the patroller—"will help you."

Troy stood quietly as his employer patted cov-aid dressing along the line of the burn. "Just grazed you." Kyger retopped the container. "You were lucky."

"It was dark and he was off orbit."

But Kyger was watching him with an intent stare as if he could see straight into Troy's memory and pick out the events as they had really happened—the incredible fact that a warning had struck from an animal's mind to his.

"He must have been badly jigged," Kyger commented. "So much so that I wonder. A sleeper makes this a Guild job—and I have one or two unfriends around here who might just employ such means to make trouble for me." He was frowning a little. "Only Guild men do not get jigged—"

"A novice might."

Kyger spread both hands on the top of his desk. "A novice? What do *you* know about this, Horan?"

"I noticed a new buy-in man at the warehouse before they tried to lift us on the street." Troy trusted now to Kyger's own background. To a merchant-born he would not have made such an admission, unless the matter had proved far more serious than it was. But to a spacer who had himself lived by a more flexible code of ethics—or rather, a different code of ethics—he could confess that much.

"A proving job for a novice." Kyger considered that. "Might fit this flight pattern, at that. This buy-in man knows you?"

"He saw me at the warehouse—just as I saw him."

"Any challenge between you two?"

"If you mean was this personal—no. He was Dipple and I knew him by name, but we never messed together."

"Silly jig, hitting here. Unless it was just for nuisance value. There is nothing he could pick up to trot to the pass-boys."

Troy wondered about that himself. Portable property was to be had for the ingenious lifts of the Guild anywhere in Tikil, where theft had become both a business and a fine art. Why would anyone try to lift living creatures, most of which required special food and attention? There was only one possibility.

"Some one-of-a-kind already promised?" he hazarded, knowing Kyger's promises to his elite customers. A unique pet, certified to the the only one of its kind on Korwar, might be an inducement.

"No profit in that. It would have to be kept under cover." Kyger put his finger on the weakness in that. Yes, the value of such a pet to the vain owner would be largely in its display before the envious.

"To keep someone else from having it?"

Again that disconcerting stare from Kyger. Troy thought he had found another small piece in this match puzzle. That had hit, if not straight to the heart of the target, reasonably near.

"Might be. That makes a spot more sense. You can bunk in. I might cover the rest of the night watch."

That was straight dismissal. Troy went back to his bunk, this time easing out of his clothes. The dressing had taken most of the smart out of his burn. But his mind was active and he did not feel in the least inclined to sleep. He closed his eyes, trying to will relaxation.

Instead, as if some tenuous circle of thought had coiled out into the air—as Lang Horan's rupan rope had done so accurately years before to catch and hold a twisting, bucking quarry—Troy's heightened sensitivity touched and held something never intended to join more than one pair of minds under that roof this night.

"He died quick. No time to see the report before put away—"

"Must return!" That was an order, final and harsh.

"Not so. No good. Man saw Shang look for report. Was suspicious!"

"There must be no suspicion!" Again the harshness.

And now there was no more protest in words, rather a thread of fear, a thread that grew into a choking rope. Troy's eyes opened. He sat up on the bunk, alive and vibrating to that fear as if its force raged in him also.

But if there was fear in that band of communication, there

was also something else he recognized—a determination to fight.
And to that his sympathy responded.

"If there is suspicion, there will be questions."

Silence from the harsh one. Was that marking thoughtful consideration of the argument? Or rejection of its validity? Troy's
hands were sweat-wet and now his fingers clenched into fists. If
what he suspected was true—The kinkajou and Kyger? But why?
How? Terran animals able to communicate being used for a set
purpose? Yet Kyger was no Terran—or was he? Troy himself was
too ignorant of other worlds, except for the people of the Dipple,
to make a positive identification. He remembered Kyger's own
questions about his past on the day he had been hired.

Terra was the center of the Confederation—or had been before
the war. But she had not come out well at the end of that con-
flict; too many of her allies had gone down to defeat. From the
dominant voice she had sunk to a second-rate, even third-rate,
power at the conference tables. The Council and the Octed of the
Rim maneuvered for first power, while the old Confederation had
fractured into at least three collections of smaller rulerships. His
thoughts were broken once more by that unidentifiable thought
stream—again the master voice: "Who came tonight?"

"One who knew nothing. He was an enemy outside the scheme.
There was no touch."

"Yet he could have been hired by another. Traps need bait."

Troy read the thought behind that last. So—if he were right and
it was the kinkajou and Kyger who were talking so—then such
an animal might well be stolen to serve as bait for its master.

But why had not the animal reported Troy's ability to receive
the mind touch, if not with the ease and clarity of this exchange,
then after a fashion? Or did the kinkajou, fearing its master,
hold Troy in reserve as a possible escape, as he had been for it
at the Di villa?

"An enemy outside the scheme!" The master voice picked that
up now. "Against me?"

"Against you," the kinkajou (if it was that) agreed. "He was paid
to cause trouble, bring you into the shop that he might kill—"

"Kill." That word throbbed in Troy's head. He strained to catch
an answer. But there was no more that night. At last he slept

fitfully, awaking now and then to lie silent, listening not only with his ears but with the portion of his brain that had tapped the exchange. But save for the sound of the birds and animals coming out of the daze of the sleeper to their normal nocturnal restlessness, he heard nothing on either plane of the senses.

In the morning, after the general round of cage tending and feeding was over, Kyger summoned Troy to the fussel hawk. The big bird was definitely emerging from its sullenness of the landing. It held its crested head high, turned it alertly from side to side. Still young enough to have some of its adolescent tail plumage, it was yet a strikingly beautiful bird with its brilliant, iridescent-black rakish crest above its bright golden head, back-patched by warrior scarlet. The golden glow of breast and the scarlet of back were blended on the strongly pinioned wings to a warm orange beneath which the darker tail and black legs again made contrast. But it was not for beauty alone that the fussel was esteemed.

On countless worlds—human, humanoid, and even nonhuman— intelligences had trained birds of falcon and hawklike strains to be hunter-companions. And now when the highly civilized were returning to more primitive skills and amusements for pleasure, hunting—not with high-power kill weapons, but with hawk or other trained birds and animals—was well established. The fussel—with its intelligence, its ability to be easily trained through the right handling, and its power to capture rather than kill a quarry upon demand—was a highly valued item of sale for any trainer.

Now, seeing the stance of the bird, Troy drew his fingers slowly, enticingly, across the front of the cage. Unlike its attitude of only two days earlier, it made no lightning stab to punish such impudence. Instead, deep in its throat, the bird gave a sound of interested inquiry and moved along the perch toward the door opening of the cage as if awaiting release.

"Shall I man him?" Troy asked.

Kyger snapped his fingers at the opposite side of the cage. That act, which had brought the fussel into raging battle before, now only led it to turn its head. Then it looked back again expectantly at the cage door.

"Here." Kyger tossed the hawker's glove to Troy. As the latter drew it on, the fussel uttered its soft cry, this time with a half-coaxing note.

Horan loosened the door, extended protected hand and wrist into the cage. The fussel ducked its head, not to stab, but to draw its curved beak along the tough fabric of the glove. Then sedately it moved from perch to wrist, and Troy carefully lifted the bird out into the open of the corridor into which they had moved the cage for this experiment.

"Olllahuuu!"

Both men turned quickly at the Hunter's call of appreciation. Rerne stood there, smiling a little.

"Your friend here looks eager for a casting," he remarked.

The fussel mantled, raising wings wide in display, shaking them a little as if glad to be free of the cage. The clawhold on Troy's wrist was firm, and the bird gave no sign of wanting to quit that post.

"Truly a beauty," Rerne complimented Kyger. "If he performs as well as he looks, you have already made a sale, Merchant."

"He is yours to try, Gentle Homo."

"When better than now? It seems that there is an earlier demand for my services in the Wild than I had thought. I am come one day ahead of time to claim this man of yours and the bird."

Kyger made no protest. In fact the speed with which he equipped Troy with the loan of a camp kit and the affability with which he saw them both away from the shop made Horan uneasy. He had had no chance to visit the kinkajou alone. And when he had been engaged in cage cleaning earlier that day, Kyger or one of the yardmen had been in and out of the room and the animal had remained in its tight ball. He wished that he could have taken it with him, but there was no possible way of explaining such a request. And he had to leave with a small doubt—of what he could not honestly have said—still worrying him.

Rerne's flitter was strictly utilitarian, though with compact storage space and the built-in necessities for a flyer that might also provide a temporary camp shelter in the wilderness. Oddly enough he had no pilot, and when Troy, with the fussel again in the transport cage, climbed into the passenger compartment, he found no other but the Hunter awaiting him there. Nor did Rerne prove talkative. His city finery was gone with his city manners. Now he wore soft hide breeches, made of some dappled skin, pale fawn and white, and tanned to suppleness of fabric. His jerkin was of the same, sleeveless and cut low on the chest so his own golden-tanned skin showed in a wide V close to the same shade as the garment. The rings of precious metal that had held his hair had been traded for thongs confining the locks as tightly but far more inconspicuously. And about his waist was a belt, plain of any jeweled ornament, but supporting stunner, bush knife, and an array of small tools and gadgets, each in its own loop.

Under his expert control the flitter spiraled well up above the conventional traffic lanes between villas and city and headed northeast. Beneath them carefully tended gardens, or as carefully nurtured "wild" gardens grew farther and farther apart. And as they topped a mountain range, they put behind them all the year-around residences of Tikil. There was a scattering of holiday houses and hunting lodges in the stretch before they came to the Mountains of Larsh—and the territory below, as uninhabited as it looked, was still under the dominion of man.

But beyond the Larsh, into the real Wild, then man's hand lay far lighter. The Hunting Clans had deliberately kept it so and profited thereby. Through the years they had made a mystery of the Wild, and now no one ventured without their guidance past the Larsh.

In the cabin of the flitter the quiet was suddenly broken by a call from the fussel—a cry that held a demand. As Troy tried to sooth the captive, Rerne spoke for the first time since they had taken off: "Try him out of the cage."

Troy was doubtful. If the hawk would refuse the wrist, take to wing, or try to, in this confined space, that action would make for trouble. On the other hand, if the bird was to be of any use in the future, it must learn to accept such transportation free of the cage. A fussel caged too much lost spirit. He pulled on his glove, offered his wrist through the half-open door, and felt the firm grip of the talons through the fabric. Carefully he brought his arm across his knees, the fussel resting quietly, though its crested head turned from side to side as it eyed the cabin and the open skies beyond the bubble of their covering. As it showed no disquiet, Troy relaxed a little, enough to glance himself at that rising wall of saw-toothed peaks which was the Larsh, gnawing at the afternoon sky.

They did not fly directly across that barrier range. Instead Rerne turned more to the north so that they followed along its broken wall. And they had covered at least an hour's flying time on that course before they took a gateway of a pass between two grim peaks and saw before them a hazy murk hiding the other world Tikil knew little about.

Rerne sent the flitter spiraling down, now that they were across the heights. There was a raveling of lesser peaks and foothills, bright-green streaks marking at least two rivers of some size. Troy leaned against the bubble, trying to see more of the spread beneath. There appeared to be a fog rising with the coming of evening, a thick scum of stuff closing between the flitter and the ground.

With a mutter of impatience, the Hunter again altered course northward. And they had not gone very far before a light flashed red on his control board. When they continued on their path without any deviation, those flashes grew closer together so that the light seemed hardly to blink at all.

"Warn off!" The words were clipped, with a patroller's snap—though the law of Tikil did not operate east of the Larsh.

Rerne spoke into his own mike. "Acknowledge warn off. This is Rernes' Donerabon."

"Correct. Warn off withdrawn," replied the com.

Troy longed to ask a question. And then Rerne spoke, not to the mike, but to his seatmate. "To your right—watch now as we make the crossover."

The flitter dipped, sideslipped down a long descent. There were no streamers of mist to hide the ground here. No vegetation either. In curdled expanse of rock and sand was a huddle of structures, unmistakably, even from this distance, not the work of nature.

Troy studied them avidly. "What is that?"

"Ruhkarv—the 'accursed place.'"

# SIX

They did not pass directly over that outcropping of alien handiwork, older than the first human landing on Korwar, but headed north once more. Troy knew from reports that what he saw now as lumpy protuberances aboveground were only a fraction of the ruins themselves, as they extended in corridors and chambers layers deep and perhaps miles wide under the surface, for Ruhkarv had never been fully explored.

"The treasure—" he murmured.

Beside him Rerne laughed without any touch of humor. "If that exists outside vivid imaginations, it is never going to be found. Not after the end of the Fauklow expedition."

They had already swept past the open land that held the ruins, were faced again by the wealth of vegetation that ringed the barren waste of Ruhkarv. And Troy was struck by that oddity of the land.

"Why the desert just about the ruins?" he asked, too interested in what he saw to pay the usual deference to the rank of his pilot.

"That is something for which you will find half-a-dozen explanations," Rerne returned, "any one of them logical—and probably wrong. Ruhkarv exists as it always has since the First-Ship exploration party charted it two centuries ago. Why it continues to exist is something Fauklow may have discovered—before he and his men went mad and killed themselves or each other."

"Did their recaller work?"

Rerne answered obliquely. "The tracer of the rescue party registered some form of wave broadcast—well under the surface—when they came in. They blanketed it at once when they saw what had happened to Fauklow and the others they were able to find. All Ruhkarv is off limits now—under a tonal barrier. No flitter can land within two miles of the only known entrance to the underways. We do pick up some empty-headed treasure hunter now and then, prowling about, hunting a way past the barrier. Usually a trip to our headquarters and enforced inspection of the tri-dees we took of Fauklow's end instantly cures his desire to go exploring."

"If the recaller worked—" Troy speculated as to what might have happened down in those hidden passages. Fauklow had been a noted archaeologist with several outstanding successes at re-creating prehuman civilizations via the recaller, a machine still partially in the experimental stage. Planted anywhere within a structure that had once been inhabited by sentient beings, it could produce—under the right conditions—certain shadowy "pictures" of scenes that had once occurred at the site well back in time. While authorities still argued over dating, over the validity of some of the scenes Fauklow had recorded, yet the most skeptical admitted that he had caught something out of the past. And oftentimes those wispy ghosts appearing on his plates or films were the starting point for new and richly rewarding investigation.

The riddle of Ruhkarv had drawn him three years earlier. While men had prowled the upper layers of the underground citadel, they had found nothing except bare corridors and chambers. The Council had willingly granted Fauklow permission to try out the recaller, with prudent contracts and precautions about securing to Korwar the possession of any outstanding finds that might result from the use of his machine. But the real answer had been a bloody massacre, the details of which were never made public. Men who had worked together for years as a well-running team had seemingly, by the evidence, gone stark mad and created a horror.

"If the recaller worked," Rerne answered, "it did so too well. The mop-up crew did not locate it—so the thing must have been planted well down. And no one hunted it there. It was shorted anyway as soon as we guessed what had happened. Ah—there is our beacon."

Through the gathering twilight the quick flash of a ground light shone clearly. Rerne circled, set the flitter down neatly on a pocket of landing field within a fringe of towering tree giants that effectively shut off the paling gold of the sky except just over the heads of the disembarking men. The fussel on Troy's wrist fanned wings and uttered a new cry, not guttural in the throat, but pealing up a range of notes.

Rerne laughed. "To work, eh, feathered brother? Wait until the dawning and we shall give you strong winds to ride. That is a true promise."

Two men stepped from between the trunks of the tree wall. Like Rerne, they were leather-clad, and in addition one had a long hunting bow projecting beyond his shoulder. They glanced briefly at Troy but had more attention for the bird on his wrist.

"From Kyger's." Without other greeting Rerne indicated the fussel. "And this is Troy Horan who has the manning of him."

Again each of the foresters favored him with a raking glance that seemed, in an instant's space, to classify him.

"To the fire, to the fireside, be welcome." The elder of the two gave a strictly impersonal twist to what was evidently a set formula of welcome. Troy was aware that in this world he was an interloper, to be tolerated because of the man who brought him.

And while he had long known and accepted Tikil's evaluation of the Dipple dwellers, yet here this had a power to hurt, perhaps the more so because of the different attitude Rerne had shown. Now the Hunter came to his aid again.

"A rider from Norden," he said quietly with no traceable inflection of rebuke in his voice, "will always be welcome to the fireside of the 'Donerabon.'"

But inside Troy there was still a smart. "Norden's plains have no riders now." He pointed out the truth. "I am a Dippleman, Gentle Homo."

"There are plains in a man's mind," Rerne replied obscurely. "Leave the fussel uncaged if he will ride easy. We shelter in the Five League Post tonight."

There was a trail between the trees ringing in the landing clearing, firm enough to be followed in the half-light. Yet Troy was certain that the three men of the Wild ranger patrol could have found it in the pitch-darkness. It led steadily up slope until outcrops of rock broke through the clumps of brush and the thinning stands of trees, and they came out on a broad ledge hanging above the end of a small lake.

The lodge was not set on that ledge, but in the cliff wall backing it. For some reason the men who patrolled this wilderness had sought to conceal their living quarters with as much cunning as if they were spies stationed behind enemy lines. Once past the well-hidden doorway, Troy found himself in a large room that served as general living quarters, though screened alcoves along the back wall served for bunk rooms.

There was no heating unit. But a broad platform of stone with an upper opening in the rock roof supported smouldering wood, wood that gave off a spicy, aromatic fragrance as it was eaten into ashes. A flooring of wooden planks had been fitted over the rock beneath their boots, and here and there lay shaggy pelts to serve as small rugs while on the walls were shelves holding not only the familiar boxes of reading tapes, but bits of gleaming rock, some small carvings. Brilliant birdskins had been pieced together in an intricate patchwork pattern to cover six feet of the opposite wall.

It was very far removed from Tikil and the ways of Tikil. But in Troy old memories stirred again. The homestead on Norden had not been quite so rugged, but it had been constructed of wood and stone by men who relied more upon their own strength and skill of hands than upon the products of machines.

The fussel called and was answered from one of the alcoves—not in its own cry, but with a similar note. Troy's other hand shot out to imprison the legs of the hawk before it could fly. But the fussel, stretching out its red-patched neck, its black crest quivering erect, merely uttered a deeper, rasping inquiry. Rerne strode forward, pushed aside the screen. There were three perches in the alcove, one occupied by a bird very different from the one Troy bore.

Where the fussel was sunlit fire, this was a drifting shadow of smoke. Its round head was crestless, but the tufted ears stood erect, well above the downy, haze-gray covering on the skull. Its eyes were unusually large and in the subdued light showed dark as if all pupil. In body it was as large as the fussel, its powerful taloned claws proclaiming it a hunter, as did the tearing curve of its beak.

Now it watched the fussel steadily, but showed only interest, no antagonism. One of the foresters presented a gloved wrist, and it made a bounding leap to that new perch.

"An owhee," Rerne said. "They will willingly share quarters with a fussel."

Troy had heard of the peerless night-hunters but had not seen one before. He watched the ranger take it to the door of the lodge and give it a gentle toss to wing away in the twilight. And a moment later they heard its hunting call: "OOOooowheeee!"

Rerne nodded at the perches and Troy went to let the fussel make a choice. After a moment of inspection, the bird put claw on the end one and settled there, waiting for Troy to offer him his evening bait.

He who flew the owhee and his partner of the resident staff did not linger after Rerne, Troy, and their kit were in the lodge house. Each forest ranger had a length of trail to patrol by night as well as by day. They said very little, and Troy suspected that it was his presence that kept the conversation to reports, questions, and answers. He tended the fussel and tried to keep out of the way.

But when both had gone and Rerne brought out a pack of Quik-rations, they settled by the fire, which the Hunter poked into renewed life. There were no chairs, only wide, thick cushions of hide stuffed with something that gave forth a pleasant herbal smell when crushed beneath one's weight.

As they shared the contents of the food pack, the Hunter talked and Troy listened. This was the stuff of the other's days—the study of the Wild, the policing of it after a fashion, not to interfere with nature, only to aid her where and when they could, to make sure that the natural destruction wrought by man himself wherever and whenever he came into new territory did not upset delicate ecological balances.

There were stands of fabulous woods that could be cut—but only under the supervision of the Hunting Clans. There were herbs to be sought for the healing fraternities of other worlds, studies made of the native animals. The Wild was a storehouse to which the Clans held the keys—keeping them by force if necessary.

In the tree-filled valleys, on the spreading plains yet farther to the east, battles had been fought between poachers and guardians. And only because Korwar had been proclaimed a pleasure planet did the Clans have the backing to keep the looters out. Most of this Troy knew, vaguely, but now Rerne spoke of times and places, named names.

The story was absorbing, but Troy was no child to be beguiled by stories. He began to wonder at the reason for Rerne's talkativeness.

"There is no carbite on Korwar," Rerne continued. "But let its equal be found here—and let the barriers against mineral exploration go down—"

"Is there any chance of that happening?" Troy ventured, suddenly aware that he, too, was now thinking as a partisan, ready to protect the Wild against willful destruction. Something in him was stirring sluggishly, pressing bonds he himself had welded into place as a self-protection. Like the hawk, he wanted to test his wings against a free and open sky.

Rerne's lips twisted wryly. "We have learned very little, most of our species. I can name you half a hundred planets that have been wrecked by greed. No, not just those burned off during the war, but killed deliberately over a period of years. As long as we can keep Korwar as a pleasant haven for the overlords of other worlds, some of them the greed-wrecked ones, we can hold this one inviolate. One does not want such desolation in one's own back yard. So far those of the villas have the power, the wealth, to retain Korwar as their unspoiled play place. But how long will it continue to be so? There may be other treasures here than those fabled to lie in Ruhkarv, and far more easily found!"

"You have had two hundred years," Troy said, with an old

bitterness darkening that elation of moments earlier. "Norden had less than a hundred—thanks to Sattor Commander Di!"

"No length of years will satisfy a man when he sees the end of a way of life he is willing to fight for. What does the past matter when the future swoops for the kill? Yes, Sattor Commander Di—who died of poison in his own garden house and whose murderer is yet to be found—and even the method by which the poison reached him determined—has to answer for Norden."

How did Rerne know all that about Di? The fact of poison had not been broadcast on the general coms. Troy felt like a sofaru rat over which the shadow of a diving fussel had fallen, powerless before the strike of an enemy not of his own element. Was *this* behind Rerne's talk, merely a softening-up process to prepare him for subtle questioning about the kinkajou? Or was his own half-guilty feeling suggesting that?

But the Hunter did not enlarge upon the case of Sattor Commander Di. His explorations into the past were not so immediate. Rather now he led Troy to talk about his own childhood. Though in another Korwarian Horan might have considered that questioning presumptuous, there was something about Rerne's interest that seemed genuine, so that the younger man answered truthfully instead of with the evasions he had used so long for a shield—including the fact that his memories of Norden's plains and the free life there were hazy now.

"There are plains here, too. You might consider that," Rerne suggested cryptically as he arose in one lithe movement. "Given time, the right man might learn much. The bunk at that end is yours, Horan. No evil dreams ride your night—" Again the phrase had some of the formality of a ritual dismissal. Troy looked in upon the fussel, saw that it was asleep with one foot drawn up into its under feathers after the manner of its kind, and then went to the bunk Rerne had indicated.

There was no foam plast filling its box shape. Inside dried grasses and leaves gave under him, then remolded about his body, and the fine scent of them filled his nostrils as he fell asleep easily. He did not dream at all.

When he awoke, the door of the big room stood ajar and from

that direction he heard the calls of birds. Still rubbing sleep from his eyes, Troy rolled out of the bunk. The fire on the hearth was out and there was no one else in the room. But the clean smell of a new day in the Wild drew him out on the ledge, to stand looking down into the valley of the lake.

Something rose and fell with a regular stroke not far from the shore, and he realized he was watching a swimmer. A series of steps cut in the rock led down from the ledge, and Troy followed them. Then a loose sleeping robe draped over a bush beckoned him on and he shed his own in turn, testing the temperature of the water with his toes, plunging into it in a clumsy dive before he could change his mind because of that chill greeting.

Troy floundered along the shore, being no expert as was that other now heading, with clean arm sweeps and effortless kicks, back from the center. His threshings disturbed mats of floating blossoms shed by trees bordering a rill that fed the lake at this point, and the bruised petals patterned his wet skin as he found sandy footing and stood up, shivering.

"Storm-cold, Gentle Homo," he commented as Rerne waded in.

The other stopped to wring water from his braided hair knot and then, surveying Troy's dappled body, he laughed.

"A new refinement—flower baths?"

Troy echoed that laugh as he skimmed the wet masses from him. "Not of my choice, Gentle Homo."

"The name is Rerne. We do not follow the paths of Tikil here, Horan." The other was using his nightrobe as a towel, kicking his feet into sandals. With the robe now draped cloakwise about him, he stood for a moment looking out over the lake, and his face was oddly relaxed, much more alive than Troy had ever seen it.

"A fair day. We shall go to the plateau above Stansill and see just how good our feathered one really is."

The flitter took them east and north again. And once more the vegetation beneath them thinned. But not to a waste scar such as that which held Ruhkarv, rather to open plains of tall grasses and scattered, low-growing shrubs. Twice Rerne buzzed the flyer above herds of ruminants, and horned heads tossed angrily before the heavy-shouldered beasts pounded away, tasseled tails high in wrath.

"Pansta," Rerne identified them. "Wild cattle of a sort."

"But they are scaled—or at least they look so!" Troy protested, thinking of his own lost tupan that had grazed so and might have run from a buzzing flitter in the same pattern.

"Not scaled as a fish or a reptile," Rerne corrected. "Those are plates of hardened flesh—something like an insect's wingcasing shell. The herds are dwindling every year, fewer calves born; we do not yet know why. We have reason to believe that they were once domesticated."

"By those of Ruhkarv?"

"Perhaps. Though who or what those of Ruhkarv were—" Rerne shrugged.

"Did they leave only one ruin behind them? I know only of Ruhkarv."

"And that is another mystery. Why a single known city for a civilization? Were they only an outpost of some long-lost stellar empire vanished before man took to space? That was one theory Fauklow wanted to prove or disprove. There is one other trace of them on Korwar—north beyond the plains. But that is all—and that is a very small post. I do not think they were native here. Just as the pansta are so alien to the other animals of the Wild that they do not seem to be native either. The feral herds of a long-gone race, which have outlasted their unknown masters."

The edge of the plains where the pansta ran dropped behind them, and now there were ridges and rising slopes once again, until the flitter climbed to a tableland open to the sky, seeming otherwise cut off from any contact with the lower stretches. Under the golden light of a perfect morning there spread a patched flooring of flowering grasses, a few scattered trees, so removed from any touch of man's passing that Troy thought they might have been the first to find that place if his companion's knowledge of it had not argued otherwise.

Rerne brought the flitter down on a stretch of gravel beside quiet water that was neither as large as a lake nor as small as a pond. They climbed out and stood with the breeze pushing against their bodies. The fussel spread wings, gave voice.

"Let him hunt! Ollllahuuuu!"

Troy gave the wrist flex that was a signal of freedom to the bird he bore. And the fussel arose in great sweeps, beating into the topaz sky until neither man could see him clearly.

# SEVEN

The sun was hot, and from under and around Troy as he lay, the smell of the grass flowers and the grass itself was heady in his nostrils, long pinched by the town and the Dipple. He was relaxed, drowsy, yet not ready to sleep.

It had been a wonderful morning on this piece of Korwar raised into the skies and kept inviolate. Now even the fussel had had enough of the freedom of the wind and the clouds and was content to perch on a tree limb Troy had trimmed and set in the ground for the bird's comfort.

Here the insects seemed few or innocuous. There was no stinging or biting to plague the would-be sleeper. Yet a part of Troy argued that this was very fleeting and that it was a pity to waste a moment in such sloth.

He levered himself up from the warmth. Avoiding the fussel's perch and Rerne's chosen couch, he walked out alone into the open, away from the flitter and all intrusions of Tikil. And as he stood there, the wind trying in vain to pull at his close-cropped hair, pushing protestingly against his straight body, Troy suddenly had a mental picture of a far different place—an artificially lighted room ranked with cages, and the brown-furred back of a creature that had curled into a ball to escape.

The cats—the kinkajou—Here was the fussel, intelligent after its kind—to be trained as another, if beloved, tool or weapon for the use of man. But the Terran creatures—there was a difference, as if somehow they had taken a huge step forward to close ranks with man himself. And Troy knew a tiny flame of excitement. What if that were true? The new world it would open!

He glanced back at Rerne, more than half tempted now to share with the Hunter what was hardly a definite secret—more a series of guesses and surmises. Somehow he thought that in Rerne he would find a believer. Nowhere else on Korwar had he met another with whom he dared be himself, Troy Horan—not a Dippleman, but a free equal. Ever since they had entered the Wild together, this sense of being alive and real again—not aloof from his fellows, but entering once more into a pattern that made for security and solidity—had been growing in him. Now Troy moved slowly, still wary of the wisdom of his half-made decision, but drawn to it. He turned toward Rerne—too late, for the sky was no longer an unoccupied arch of gold. There was a second flitter descending at a speed and angle of approach that suggested urgency.

Rerne sat up in his grassy nest, instantly alert and ready for action. The flyer touched earth not far from their own flitter. The man swinging out of its cabin wore not the tanned-hide uniform of a ranger on duty, but the more elaborate kilt and tunic of a city dweller. He spoke hastily to the Hunter, and then Rerne beckoned Troy to join them.

"Harse will fly you back to Tikil," he said abruptly, making no explanation for the change of plan. "Tell Kyger that I want the fussel. I will call for it later." He paused, his gaze lingering for a second or two on Troy, almost as if he wanted to add something to that rather curt dismissal. But then he turned away, without any other farewell, climbing into his own flitter.

Troy, chilled, shut out again, a little angry at his own thoughts of only a few moments before, took the fussel on his wrist and joined Harse in the second flyer. Rerne's ship took off in a steep climb and continued north—toward the Clan holdings.

Harse chose the shortest lane back to Tikil. It was late afternoon when, after steady flight, Troy once more entered Kyger's shop. The merchant met him in the courtyard corridor.

"Hunter Rerne?" The ex-spacer looked beyond Troy in search of the other.

Troy explained. Kyger heard him out, his fingers tracing the scar on his cheek as he listened. And it seemed to the younger man that the merchant was waiting to hear something of greater importance than just the confirmation of the fussel's sale.

"Cage it then," Kyger ordered. "And you are in time to help with the last feeding. Get to it!"

One of the yardmen was busy with the water pans in the animal room, but he did not look up as Troy went down the line of cages to that which had held the kinkajou. Only this time there was no round ball of fur in its corner. Another quite different creature, pointed-nosed, sharp-eyed, gazed back at him.

"Back, eh?" The yardman lounged over to lean against the wall. "'Bout time you got to it, Dippleman. We have done your work an' ours too, an' we have had 'bout enough of that. How did your ride with one of the lords-high-an'-mighty go?"

"Sold the fussel." Troy made a noncommittal answer. He was more interested in what had happened here. Though one Terran animal had disappeared during his absence from the shop, here was another established in the same cage, for he was sure that this newcomer was the beast Kyger had shown to the Grand Leader One, via tri-dee, as a fox.

One Terran animal—no, two! He saw the second one now, curled up much as the kinkajou had been, its back to the world, in the far part of the cage. And he noted that the eyes of the one on guard were as searching in their inspection of him as had been the eyes of the cats. The one on guard—why had he thought that?

"One guards—one sleeps—"

Out of nowhere had come the answer. The fox seated himself now, much as the cats had done in their traveling cage, no longer so wary, more as if ready for some answering move on Troy's part.

"New—what are they?" Troy appealed to the yardman merely to cover his interest in the occupants of the cage.

"Extra-special. And you do not take care of these, Dippleman. Boss's orders. He takes care of them himself."

"Horan!"

Hoping he was able to disguise his somewhat guilty start, Troy glanced back to see Kyger standing at the door of the cage room beckoning.

"Get over here and help Jingu." He shepherded Troy into the tank room where the marine creatures were on display.

On the table at the far end of the room stood a traveling container into which Jingu, the attendant of those particular wares, was measuring a quantity of liquid with an oily sheen to it. A small aquarium containing the same liquid stood before him. And plastered against the side of that was something Troy, at first sight, could not believe existed outside the imagination of some V-dee fantasy creator.

He had seen many weird life forms, either in the flesh or in Kyger's range of tri-dees. But this was not strange; it was impossible—impossible with a kind of stomach-turning horror. He did not want to look at it and yet his eyes were continually drawn back to the aquarium, and, when the thing moved, he fought an answering heave to his stomach.

Leaning against the end of the table, intent upon Jingu's task, was a stranger, a small man wearing the tunic of one of the minor administrative bureaus. He was a colorless man whom one might not have noted or remembered unless seen as he was now, both hands set on the table top as if to lever his slack-muscled body closer to the monster in the aquarium, his eyes avid with—Troy realized—greed, his pale tongue moving back and forth like a lizard's over pale lips. He turned his head as they came up and his eyes were bright.

"Beautiful, Merchant Kyger, beautiful!"

Kyger regarded the aquarium occupant bleakly. "Not to me, Citizen. Those hur-hurs are"—he shook his head as might a man at a loss for a descriptive word pungent enough, and then ended rather mildly—"hardly considered beautiful, Citizen Dragur."

The small man might have been the fussel lifting its wings, ready to dart head forward in a beak-sharp attack. "They are a rarity, Merchant Kyger, and of their kind beautiful!" He bristled. "A splendid addition to my collection." He looked from Kyger to Troy. "This young man is to aid in the transporting? I trust that he knows how to handle such valuables safely? I shall hold you responsible, Kyger, until this magnificent specimen is safely installed in my pond room."

Troy opened his mouth to deny that he was going to have any part in the transportation of the hur-hur. Then he caught Kyger's glare and remembered that the seven-day contract was close to renewal time. After all, the carrying jug, or bucket, or whatever they termed it, which Jingu was filling so carefully, did have solid sides, and a cover was waiting to be placed on it. If he did lug the thing around, he did not have to continue to look at it.

Jingu now took up a rod and inserted it carefully, a few inches at a time, beneath the surface of the water in the aquarium. Then he prodded the hur-hur gently. Troy, unable to look away, watched with fascinated disgust as the monster embraced the rod with its profusion of thread-thin tentacles, planting the suckers beading those same tentacles fast on the rod. Then Jingu whipped the rod and hur-hur out of the aquarium into the container and clapped on the lid, adjusting a carrying strap.

Troy lifted the cylinder gingerly, felt it quiver between his hands as apparently the hur-hur chose to resent its new prison with some spirited movements. His fingers shrank from even that contact with the thing inside.

"Be careful!" Dragur shuffled along beside him as he steadied the strap across his shoulder. But Kyger came to his employee's rescue.

"They are not as fragile as all that, Citizen. And here are your obaws for feeding."

He almost thrust a small cage into his customer's hold. The small animals inside were running madly about, squeaking wildly as if they had foreknowledge of their dismal future. Troy, knowing just what that future was in connection with the hur-hur, fought another sharp skirmish with his stomach.

His task was not just to carry the container as far as the flitter awaiting Citizen Dragur, Troy discovered, but to accompany the patron to his home, insuring the safety of the hur-hur while Dragur himself piloted the flyer, at a pace hardly faster than a brisk walk on the ground. Dragur, unlike Rerne, proved to be a babbler. Not that much of his conversation was directed to Horan.

Instead, the words that flowed were thoughts uttered aloud and mainly concerned with his now present ability to confound some fellow collector by the name of Supervisor Mazeli, who might outrank Dragur in the hierarchy of the department in which they were both incarcerated until they reached age-for-ease pay, but whose ambitious collection of marine life did *not* embrace a hur-hur.

"Beautiful!" Dragur crawled the flitter across an intersection of avenues, turned into the slightly wider one that led to the outskirts of Tikil. "He will never believe it—never! Next Fellowsday I shall invite him and, say, Wilvins and Sorker. And then I shall escort him around the room, show him the Lupan snails, and the throwworms, give him a chance to enlarge on what *he* has—then—" Dragur lifted one hand from the controls, reached out to pat the top of the container now riding on Troy's knees. "Then—the hur-hur! He will never, never be able to match it. Never!"

For the first time the small man seemed to recollect he did have a human companion in the flitter. "That is correct, is it not, young man? When Merchant Kyger gives a certificate of one-of-a-kind, he does not import during the lifetime of the first specimen? That is truly correct?"

Troy had not heard of that arrangement, but prudence dictated a reply in the affirmative. "I believe so, Citizen."

"Then Mazeli will never have a hur-hur—never! Their life span is two hundred years—maybe three—and Kyger has certified that this is a young one. Oh, Mazeli may wish but he cannot have! Not one such as you, my little beauty!" Dragur delivered another pat to the top of the cylinder. And perhaps some of this elation did register on the monstrosity inside, for the thing gave such a determined lurch against one side that Troy had to hold it steady with both hands.

"Careful! Careful! I say, young man! What are you doing?" Dragur brought the flitter to a complete stop and fronted Troy indignantly.

"I think it is excited, Citizen." Troy held the quivering container with both hands. "It probably wants back in an aquarium."

"Yes, of course." This time Dragur started the flitter with a jerk, and his rate of speed increased appreciably. "We shall soon be there, very soon now—"

Dragur had one of the small share-houses along the merchant zone. He unsealed the palm lock of the door with one hand, waved Troy in with the other. But the atmosphere that met Horan upon entrance was anything but enticing.

There were strange smells to be met in plenty at Kyger's, but a clever system of ventilation and deodorization kept the air from anything but a suggestion of the wares to be offered under that roof. Here the marine reek of the fish room at the shop was multiplied a thousand times.

What had been intended as the meeting room of the share-house was now a miniature sea bottom. The light itself was subdued, in a manner greenish, when compared to the daylight entering through specially tinted panels. And aquariums were set along the walls in banks with what might be a naturally formed pool in the center.

"Stand where you are, right where you are, young man!" Dragur pushed ahead, skirted the floor pool, and approached a table in the darkest corner of that dim chamber. He pulled and pushed at an empty aquarium there until he had it in line with its fellows and then proceeded to lift, with every appearance of exertion, a series of glass containers, pouring from first one and then the other, now and then leaning well over to sniff loudly and rather dramatically at the mixture.

Troy shifted his feet. The weight of the container was not light, and it kept jerking on the shoulder strap as the hur-hur continued to resent transportation. Horan was eager to be out of this cave of bad smells and marine monsters, for some of the things that bumped sides of bowls and aquariums to stare at him, or seem to stare at him, were not far removed from the hur-hur in general frightfulness.

At last the concoction appeared to satisfy Dragur. He added, with the air of an artist supplying the last touch to a masterpiece, a long string of what looked like badly decayed root fibers and beckoned to Troy.

Did Dragur think that *he* was going to transfer the hur-hur via the rod method Jingu had used? If so, this customer was not going to be a satisfied one. Troy had no intention of trying such action.

But apparently Dragur had no idea of leaving such a delicate task to a novice. He waved Troy away again as soon as the other had put down the container and took off the lid. Playing the hur-hur into clinging once more to the rod, the little man whipped the creature with even more dexterity than Jingu had displayed into its new home.

"Now!" Dragur gave the shop container back to Troy. "We must let it alone, strictly alone, two days—maybe three—only visiting it for feeding."

Troy wondered if the other imagined that he was going to be in this smelly room for another few moments, let alone two or three days! "Is that all, Citizen?" He asked firmly.

Dragur again seemed to notice him as a person. "What? Ha—yes, that will be all, young man. I have not seen you before, have I? You did not come with me last time for a delivery."

"No. I am new at Kyger's."

"Yes, it was Zul who came last time, I remember. And who are you, young man?"

"Troy Horan."

"Horan? Horan—that is an off-world name, surely?"

"I am from Norden," Troy returned as he edged toward the outer door with its promise of fresh air.

"Norden?" Dragur blinked as if trying to visualize some solar chart on which he could place Norden with dispatch and precision. "You are a former spacer then, as is Merchant Kyger?"

"I am from the Dipple."

"Oh." Dragur displayed the conventional citizen's reaction to that, embarrassment intermixed with irritation. "Assure Merchant Kyger that I am pleased, very pleased. I shall be in myself, of course, with my supply list. And please remind him that this is a one-of-a-species sale—that must be plain, very plain."

"I am sure the merchant understands, Citizen."

Dragur followed him to the door, pointed out the nearest roll walk. He did not reenter the house until Troy was several paces away. Probably, thought Horan bitterly, he just wants to make sure a Dippleman is well off the premises.

But this was not the end of a day of minor irritations and disappointments. The morning had begun so well with the awakening in the lodge of the Wild. It was ending in the evening in Tikil with his re-entering the shop to discover Zul very much the master of the cage room. Though the small yellow man walked with a limp, he walked briskly, and he did not welcome Troy back.

End of the seven-day contract—Troy was very conscious of that. He could continue here to the limit of that time and then Kyger was under no obligation to renew. With Zul back he probably would not. When Troy brought in water for the fox cage, the other waved him off, attending to the Terran animals himself. In fact he zealously preempted so many of the tasks Troy had done that the latter was elbowed out of the work almost entirely. And each time Horan saw Kyger he expected to be told that his employment would be over as soon as it was legally possible to dismiss him.

However, the merchant said nothing—until a few moments immediately preceding the official closing of the shop. Then Troy was summoned to where Kyger and Zul stood by the door of the animal room. And he could see that Zul was not pleased.

"You will take the night inspection tours as usual," Kyger ordered. His broad fingers rested on Zul's shoulder, and now he pulled the smaller man with him as easily as if Zul were powerless in his hold. The yellow man favored Troy with a glare that made the latter wish, not for the first time, that he had a right to wear a belt knife.

With the shop closed and the animals settled, Troy made his first round, starting with the now silent customers' lounges, checking each room. What he was hunting, or why he had this growing compulsion that was almost a search, he could not have told.

The lounges contained nothing out of the ordinary; the bird room was as always. He lingered before the fussel. It was hard to remember this morning. The bird permitted him to run a forefinger along its crest, drew the bill that could stab and kill across his hand in return.

Then he was in the animal room. And now he thought he knew what had driven him to this restless seeking. What *had* become of the kinkajou? No one had mentioned it since his return. The foxes had been settled in its place as if they had been there for days. Had it been returned to the Sattor Commander Di's heirs as a valuable part of his estate?

Suddenly Troy knew that he would have to discover what had become of the animal that had claimed his aid and that he might have unknowingly left unprotected, for he remembered all too well the strange conversation in the night.

On impulse he turned and left the cage room, walked straight to his bunk and stretched out on it. If he could not find the kinkajou one way, there was a chance—just a very faint chance—another and more devious path might serve.

# EIGHT

Troy's eyes were shut. He willed nerves and muscles to relax, trying to hit by chance, since he had no better guide, on the pattern that had aided him that other night to tune in upon the exchange that was not conversation. Through the coms all the usual noises from the bird and animal rooms reached him, and he tried not to listen.

"—here. Out—"

Not really words, rather impressions—a signal, a plea. Troy's eyes opened; he sat up—and that whisper of contact was gone. Angry at his own lack of control, he settled himself once more on the bunk, tried again to tap that band of communication.

"Out—out—danger—"

He lay, hardly breathing, trying to hold that line.

"Out—"

Yes, it was a plea; he was certain of that. But there was no way of discovering from whom or from where it came. He might have stumbled upon a small loop of rope in the middle of a large room, to be told to find the coil from which it had been cut.

"Where?" He tried to frame that word in his own mind, force the inquiry into the band he could not locate.

Then he received an impression of surprise—so strong it was like an exclamation his ears could pick up.

"Who? Who?" The query was eager, demanding.

"Troy—" He thought his own name but was answered by a sense of bafflement, disappointment. Maybe names meant nothing in this eerie exchange. Troy tried to build up a mental picture of his own face as he had seen it in mirrors. He thought intensely of that face, of each detail of his own features.

The sensation of bafflement faded, though he was sure he had not lost contact.

"Who?" he asked silently in return, certain that he was communicating with the kinkajou.

But instead an oddly shaped and distorted picture of a triangular mask, sharp-pointed nose, glittering eyes, pricked ears—the fox!

Troy slipped out of his bunk. He did not foresee any trouble. If Kyger or Zul turned up, he could always say he was investigating some unusual sound. Yet he took the stunner from its wall niche before he left the small room and went as noiselessly as he could down the corridor to the animal room.

There was a cover over the front of the fox cage. Troy raised that flap. Both animals sat there, watching him. He glanced about the room. Even in the dim night light he could see nothing amiss. This could not be a case of an intruder as it had been when the kinkajou's warning had saved his life.

"What is wrong?" At the moment there was nothing strange in his standing there thinking that question at a pair of Terran foxes.

"The big one—he threatens."

It was as if someone with a strictly curtailed number of words was trying to convey a complex thought. The big one—Kyger?

"Yes!" The assent was quick, eager.

"What is wrong?"

"He fears—thinks better dead—"

"Who is better dead?" Troy's grip on the stunner tightened. He felt a cold stab between his shoulders giving birth to a chill that had nothing to do with the temperature of the room.

"Those who know—all those who know—"

"Me?" Troy countered quickly. Though of what Kyger might suspect him or why he had no idea.

There was no answer. Either he had presented them with a new puzzle, or, unable to give a definite reply, they gave none at all.

"You?"

"Yes—" But there was an element of doubt in that yes.

"Others like you?" Troy pushed.

"Yes!" Now there was no mistaking the vehemence of that.

He thought of the kinkajou. One of the foxes reared, put front paws against the screening of the cage. "It was here. Now it is there."

"Where?" Troy tried to follow.

His mind pictured for him a cage, hooded and stored—but not in any room of the shop he had seen.

"In the yard pens?" he asked.

There was a long moment before the answer came and then it was evasive.

"Cool air, many smells—maybe outside."

Was the fox only relaying for the kinkajou? Troy thought that might be true.

"Cage covered—not to see—"

That fitted. The animal might well be in one of the outside pens still in a carrying cage. But to find it tonight would be a risky project, and what could he do if he did locate it?

"Hide!"

They had picked that out of his thoughts, replied to it. The standing fox was panting a little, its red tongue lolling from its jaws.

Troy considered the problem. For some reason Kyger had hidden the kinkajou, intending to get rid of it. To meddle in this at all was simply asking for trouble. Not only would the merchant break contract, but he was entitled to black-list Troy with the C.L.C. so that he could never hope for another day's labor on Korwar. That had happened to Dipplemen in the past, and for less cause. He had only to fasten down the cover of the foxes' cage, leave the room, forget everything, and he was safe.

How safe? He stared down at the fox. The kinkajou, the foxes, even the cats, all knew that he was able to communicate with them. Suppose they passed the information on to Kyger? That interrupted conversation the other night—if Kyger knew he had "heard" that—Yes, a refusal to help might cut two ways now.

He jerked the flap of the cage cover into place, making no further attempt to talk to the foxes. Then, thrusting the stunner into the top of his rider's belt, he padded to the rear door and let himself out cautiously, ducking into a convenient pool of shadow.

Just as he patrolled the shop during the night, the senior yardman made the rounds out here. And Troy's presence near some of the larger animal pens could arouse their inhabitants to noisy protest, betraying him at once. Nor did Horan have the least idea in which of these enclosures the kinkajou was now housed, if it was here at all.

He slipped along the wall, his left shoulder against it, making a quick dart across an open space to the shelter of a doorway. From that came the scent of hay, seeds, dried vegetation. And those mingled odors took him back to his twenty-four hours in the Wild. Perhaps it was then that the first flick of an idea was born—not concrete enough yet to be called a plan, just a hazy half-dream suggesting a way of escape if Kyger did dismiss him again to the Dipple.

Troy felt the door yield to his gentle push and he went in. Under his hand the panel swung almost closed once more, but through the crack he was able to reconnoiter the rest of the courtyard. In which of the pens and cages about its circumference could what he sought be effectively hidden? And would Kyger have undertaken that mission himself or left it to one of the yardmen—or Zul?

Kyger—or Zul, the most likely. Zul had not wanted Troy to be left in the shop tonight; he was certain of that. He wished he knew where that small man was right now.

There was a stir by the door that gave on the passage leading to Kyger's private apartment. A figure moved into the open and Troy saw Zul, by his present actions a Zul who did not want to be observed, for, as Troy had done, the other took advantage of every shadow to cover his journey along the row of pens.

Perhaps the creatures penned there were used to his scent and such nighttime journeys, for none of them roused. Then Zul disappeared, seemingly into a patch of wall. Where his flitting had been soundless, the tap of footsteps now sounded briskly down the opposite side of the yard, and Troy held his breath as they approached the supply room. He gently eased the panel fully shut and waited tensely to see if the patrolling guard would try it.

When the footfalls passed without pausing, Horan again opened the door a crack. He could not see the retreating yardman from this position, but he heard the door at the other end of the court close. Then he saw Zul detach himself from the wall and move on. So—Zul was keeping this a secret from the regular guard? That was most interesting.

Two, three more pens the other passed. Then he stopped before the last in that row, a larger enclosure where two small trasi from Longus were kept. They were very tame and most affectionate creatures of a subspecies of deer.

The pen door opened and Zul disappeared within, the darkness there hiding him entirely.

"Obey!"

Troy's hand went to his head at the force of that menacing thought-order, which struck like a blow. But to it there was not the faintest trace of an answer, either agreement or protest. Somehow Troy could imagine Zul stooped above a shrouded cage, trying to arouse a ball of fur that remained stubbornly impervious to his commands.

"Listen!" Again that whip crack of order. "You will obey!"

Again only complete silence. Will against will—animal opposing man? Troy leaned his forehead against the cool surface of the door behind which he half crouched, trying with every fiber of will and strength to listen in on the duel that he was sure was being waged across the courtyard.

Minutes dragged. Then Zul slid out of the pen, made his way back along the wall, disappeared into the same passage the spacers used when they visited the shop. Troy counted slowly under his breath. When he reached fifty and there was no movement in the courtyard, he came out of the storeroom, went to the trasi pen.

The animals stirred as he lifted the latch and let himself in. Only a little of the limited light in the yard reached here, and at first he thought that he must have been mistaken; there was no cage in sight. He stooped, brushed through the hay piled against the far wall, to bark his knuckles painfully against solid surface. Then he hunkered down, feeling over the covered cage for the fastenings. They had been doubly tied and he had difficulty in loosening them.

Though the kinkajou must have been aware of his efforts, it made no move, neither a stir nor a mind touch. The flap of the cover was up now, but Troy could not see into the cage. He unfastened the catch of the door.

Troy fell back as a half-seen thing flashed into the loose hay, tossing up a small whirlwind of scattered wisps, squeezed under the bottom of the pen door and was gone—before the man half comprehended that the captive had been poised ready for escape. There was no use now trying to find it in the courtyard. There were a hundred places that might have been designed to conceal a fast-moving arboreal animal such as the kinkajou—which left Troy where?

He snapped shut the cage, refastened the covering the same way he had found it. Brushing hay from his coveralls, he detached a last telltale length from his belt. There was no use in looking for more trouble. The kinkajou was loose, and he could not help believing that the animal was far safer at this moment than it had been in that cage. Let its empty prison provide a morning mystery for Kyger or Zul.

Troy went back to his bunk. He was convinced now that his employer had a part in a game more important than smuggling, a game in which the animals were involved. And as he dozed off, he wondered just how many four-footed Terrans with strange mental powers had been loosed on Korwar—and why.

If the kinkajou had been missed, there was no alarm given the next day. The routine followed the same pattern it had every morning that Troy had been employed by Kyger's, with the exception that Zul now took over a major portion of the indoor work and Troy was relegated to sweeping and cleaning jobs, which were the least desirable. But at noon he was summoned to the bird room, for it appeared that competent as he might be in other ways, Zul was not the handler favored by the fussel.

Troy could hear the bird's angry screams while he was still in the corridor. And Kyger, scowling, stood waving him to hurry. Zul, chattering in some language other than Galbasic, was fairly dancing in his own heat of rage, a bleeding hand held now and again to his wide-lipped mouth as he sucked a deep tear in the flesh.

Troy spoke to the merchant. "We shall have to have quiet."

Kyger nodded, reached out for Zul, and manhandled the struggling man out. The fussel was beating its wings, its beak stretched to the limit as it screamed.

Troy approached the bird slowly, crooning a monotone of such small soothing sounds as, he had discovered during his night rounds, combatted the suspicions and alarms of any disturbed cage dweller. There was no hurrying this. To arouse the fussel to the state of fighting against the cage would be to damage the bird, if not physically, then emotionally. Troy summoned all his concentration of mind and body, unconsciously trying to reach the bird's mind by the same method he had used to communicate with the Terran animals. He was aware of no response in return, but the fussel did quiet, until, at last, Troy could take it out on his wrist. He moved to the door, eager to walk the bird in the open where it might lose its agitation.

Kyger stood aside for him. "The courtyard," he suggested. "I will see you have it free for a space."

An hour later the great hawk was restored to good humor and Troy returned it to the cage. He was pulling off his glove when Kyger joined him.

"That was well done. We can use you on staff. Will you take full contract?"

This was what he had hardly dared hope for—a contract that would register him as a subcitizen! He would be free of the Dipple forever, since you were not demoted from a full contract except for a very serious criminal cause; the laws of Korwar would operate in his favor, not against him, from now on. Yet—there were all those nagging little doubts, and the affair of the kinkajou. Beneath that was something else as well, the feeling that he did not want to be a loyal employee of Kyger's, tied by custom and ethics to the purposes of the shop. What he did want he had sensed only vaguely that morning on the plateau in the Wild—a freedom not to be found in Tikil. But that was stupid. Troy disciplined his wishes never to be realized and looked to his employer with all the gratitude he could muster.

"Yes, Merchant, I accept."

"Another day for the old contract to run—then the new. Meanwhile"—Kyger observed the fussel—"we don't want any more trouble with this one. I will com the Hunter Headquarters in the city and if they will accept delivery on Rerne's behalf, you can take the bird there tonight."

But within the hour Zul brought a message from Kyger, and Troy came to the office to find the merchant striding up and down, his fingers picking at his scar. He had never given the impression of an easily disturbed man, but he was not the calm and confident purveyor of luxuries to Tikil now.

"We close early," he told Troy. "Do not answer any queries on the door com. And make your rounds on time. I will not be here—but if there is any trouble, hit the alarms at once. Do not try to handle it yourself. The patrollers will take over."

What did Kyger expect, an armed invasion? Troy knew that this was not the time to ask anything. The other had gathered up a hooded night cloak—usually the garment for one venturing into the less reputable portions of the town—and he was wearing his service blaster. It was a certain bleak look in his eyes, a set to his jaw, that warned off questions.

To Troy's satisfaction Zul accompanied his master. Now, with the shop closed and yet the hour early, he would have a chance to look about the courtyard. He did not believe that the kinkajou would remain in hiding there unless the fact that it must have imported food would tie it to the source of supply. But maybe he could prove or disprove that theory tonight.

There were only two places that had not been open to constant view during the day—the storeroom in which he had taken refuge the night before and Kyger's own quarters. The latter he had no hope of exploring. They would be locked, to be opened only by the pressure of the merchant's own hand—or a blaster.

But the storeroom, filled with boxes, bales, containers, had a score of hiding places into which a frightened animal could tuck itself. The foxes in the animal room—the kinkajou free. Troy could not rid himself of the thought that those three might be in contact. Would he be able to reach and influence the fugitive through the two still in the cage? And why were they still in the shop? To Troy's knowledge there had been no message sent to the Grand Leader One that her pets had arrived.

Armed with a food box, he went to the animal room. Again the foxes' prison was curtained. Troy loosened the flap. One of the animals was sleeping, or seeming to sleep. The other also sprawled, its eyes half closed. And seeing them, Troy could almost doubt his belief in their powers.

"Where is the other?" he thought, trying to get into that demand a little of the force Zul had used in his questioning of the kinkajou.

The waking fox yawned, then brought its jaws together with a snap, its eyes still bemused—with no outward interest in Troy at all. The man tried again, throttling down his impatience, using the same gentle approach he had brought to the soothing of the fussel—with no result. If there was any contact between the foxes and the fugitive, they would not employ it for Troy. He would have to hunt on his own.

He was on his way back to the courtyard when the com shrilled, drawing him to the nearest viewplate. The clouded image there settled into a rather fuzzy focus of Kyger's features.

"Horan?"

Troy thumbed the answer lever. "Here, Merchant."

"You will turn guard duty over to Jingu and deliver the fussel to the Hunter Headquarters in the Torrent District. Understand?"

"Understood," Troy assented. There went his hopes for exploring the storeroom. He went to tidy his clothes, and then to select a traveling cage for the bird. Would Rerne be there, back from his mysterious errand? He found himself hoping so.

# NINE

Tikil at night, or at least during the early hours of the night, was more crowded than by day. Horan called an accommodation flitter for his crosstown journey to the Hunter Headquarters, but he decided to use the roll walk on his return. He was going toward it when Harse hailed him, just in front of the building.

"You seek Rerne?"

"I brought the fussel, by Merchant Kyger's orders." Troy was put on the defensive by the other's attitude. During their brief time together Rerne had never made him conscious of the Dipple. With the other rangers Horan was ever aware of his knifeless belt and the fact he was a planetless man.

"There is a message," Harse replied aloofly. "Rerne wishes to speak with you—"

"But I was just told he is not here."

"So he is elsewhere. Come!"

Troy was tempted to reply "no" to that curt order. After all, he was not under contract to Rerne. Yet he could not deny that he was interested to learn why Harse had been sent to find him.

The other was as adept at threading a fast passage through the crowds as he might have been in finding a path through the forests. And he brought Troy not to any office or lounge, but to one of those small eating places that sprang up overnight by public favor and disappeared as quickly when some newer attraction drew the fickle pleasure seekers.

"Fourth booth," Harse said and left him.

Troy pushed his way in and discovered that his shop livery did not make him conspicuous here. This cafe definitely catered to subcitizens and the lower ranks of shop employees. Two of the booths were curtained, signifying private parties. But there were two men without feminine company in the one to which he had been directed.

Rerne, wearing shop livery, sat with his back against the wall. And with him was an older man in a dark tunic lacking any emblems of rank, yet equipped with that indefinable aura of authority that Troy recognized as the inborn assurance of a man who has held responsibility from his early years.

"Horan—" Rerne uttered his name in what might be a greeting, but more likely was an introduction for the stranger's benefit.

"Rogarkil." Now the stranger nodded to Troy.

"You have taken permanent contract with Kyger?" Rerne shot that question at him bluntly, even as he waved the younger man to a seat.

"I will—tomorrow—" A subtle tone in the other's demand made him uneasy, put him on the defensive—why, he could not have said.

"You are now under a short-term one?" That was Rogarkil.

"That is so."

"And if you should be offered employment elsewhere?"

"I have given my word to Merchant Kyger. He would have to agree to my going."

Rogarkil smiled wryly. "There are always such disadvantages when one deals with honorable men. And to deal with dishonorable ones is to lose before one takes the first stride in a race. So at this hour you are still Merchant Kyger's man?"

"I am."

What did they want of him? This talk of honor and dishonor made Troy uncomfortable. But Rerne did not give him time to speculate about the meanings that might lie behind their fencing blades of words.

"There are questions you can answer, which will in no way break contract. For example: Is it not true that Merchant Kyger is now in the process of importing a Terran animal known as a fox at the express order of the Great Leader?"

"You yourself heard that order given, Gentle Homo."

"And he has imported other Terran animals?"

"As you say, Gentle Homo, he has imported other Terran animals. This must be general knowledge, since the display of such pets is the pleasure of those who buy them."

"A pair of cats for the Gentle Fem San duk Var, a kinkajou for Sattor Commander Di—"

"I am a cleaner of cages and do general labor for the worthy merchant," Troy returned stiffly. "I do not make sales, nor do I see many of the great ones who buy."

"But among those cages that you clean," cut in Rogarkil, "are doubtless those of some of these exotics. You have seen some of them with your own eyes, young man?"

Troy kept strictly to the record. "I was with Subcitizen Zul when he went to the port to accept delivery of the cats—"

"And you met with some trouble that morning—"

Troy looked slowly from one man to the other. "Gentle Homos," he said softly, "if I speak now to patrollers not in uniform, I have the right to know that fact. There is still law to protect a man in Tikil—even one from the Dipple."

Rogarkil grimaced. "Yes, you are entirely within your rights, young man, to deliver such a counterthrust as that. No, we are not patrollers—nor do we represent the law of Tikil. This is a Clan matter. Do you understand what that means?"

"Even in the Dipple, Gentle Homo, men have ears and lips. Yes, I know that the Clans are older than the city law, that they are rumored to have powers even beyond those of the Council Governor-General. But they are of the Clans and for the Clans. I am of the Dipple and if I am to climb out of the Dipple, I must do so under the laws of Tikil. Why you ask me these questions I do not know, but I hold by contract rights. This much I will say—and it is no more than you can learn from the patroller records—I have seen the cats. And I took the kinkajou from the villa of Sattor Commander Di. It had been frightened by rough handling there. I have seen the foxes, which are now in the shop. Why should these facts be of any importance?"

"That is what we are striving to learn," Rogarkil answered enigmatically. "You are right, Horan. Clan law does not run in Tikil. But remember that it does run elsewhere—"

"A threat—or a warning, Gentle Homo?"

"A warning. We have reason to believe that you walk on the rim of a whirlpool, young man. Take good care that you do not leap into its current."

"That is all you have to ask me?"

Rogarkil waved his hand in dismissal. But Rerne arose as Troy did.

"I will see Merchant Kyger."

"Not tonight. The shop is closed."

Both men eyed him now as if he had made some fateful announcement.

"Why?"

"Kyger had an errand—"

Rerne turned to his companion, spoke a sharply accented sentence in a language that was not Galbasic. Rogarkil asked Troy another question: "Is not this foreign to your regular routine?"

"Yes."

"So—well, maybe Merchant Kyger's personal affairs are beginning to press him more acutely," he commented. "One cannot carry a knife in two quarrels and give equal attention to both. But the foxes are still there?" He turned to Troy. "And where is the kinkajou you took from Di's villa—also in the shop?"

Troy shrugged. "When I returned from the Wild, it was gone from the cage room. Perhaps it was restored to the Sattor Commander's heirs. It is a very valuable asset of the estate."

"Kyger did not return it so," Rerne stated with finality. He was watching Troy narrowly now, coldly.

"It was gone from its cage." Troy repeated the part-truth stubbornly. He was not going to add to that when he did not know the game they were playing—the nature of this "whirlpool" in which he, too, could be trapped.

"The boy is right, of course," Rogarkil said. "Employed as casual labor, he would have no reason to know more than he has noticed. And he is a man under contract, apart from our problems. It is a pity this is so now, Horan. Under other circumstances we might have been of mutual assistance to one another. A rider of Norden is not too far removed in aspirations and desires from a Hunter of Korwar."

"There are no riders on Norden today," Troy pointed out. He was watching Rerne, and again it seemed to him that the Hunter was two-minded, about to speak and then thinking better of it. Instead he nodded and Troy took that gesture for one of dismissal. He lifted his own hand in a small salute—one of equality though he was not aware of that—and walked away from the booth. Why was he gnawed by the feeling that he had just slammed a door irrevocably, a door that might have opened on a new world? There was an ache of disappointment in him that was like the bite of an old unappeasable hunger.

He pushed through the crowds, hardly noticing those about him, made his way back to the shop and the side entrance into the courtyard. Slapping his hand against the signal plate, he waited for the night yardman to activate the open beam for him. But instead, at that touch from his open palm, the panel swung inward and he was looking down the short covered way, a way that was unnaturally dim as if the usual night-radiance bars there had been set at least two notches lower than was normal.

Troy's stunner was in the bunk room. He was unarmed, and he had no intention of walking that courtyard without some form of defense. The door had no right to be open; the dimmed lights underlined that silent warning. He could well be facing a trap.

Now he unfastened the polished silver buckles of his belt. The strip of metal-encrusted leather was the only thing on him that could serve as a weapon. With one end grasped tightly in his fist, the length ready to use as a lash, he edged along the wall of the passage, listening to catch any sound from the courtyard beyond.

The mild complaints of the animals penned there could cover an attack. But from whom and for what purpose? Troy reached the end of the passage, flattened his body against the wall just inside the entrance, and surveyed the open. There was something wrong about the south side—

Then he pinpointed that difference. The door that led to Kyger's private quarters, which he had never seen open, stood ajar now—painting an unfamiliar shadow across a section of pavement. And in the center of the yard stood a flitter. Whether it was the shop flyer he could not tell.

The open door and that waiting flyer were not all. There was an atmosphere of sharp expectancy about the whole scene—as if the stage awaited actors. Maybe the animals were sensitive to that also, for there were only the most subdued sounds from the pens. Again Troy smelled "trap" as if it were a tangible odor in the air. But somehow he could not believe it was set for him.

Kyger then? That fitted better. He had had hints of some personal difficulty—perhaps even a knife feud—engulfing the merchant. And there was the Clan's concern with the ex-spacer, too. Troy Horan was very small fry indeed. This suggested an operation on a much more important scale.

Prudence dictated his getting across that courtyard, into his own bunk room, without any exploration—if he could make it unobserved by what might hide out there. And what about Zul? The little man had left with Kyger—but what if he had returned separately? The yardmen? From what he could see, there was no indication that there was any human anywhere in the store block.

A flicker of movement, not in the courtyard but on the top of one of the blocks of pens, drew Troy's eyes. There was a second such. Something small, dark, fluidly supple, had crossed a patch of light, been followed by another such. Far too small to be Zul—animals loose from some cage? But why on the roof coming *in*? The shadows into which both had slipped were far too deep for his sight to penetrate, and the speed with which they had disappeared suggested they might already be far away from that point.

A gathering—why did he think of that? Troy measured the distance between him and the nearest cover. Then, with as much speed as he could muster, he made that leap, stood listening once more, his breath coming raspingly.

Another surge of shadow, drawn toward that half-open door of Kyger's. This moving, not with the slinking glide of the patch on the roof, but in a quick, scuttling dash, again too hurried for Troy to see clearly. But he was sure it whipped about the edge of the door, went into the merchant's private quarters.

Troy made his own advancing rush. Then he saw round balls of green turned up toward him from close to ground level, feral animal eyes. The belt swung in his hand, his reaction to being so startled. They were gone as another form went through the door.

His earlier alarm had been tinged with curiosity. Now there was another emotion feeding it. Just as those shadows had gone to the waiting door, so did he have to follow. He crossed the last few feet and entered, somehow expecting an attack.

Here the sounds from the courtyard were muted. But there was that which was not a sound, rather a thrumming in the blood, a throb in the ears—less than audible sound, or more. He knew of whistles, animal and bird calls, that sounded notes beyond the human range of hearing. Yet he could feel this that he could not hear, and it was an irritant, a disturbance that nourished fear. But he could not turn his back upon it.

Troy groped his way forward, for there was no night ray on. Then his foot touched a rising surface and he explored a stairway with his hands. Step by step he climbed, the thick substance of the footing soaking up any sound of his boots. The throb was beating more heavily through his body as he went.

The stairway ended. He stood listening—and knew that no longer was he alone, though no sound, not even that of a hurried breath, betrayed whoever, or whatever, shared that darkness with him.

Troy had no idea of the geography of the space in which he now was, and there could not be any open window slits, for the dark was complete. He kept stern rein on his imagination, which tended to people this place with shapes that crept and slunk toward the target—which was himself. On impulse he squatted on his heels, marked off a foot or so on the belt he held, and swung it from left to right at floor level. Sure of that much clear space, he inched on to try the same maneuver again.

How long he might have taken to make the trip across the hall Troy was never to know, for a sudden shaft of light speared dazzlingly from right to left some feet away. And as his eyes adjusted to that, Troy saw it issued from a panel door not quite closed.

He was in a hallway from which three such doors issued, all of them on his right. And it was the last one that showed the light. No sound—but he could not retreat now. Someone—or something—knew he was there, was waiting. And he had to face it.

On his feet again, Troy moved lightly and swiftly to that panel. His hand touched its surface—now he could look in, though he was not sure the man in that room could see him.

Kyger sat there, not in the enveloping embrace of an eazi-rest, but upright on a queer, backless, armless stool, his shoulders against the wall. And between his hands was a cylinder perhaps a foot in diameter, one end resting on the floor guarded by his firmly planted boots, its top slightly below his chin.

No man could sit that quietly, not if he was conscious. Yet Kyger's eyes were open, staring—not at Troy as the other first supposed, but beyond and through him, as if the younger man had no existence. And that frozen stare moved Troy forward, made him push open the panel and step within.

Kyger did not stir. Troy, tongue running across suddenly dry lips, came on. It was an oddly bare room. There was Kyger on his stool, gripping his cylinder. There was a series of small pol-ished cabinets, all closed and with plainly visible thumb locks, and that was all.

Troy spoke and then wished he had not as his words echoed hollowly. "Merchant Kyger—is there something wrong?"

Kyger continued to stare and Troy at last knew the truth—Kyger was a dead man. He whirled, seeking behind him the one who had put on the light—to see nothing save a wall on which there were patterned lines of red, black, and white laid down in a map's design. A map of Tikil, he realized as he surveyed it, in which the open door panel had left a break in the eastern section.

Purposefully Troy moved to the right of the seated man. He could see no wound, no indication of any violence. Yet Kyger had not died naturally—his position, this room, argued that. And what of the thing or things that he had seen precede him through the downstairs door?

Leaving the panel open for light, Troy went back into the hall, pushed open both other doors. One gave on a bedchamber, the other on a small lounge-diner, both empty.

He went back to Kyger's room. And now, fronting him out of nowhere, were those shadows—the black cat and its blue-gray mate, the kinkajou, no longer an indifferent ball but very much alert, the two foxes he could have sworn were safe in their cage in the other building. It looked as if the full roll of Terran imports to Korwar was before him now. And their lips were drawn back from their teeth, the hair of the cats was roughened on their arched backs, their united menace could be felt as a blow.

"No!" Oddly enough he answered that unvoiced rage and fear with word and gesture, dropping the belt, holding his hands up and palm out to them as if he faced another of his own species.

The black cat relaxed first, pacing forward a paw's length or so, and Troy dropped on one knee. "No," he repeated as firmly but in a lower tone. Then he held out his hand as he had seen Kyger do on the morning they had first uncrated the cats in the courtyard.

A delicate sniff or two, and then sharp teeth closed on the back of his wrist, not to hurt, he knew, but as if to seal some agreement. Troy did not have a chance to learn more, for there was a sound from below. Someone who had no reason to disguise his coming was climbing the stairs.

Troy strode to the panel of the hall door. Then he knew that his silhouette could be seen from below, and he ducked to one side. It was the action of only a few seconds, but when he glanced at the animals, they were gone. Where they had vanished to he could not guess, but that they had their suspicions concerning the newcomer he could deduce from that disappearance.

There was no such escape for him. Troy stepped back a little, picked up his belt, and, with it ready in his hand, stood waiting.

Zul came into the path of the light. He gave Troy a wide-eyed stare, looked beyond to the motionless Kyger. Then, his lips pulled tight against his teeth, just as the animals had snarled, he launched himself at Troy, his knife out, a vicious streak of fire in his hand.

# TEN

Troy dodged and licked out with his belt lash for the wrist of Zul's knife hand. The buckle-loaded tip found its mark, and the smaller man yelped and swung around so that his outflung, balancing arm brushed against the tube Kyger's dead fingers steadied. The cylinder fell and the body of the merchant followed it, wilting bonelessly to the floor. Zul screeched, a cry as high and unhuman as any the animals or birds could have uttered.

At the same time Troy felt a cessation of that thrumming throb. The tube rolled toward him, and Zul, seeming to forget his rage of only seconds earlier, made a grab for it.

Troy kicked, sending the tube spinning. Then he brought the edge of his hand down across Zul's neck, dropping the little man to lie on the floor gasping. Troy had leisure to collect both knife and cylinder before Zul sat up, still breathing in hoarse rasps.

With the knife and tube laid on top of a cabinet, Troy advanced on Zul. It was like trying to master by force a frenzied animal, one that scratched and bit. In spite of his repugnance, Troy was forced to knock the smaller man out in order to fasten his hands behind him with his own belt.

Troy was rebuckling his rider's broad cincture when he saw Zul's eyes open and take in the limp body of Kyger. The small man's face twisted in a grimace Troy could not read. Then he strained to raise his head from the floor, looked about eagerly, as if he wanted something more important for the moment than Troy. His attention centered on the tube where it lay with one end projecting over the edge of the cabinet, and he actually began to wriggle his body across the floor toward it.

Troy stepped between. Zul's grimace was now an open snarl. He spat, struggled to lever himself from the floor.

Troy picked up the tube and took it with him as he moved to the red alarm button on the wall. The quicker he summoned the authorities, the less trouble he would have in telling his own tale.

"No!" For the first time Zul spoke intelligibly. "Not the patrollers!"

"Why not? I have nothing to hide. Have you?"

Zul's frantic squirming across the room had brought him to the row of cabinets. Now he wriggled his shoulders up against that support so that he was sitting, not lying.

"No patrollers!" he repeated, and his words now held the tone of an order rather than a plea. "Not yet—"

"Why?"

Zul's dark eyes were again focused on the tube Troy held. He was plainly a man torn between the need for secrecy and the necessity of having help.

Troy pressed. "Because of the animals—the Terran animals?"

Zul froze, his small body suddenly rigid, his face the personified mask of surprise—and perhaps some other emotions Troy could not read.

"What do you know?" His words were harsh, rasping, as if he had to fight for the breath to expel them.

"Enough." Troy hoped that ambiguity would force some revelation out of his captive.

Zul's tongue tip wet his lips. He hitched his shoulders along the cabinets as if to reach Troy.

"They must be killed—quickly—before the patrollers are called."

Troy was startled. Death for those who had met him in this room was the last thing he would have expected from Zul. And certainly he had no intention of yielding to that.

"Why?"

Zul's eyes changed, became sly and suspicious once again. "If you do not know, Dippleman, then you know nothing. They are a danger—to all of us under this roof they are a great danger, now that their master is dead. You will kill, or you will wish that you had died also."

Troy covered the space between them in one long-legged stride. He stooped, caught Zul by the collar of his tunic, and pulled him to his feet, holding him pinned against a cabinet.

"You will tell me why these animals are a danger," he said softly, trying to put into that speech all the force and menace he could muster.

"Because"—Zul's eyes were lifted to Troy's; apparently he was making a last throw, which might or might not contain the truth—"they are more than animals. They think, they take orders, they report—"

"What orders do they take, and to whom do they report?"

Zul swallowed visibly. There were small beads of oily moisture forming on his forehead just below the tight knots of his hair. Yet Troy sensed that he was not afraid of his captor, but of something else. "They take their orders from him who summons them." Zul's eyes flicked to the tube and back again to Troy's face. "And they report to him—"

"What?"

"Information."

Puzzle pieces clicked together in Troy's mind. Pets—with the ability to understand their masters' or mistresses' actions, to collect information—planted in households where information worth a high price could be gathered!

"And Kyger did this?" That was a statement as well as a question.

"Yes. Now the animals must be summoned and killed before the patrollers arrive. Give me the caller."

"I think not." So Zul did not know that the animals had already arrived to answer the call of a dead or dying man. And as Troy made a decision of his own, he was answered by a thrust of emotion from the seemingly empty spaces of the room—fear, such as had moved the kinkajou to his arms in the garden, a determination to fight, perhaps, too, a vague plea. And he knew that he was again tuned in on the hidden five. If the animals had been used by Kyger in some scheme, certainly they had only been tools.

"Let the patrollers get them," Zul continued, "and they will have them under probes to learn what they can—and kill them afterwards. Is it not better to kill them cleanly before that is done?"

Troy stiffened, felt his own reaction intensified as the others picked it up. What Zul said made such good sense it presented a new form of danger, and a very big one. But his own thoughts were racing ahead.

So far only those in this room knew that Kyger was dead, with the exception of his killer—which gave Troy a small measure of time. He knew that he could not let Zul kill the animals, and he would fight to keep them from falling into the hands of those who would wring secrets out of them via the probes.

Flight—But where? Memory painted for him a picture of that plateau high in the clean wind. Not perhaps there—but the Wild that stretched over half of this continent. To shake one man and five small animals out of that would be a long and arduous task, and before it was done perhaps he could find a solution to their problem in another way.

"You'll have to let me call them—and kill them quickly!" Zul was losing control, his voice rasping louder as he watched Troy with narrowed eyes.

"Be quiet!" Troy enforced that order by planting his hand over the other's mouth. Holding Zul so in spite of his renewed writhings, Horan tried to contact the animals.

"Go together—away from here." He thought those words with all the emphasis he could, not trying to analyze why he must champion the five, only knowing that it was very important to do so—not only for them but for him.

If Zul understood what he was doing, he gave no sign of it. As he fought to be free of Troy's hold, his eyes were now wild above the temporary gag of the other's palm.

There was again a flicker of movement, which Troy caught only from the corners of his eyes. The black cat materialized as if from the flooring, came stealthily, with its belly fur brushing the carpet, skirting Kyger's outflung arm. And Zul, sighting it over Troy's hand, was still. Troy waited as the cat reached them, to front Zul with a silent, menacing snarl, hatred expressed in every fluid line of its body.

"They do not need to be called, Zul," Troy said softly, "for they are here. And from here they shall go safely."

So they came—the other cat in a swift spring, the foxes side by side, and last of all the kinkajou in a rush that brought it to Troy, to climb up his body as if it were a tree.

"We shall all go together for a little, Zul." Troy swung the smaller man about, held him before him with one hand as he transferred Zul's knife to his own belt. He dropped the tube to the floor, and the black cat went into instant action, setting it rolling with small paw taps until the cylinder disappeared under one of the cabinets. Now all the animals, save the kinkajou which rode on Troy's shoulder, its tail loosely coiled about the man's neck, slipped out the door.

Zul might have been shocked speechless by the appearance of that furred company and their cooperation with Troy. He obeyed the other's push like a controlled robot, and all his struggles ceased as they went down the stairs, heading toward the courtyard.

One part of Troy's mind considered the matter of supplies—and the flitter. So much depended now on chance and luck, and he would have to hope for help from both.

Still holding Zul, he paused just within the passage door and looked out into the courtyard. The flitter was just where he had seen it last. From the pens and cages came the usual night sounds. And there was no sign of the yardman who should have been on duty.

Troy caught a stir at the side of the flitter, knew that the animals had picked that much of his intention from his mind. At this hour the air lanes would be crowded with villa dwellers returning home from night spots in Tikil. He would have that traffic for cover from the patrollers.

Now that he had made his decision, Troy had to throttle down the excitement bubbling in him. For the first time in years he was going to sample freedom. He had had a very small taste of that on the expedition with Rerne, but this time the choice was his alone.

Zul remained the immediate problem. Troy continued to propel the other before him until they reached the storeroom. Since they had left the room in which Kyger lay, the other had not struggled. It might have been that he had no more desire than Troy to draw attention to their activities.

Inside, Troy shoved his captive into a corner and worked fast. He knew that Kyger had made a point of supplying the Terran animals with special imported food, and he tossed into a sack such containers of that as he could find. Zul's knife was in his belt and in addition the flitter would have a stunner in its arms locker. He drew the cord of the sack tight, with Zul watching him. The latter spoke and Troy knew he meant every word he said.

"We shall hunt and we shall kill. And the patrollers will hunt also. There is no place you can hide that one or the other of us will not find. And for you also there will be death now."

"Because I know too much?" Troy suggested.

"Because of that—and because of this. We cannot allow knowledge of this thing."

"And you will set the patrollers on me—"

Zul grinned. "There will be no need to tell them of the animals. They will come and find a dead man where one of his hirelings has fled. That is a story that needs no telling, even to the most stupid."

"Suppose they find that two have fled?" Troy asked. He had no wish to take Zul along; that would be like fitting a triggered egg bomb into the flitter. But the disappearance of two of Kyger's employees at the same time, and one of them an old associate of the ex-spacer, might muddy the trail as far as the law was concerned.

Slinging the bag over his shoulder, he closed on Zul again, herding him out of the storeroom in the direction of the flitter. But that plan was to go awry. There was a sudden shout from the passage leading to Kyger's quarters. Zul relaxed, made himself a dead weight that Troy could not hope to manhandle into the flyer without a loss of precious time. He leaped over the prone man and scrambled into the flitter, hoping the animals were already on board.

"Here!" Out of nowhere came that reassurance as Troy took the lift control and raised the machine out of the well of the courtyard. Lights showed in the forepart of Kyger's rooms. Perhaps one of the yardmen had discovered the body. Troy must make the best use of the small head start that he had.

The main stream of the late traffic went north, not east, and he would have to weave into that, not making the necessary turn until he was well over the villa section. Also the flitter must keep within the lawful speed of the passenger lanes.

Troy triggered the com on the control panel and listened intently for any hint that the alarm had been raised behind him. Zul's words had not been an idle threat. However, once in the Wild, he did not fear the patrollers too much.

What did concern him was the Clan rangers, organized to track down just such unauthorized invasions as his own. They knew the wilderness intimately. This realization made future prospects suddenly far more bleak for Troy, and they grew grimmer the farther he flew. Yet he had made his choice and there was no turning back.

Rerne! If cornered, dare he appeal to the Hunter? Once more he experienced the odd duality he had known that morning on the plateau. Part of him was untrusting, wary, disillusioned, and another segment pulled toward confidence in the ranger, a longing for the freedom in which he and his kind walked under an open sky.

A patroller cruised above his flitter, and Troy sat stiff and tense, waiting for the order to land. Then the official flyer darted away, and he drew a really deep breath once more. The traffic about him was thinning. Soon he would have to make his dash out of the regular lanes into what he hoped would be the concealment of the night. He saw the twinkle of villa lights, two of them among the rising heights. Snapping off his lawful lights, he banked to the right, coming around to head eastward in a burst of speed that should tear him well away from the city lanes before he was noticed.

But it was several very long moments before he could be sure of that escape. So far there had been no warning broadcast on the com. Certainly if the men in the shop had been aroused, they would have called in the patrollers and there would be a blanket alarm out for the stolen flitter. Zul—was Zul still determined to hold off the law as long as he could to serve his own purposes?

And in the last warning the little man had said "we"—not "I". Who were "we"? If Kyger was not the master of the animals—and Zul was certainly a subordinate—then who was? Someone in Tikil with power enough to delay the official hunt so that a private and deadly one could be put into motion? Zul had warned Troy that he would be the quarry of two chases. And in the Wild perhaps tailed by the Clans as well.

Troy's lips shaped a mirthless smile. Too many hunting parties might just foul each other. He would not speculate on chances that might not exist. One move at a time was all anyone could make.

The flitter sped on into the night, northeast. Before daylight caught them and he would have to set down, they should be well into the wilderness. And, remembering the mountain chains Rerne had lifted them above, he set the flyer to climbing, though the automatic alarm system was on and the autopilot would avoid any crash against an unseen peak.

He became conscious of warmth against his thigh and side, the soft touch of a small paw on his nervously rigid arm. The kinkajou was pressed against him, and the rest of that odd crew had climbed into the other half of the driver's seat. Troy began to talk, not knowing how much of what he said reached their minds, but driven by the impulse to put his nebulous plans into words.

"There is the Wild ahead—and only the rangers and the native animals in it. Such a place should hold many hiding places for such as we—"

"And good hunting." From one of them had come that quick reply. He sensed a rising excitement that was born not of fear or the need for defense but of anticipation—an emotion that all five of them shared.

"Good hunting." He confirmed that. "Trees, and plains, mountains, rivers, rocks—"

"It is good to run free." Out of the general aura of satisfaction those definite words arose.

"It is good to run free!" Troy echoed. Free of the Dipple, of Tikil—of the ways of men, which he had endured only because of his own stubborn determination not to be broken.

Overhead the stars made a clear, cold pattern, and the green round of the moon, rising above the mountains, showed snow caps like clear jade. The fugitives were across the first rim of the Larsh—into the Wild—and still no hint that the chase was up behind. Troy knew again the heady exultation of one who is pulling off an odds-against mission. He had no map, no points of reference, but he was certain that to simply continue northeast would bring him out along the fringe of the plains.

He set the controls on complete autopilot, stretched his arms wide. His shoulders ached from the rigid tension that had held him during the first hours of flight.

"By dawn," he told his companions, "we shall be down—in a big country where there are no trails."

The kinkajou had crowded into his lap, was curling up against him. And now the black cat was at his side, sitting upright, watching the night sky outside the bubble of the flitter, as if it had now accepted Troy as one of its own kind.

He must have drowsed, for the red snap of light on the control panel brought him awake with the stupid dullness of a too quickly aroused sleeper.

"Warn off! Warn off!"

Troy had heard just that same metallic voice before, but he could not remember when or why.

His hands went to the controls. He thumbed the autopilot release, but it did not give. As he hammered at it with his fist, that blink of light became steady and he remembered—Ruhkarv!

"Warn off!"

Troy reached for the mike, to say the words that would end their escape attempt. But that move came too late. The red light was now a beam. Out of the night blossomed a huge burst of eye-searing white. The flitter lurched, lost speed, started down.

# ELEVEN

Afterwards Troy could recall little of that crazy falling-leaf descent that threw them from one side of the pilot's seat to the other. They were not quite helpless before the force that had shaken them off course and out of the sky, for the accident-safety ray had flashed on automatically, bringing them down to ground level at a speed under that of a direct crash. Troy fought the controls, beat at the lock with the full force of his wrists and arms. Something gave and for an instant or so the flitter was his again. He tried to put the nose up and the flyer gave a giant hop.

If that action did not win them the sky again, it did carry the flyer—with the effect of bursting through a taut curtain—beyond the influence of the thing that had grabbed them out of the air. Troy felt the flitter wheels strike, bouncing them up. They flattened off in a second crash, and it was dark—moon and stars blotted out.

His chest hurt and his head ached. In his mouth was the unforgettable flat sweet taste of blood. Before him was darkness, but from behind came a measure of light that he could sight as he tried to turn his head.

"Out—out—" That was a plea rising to a kind of frenzy. Troy

could feel movement beside him, back and forth across his bruised body until he grunted with pain.

Somehow he forced up his left arm, worked at the catch of the cabin door, lunging against that stubborn barrier with the strength of his shoulder. The panel gave, tumbling him out, and small paws thudded on him as their owners raced into the open.

Troy pulled himself up and tried to see where they had come to earth. Under him the surface of the ground seemed singularly smooth. His hand, questing over it, scraped up the grit of sand that lay in a drifted skim on stone or rock, very level stone or rock. As he twisted fully around, he could see the shaft of moonlight better. Behind—yes—the flitter had in some incredible way fitted itself nose first into a crevice where an arch of roof shut off the sky.

Troy worked his way around the wreckage to the light. But it was after he had crawled those few feet that he realized what had happened and how chance, the protective device of the Clans, and his own last-moment attempt to control the flitter had landed them in an unusual hiding place. Those rounded domes and crumbling walls, blind of any window or door opening were set deep in the sand of a desert waste. He had crashed straight into the heart of Ruhkarv itself.

"Where—?" He tried to summon the animals—and since he had no names to call, he pictured them mentally. The cats, black and gray-blue, the foxes, russet and cream, the kinkajou, where were they? Hurt? Still about?

"Come—come back!" He called softly aloud, heard odd echoes reply from the ruins about. Outside now, he could look around, see how the flyer had nosed into a dome that had a crumbled opening in one side.

A shadow leaped from one of the broken arches, pattered to him. The kinkajou had answered his call. It leaped to his shoulder, coiling its flexible tail about his upper arm in a grip tight enough to pinch. Troy reached up his other hand, caressed the round head butting against his cheek.

Then the foxes returned in a swift lope, stopping before him, their pointed noses up, testing the wind, their eyes agleam.

"Come," Troy coaxed the cats. When there was no answer,

he detached the kinkajou, started back into the dome cave to explore the wreck. In the pocket of the door he had wrenched open he found an atom torch and thumbed its button. The cone of light made clear the nose of the flyer embedded in the space of the dome as a too thick thread might have been forced into the eye of a needle.

Troy flashed the light into the machine and then stood very still as he saw a small limp body. Blue eyes wide with pain were raised to his. The gray-blue cat lay flat, its mouth open, panting. Now and again it licked a foreleg that was clamped tight between two buckled pieces of metal. Above it crouched its black mate, who, upon seeing Troy, uttered a series of sharp, demanding cries.

Setting down the torch, Troy went to work to free the delicate leg. Then he carried the cat into the open, placing it on the ground until he could salvage the aid kit of the flyer.

By the time the first thin streaks of false dawn were in the sky, he had done what he could. The leg had been set and treated. He had dragged out of the flitter the food bag, the stunner, and some of the kit tools, which he festooned from his own belt. As time had passed and no one had invaded the forbidden area of the ruins to gather them up prisoners, Troy began to believe that they had been brought down by some automatic guard device and that on foot they still had a chance to escape capture. But whether the Clans had set other guards about Ruhkarv, which might now keep them inside, he did not know.

The foxes and the black cat melted into the shadows, leaving Troy to his collection of equipment. Only the kinkajou remained to watch and at last to come to his aid, dragging small objects from the wrecked flyer to pile by the dome. Troy sat back on his heels. He had been so busy that he had not had time to consider the future further than the next job to be done, for he had been driven by a sense of working against time.

"Wall—wall that cannot be seen—" The black cat stepped out from a neighboring dome and came directly to the man.

"Wall around here?" Troy's hand swept in a gesture to indicate the ruins.

"Yes. We have tried to cross many places."

One of Troy's fears had materialized. The Clans must have set a barrier about Ruhkarv. Intended to bar interlopers, it would make him and the animals prisoners within. How he had managed to pierce it with the flitter was a mystery.

"There are many dens—maybe hunting in them—" One of the foxes drifted into the open. The cat had gone to its injured mate, was licking its head caressingly.

"Danger underground here." Troy countered that half suggestion from the prick-eared scout.

"Not now." The report was emphatic and Troy wondered. Before Fauklow's expedition with the recaller had turned the name of Ruhkarv into a synonym for nightmare, the upper galleries of the strange city or structure had been explored with impunity by a handful of the curious. If it had been only the action of the recaller that had damned the place—well, the rangers had put an end to the machine's broadcasts, according to Rerne, and the undersurface passages might give the fugitives shelter for a time. He would have to have some rest, Troy knew, and perhaps here in the heart of a forbidden territory they had found temporary safety after all.

"We go then—to a safe den."

With the food bag over his shoulder, the injured cat held as comfortably as he could manage against his chest, and the stunner ready in his free hand, Troy moved out. The kinkajou rode on his shoulder, making small twittering noises and now and then patting its two-legged steed with a forepaw as if to make Troy continually aware of its presence. The foxes and the black cat guided him to another dome, in which a large segment of wall had been cut through in the past, either by one of the early treasure seekers or by the ill-fated Fauklow men.

All the fantastic tales that had been told of this place were peopling the dusk Troy faced with a myriad of nightmares, but the readiness of the animals to explore was his insurance. Troy knew that their senses were far keener and more to be relied upon than his own, and that they would give warning of any trouble ahead. He snapped on the atom torch he had slung from his belt, watched the cone of light bob and wave across flooring and walls as it swung to the rhythm of his walk.

There was nothing to be seen but walls and a pavement of blocks, fitted together with precision and skill. At the far side of the dome was the dark mouth of a ramp leading down into the real Ruhkarv. That murk had a quality close to fog, Troy thought—as if the dark itself swirled about with independent motion. And even the atom light was sapped, weakened by it. Yet the lead fox had already padded down into those depths, and its mate and the cat were waiting for Troy almost impatiently.

"This is a place where there has been great danger," Troy warned, combining words with the mental reach.

"Nothing here—" He was sure that impatient overtone came from the black cat.

"Nothing here," Troy repeated even as his boots clicked on that sloping length of stone, "but perhaps farther on—"

"There is water."

Troy was startled at that confident interruption. They had the supplies from the flitter, but the problem of water had nagged at him. If somewhere within this maze the animals had located water, they were even better provided for than he had dared to hope.

"Where?"

"We go—"

The ramp carried him down through three levels of side corridors, all empty as far as the beams of the atom light could disclose, all exactly alike, so that Troy began to think a man might well become lost in such a place without a guide. And he tried to set his own entrance path in his head, memorizing each corridor by counting.

Somewhere there must be an unseen air system, for the atmosphere, though dry and acrid, remained breathable, and he was sure that now and then from one of the offshoot corridors he scented a whiff of some fresh import from the surface.

At the fourth level, though the ramp continued on to Korwarian depths, Troy found the three scouts waiting for him. And now, unless his sense of direction was completely bemused, they took a way that headed directly east. For a moment he dared to wonder if some one of these long hallways might not take them outside the range of the blocking-wave wall so that they could emerge free in the Wild.

Stark walls of red-gray stone, paved footing—nothing else, save
the fine sifting of centuries of dust, which arose almost ankle-high
and muffled the sounds of his own footfalls. Twice only were
those walls broken by round openings, but when he swung the
beam of the torch in, he saw nothing save a bare, circular cell
hardly large enough for a man to crouch in, without any other
opening. The purpose of such rooms—if rooms they could be
called—remained another of the Ruhkarv mysteries.

But their journey was not to continue so easily. The eastern
corridor ended in a huge well, and again a descending ramp faced
them, curving about the side of that opening, narrow enough to
make Troy thoughtful, though the slope was not too steep as far
as he could sight with the torch's aid. Again the scouts moved
ahead, and there was nothing to do except follow.

As he went down, there was a change in the air—not a freshness, but a rise of moisture. As the wall against which he steadied himself from time to time began to grow clammy under his
fingers, he knew that the fox had been right. Somewhere below
was a source of water—a large one, if he could judge by the
present evidence.

As the moisture content grew, he was aware of a fetid under
scent—not exactly the stagnant stench of an undrained and
unrenewed pond under the sun, but the hint of something ill
about that water. However, there were trickles of damp on the
walls and his thirst grew.

Around and around—the coiled spring of the ramp inside
the well began to form a dizzying pattern. There was no break
here made by side corridors. Troy lost track of time; his legs
ached, and every bruise on his body added to his punishment.
He was sure now that if he should try to reverse his path and
reach the surface—or even the last corridor from which this
drop had issued, he would not be able to summon up strength
enough to finish. There was only the need to get to the bottom
of the well, out on the level somewhere where he could drop
down and rest.

And finally the torch did show him a pavement. Troy reached
it in a long stride and flashed the light about the bottom of the
well. There was water right enough, but—as dry as his mouth now

was, as much as his body cried out for a drink—he could not bring himself to approach closely that sullenly flowing runnel.

The water was a ribbon of oily black, looking as thick and turgid as if the substance were more than half slime, and it moved with sluggish ripples on its surface from one side of the pit to the other, filling to within a few inches of the pavement surface a stone trough that had been constructed to carry it.

The inlet and outlet for that yard-wide flow were large circular openings—the inlet situated under the rise of the ramp from the floor. And except for those there was no other way out—save the ramp down which he had just come. But the black cat and the foxes were at the mouth of the inflow tunnel, and when Troy walked to that point, he saw that the tunnel was larger than the stream at floor level, leaving a narrow path to the right of the water.

"Out?" he asked, and that single word echoed hollowly until the boom hurt his ears. The kinkajou chattered angrily, and the cat in Troy's hold pressed the good foreleg hard against his chest and added a protesting wail. But the three animals before him glanced up and then away again, into the tunnel, telling him as plainly as with words or the mind touch that this was indeed the proper exit.

The ripples on the water, as Troy passed along so close to it, began to take on a rather ominous and sinister significance, and he wondered just how deep that trough really was, for some of the ripples went against the current, suggesting action under the dark surface of the flood—some thing or things moving independently against the flow of the water. For an anxious while one such V of ripples accompanied Troy at his own pace. Time and time again he paused to flash the torch directly on that disturbance—to sight nothing in the inky liquid.

That slight fetid odor was growing stronger, yet again he felt a puff of renewing air, though through what channel in the walls he could not guess. But the gleam of his torch began to pick up small answering sparks of light along the walls. From pinpricks scattered without apparent pattern they grew thicker, set in clusters. And once, when he turned his head to watch a particularly large and suspicious line of ripples, Troy saw that those sparks of light behind him, awakened by the torchlight, did not lose their gleam but continued as small patches with a bluish glow. He tried the experiment of snapping the torch off for a moment and looked about him. Where the atom light had touched, that blue glow remained. But ahead the way was still dark. Whatever those flecks might be, they needed the radiance from the light to set them actually working.

The patches of such light grew larger, and now he thought he could trace a kind of design—like a sharply peaked zigzag—in their general setting, which argued that they were not native to the rock blocks of which these walls were fashioned but placed there with a purpose by the unknown builders. At last he was backed by an eerie glow walling in the stream along which he walked.

His torch found an opening in the wall ahead. The cat awaited him there, but the foxes were not to be seen. Troy pushed on, eager to be out of the tunnel and its attendant water channel.

When he came out, he was not in another corridor or room—but he stepped into what might have once been some vast underground cavern adapted by the unknown builders of Ruhkarv to their own peculiar uses. His torch beam was swallowed up by the vastness of the open expanse and he halted, a little daunted by what faced him. Here was a city in miniature, open ways running between walls of separate, roofless enclosures. And yet the substance of those walls—! It was from here that the fetid odor had come. He could not be sure, yet somehow he shrank from putting his guess to the test of actually laying his hand upon one of those slimily moist surfaces—but it looked at first, and even after a more careful examination, as if those walls grew out of the ground, that they were giant slabs of an unknown fungus.

There was an open space of white-gray soil, neither sand nor gravel but possessing a granular appearance, between the mouth of the water tunnel and the beginning of the first of those structures, and Troy was in no hurry to cross it.

"A road around—"

One or all of his guides had picked his feelings of repugnance out of his mind, and he knew then that they shared it in a measure.

"Come!" The last was urgent and Troy broke into a clumsy

trot, not sure now just how long he could keep moving at all. He rounded an outthrust suburb of the fungus town and saw something else—a shaft of brightness that was so clean, so much of the world that he knew, that he threw himself toward it, his trot lengthening into a run.

There was an island of sanity in the midst of what was not of his world, nor, he suspected, of any human world. From some break in the arch overhead, through what unknown trick of nature—or of the architects of this place—he would never know, a shaft of sun struck here. And there was water, a small pool of it fed by a runnel through the sand. Clear water with none of the turgid rolling of the stream that had led them here. Troy put down the injured cat where it could lap beside its mate, scooped up a palmful to wet lips and chin as he sucked avidly.

Two, three tiny plants, frail as lace, grew on the bank of that pool. Troy drank again blissfully and then opened the supply bag, sharing its contents among his band, taking himself the concentrates that would give him days of energy.

Was there any other way out of this dead, fungoid world? At the moment he was too tired to care. With his head pillowed on the food bag, Troy curled up, weak with exhaustion, aware that the animals were gathering in about him, as if they, too, distrusted what lay beyond the circle of sunlight.

Did anything live here? The ripples in the water had been suggestive. And there might be other creatures to whom the fungus-walled streets were home. But Troy could no longer summon the strength to stand guard. He felt the warmth of small furred bodies pressed against his, and that was the last he remembered.

# TWELVE

He might have been asleep only for a moment, Troy thought when he roused. The sun patch still lit the pool. There had been no change in his surroundings, save that the animals, except for the injured cat, were gone. The cat raised its head from licking the splinted leg and made an inquiring noise deep in its throat as Horan sat up, rubbing his arm across his eyes. He shook his head, still a little bemused, wondering vaguely if he had slept the clock around.

Then out of the murk of the fungus growth trotted the black cat, its head held high as it dragged the body of a limp thing across the coarse earth. Paying no attention to Troy, it brought the weird underground dweller to its mate.

The dead creature was in its way as hideous as the hur-hur, a nightmare combination of many legs, stalked eyes, segmented, plated body. But apparently to both felines it was a very acceptable form of food and they dined amiably together.

If the Terran animals were able to forage for themselves even in this hole in the ground, Troy had proof of another of Kyger's secrets. They had *not* needed the special food that had been so ceremoniously delivered at a suitably high price to the quondam owners in Tikil.

"Good hunting?" he asked the black casually.

The cat was meticulously washing itself with tongue and paw.

"Good hunting," it agreed.

"The others also have good hunting?" Troy wondered where in that unwholesome fungoid growth the missing three hunted and what they pursued.

"They eat," the cat answered with finality.

Troy stood up, stretched the cramps out of his sore body. He had no intention of remaining in this cavern, or underground city, or whatever it might be.

"There is a way out?" he asked the cat, and received the odd mental equivalent of what might have been a shrug. It was plain that hunting had been of more importance than exploration for another passage as far as that independent animal was concerned.

Troy sat down again to study both cats. The injured one was still eating, with neatness, but hungrily. He was sure that it was not unaware of the exchange between its mate and himself.

Horan had no control over the five Terran animals, and he knew it. By some freak of chance he was able to communicate with them after a disjointed fashion. But he was very sure that their communication with Kyger had been much clearer and fuller—perhaps through the aid of that odd summoning device he had seen in the dead man's hands.

They had accompanied him in the flight from Tikil because that had suited their purpose also, just as they had guided him to this particular hole. Yet he knew well that if they wished they would leave him as readily, unless he could establish some closer tie with them. The position was changed—in Tikil he had been in command because that was man's place. Here the animals had found their own; they no longer needed him.

It was disquieting to face the fact that his somewhat rosy dreams of cooperation between man and animal might be just that—dreams. He could fly the fussel to his will and that bird would know the pleasure of the hunt and still return on call. But these hunters had wills and minds of their own, and if they gave companionship, it would be by free will. The age-old balance of man and animal had tipped. There would be a cool examination from the other side, no surrender but perhaps an alliance.

And such thoughts could lead Troy now to understand Zul's demand that the animals be killed. Few men were going to accept readily a copartnership with creatures they had always considered property. There would lurk a threat to the supremacy man believed in.

Yet Troy knew that he could not have left any of the animals in Tikil, nor yielded to Zul's demands. Why? Why did he feel that way about them? He was uneasy now, almost unhappy, as he realized that he was not dealing with pets, that he must put aside his conception of these five as playthings to be owned and ordered about. Neither were they humans whose thinking processes and reactions he could in a manner anticipate.

The black cat ceased washing, sat upright, the tip of its tail folded neatly over its paws, its blue eyes regarding Troy. And the man stirred uneasily under that unwinking stare.

"You wish a way out?"

"Yes." Troy answered that simply. With this new humbleness he was willing to accept what the other would give.

"This place—not man's—not ours—"

Troy nodded. "Before man—something like man but different."

"There is danger—old danger here." There was a new touch of thought like a new voice. The gray-blue cat had finished its meal and was looking over the good paw, raised to its mouth for a tonguing, at Troy.

"There was a bad thing happened here to men—some years ago."

Both cats appeared to consider that. Perhaps their minds linked in a thread of communication he could not reach.

"You are not of those we know." That was the black cat. Troy discovered that he could now distinguish one's thought touch from another's. The animals had come to be definite and sepa- rate personalities to him and closer in companionship because of that very fact. Sometimes he was so certain of a comrade at hand that it was a shock to realize that the mind he could touch was outwardly clothed in fur and was borne by four feet, not two.

"No."

"Few men know our speech—and those must use the caller.

Yet from the first you could contact us without that. You are a
different kind of man." That was the gray-blue cat.

"I do not know. You mean that you cannot 'talk' to everyone?"

"True. To the big man we talked—because that was set upon
us—just as we had to obey the caller when he used it. But it
was not set upon us to talk to you—yet you heard. And you are
not one-who-is-to-be-obeyed."

Set upon them—did they mean that they had been conditioned
to obey orders and "talk" with certain humans?

"No," Troy agreed. "I do not know why I hear your 'talk,' but
I do."

"Now that the big man is gone, we are hunted."

"That is so."

"It is as was told us. We should be hunted if we tried to be
free."

"We are free," the black cat interrupted. "We might leave you,
man, and you could not find us here unless we willed it so."

"That is true."

Again the pause, those unblinking stares. The black cat moved.
It came to him, its tail erect. Then it sat upon its hind legs.
Horan put out his hand diffidently, felt the quick rasp of a rough
tongue for an instant on his thumb.

"There will be a way out."

The cat's head turned toward the fungus town. It stared as
intently in that direction as it had toward Troy a moment earlier.
And the man was not surprised when out of that unwholesome
maze trotted the fox pair, followed by the kinkajou. They came
to stand before Troy, the black cat a little to one side, and the
man caught little flickers of their unheard speech.

"Not one-to-be-obeyed—hunts in our paths—will let us walk
free—"

It was the black cat who continued as spokesman. "We shall
hunt your way for you now, man. But we are free to go."

"You are free to go. I share my path; I do not order you
to walk upon it also." He searched for phrases to express his
acceptance of the bargain they offered and his willingness to be
bound by their conditions.

"A way out—" The cat turned to the others. The foxes lapped at the pool and then loped away. The kinkajou dabbled its front paws in the water. Troy offered it a pressed-food biscuit and it ate with noisy crunchings. Then it turned to the cavern wall at their back and frisked away along its foot.

"We shall go this way." The cat nodded to the right of the pool, along that clean strip of ground between the fungoid growth and the cavern wall.

Troy emptied two of the containers of dry food, rinsed them, and filled them with water as a reserve supply. Both cats drank slowly. Then Troy picked up the injured one, who settled comfortably in the crook of his arm. The black darted away.

Horan walked at a reasonable pace, studying his surroundings as he went. To the glance there was no alteration in either the fungus walls or the rock barrier to his right. But as he drew farther away from the splotch of sunlight, he switched on his atom torch.

The cat stirred in his hold, its head—with ears sharply pointed—swung to face the fungus.

"There is something there—alive?" Troy's hand went to the stunner in a belt loop.

"Old thing—not alive," the thought answer came readily. "Sargon finds—"

"Sargon?"

The wavering picture of the male fox crossed his mind. "You are named?" he asked eagerly. Somehow names made them seem less aloof and untouchable, closer to his own kind.

"Man's names!" There was disdain in that, hinting that there were other forms of identification more subtle and intelligent, beyond the reach of a mere human. And Troy, reading that into the cat's reply, smiled.

"But I am a man. May I not use man's names?"

The logic of that appealed to the dainty lady he carried. "Sargon and Sheba." Fleeing fox faces flashed into his mind. "Shang"—that was the kinkajou. "Simba, Sahiba," her mate and herself.

"Troy Horan," he answered gravely aloud, to complete the round of introduction. Then he came back to her report. "This old thing—it was made—or did it once live?"

"It once lived." Sahiba relayed the fox's report promptly. "It was not man—not we—different."

Troy's curiosity was aroused, not enough, however, to draw him into the paths threading the forbidding fungoid town. But as they passed that point he wondered if the remains of one of the original inhabitants of Ruhkarv could lie there.

"An opening—" Sahiba relayed a new message. "Shang has discovered an opening—up—" She pointed with her good paw to the cavern wall.

Troy altered course, came up a slight slope, and found the kinkajou chattering excitedly and clinging head down to a knob that overhung a crevice in the wall. Troy flashed the torch into that dark pocket. There was no rear barrier; it was a narrow passage. Yet it did not have any facing of worked stone as had the other corridor entrances, and it might not lead far.

The foxes and Simba came from different directions and stood sniffing the air in the rocky slit. Troy was conscious of that too—a faint, fresh current, stirring the fetid breath of the fungus, hinting of another and cleaner place. This must be a way out.

Yet the waiting animals did not seem in any hurry to take that path.

"Danger?" asked Troy, willing to accept their hesitation as a warning.

Simba advanced to the overhang of the opening, his head held high, his whiskers quivering a little, as he investigated by scent.

"Something waiting—for a long time waiting—"

"Man? Animal?"

But Simba appeared baffled. "A long time waiting," he repeated. "Maybe no longer alive—but still waiting."

Troy tried to sift some coherent meaning out of that. The kinkajou made him start as it leaped from the rock perch to his shoulder.

"It is quiet." Shang broke in over Simba's caution. "We go outside—this way outside—"

But Troy asked Simba for the final verdict. "Do we go?"

The cat glanced up at him, and there was a flash of something warm upon the meeting of their eyes, as if Troy in his deference to the other's judgment had advanced another step on the narrow road of understanding between them.

"We go—taking care. This thing I do not understand."

The foxes were apparently content to follow Simba's lead. And the three trotted into the crevice, while Troy came behind, the atom torch showing that this way was indeed a slit in the rock wall and no worked passage.

Though the break was higher than his head by several feet, it was none too wide, and Troy hoped that it would not narrow past his using. Now that he was well inside and away from the cavern, the freshness of the air current blowing softly against his face was all the more noticeable. He was sure that in that breeze was the scent of natural growing things and not just the mustiness of the Ruhkarv paths.

They had not gone far before the pathway began to slope upward, confirming his belief that it connected somehow with the outside world. At first, that slope was easy, and then it became steeper, until at last Troy was forced to transfer Sahiba to the ration bag on his back and use both hands to climb some sections. His less sensitive nose registered more than just fresh air now. There was an unusual fragrance, which was certainly not normal in this slit of rock, more appropriate to a garden under a sun hot enough to draw perfume from aromatic plants and flowers. Yet beneath that almost cloying scent lay a hint of another odor, a far less pleasant one—the flowers of his imagining might be rooted in a slime of decay.

The torch showed him another climb. Luckily the surface was rough and furnished handholds. Shang and Simba went up it fluidly, the foxes in a more scrambling fashion. Then Troy reached the top and was greeted by a glow of daylight. He snapped off the torch and advanced eagerly.

"No!" That warning came emphatically from more than one of the animals. Troy stiffened, studied the path ahead, saw now that between him and the open was a grating or mesh of netting.

He stood still. The cat and the foxes were outlined clearly against that mesh.

"Gone—"

A flicker of thought, which was permission for him to come

on. There *was* a meshwork over the way into the open. And through it he could see vegetation and a brightness that could only be daylight. The mesh itself was of a sickly white color and was formed in concentric rings with a thick blob like a knob in the center.

Troy approached it gingerly, noting that the cat and the foxes did not get within touching distance. Now he noticed something else—that along the rings of the netting were the remains of numerous insects, ragged tatters of wings, scraps of carcasses, all clinging to the surface of those thick cords. He drew the knife from his belt and sliced down with a quick slash, only to have the cord give very slightly beneath his blow. Then the blade rebounded as if he had struck at some indestructible elastic substance.

The cord stuck to the blade so that it was carried upward on the rebound, and he had to give a hard jerk to free it. A second such experiment nearly pulled the knife out of his grasp. Not only was the stuff elastic and incredibly tough, but it was coated with something like glue, and he did not think it was any product of man—or of man's remote star-born cousins.

There was clearly no cutting through it. But there was another weapon he could use. Troy set down the bag in which Sahiba rode and investigated the loot he had brought with him from the wrecked flitter. There was a small tube, meant originally for a distress flare, but with another possible use.

Troy examined the webbing as well as he could without touching it. The strands were coated with thick beads of dust. It had been in place there for a long time. Unscrewing the head of the flare and holding the other end of the tube, he aimed it at the center of the web.

Violent red flame thrust like a spear at the net. There was an answering flower of fire running from the point of impact along the cords to their fastening points on the rock about the opening, a stench that set Troy to coughing. Then—there was nothing at all fronting them but the open path and some trails of smoke wreathing from the stone.

They waited for those to clear before Simba took a running leap to cross the fire-blackened space, the foxes following him eagerly. Troy, again carrying Sahiba and Shang, brought up the rear.

He was well away from the cliff before he realized that they might have made their escape from the cavern of the fungus town, but they were not yet on the open surface of Korwar. There was vegetation here, growing rankly in an approximation of sunlight, a light that filtered down from a vast expanse of roof crossed and crisscrossed with bars or beams set in zigzag patterns like those formed by the light sparks in the water tunnel. Between that patching of bars was a cream-white surface, which, seen from ground level, could have been sand held up by some invisible means.

As Troy studied that, he saw a puff of golden vapor exhaled from a section of crosshatched bars. The tiny cloud floated softly down until it was midway between the roof and earth, and then it discharged its bulk in a small shower, spattering big drops of liquid on the leaves of the plants immediately below.

And now Troy could see radical differences between those plants and the ordinary vegetation of the surface. Not far away a huge four-petaled flower—the petals a vivid cream, its heart a striking orange-red—hung without any stem Troy could detect, in a rounded opening among shaggy bushes.

The heavy, almost oppressive fragrance he had first noted in the passage came from that. Simba, nose extended, stalked toward the blossom. Then the cat arched its back and spat, its ears flattened to its skull. Troy, coming in answer to the wave of disgust and warning from the animal, found his boots crunching the husks of small bodies, charnel house debris. His sickened reaction made him slice at the horrible flower—to discover it was not a flower but a cunning weave of sticky threads. And, as his knife blade tore through them, the orange-red heart came to life, leaping from the trap, darting straight at him.

Troy had a confused impression of many-legged thing with a gaping mouth, a thorned tail ready to sting. But Simba struck with a heavy clawed paw, throwing the creature up into the air. As it smashed to the ground, Sargon pounded it into the earth in a flattened smear. The fox sniffed and then drew back, his head down, his paws rubbing frantically at his nose.

Simba, tail moving in angry sweeps from side to side, sat half crouched as if awaiting a second attack.

"This is a bad place," Sahiba stated flatly. And Troy was ready to agree with her.

Oddly enough it was Shang, the kinkajou, who took the lead. He leaped from Troy's shoulder to the top of the nearest tall bush, and in a moment was only to be marked by a thrashing of branches as he headed into the miniature wilds. Troy dodged another made-to-order rain cloud and sat down to share out supplies with his oddly assorted company. They would need food and water before they tried to solve this latest riddle.

# THIRTEEN

The same wild waving of leafed branches that had marked Shang's departure heralded his return. He made a flying leap from a nearby bush top to the ground, raising small spurts of dust as he raced toward Troy.

"Man thing!" There was excitement in that report, enough to make Troy set down a water container hastily, not quite sure whether Shang meant an animate or inanimate find.

"Where?" Troy asked, and then added quickly, "What?"

Shang raised a front paw and gestured to the miniature wilderness. He seemed unable to define the "what" at all. Troy looked to the cats; he had come to accept their superior judgment in such matters.

Simba faced the screen of vegetation, and Horan, alert now to the slight changes he might not have noted hours earlier, marked that twitch of whiskered muzzle. Sahiba, limping clumsily, left his side, joined her mate, and sat in the same listening attitude.

"Call thing—" It was Simba who reported.

Troy experienced a flicker of uneasiness. There had been a "call thing" associated with Ruhkarv, and he did not want to have any close connection with that, certainly not with what rumor and legend suggested that it had called.

"Old?" He did not know how Simba could pick the answer to that out of the air, or out of Shang and the messages the air brought feline senses.

"Not old."

"A man with it?"

Simba's blue eyes, with their unreadable depths, lifted from the foliage wall to Troy's. He caught the cat's puzzlement, as if Simba was able to pluck a confused series of impressions from channels closed to the man, but as if important sequences in that series were lacking.

"Man thing—" Shang was fairly dancing up and down with eagerness, running a few steps toward the wilderness, retreating to peer at Troy, plainly urging that his find be examined by Horan. But the man continued to wait for the cats' verdict.

"Dangerous?"

To that again neither Sahiba nor Simba made a direct answer. But the urge to caution was intensified. Then Sargon and Sheba went purposefully off into the brush as if obeying some order. Troy repacked the supplies, picked up Sahiba. He studied the matted growth before him, looking for a path, or at least a thinner patch through which he might force his way.

The light from the odd roofing overhead, which had been day-bright when he had found his way into this place, was fading, and Troy did not much relish plunging into the tangle. But, sighting a space between two bushes, he pushed in resolutely.

Within seconds he was completely lost. It was impossible to keep any sort of straight course, and he had to use his knife to get free of vines and sprawling branches. The whole growth might have been intelligently planted to form a giant trap or barrier. It was Sahiba who relayed the suggestions of the scouts and Shang who roamed from bush to bush, coming back to coax him on.

Then Troy half fell through a mass of foliage, as a tough vine gave way, and was once more in the open—facing a nightmare scene.

There was an opening in the wall here, with a well-cleared, paved space before it. And in the center of that, facing the opening, was a small machine, a machine akin to his own time and culture. A cone of meta-plast was pointed with its large end toward the wall opening, and, as Troy stepped onto the pavement, he was immediately conscious of the fact that a faint vibration came from that machine. It was not only in working order—it was running!

Cat, foxes, kinkajou—the animals were lined up well to the left of the machine, facing the opening—waiting—

Troy's cry was half choked in his throat as he looked beyond the machine, along the line of that pointed cone. It must—surely it must have once been human, that thing trembling a little, spread-eagled on just such a webbing as had choked the passage from the fungus cavern. Yet this was a dried rag-fashioned creature from which not only life but much of the bulk of body had vanished. The head, which still showed a thatch of dust-stiffened hair, lolled forward on the rack of bones that was the chest, and Troy was glad he could not see the features.

He surveyed the webbing, seeing not only that it covered the opening and held its long-dead prisoner upright, frail as that structure of skin and bones was, but that the cords also ran along the walls to form a pattern of stripes, some as fine as thread, others as thick as one of his fingers. And the thing that had woven the web could not have been one of the orange-red lily hearts. It must have been larger than the Terran animals.

Had been—must have been? What was there to prove that the weaver was now gone? The captive was dead. Troy thought he could guess how long he had been there—just as he knew what machine stood before them, its powers dampened out, mercifully, but still in operation. This was part of the horror that had put Ruhkarv out of bounds for his kind. The recaller had been set here, a point Fauklow had selected because his knowledge of nonhuman remains had indicated there might be a response. And there had been a response—too concrete a one.

Elsewhere the recaller had summoned only the pallid tatters of ghostly memories. Here some freak of time, space, or unknown nature had given body to a ghost and the power to use it! Out of a far and devious past and the corridors of Ruhkarv had come a creature, intelligent or not, ruler of those ways once, or a prowler in them, as great an enemy to the builders as it was to the Fauklow men, which had had the energy to revive and attack its arousers.

And perhaps the maker of that web had been only one of a number of monsters that had crawled out of the caverns of Ruhkarv. Most of the bodies of the explorers had been found aboveground with indications that they had, toward the end of their suffering, battled insanely against each other. Horrors driving them in a mad flight to the surface.

To the surface! That registered in Troy's mind now as he strove desperately to keep his imagination under control, to observe without trying to reconstruct what had happened here. Fauklow's men had set up the recaller, and they had fled from this point. So there was an exit to the surface somewhere from this chamber—did it lead through that opening before him?

He thought not. There would be no reason to aim the recaller on the back trail of the passage that had brought explorers here. No, that opening had had some significance for the dead archaeologist, but not as a door of escape. The old story of the treasure of Ruhkarv—had Fauklow found some clue that had led him to believe he could summon a whisper from the past to reveal the hiding place of the treasure?

Troy only knew that nothing would have led him to explore that dark tunnel mouth behind the spread and wasted body of a man who might have tried just that. He glanced at the animals. They were intent upon the scene, but not hostile.

"Dead only?" he asked.

Sahiba pushed back against his shoulder, her good foreleg rigid on his arm.

"Dead here—" But there remained an odd note of puzzlement in that reply.

"Here?" he echoed.

"It is here—yet it is not here." She shook her head.

Troy could not be sure of what she was trying to tell him. "The man is dead."

"Yes."

"And that which made the net?"

"It is"—the gray-blue head moved, soft fur rubbing his shoulder—"dead here—but waiting."

"The recaller!" Troy thought he knew now. Blanketed by the quencher beam from the rangers' installation, the machine could no longer materialize the uncanny thing from the past. But under that blanket the recaller still ran. Let anything again lift the quencher and the weaver of those webs would return!

Troy stared at the array of dials and buttons on the small control board set into the back of the machine. There was no way of his knowing which of those would close down the dangerous ray, and he had no intention of experimenting.

Simba crept slowly toward the web and the captive there. He might have been a hunter stalking prey. One black foreleg stretched, a paw with claws extended patted the drift of dust that lay at the foot of the webbing. Something bright spun from that dust and Simba followed it, keeping it rolling away from the opening, back, until it struck against Troy's boot.

The man stooped to pick it up. By the slick, cold feel he knew he held a ring of metal, a deep crimson-red. But as his fingers closed on it, there was a change in that plain blood-colored band. Sparks flashed on it, single and in pinpointed clusters, just as they had appeared on the walls of the water tunnel. And Troy believed that on his palm now rested no memento from the body of the unknown dead captive, but something that was native to these chambers and halls from the beginning, perhaps the only piece of the lost treasure of Ruhkarv that men of his own time would ever see. Had that, too, been summoned out of the past, given substance by some chance of the recaller? Or had it been found in the tunnel by the web captive, who had fled carrying it—only to be taken just as he was within sight of freedom?

On the band the sparks winked faster. Also—Troy frowned, completely puzzled. He had picked up a ring only a size too large for any of his fingers; now he was holding a much larger loop. Sahiba sniffed, then put out a paw, touched the hoop. It spanned his palm. Troy pushed his fingers together, inserted them. The band moved down, closed about his wrist, tightened there.

Startled, he jerked and tugged at it, only to find the bracelet now immovable, not tight enough to pinch the flesh, but resting as if it had been fashioned exactly to the measure of his arm. Yet under his exploring fingers the metal was solid surface, with no discernible joints or stretching bands to account for the alteration in size.

Sahiba patted it, apparently attracted by the winks of light still flickering on and off around it. Was it only a piece of personal ornamentation—or some outlandish weapon defensive or offensive?

"Good or bad?" he asked aloud, wondering if the acute senses of the animals could give him a reply to that.

"Old thing." Sahiba yawned.

"A way out?" Troy returned to the main problem. Perhaps some kind of trail would be marked in the earth of the garden away from this point. He walked along the edge of the pavement on which the recaller had been set, searching for any trace of the route taken coming or going by those who had brought the machine here and then must have fled or been driven back to the surface.

Simba and the foxes accompanied him, then darted ahead, while Shang swung into the bushes again. They reached the end of that rectangle of pavement, and there Troy had eyes keen enough to pick out old scars of lopped branches, once again woven with a cloak of thick growth but still to be seen. He swung his knife, cutting a new way by those guides.

The light from overhead had dimmed into what was more night than dusk when he came out facing the foot of one of those ramps such as had led them down into this strange territory hours—or was it days?—earlier. He had lost all sense of time.

They made camp in a pocket of bare earth with the slope of the ramp at their backs. Troy eyed the now dark jungle distrustfully. So far only the lily hearts had been sighted as living things. But that did not mean that there were no other, just-as-vicious unknowns. And perhaps, as on the upper surface of Korwar, nocturnal hunters were more to be feared than those who stalked by day. Now more than ever he was dependent upon the senses of his companions. And that balance had shifted again—here man might be a liability to the Terrans.

He shared out supplies, noting that the animals made no move to hunt their own food.

"Hunting bad?"

Simba regarded the now gray-black mass of vegetation.

"There is hunting—for others—"

"Others—" That word might not echo in the air, but it did repeat itself in Troy's mind. He tried not to think of the captive in the web. Yes, there had been cruel hunting for others here.

"That which caught the man?" Against his will almost, Troy pressed the point. Did darkness activate what the recaller had summoned out of the past? With that thrust of apprehension, to be fed by his species' age-old distrust of the dark, Troy put out a hand to gather up the supply bag. Tired as he was, he had the atom torch, and he could keep going on the ramp until he dropped rather than face that weaver of webs. The residue of terror here bit at him now.

"No." Simba seemed assured of that. "Other things—this their place—"

As though on cue there came a cry out of the miniature jungle, a long, wavering screech that was made up of pain, terror, and the approach of death. Yet it was no cry that could have come from any animal he had ever known. And those he did know retreated, edging in around him, their heads turned to the jungle, their eyes alert, their lips lifted in snarls of warning.

"Out of here!" Troy's torch snapped on. "Up—"

He did not have to urge. The foxes sprang from the camp site to the ramp; the kinkajou was already racing after them. As Troy, carrying Sahiba and the bag, started that same climb, Simba fell in behind, looking back over his shoulder now and again, a low growl coming from his throat to warn off would-be trailers.

They went on climbing, the torch showing only the rise before them. Soon they were above the surface of the garden cavern, now in a sloping tunnel enclosed by rock walls.

They came to a level with corridors starring out at five different points, bare corridors in which his torch showed the dust disturbed, perhaps by the feet of the men who had planted the recaller and died for it. Another length of walled-in climbing, then again corridors—four this time.

Troy's ribs ached; his breath came in heaving gasps. More and more often he had to pause to rest. But he was driven now by the need to gain the open air and the world he knew. How long that climb continued he could not have told, for at last he moved through a daze of fatigue, weaving and staggering from wall to wall on the ramp, no longer aware of any communication with the animals, or even if they were still with him. It seemed that the residue of terror that had sent him out of that cavern grew stronger instead of weaker as he went, until it blanketed out his normal reactions and whipped him on and on—

Then there was gray light—and cool air, fresh air—air that bore with it the burden of fine rain, but which cleansed him and fought the shadows in his mind. Troy reeled, caught at a block of masonry, dimly conscious that he was out in the open now and that he was done. With that crumbling wall as a prop to keep him from crashing on his face, he slid down and lay on his back, the soft steady rain pouring over his face and body, plastering his clothing to him.

"Danger!" That word rang in his head as a shout might have torn at his eardrums. Troy raised his head groggily. The rain was over. There was a patch of sunlight on the ground just beyond his hand. He shook his head, trying to wake up fully.

Then he heard more than that mental warning. He heard the sound made by a flitter hovering over a landing site in a cramped space. A flitter!

More by instinct than by any conscious move, Troy drew back against the wall that had given him partial shelter, trying to locate the machine, which, by the sound, must be very close. Around him were the domes and walls of surface Ruhkarv. There could be only one reason why anyone had invaded this forbidden territory—they must have traced him here. And who were "they"? The patrollers, Zul—or the rangers on their usual duty of keeping the unauthorized out of this danger zone?

For the first time he looked about for the animals. And they were nowhere to be seen. Even the injured Sahiba had disappeared. Yet they had warned him mentally—or had they? Perhaps he was only still tuned in on some wavelength of their intercommunication.

The sound of the flitter grew louder, and Troy tried to squeeze his bulk smaller in the shadow of the wall. He saw the flyer as it crossed between two domes. It was that of a ranger.

Troy crept backward, angling toward the mouth of the ramp. He discovered that the fact he might be the object of an air search removed a great deal of the nebulous distaste he had known in the depths. Then, to his astonishment, for he had felt very naked and plainly in sight, he watched the flitter keep straight on course and vanish behind the rise of another dome, the sound of its passing dying away in the distance. With a sigh of relief he sat up.

"Simba, Sahiba—" He pictured the cats in his mind, aimed his mental call.

"One comes."

Troy was not sure of the direction of that ambiguous answer.

"The flitter has gone." He tried to reassure the furred company, to summon one of them into sight.

"One comes." It was repeated. "One comes from the big man."

From the big man—Kyger! Zul?

"Where?" Troy pushed that effort at communication to the top pitch he could hold. For a long moment he feared they had cut their contact, refusing to answer. Then Shang frisked around the swell of the dome behind which the flitter had disappeared, showed himself to Troy, and was gone again.

With far less speed and agility the man followed that lead, crossing the space between wall and dome with care as to his path but as quickly as he could. Then, one hand braced against the side of the structure, the other gripping his stunner, he began a slow and, he hoped, a noiseless journey. He could hear the buzz of a few insects. But there were no birds here, no sign of life in this desolation that was the upper cover of Ruhkarv. And he caught no sign of the animals save that momentary glimpse of Shang.

# FOURTEEN

◇

**P**erhaps it was because his body was pressed so tightly to the masonry of the dome that Troy caught the first vibration, a faint tingle through blood and bone that was familiar, bringing with it a vague memory of darkness and suspense. That throb grew faster, and it pulled, pulled against his intelligence, against the need for caution, making Troy want to run toward its source.

He battled that impulse, holding to cover, but moving on with that hardly heard beat for his goal, that thrumming which registered on his nerves and muscles before it did on his eardrums. And along with his involuntary answer to that call, there came now another emotion—not his, but the animals'! A desperation—the hopeless fear of bound and helpless prisoners.

Tasting their fear, Troy guessed the truth. Somewhere ahead Zul was using the cylinder that had rested in Kyger's lifeless hands. And the animals, conditioned to answer its summons, were being drawn to their own end without any chance to fight for their freedom. Just as that cord within him, which was able to serve as a communicating link from their brains to his, was also responding—

Only he had not been conditioned—he could fight back! And Zul would lead him straight to where he wanted to go.

Troy ceased to resist, allowed his hidden compass to guide him. But, though he followed the line of that infernal piping, he still kept to cover.

Between two more domes, then into a space of open land with straight towers of rock outcrops. As soon as Troy was sure of his goal, he swung to the right, pulling out of the direct line of the piping, circling to bring up to the rear of the suspected ambush. Was Zul alone? So much depended upon that.

Troy reached the first of the rock outcrops, went in a half stoop to round it and thread a path of his own. The piping still continued, which meant that Zul had not yet pulled the animals out of hiding. But, as Troy came to the tallest pillar in that broken land, it stopped abruptly, and then he knew that he must trade caution for speed.

His stunner ready, he whipped around the base of that tower to find the scene he had expected. Zul was there, and between his knees was the tube from Kyger's chambers. He had one hand still cupping its length. The other, with wrist steadied on the head of the cylinder, grasped a blaster. While facing him, crouching, snarling, betraying in their tense bodies their hatred and their fear—and helplessness—were the animals.

Troy snapped the stunner, aiming for the difficult point of that bony yellow wrist. A head target would have been best—but even as he blacked out under the bolt, Zul could still have triggered his blaster. Now the numbing beam struck the curled fingers with better success than Troy had dared to hope for. Zul cried out with the shock and surprise, his voice thinned by rocky echoes. The blaster spun from his deadened fingers. Grabbing for it with his other hand, he lost his hold on the tube.

When Troy thumbed for a second stunner shot, the release light did not spark. Charge exhausted! He sprang into the open, running for the blaster. Zul was down on his knees, his numbed hand folded up against his chest, the other within fingertip reach of the blaster grip. Troy swung a boot toe forward, kicked the blaster away from Zul but out of his own path also.

Zul was well-versed in rough-and-tumble. The hand that had been straining for the blaster grip struck out at Troy's ankle, fingers raked across his boot, sending him enough off balance to stagger a step or two beyond the smaller man. Horan brought up against one of the rock pillars with force enough to awaken the pain in his old bruises, and clawed about breathlessly just in time to face death.

Erupting from his half crouch, the blade of a knife glinting in the sun, Zul came at him. Troy knew his attack would end in the vicious up-cut that would finish the fight and him in one skilled stroke if he could not counter it. He was no knife fighter and Zul was.

But Zul's right hand was numbed and perhaps he was awkward with the left. There was only that one small chance. Troy swerved and struck for Zul's head with the barrel of the stunner. The jar of that blow getting home was followed by a thud against his own ribs, so sharp and painful as to bring a yelp of agony out of him.

Zul staggered against the rock, recoiled, and slumped to the ground. Troy, hands pressed to his side, needed the support of the pillar or he would have joined him. He looked down, expecting to see the hilt of the blade projecting from his flesh. But on the ground at his feet lay the knife snapped in two pieces, and there was a line of welling red on his arm above and below the strange wristlet he had brought out of Ruhkarv. Dazed, he watched the blood gather and drip, realizing tardily that a super-steel blade meeting that red band had been broken like a stick of dead wood and that, thanks to the bracelet, he was still alive.

Holding his arm pressed tightly to his side to slow the flow of blood, Troy stooped over Zul. The yellow man lay limply on the ground but he was still breathing.

"Behind you—"

Troy tried to turn, tripped on Zul's outflung arm, and went to his knees, so saving his life, for he cowered just beyond the searing edge of a blaster beam. He coughed in the ozone stench of the discharge. Then, obeying the instinct of self-preservation, he rolled across the ground, sick with the torment of his side and arm, gaining cover behind another rock pillar. So Zul had at least one companion. And disarmed and wounded, Troy would now be hunted down, with all the advantages on the side of the hunter.

In his desire to hide, Troy knew of only one place—the depths of Ruhkarv. Its evil reputation might slow up pursuit, give him a breathing space. If he could only have reached the blaster he had stunned out of Zul's hand! But there was no chance to hunt for that now—not with a sniper ready to fry him if he ventured into the open.

"The depths," he thought fuzzily, trying to contact the animals, sure that they had scattered into hiding when he had broken Zul's spell-binding with the tube.

The tube! With that in Zul's or another's hands the fugitives had no chance at all. Troy looked about him a little wildly. There it lay—one end projecting beyond a stone. To leave that intact meant disaster. Horan hunted for a weapon—any kind of weapon.

He chose a stone block detached from a nearby dome, of a size to fit his hand. And he hurled it—to strike hard and true. Under its impact the tube cracked, the end shattered, past any repair, he trusted. Their luck had held—this far.

Then, his throbbing arm tight against his chest, Troy scuttled away, expecting every moment to see the flash of another blaster beam or feel his flesh crisp under the beam he did not see.

Somehow he made it, falling rather than running into the open mouth of the ramp up which they had come hours before with such hope. And that beam he had been anticipating struck as he fell and rolled down the inside slope. He saw the brilliant, eye-searing flash and heard the crackle as it lapped stone. Then he was beyond its reach, only aware that somehow he was still alive, if badly battered.

Would his tracker come boldly on? Troy tried to listen. He could not see well; his eyes were still dazzled by the last shot. What he did hear was the return of the flitter, or else another flyer. And that might have provided a signal of sorts, for dark shapes flowed over the edge of the ramp above, visible only for a second or two against the circle of the daylight. The animals were on their way to join him.

Together they retired to the first level of corridors and there paused. There was no sound from above. Had the rangers' scout seen the activity in the ruins and landed to investigate? Troy knew that he had left Zul partially stunned but still able to join the chase. If he only had the blaster that the other had dropped in their first encounter—

"It is here."

Sahiba! Troy dared for an instant to snap on the atom torch. The gray-blue cat, her splinted leg held at an awkward angle, was half lying, half sitting, close to him, and next to her was her mate. And in front of Simba rested the weapon Troy had longed for. He caught it up, feeling the dampness of the cat's mouth-carry on the slender barrel, checking the charge. That was less than a third expended. Now he could defend them.

"They come." That was Sargon.

"How many?" Troy demanded.

"One—there are others—still above—"

One. Zul, or the unseen with the blaster? Troy eyed the corridors issuing from the ramp, then flashed off his torch. To venture blindly along any of those might be to lose oneself entirely. Better the dangers he knew than a new host, especially with the hunt behind, for Troy was certain that Zul was not going to give up. And he tried to plan ahead. Perhaps in that tangled jungle below he could find the means of turning tables on the other.

There was the problem of water and food. His bag of supplies had been abandoned in the open. But there was water below, and perhaps food, if he was not dainty. He knew that the animals had found edible prey in the fungoid cavern.

"Down!" He picked up Sahiba, unsealing the front of his tunic and settling the cat into an improvised carrying bag, which left his good arm free. The cuts on his left forearm had stopped bleeding, but he feared to use it freely lest they begin to ooze again.

Though no sounds save his own breathing, the faint scurrying that marked the going of the animals, and the thin click of his boots reached his ears, Troy's scouts assured him that the pursuit was still in progress as they retreated to the level of the next set of corridors and on back to the haunted wilderness cavern. He went without the torch, feeling his way, and now the pallid seep of light below marked their goal.

When he dropped from the foot of the ramp, Troy discovered the weird daylight was again in effect. Perhaps it was true sunlight beamed through some unknown process of Ruhkarv's builders into this hollow. There was a line of clouds discharging their burden of rain, and Troy dodged to a dry space beyond. He came against the rock wall where a filament of gray-white stuff clung, and his shoulder brushed against it—to adhere so that he had to jerk to free himself.

That was one of the web cords—strung all the way from the opening—which had made a fatal trap for Fauklow's man.

With the glimmering of an idea, Troy examined the length carefully. He discovered that it was not plastered to the stone surface along its entire side, as he had first feared, but attached at intervals by thicker portions. Thrusting his blaster into his belt, he pried between two of those buttons and, either because the cord was old or because it had never been meant to grip too tightly except at those points, he freed a loop.

Troy worked fast. There were other cords, some thinner, one or two as thick, and he moved them with caution, picking the suckers away from the wall. The outer sides were adhesive in the extreme. Sometimes the ends he loosened flopped and became irretrievably glued together before he could prevent their touching.

But even laboring one-handed he had a net of sorts, though very crude and far from the perfect mesh he had seen set over two of the cavern entrances. With infinite care he spread his trap at the foot of the ramp before the chopped-out trail that marked their former trip through the jungle. Why he had been allowed time enough to finish the job he did not know. But the animals posted on the ramp had not given the alarm.

At Troy's signal they leaped free of the tangle now lightly covered with dust and trampled leaves. To the man's eye the net was well hidden, and he hoped his pursuers would be as blind. Then they took cover, the animals—except Sahiba—under the fringe of vegetation, Troy and Sahiba in the pocket between wall and ramp.

They had set the trap. But was a trap any good without bait? There had been no sight or sound of the enemy for more than an hour. Had the other—or others—stopped to explore the level corridors?

Man had only a scant portion of the patience of the four-footed hunters, as Troy was to discover. His skin itched; his side and arm throbbed. Hunger and thirst clawed at his insides. A hundred minor irritations of which he would not have ordinarily been conscious arose to the point of torment. The sinister vegetation that had repelled him earlier now beckoned with a promise of food and water—somewhere—somehow—

And under that physical discomfort lay the malaise of spirit that had troubled him before when night had caught him in this place—the suggestion that there were unseen terrors here worse than any danger he could face body to body, weapon to weapon.

Troy battled discomfort, vague fears, held himself taut, hoping his forlorn hope would work. But how long he could keep this watch he did not know. A trap—but a trap needed bait.

A bush trembled. Shang sprang from its crown onto the ramp. He stood so for a moment, his prehensile tail curled up in a question mark, hindquarters up slope, his round head atilt as he looked down at Troy.

"No." The man protested. The kinkajou could move fast, Troy would bear witness to that, but not fast enough to escape a blaster bolt.

But the animal did not heed him. Out of reach, the kinkajou was now out of sight as well, up the ramp. The bait had been provided.

Sahiba shifted her weight inside his tunic, making Troy catch his breath as one of her hind paws scraped his tender ribs.

"One comes?" he asked hopefully.

His less able sense of contact caught again the fringe of their joint concentration, the filament that must unite them to Shang up there in the danger of the higher levels. And Troy, impatient, knew that he could not badger them with questions now.

Time crept. Once more dusk was growing in the jungle, patch of shadow united with patch of shadow, and did not retreat but became solid.

"One comes!" Sahiba dug the claws of her good forepaw into Troy's flesh, jerking him out of a nod. He drew the blaster, took the cat out of his tunic, and set her in safety behind him.

A scurry on the ramp. Shang flew through the air from

the stone to the bushes. And now—louder—the click of shod feet—human feet.

Above, a flicker of light—gone almost as instantly as Troy had sighted it. An atom torch snapped on and off again? He was sure that the newcomer must have seen the thin light of the cavern and would now proceed guided by that alone.

"Zul?" He beamed that at Shang.

"No."

If not Zul, then it must be that unknown who had sniped with the blaster. Troy readied his own weapon. Whether he could burn down another human being, even when fighting for his life, he was not sure. The struggles in the Dipple had always been man to man, fist and foot. And a knife was an accepted combat arm anywhere on Korwar, in fact across the stellar lanes. But this thing in his hand—he did not know, though he was very sure no such scruples would check the other.

The click of boots was still. Had the other halted—or turned back?

"No!" A reply concentrated in force from the animals.

Then it was stealth. Troy crouched, steadied his blaster hand against the wall. Yet for all his long period of waiting he was not quite prepared for the sudden spring from the head of the ramp.

His own slight movement might have spiked that attack and almost spoiled his plan. But Troy had planted the net well. The man fell short and his landing was not clean. He went to his hands and knees, to be enmeshed in the sticky ropes, which, as he rolled and fought, only tied the more tightly about his body.

Troy stood away from the wall. He would not be forced to fire after all. The other was doing a good job of making himself a prisoner.

"Another—"

The warning startled Troy out of his absorption in the struggle. Simba advanced into the open, avoiding the flopping captive, to stand at the foot of the ramp looking up.

Then a blaster bolt crackled—striking not for Troy, as he had expected, but at the writhing figure on the ground, close enough to singe some of the cords so that they flaked away from smoldering clothing. The bound man gave a mighty heave and rolled, as a second bolt burned the soil where he had lain and cut a blackened slash into the jungle.

And by that flash Troy saw the hide tunic the other wore. The trapped man was not Zul but one of the rangers. Horan snapped an answering bolt recklessly up the ramp. There was a cry and a figure staggered into view, slipped, rolled to the cavern floor. When it did not stir again, Troy went to the ranger.

"I thought I might find you here, Horan."

He was looking down at Rerne. And his first impulse to free the other died. Once he had almost turned to this man for help. Now all the instincts of the hunted brought back his long-seated suspicions. He might well have as good a reason to fear Rerne as he did Zul. Not that the ranger would blast him without warning, but the Clans had their own laws and those laws were obeyed in the Wild. Troy did not sheathe the blaster, but over its barrel he regarded the Hunter narrowly.

"Do not be a fool," Rerne had stopped struggling, but he was trying to raise his head and shoulders from the ground. "You are being hunted."

"I know," Troy interrupted. "You are here—"

Rerne frowned. "You have more after you than Clan rangers, boy. Including some who want you dead, not alive. Ha—"

His gaze swept from Troy to a point nearer ground level. Troy follow the path of his eyes. Shang, Simba, Sargon, and Sheba had materialized in their usual noiseless fashion, were seated at their ease inspecting Rerne with that measuring stare Troy could still find disconcerting when it was turned in his direction. Sahiba came limping from the place where he had left her for safety.

"So—" Rerne returned the steady-eyed regard of the animals, his expression eager. "These are the present most-wanted criminals of Korwar."

# FIFTEEN

**M**ost wanted, maybe,"—Troy's voice was soft, cold, one he had never used before to any man outside the Dipple—"but not criminals, Rerne." No more subservient "Hunter" or "Gentle Homo." This was not Tikil but a place into which the men of Tikil feared to go, and he was no longer a weaponless city laborer but one of a company who were ready to fight for what the Dipple had never held—freedom.

"You know how they served Kyger?" Rerne asked almost casually.

"I know."

"But you could not have been a part of that—or could you?" That last portion of the question might be one Rerne was asking himself—had been asking himself—for some time. He was studying Troy with a stare almost as unblinking as that Simba could turn upon one.

"No, I was not a part of Kyger's schemes, whatever those were. And I did not kill him—if you have any doubts about that. But neither are we criminals."

"We?"

Troy took a step backward to join the half circle of animals. They stood together now, presenting a united front to the ranger. Rerne nodded.

"I see, it is indeed 'we.'"

"And what do you propose to do about it?" Troy challenged.

"It is not what I propose to do, Horan. We shall all probably die unless we can work together to find a safe way out of here." But he sounded calm enough. "You are being hunted by more than just Clan rangers—in fact, the rangers could be the least of your worries. And it seems that the order is out to blast before asking questions—blast on sight."

"Your orders?" Troy brought up his own weapon.

"Hardly. And when they hear about it, the Clan shall take steps. That I promise you." There was ice in that, and Troy, noting the narrowing of the other's eyes, the slight twist of his lips, estimated the quality of the anger this man held under rigid control. "It is easy to eliminate a fugitive and afterwards swear that his death was all an unfortunate mistake—the game our friend over there was trying to play." He jerked his head toward the body at the foot of the ramp. "You have one chance in a thousand of escaping one or another of the packs after you now or—" He was summarily interrupted.

"One comes." Simba padded to the foot of the ramp again.

Troy hesitated. He could leave Rerne where he was, neatly packaged, for either the ranger's own men or someone else to discover—and melt back into the jungle, eventually seeking the yet lower level of the fungoid cavern, retracing their whole journey through Ruhkarv. Or he could make a stand here and fight.

Rerne's eyes traveled from cat to man and back again. "We are about to entertain another visitor?"

"*We?*" This time it was Troy who accented the pronoun.

"It could not be my men coming now."

And Troy believed him. That meant it was truly the enemy.

"You have a choice," Rerne pointed out. "Take to the bush over there and they will have a difficult time beating you out of it—"

"And you?"

"Since you can name me one of your pursuers, should that matter?" There was a grim lightness in that.

"The other one tried to burn you."

"As I said, they are working on the principle that accidents will happen and a dead man one has to explain is better than a live witness who can explain for himself."

Troy made the only possible choice. Hooking his fingers in the nearest loop of the cords about the ranger, he jerked the man under the overhang of the ramp. There was no time now to try to free Rerne, even if he were yet sure he wanted to. But he knew he could not leave the other helpless to take a blasting from Zul or one of Zul's crowd.

"Zul?" he asked Simba.

"Zul," the cat replied with sure authority.

There was no time either in which to rig another trap, and Troy was sure the other came armed. Nor could he count on another shot as lucky as the one that had brought down the earlier assailant. Now he squatted beside Rerne, hoping for a workable ambush.

"Get me loose!" The ranger's shoulders heaved as he worked his muscles against the cords of the webbing.

"Nothing will cut those except heat," Troy told him absently, most of his attention on what might be happening up ramp.

"What is this stuff?" Rerne demanded, his voice a whisper.

"Part of a web—taken from the wall over there." Troy nodded to the stretch of rock where strips of cord and thread still hung in tatters. Rerne gave a small gasp and was silent.

The light was fading steadily into a dark that had none of the quality of the upper-surface night. Troy remembered his first stay in this place, his belief that the jungle had its own brand of very dangerous life. There was one place free of that growth—the section of pavement where the recaller stood. And as long as that machine was deadened—

If Zul did not come soon, should they try to reach that? Troy seesawed between one plan and the other. Wait here for Zul and try to shoot as soon as he appeared on the ramp, when he could not be too sure of his aim in the failing light? Or free Rerne's legs and bundle the ranger along to that haunted spot beside the recaller with the warning of that shriveled, long-dead thing set up to stare at them through the night hours?

"Zul?" Again he asked that of those who were quicker than he to know whether danger ran or crept toward them now.

Simba again answered, but this time with a puzzled shading to his mind speech. "Zul begins to fear—"

"Us?" Troy could hardly believe that. He knew well that Zul had had no fear when they had fought above, that Zul looked upon the animals as creatures he could control, could entice helpless to their deaths. What and why did he fear now? Or was it the presence of Rerne that was a restraining factor? Could Troy somehow use the Hunter to bargain with?

"Zul fears what he cannot see," Simba reported, still that puzzlement coloring his reply.

For a moment Simba's report fed Troy's own latent uneasiness. With the dusk closing in about them and the only too clearly remembered picture of the captive in the web at the back of his mind, he thought he knew what could plague a man, eating at his nerves until he had to get out of this hidden pocket within Ruhkarv. But Zul had not been here; he could not know of the web, or the recaller, or guess at what might have been summoned and now, according to the animals, still hovered just beyond the bonds of living consciousness. Why did Zul fear?

"He does not see," Sahiba cut in, "not with his eyes—only with his far thoughts. But he is a kind who feels trouble before him."

"He is able to speak to you then?"

"No." That was Sargon. "Not without the aid of the thing-which-calls. But Zul sees many shadows now and each holds an enemy." The fox trotted out of hiding, made a detour about the body of the dead man, and advanced a foot or so up the ramp, surveying the gloom above. "He wishes to come, yet his fears hold him back."

And did Zul have a right to fear? Troy watched the now night-disguised splotch of the jungle. And he knew that he could no longer plan to pass through even a fringe of it, much less intrude upon that open space about the recaller. It was as if that thing, which lurked—not alive, yet not wholly in the dead past either—sucked vitality from the dark, made itself substance that could not be seen with the eyes, but which could be sensed by that other thing inside one, the thing that allowed him to communicate with the animals.

"What is it?" Rerne, too, his shoulders braced against the rock wall, was staring into that mass of vegetation. "What walks there?"

"Nothing alive—I hope." Troy went down on one knee, sparked his blaster on low power, and touched lightly the coils of webbing still encircling the other's legs. The strands shriveled and were gone.

"Nothing alive?" Rerne repeated questioningly.

"The recaller Fauklow brought is out there. Your machine muted it, but the power is still on—blanketed. They tell me that what it summoned is still partly in this dimension."

"What! And I take it that our friend above is reluctant to descend into what may prove to be a dragon's jaws?"

Troy sat back on his heels. Had Rerne been able to tune in on that conversation between Troy and the animals? But he was certain that the animals would have known of such eavesdropping and would have warned him.

"You communicate with the animals somehow," Rerne continued. "And now you suspect that I can also."

Troy nodded.

"Mental contact." That was a stated fact, not a question. "No, I have been guessing only. And this I do know, Zul is of unusual stock. Most of us now are a mingling of many races, the result of centuries of stellar colonization. He is a primitive out of Terra—pure Bushman—a race of hunters and desert dwellers with an inborn instinct for the Wild such as few others have today. And such primitives keep senses we have lost. If he sniffs your demon, then I do not think that mere duty will drive him down. Rather he will comfort his conscience with the belief that the demon will account for us—if he sits over the exit and so locks us in. And at that, I can almost find myself agreeing with such reasoning."

Rerne moved his shoulders again, straining at the remaining cords. "This is not a place in which I would choose to spend the night," he confessed, and there was no light touch to those words.

"You were here when Fauklow was found?"

"Not here. We did not know this particular beauty spot existed.

After what we saw aloft there was no nonsense about exploring below ground. We thought we had accounted for the recaller, though. That must be seen to. That is, if I ever get out of here to report it."

"He can wait up there a long time—pick us off easily if we try to pass." Troy wondered if now was the time to reveal the alternate route to the surface. Without food and water—no, he was not sure they could make it back the longer way around.

"Yes, any one of those level corridors would make him a good cover for ambush. But if we cannot get up, we can bring help from the surface to take him in the rear." Again Rerne tried to flex his upper arms. "If you will just loose me the rest of the way, Horan, I can bring in reinforcements."

"No." Troy's dissent was flat and quick.

"Why?" Rerne did not sound angry, merely interested.

"We are criminals—remember?"

"Where there is a common enemy there can be a truce. In the Wild I do have some small authority."

Troy considered that. Trust was a rare commodity in the Dipple. If he gave his now to this man, as he was so greatly tempted to do, he would be putting a weapon in Rerne's hands just as surely as if he were to hand over the blaster. And again his suspicion warred with his desire to believe in the other.

"A truce, until we are out of here," Rerne suggested. "I am willing to swear knife oath if you wish."

Troy shook his head. "Your word, no oaths—if I accept." He paid that much tribute openly to the ranger. "Truce and a head start for me, with them."

"The chase will be up again," Rerne warned. "You have no chance with the Clans out to quarter the field. Better surrender and let the law decide."

"The law?" Troy laughed harshly. "Which law, Hunter—Clan right, patrollers' code, or Zul's extermination policy? I know we are fair game. No, give me your promise that we can have a start of at least half a day."

"That is freely yours, for what you can make of it, which I am afraid will be very little."

"We shall take our chances." Troy applied heat to the other's remaining bonds.

"Always *we*. Why, Horan?" Rerne rubbed his wrists.

"Men have used animals as tools," Troy said slowly, trying to fit into words something he did not wholly understand himself. "Now some men, somewhere, have made better tools, tools so good they can turn and cut the maker. But that is not the fault of the tools—that they are no longer tools but—"

"Perhaps companions?" Rerne ended for him, his fingers still stroking his ridged flesh, but his eyes very intent on Troy.

"How did you know?" the younger man was startled into demanding.

"Let us say that I am also a workman who can admire fine tools, even when they have ceased, as you point out, to be any longer tools."

Troy grasped at that hint of sympathy. "You understand—"

"Only too well. Most of our breed want tools, not companions. And the age-old fear of man, that he will lose his supremacy, will bring all the hawks and hunters of the galaxy down on your trail, Horan. Do not expect any aid from your own species when it is threatened by powers it cannot and does not want to understand. But you will have your truce—and your head start—and what you do with them is up to you. Now, let us see what we can do about getting a clear road out of here before what prowls over there takes a fancy to come out." Rerne waved a hand toward the jungle.

He slipped a small object from a loop on his belt. On its surface was a tiny dial he set with care, holding it into the beam of an atom torch. Then he smiled at Troy.

"Broadcaster. It is beamed for a ranger aid call, and I have alternated that with a warning code, so they will not head blindly into any ambush of Zul's. He may have another man with him, possibly two. We know that he went to the Guild in Tikil before he coasted in here. I think he hired blaster men."

"Then he must have robbed Kyger's. He would not have credits enough on his own to pay blaster man prices to the Thieves' Guild."

"Did you ever think that perhaps Kyger was not the top man

of his organization on Korwar?" returned Rerne. "If he was not, then it is up to that head to close down the whole enterprise as quickly and with as little fuss as possible. You have already been posted in Tikil as a murderer who has stolen valuable animals. Someone issued that complaint."

"I thought that would happen." Troy governed his dismay speedily. Posted as a murderer! Which meant that even the city patrollers could shoot first and ask troublesome questions after. Only this was the Wild, not Tikil, and he thought he had an advantage over that set of trackers here.

"You say that you did not kill him?"

"I found him dead." Swiftly Troy outlined the events before his escape from the shop and from Tikil that night.

"That account I can readily believe. Kyger had some odd acquaintances and had stepped hard on the wrong toes," Rerne commented obscurely, "apart from these other activities. And do you realize that I can supply you with an alibi? At the time Kyger died you were with Rogarkil and me."

"Did you say that to the patrollers?" Troy's throat felt tight. If that was the truth, why had Rerne not cleared him?

"Not so far—"

"You wanted a bargaining point to use with me?" Troy demanded. That seesaw of belief, then suspicion, within him swung once more to the chilling side.

"Perhaps."

"I am not interested. I will take what I have." Troy was cooling rapidly. He was sure Rerne would keep his word to the strict letter of his promise. But why the ranger had revealed this other matter—that he could clear Troy with the law of the city but had not done so—remained a mystery. It smelled of the desire to push Horan into some pattern of Clan devising, just as he and the other had obliquely suggested at that cafe meeting. And having tasted freedom, Troy was not minded to walk again another's road.

"As you wish." Rerne neither urged nor explained. He raised the miniature com unit to his ear, listened for a moment, and then nodded.

"They are coming, have laid down a haze ahead—as far as the levels. Should not be long before that reaches Zul."

So the rangers were using that most up-to-date subduing weapon—and one Zul, Troy was certain, was not armored against.

"Will they arrest Zul?"

Rerne glanced at him. "Is that what you wish?"

"Why not?"

"There is no reason to believe that Zul is top man. He was wholly Kyger's subordinate, not the other way around. Zul, left free, could lead someone to his employer."

"If that trailer had time—and the inclination," snapped Troy. "Just at present I have more important things—" He paused. Rerne was right in a way. To trace Zul's contacts to their sources. If it were not for the animals, he would like to do just that. But he must make the best use of his truce, and he could not waste time on Zul. "Your move, if you wish," he suggested.

Rerne was holding the broadcaster to his ear again. "Our move is up." He gestured to the ramp.

"Zul?"

"No sign of him. But there is a Guildsman sleeping sweetly at the second level. They have collected him for the patrollers. Let Zul believe that he has made a safe escape in his hiding place. He will sleep off the haze and he can be watched later."

So Rerne was going to investigate Zul? Though what he would make of more exact knowledge, except to use it as a lever for some Clan dispute with the authorities in Tikil, Troy did not see. He gathered up Sahiba, motioned Rerne to precede them.

"I have a blaster. You have granted me a truce. Maybe some of the rest up there will not be so generous."

Rerene smiled. "It pays to be cautious. But I think you will find I speak for the rangers. Up it is."

To Troy the climb was as long and exhausting as had been the descent of the winding way in the well. There was no one waiting at the first level of corridors. On and up, Simba and Sargon forging a little ahead, a twin pair of scouts Troy was sure no human being could equal, Shang was on his shoulder, Sheba beside him. None of the animals paid any attention to Rerne outwardly, but Troy knew they kept an expert watch on the ranger.

They passed the second level. Ahead lay the open, Troy pushed his weary brain to plan action beyond that point. He could not hope that he would have any chance at mechanical transport; his bargain did not reach that far. But the barrier about Ruhkarv must have been lowered to let the searchers in, so they could leave this scar on foot. Tired as he was, without supplies, he did not see how they would be able to cover much ground. But even if they could reach the fringe of forest lands, the animals could escape. Then he would take his chances with the men.

"Men waiting," Simba warned.

Well, that was to be expected—Rerne's men.

"Not enemies," Troy replied.

"We have you covered! Drop your blaster!"

Troy spun halfway around as he caught a glimpse of a uniformed shoulder, a hand holding a blaster. His arm, still stiff from the cut, went up and his fingers gripped Rerne, pulling the other to him as a shield. He heard a gasp from the ranger and an exclamation of anger.

"So this is the worth of a Clansman's word!" Troy spat. "Would your knife oath have held any better?" Then he raised his voice to reach the others. "We got out—this Hunter lord with us. Any attempted burn-down and he roasts too!"

Rerne offered no resistance as Troy propelled him ahead into the open. There was a muttering behind but no bolt to shatter the gloom.

# SIXTEEN

Rerne was oddly silent; he had made no reply to Troy's accusation. That bothered the younger man; he wanted an explanation, to know that the other had not purposely led him into a trap. Now that he had a moment to think, he believed that scrap of uniform so briefly glimpsed had not been ranger dress.

"Men here—" Again that alert from the animals.

Troy, holding the unresisting Rerne to him, stood—back to the dome wall—surveying the scene. He could see those others waiting—and they were unmistakably rangers, the hunting dress blending into the earth color of the ruins. A little beyond was what he had not dared to hope for—a flitter!

"Tell your men," he said harshly to his prisoner, "to stand away from the flitter—now!"

"Leave the flitter," Rerne repeated obediently, his voice as toneless as that of a com robot. His features were set and hard, and Troy sensed his rage.

The rangers moved. When they were well away from the flyer, Troy began a crablike journey in its direction, keeping Rerne between him and the Clan men, knowing the animals were well ahead of him. Then he was at his goal, his hand on the cabin door.

His anger and fear driving him, Troy swung the blaster, laid the barrel against Rerne's head. The Hunter gasped, his knees buckled, and he dropped to the ground. Troy scrambled into the flyer, knocked down the rise lever. They climbed in a jump, which shook him across the control board and made Sahiba yowl in protest as she was scraped against that obstruction. But they were safe for the moment; he was sure the zoom had lifted them out of range of blaster fire. Free and in a flitter.

He twirled the journey dial to the east, knowing that the flyer, without any tending from him, would keep straight for the heart of the Wild. They would be after him surely. But unless they had another flitter at Ruhkarv, there would be precious time lost until they could summon one, and time was all he dared hope to gain now.

Troy's eyes were fixed unseeingly on the night sky that held them. Food—water—shelter—His mind felt as sapped of energy as his body. He could not think properly. Of only one thing was he sure: a stubborn determination to set down the flyer somewhere in the Wild where the animals could take to the country for their own concealment.

"It is well." That was Simba. "Good hunting here. Men cannot shake us out of these lands."

"There is still Zul," Troy warned sluggishly.

"There is still Zul," Simba agreed. "But let Zul follow us before we lay a trap for his feet."

Troy must have slept. He aroused with light in his eyes, sat up groggily, for a moment unable to remember where he was. Then the golden sky of morning, patterned with the clouds of fair weather, recalled the immediate past. Under him the flitter rode steadily on the course he had set—eastward.

He looked down through the bubble, expecting to see the rolling plains he had hoped to find. They spread beneath him right enough, only ahead was a distant smudge of darker vegetation, the sign of a forest or more broken ground. They must have passed over a large section of the open territory during the night and were leagues deep into the reserve, farther than the Tikil hunting parties ever went. Troy rubbed his eyes, began to think again.

The only way they could be traced now was by the flitter.

Suppose he were to land by the edge of that distant wood and then send the flyer off on remote control—back to the west? One way of confusing the pursuit.

But, as he reached for the controls, to take the flyer back under manual pilotage again, his time had run out. The flitter plunged crazily, caught in the side sweep of a traction beam. Troy gave one startled look to the rear, saw another flyer boring down his track.

Perhaps a more skilled pilot could have done better. His evasive swings only kept him out of the direct core of the beam the other had trained upon his craft. He set the air speed to the top notch, striving to reach the wood before the other pinned him squarely.

At last Troy set down, felt the wheels of the flitter catch and tear through the long grass. But that grass could cover his passengers' escape. He slewed the flyer about, broadside to the first tongue of woods cover. Opening the door of the cabin before they bumped to a complete halt, he gave his last command to the animals: "Out and hide!"

Sahiba he set down himself, saw her limp into a tangle of grass with her mate, the foxes and the kinkajou already gone. Then Troy sent the flyer on, scuttling along the ground as far and as fast from the point where he had dropped his live cargo as he could get.

The flitter rocked, half lifted from the ground. Now he was pinned to his seat, helpless, unable to raise as much as a finger from the controls. They had a pinner beam on him, and he was a captive forced to wait for the arrival of his pursuer.

Unable to as much as turn his head, Troy sat sweating out the minutes of that wait. At least they wanted to take him prisoner, not just blast him out of the air as they might have done. Whether this was good or bad he had yet to learn. And whether his captors were rangers, patrollers, or Zul's ambiguous force he would know shortly.

The cabin door was pulled open. Though he could not turn his head, Troy rolled his eyes to the right far enough to see that the man who had thrust head and shoulders into that confined space was not wearing the hide forest dress of the Clans, not the uniform of a patroller. Zul's party—?

Paying little or no attention to the helpless prisoner before the controls, the other searched the floor, squeezed behind the seat to survey the storage space. Undoubtedly he was looking for the animals. And, guessing that, Troy's spirits rose a small fraction. They had either not noted his brief pause by the tongue of woodland, or they had not understood the reason for it. They had expected to find not one but six helpless in the flitter.

The man backed out of the door. "Not here." Troy heard his call.

Though he knew he could not fight the tension bands of a pinner, Troy strove to move just his hand. The blaster butt was a painful knob against his chest, held upright by his belt. If he could only close his fingers about that, the man by the door and the one he reported to—he could turn tables on both of them. But, though blood throbbed in his temples from his efforts, he was held motionless and unable to resist any attack the others chose to make.

His eyes began to ache with the strain of trying to keep watch on the door of the cabin. But he did not have too long to wait. Zul, his yellow face a mask of pure and unshielded malignancy, took the place of his hireling there. As the other had done, he searched the floor of the machine, apparently unwilling or unable to accept that first report. Then he looked directly at Troy.

"They are gone!" He said that flatly.

At least vocal cords and throat muscles were not governed by the pinner. Troy was able to answer. "Where you will not find them."

Zul did not reply to that. Withdrawing from the cabin, he gave a low-voiced order. After a moment the door beside Troy was opened, and his disobedient muscles could not save him from falling through it, dropping to the ground on his face.

But the fall had removed him from the direct line of the pinner, and now he was free to move as the others, protected by countercharge buttons, had moved within the machine. He tried to get to his knees but he was not quick enough. A sharp pain burst at the nape of his neck, and he sprawled forward again, into the trampled grass of the plains.

Troy roused to utter darkness, a black that was frightening with its suggestion of blindness. And as he tried to raise his hand to his eyes, he made the discovery that he was bound, this time by no pinner but by very real cords, which chafed his wrists, drew hard loops about his ankles. A moment's experimentation informed him that it was no easier to loosen those than it had been to fight the beam. And he also learned that the dark came from an efficient and bewildering blindfold.

Whatever the intentions of his captors, they wanted to keep him alive for the present—and in reasonably good shape. Having made sure of his status as a wrapped package, Troy tried to figure out where he now was. The vibration, the small rough jolts of a swift air flight, were transmitted to his body through the surface on which he lay. His legs were curled behind him in a manner to stiffen muscles with cramp if he did not change position, and he could not. So Troy guessed that he now lay in the storage compartment of a flitter, in either the one in which he had made the dash from Ruhkarv, or the one in which Zul had tracked him.

And with Zul in command of that party, Troy thought that they must now be headed back toward Tikil—Tikil and perhaps the man who gave the orders now that Kyger was dead. The animals—They had expected to find them in the flitter. After they had stunned him had they discovered the animals? With nothing to bring them out of the woodland as Zul had drawn them with the summoner, Troy doubted that any of those who held him prisoner could have picked up the four-footed fugitives.

He tested his hope by trying to reach one of the animals with the mind touch. There was no response; he apparently had no fellow captives. Nor could he hear anything except the normal noises of a competently piloted flitter going at top legal speed—which meant they were flying high.

He had no way of telling how long he had been unconscious. But his middle was a hollow ache of hunger, and the thirst drying his throat was an additional pain; it was hard to remember now just when he had eaten last, harder yet to think back to a full drink of water. And these torments, added to the discomfort of his present position, spoiled his efforts to plan clearly, to try to speculate concerning what lay ahead of him at the end of this journey.

Troy wriggled, trying to work his legs straighter, then became aware of a change in the tempo of their flight. The pilot was cutting air speed, with a jerk that shook the flyer every time they dropped a notch—which argued the need for saving time. They must be ready to drop into a lower lane—could they be approaching Tikil?

Lying in his cramped curl, Troy tried to sort out the few impressions he could gather through the vibration of the flyer, the difference in small sounds. Yes, they were definitely dropping to a lower lane. Then he caught the whistle of a patroller flitter.

Troy tensed. Was this flyer being overhauled by the law?

But if the pilot had been questioned, he had been able to give the right signal answer, for there was no change in the beat of the engine—they had not been ordered to set down. However, the speed decreased another notch. They were now traveling at the placid rate required for a low city lane, one used preparatory to landing.

Landing where? Troy's whole body ached now with the strain of trying to evaluate what he heard and felt. The swoop of the flitter he had been expecting. Then came the slight bound of a too-quick wheel touch, and the engine was snapped off.

Play dead, Troy thought. Let them haul him about as if he were still unconscious until he learned what he could. He forced his muscles to relax as well as he was able.

Air blew through the flitter. He heard the scrape of boots. Then another panel was opened only a few inches beyond his head. Hands, hooked in his armpits, jerked him roughly backward so that his legs hit the pavement. Grunting, the man who had unloaded him continued to drag Troy along.

But the air was providing the blindfolded prisoner with a clue to his whereabouts. Only one place had ever held that particular combination of strong odors—the courtyard of Kyger's shop. He was back to where he had started from days before!

He thudded to the ground, dropped by his guard, then heard the faint squeak of a panel door. Once more hands hooked under him and he was manhandled along. Again his nose supplied a destination. This was the storeroom off the courtyard. Troy was allowed to fall unceremoniously, his head and shoulders against a bag of grain, so that he was half sitting. He made his head loll forward in what he hoped was a convincing display of unconsciousness.

But if this convinced his captors, they were no longer willing to let him remain unaware of his plight. Out of nowhere the flat of a palm smacked one cheek, snapping his head back against the bag. And a second stinging slap shook him equally as much.

"What—?" He did not need to counterfeit that dazed query.

"Wake up, Dippleman!" That was Zul. Yet Troy was sure the small man did not have the strength to drag him here. There must be at least two of them beside him in the storeroom.

"What—?" Troy began again.

"Use your mouth for this."

A hard metal edge was thrust against his lips with force enough to pinch flesh painfully against his teeth, and then he almost choked as a substance that was neither liquid nor solid but more nearly a thick soup filled his mouth and he had to swallow, a portion trickling out greasily over his chin. It had a bitter taste, but he could not struggle against their force-feeding methods, and about a cupful of it burned down his throat into his stomach.

"Will that hold?" someone, he thought it was Zul, asked.

"Never failed yet," returned a stranger briskly. "He'll be as frisky as one of those Dandle pups of yours about five hours from now. That's what you want, is it not? Up until then you can leave him here with all the doors wide open and he will not get lost. We know our job, Citizen."

Troy's head flopped forward on his chest once more as the other released his grip. There was no need to sham helplessness. Spreading outward from that warmth in his stomach was a numbness that attacked muscles and nerves; he was completely unable to move. One of the notorious drugs used by the Guild. But, Troy thought dimly, that made this a highly expensive job—to include scientific drugging would put the price in the upper credit brackets. And where had Zul managed to lay his hands on that kind of funds—and the proper connections?

The numbness that had first affected his body now reached his mind. There was a dreamy lassitude in which nothing mattered. He lay quietly, drifting along on a softly swaying cloud that spiraled up lazily higher than any flitter could climb—

Cold—very cold—The cold centered in his head—no, in his mouth. Troy swallowed convulsively and the cold was in his throat—his middle—

"Thought you said he would be ready—" Words, the very sound of which jarred in his head.

"Does not usually work this way—unless he had an empty stomach to begin with." More words—protesting—hurting his head.

The cold spread outward, up through his shoulders, down his thighs, into his arms, hands, fingers, legs, and toes—a cold that bit, though he was unable to shiver.

"Get some sub-four into him now!" The order was rapped out in a louder tone.

More liquid splashed into his mouth, to dribble out again because he had no control over slack lips. Then his mouth was refilled, a palm held with brutal force over his lips, and he swallowed. The taste this time was sweet, cloying. But it drove out the ice as it went down him, bringing a glow, a feeling of returning energy and fitness, which was like a raw life force being pumped into his veins to supply new vigor for his body.

"That does it." The hand that had been over his lips slipped down to rest on the pulse in his throat, then farther, inside his tunic, to touch directly over his heart. "He is coming around all right. He will be ripe and ready when you want him."

The fatigue, the hunger, the thirst of which Troy had been so conscious were gone. He was fully alert, not only physically but mentally, with an added fillip of rising self-confidence—though he mistrusted the latter, for that emotion might be born of the succession of drugs they had forced into him. A haffer addict, for example, simply did not believe that failure of any of his projects was possible. Had they pumped him full of something that would make him as amenable to their will or wills as the animals had been to Kyger's summoning tube?

However, for the moment they left him. His nose told Troy he was still in the storeroom of the shop, the bag of grain propping his shoulders. Beyond that there was little that hearing, touch, or smell could add. Time had long ceased to have any meaning at all in his blindfolded world—this might be tomorrow, or several tomorrows, after that hour when he had dumped the animals in the Wild.

The animals! Once more he put his newly alerted mind to trying to establish contact with them. If they had been located and captured, he could not tell, for to all his soundless calls there came no replies.

Click of boot soles, the scrape of the door panel, boot soles again much louder. Then the smell of clothes worn about animals too long—the odor of a human body. Troy found a snatch of time in which to marvel at his heightened sense of smell.

There was a tug at the bindings about his ankles, those bonds pulled off. Then a hand dug fingers into his shoulder.

"Up and walk, Dippleman! You go on your own two feet this time."

He staggered a step or two, brought up painfully against the sharp edge of a box. The hand came again to steer him with a shove that made him waver. So propelled, he emerged into the courtyard, heard the purr of a waiting flitter ready to take off.

His guard steered him to the flyer, and he was loaded by two men, not into the driver's seat but once more into that storage space in which he had ridden back to Tikil. He was sure of only two things: that Zul was in charge of his transportation—he had heard the small man's grunt of assent from the pilot's seat before they lifted—and that the Thieves' Guild, Blasterman's Section (highest paid of all the illegal services on Korwar), was in command of the prisoner's keeping, which was enough to dampen thoroughly all hopes of escape, or even of a try at defense.

# SEVENTEEN

◈

**B**ut their lift into space was a very short one—perhaps it only cleared the division between courtyard and street. They descended gently, the wheels touched pavement, and the flitter proceeded as a ground car. Which meant that their destination was somewhere within the business sector of the city and not one of the outlying villas. A warehouse—an office? It would have to be where the entrance of a blindfolded, bound man, accompanied by at least one guard, would not attract attention. If this was night, a goal in the business district or among the warehouses would meet those requirements.

Troy tried to remember the geography of Tikil in relation to Kyger's but found that a hopeless task. Unless he was on his feet in the open, his eyes unbandaged, he could not even effectively retrace his way to the Dipple.

They turned once, twice, their speed a decorous one well within the limit. And undoubtedly they were taking every precaution against any irregularity of action or appearance that could awaken suspicion in a patroller's mind. The Guild were skilled workmen and this was a Guild protection project, which meant that Troy might well be on his way to some hidden headquarters of that power. Only he did not believe so. It was more likely he was being taken to face, or at least be inspected by, Zul's new employer.

Another turn. Neither man in the driver's seat spoke. Troy deduced by the volume of street noise that the hour must be one of late evening. They had joined homeward-bound traffic, which meant they were *not* heading toward the warehouses.

The flitter came to a stop. Troy, with his heightened sense of smell and hearing, knew that one of the men had leaned across the partition and was hanging head and shoulders above him.

"Listen, you." The words were bitten off dryly, and Troy knew that the speaker meant them. "You are going to get out and walk, Dippleman. And you are going to do it nice and easy without any noise or confusion. I'll have a nerve-block grip on you all the way. Make any trouble and you will still walk—but not nice and easy. You will sweat blood with every step. Understand?"

Troy nodded his head violently, hoping that the other could see that gesture. He had not the slightest desire to suffer the promised correction for the fault of causing his captor any trouble.

The other assisted him out of the flitter and kept a tight fingerhold on him. They walked, as his guard had promised, "nice and easy" across a strip of pavement.

Troy sniffed vegetation. They must be in a dwelling-house district. There was a slight pause, probably waiting for the householder to release a door-panel lock. Then their slow march started once again, the click of boot heels deadened by foam-set floor covering.

Troy's head jerked suddenly. Just as he had known they had returned him to Kyger's storeroom, so did he now guess where he stood. There could not be two such establishments in Tikil! But knowledge brought with it complete bewilderment—almost shock.

What did the clerk Dragur, living in the midst of a collection of marine horrors, have to do with Kyger's secret employment?

On the other hand—Troy's thoughts readjusted quickly—the colorless man's chosen hobby was an excellent cover for a connection between him and the shop, a connection above suspicion, since Dragur's enthusiasm concerning his pet monsters in their globes and aquariums had not been feigned; Troy would swear to that. His only objection to this new revelation was the character of the man himself. He simply could not visualize Dragur as the mastermind behind anything but fussy details of Korwarian bureaucracy.

Troy's ears caught the faint plop-plop of water slapping in a bowl as some inhabitant of the marine zoo moved, and he tried to remember how the room had been laid out at the time of his first visit there.

"Here is your man, Citizen, safe and in one piece." That was his guard reporting.

"Most commendable," Dragur's slightly high-pitched voice replied. "But I understand that the shipment is not complete. We were to have a complete shipment, Guildsman, complete."

"You shall have to ask this one what he did with the others, Citizen. The Big Man will settle with you on the deal. Give me the delivery release."

"Your Big Man shall also make an adjustment on the fee," Dragur snapped. "I bargained for a complete shipment. No release until that matter is settled."

"The Big Man will not feel kindly about that, Citizen." This was no threat, just a statement of fact, a fact to be accepted when the Guild made it clear.

"Oh, he will not? Well, I share his disappointment!" Dragur actually giggled. "You may tell him that as soon as you wish."

"No release, no delivery." The grip on Troy tightened.

"And you think you may march out of here, taking him with you?"

There was a long moment of silence. Troy tried to imagine what might be happening that he could not see.

"Where did you get that?" his guard asked slowly.

"I do not ask questions about the source of *your* equipment, do I?" countered Dragur. "Now you will remove your hands from my shipment and you will withdraw to your flitter. You have my permission, however, to communicate with your Big Man if you wish. I do not know whether he suffers bungling with patience or not. His reaction to your report you are better able to gauge than I. But you may mention to him, as a mitigating point, that a profitable relationship between ourselves may not be at an end, providing, of course, that we come to an equitable agreement now. I will also indicate that I have contracted for a time guardianship with your organization and that still has several hours to run. I am not in any way breaking contract."

The hand fell away from Troy. With the grunt of a baffled man who had been outmaneuvered, the guard moved from his side, and a moment later a door panel opened and closed. Troy heard Dragur laugh again.

"He will beam in his Big Man as soon as he thinks matters over. Better get a rating now than a burn later for not reporting."

"The Guildsmen like their credits." Zul spoke for the first time.

"But of course, do not all of us? On the other hand their continuing in business—at least the continuance of this particular branch of their business—depends also on a certain integrity. If they promise a shipment in full and deliver only part, then they have broken contract and must take the consequences. But that is a matter to be taken under advisement later. Now, Zul, let us make our visitor more comfortable."

Fingers pulled at the cords about Troy's wrists. His arms fell to his sides and then he rubbed his hands together. Another tug and the blindfold was a loop about his throat. He was blinking, dazzled by the light, subdued as it was, in the room.

"A most energetic young man—"

Troy centered his attention on the speaker. Dragur sat there in a most unusual chair. A tall glass slab formed the back, and in it swam with oily ease one of the miniature nightmare monsters, coming to the fore now and then as if peering over its master's shoulder, or to whisper through the transparent pane into his ear. Similar aquariums on either side, one holding carnivorous dorch crabs and the other a tramjan reef snake, served as armrests. The lid of the crab container was up, and from time to time Dragur tossed in small wriggling creatures to satisfy his pets' hunger. As an arrangement designed to make the onlooker both queasy and disinclined to argue with its owner, it was extremely successful.

But across Dragur's sharp-boned knees there also rested a nerve needler. And, seeing that, Troy could well understand the quick and almost fearful withdrawal of the Guildsman.

"You must be tired," Dragur continued in his high, fussy voice.

"So much traveling and most of it under what might be termed uncomfortable conditions. Zul, provide Horan with a seat. There is no need for you to be uncomfortable here. No—I believe in comfort. Ehh—that is it, my pretty! Jump!" He was dangling a tidbit over the crab cage. "Did you note that, my boy? Such energy, such spirit! One could not believe that a crab could actually leap, now, could one? I have discovered that many things will cause a crab, or an animal, or a man, to exert himself far past the powers one believes that nature endows him with at birth. Many things—"

"Such as a needler?"

Zul had brought a chair, not one furnished with attendant monster cages, Troy was pleased to note, and he sat down.

"A most crude stimulant to endeavor, only to be used in special cases and under special conditions. No, the action obtained under threat of punishment or death cannot be depended upon for any length of time. Just as torture is an expedient to be tried only by the unimaginative. A man will admit anything to save himself from pain when his breaking point has been found. Needlers have their places. I prefer more attractive methods."

"Such as?" Troy tried not to watch a second exhibition of profitable greed in the crab cage.

"Such as—" But whatever Dragur was about to say was silenced by a low buzz.

Zul, blaster in hand, sped across the room and vanished through an inner door. Dragur raised the needler so that the spray barrel sighted on Troy.

"Perhaps I am wrong," he said in a voice that was this time neither high nor fussy. "This may be an occasion for the cruder settlement after all. Sit where you are, Horan. The slightest move will compel me to press the trigger on this, and I think you know the results of such an action. I will also be compelled to do the same at any vocal warning from your direction. If we do have an unfriendly visitor on the way, he will encounter some surprises." With his other hand Dragur snapped down the lid of the crab cage, and in the quiet only the noises of the aquarium dwellers could be heard.

Then there was the sound of a scuffle, followed by a thud.

Dragur, Troy noted, did not turn his head in that direction; his full attention was still fixed on his prisoner.

"An intruder indeed." The agent's voice was now hardly more than a whisper. "And I believe that he has fallen into one of our amusing little traps. We shall soon know."

They did. Zul led the small procession. Behind him stumbled a man who wove about on rubbery legs, the normal gait of one who has taken a half jolt from a stunner in the motor nerves. And holding him erect and on course was the same Guildsman who had explored the flitter when Troy had been a captive to the pinner beam in the Wild. But it was the identity of the prisoner that startled Troy. Rerne!

Just as he had not expected to find the ranger in his trap in the cavern of the Ruhkarv, so he had not foreseen his arrival not only in Tikil but in this particular house.

Dragur surveyed the new captive.

"Greetings to the noble Hunter." He used the exaggerated phrase demanded by formal society with a sardonic inflection. "Not that I quite understand why one of the Clans should be moved to enter my modest home by the rear entrance and that without invitation from me. Zul, a chair for our new guest, please. We are becoming quite crowded here, are we not? So you—" He watched the Guildsman slide Rerne onto the seat of the chair Zul drew forward. "You might as well retire, guard. Be sure I shall inform your Big Man of your alert and most appreciated services. I trust, Hunter Rerne," he said to the new captive, "your head is sufficiently clear for you to note and be duly apprehensive of this importation of mine." The needler lifted a fraction of an inch and then went back into a new position, one that would share its deadly and agonizing spray between his prisoners.

"These interruptions quite put one off." Dragur shook his head. "We were in the midst of a most serious conversation, Hunter."

"Then I ask pardon for the disturbance." Again the formal words. Save for his loss of control over his muscles, it would appear that Rerne had not been stun-beamed to the point where he suffered too much.

"Most gracious of you, noble Hunter. Time presses or we could resume our conference later and in more privacy, Horan. But you have no ties with the Clans. Or have you? This sudden and unheralded arrival of the noble Hunter is provocative."

His head slightly atilt, Dragur looked speculatively from Troy to Rerne and back again.

The ranger turned a countenance of blank courtesy to his captor as he replied, "Your men left a trail that was easy enough to follow, Citizen. When a trace of that sort leads from the Wild to Tikil, we are interested."

"Interested!" Dragur repeated that word as if he would wring more than one fine shade of meaning from it. His attention returned to Troy, and the latter had his own reply ready. He did not know why Rerne had followed him here, but he was not going to be drawn into any business of the Clans.

"I have no ties with the Wild." And the emphasis he put on the statement made it sound unduly harsh in that crowded room.

"And I shall accept that assurance, Horan. It is easy to believe that you do not have much sympathy for any authority on Korwar."

"And I am not a Guildsman."

"Have I suggested such a thing?" Dragur demanded. "I merely comment upon certain unpleasant facts of life. You surely cannot nurse any fondness for the Dipple, nor accordingly for the laws that have confined you there. On the other hand"—his fingers moved to one of the seam pockets of his tunic, came out to display a white card—"this is your permission to leave this world."

"Going where?"

"Norden."

The answer was so unexpected that Troy was as shocked as if he had met a needler face on. Then caution, learned painfully through the years, took cool control of his brain again. He hoped he had given no outward sign of his shock and surprise, knowing that Dragur was perhaps the most dangerous man he had ever faced—not because of the outlawed off-world weapon he now held across his knees, but because he did not really have to use it. The agent was right; there were other ways to bend a man to his will, and he had just produced an effective one to level Troy Horan.

"Why?" Troy came out with the question flatly.

"Let us say that I have—"

"A tidbit for a crab to jump for?" Troy countered. He was afraid, afraid with a different sort of chill than that which had seeped along his backbone when he had faced the needler.

"A tidbit, just so. Norden is now under the jurisdiction of the Confederation. The Horan holding there was, I believe, the Valley of the Forest Range—a good-sized range—a very fruitful one. There was the stockade of the Home Place, and five out-towers, a fruit setting, and an excellent stand of skin-wood in the heights. Quite a pleasant little kingdom of your own, Range Master Horan, was it not? Your family and their riders must have been practically self-sufficient. Such a pity—less than a century to grow and all swept away by the arbitrary orders of one man with his mind on a war that did not even come near that planet. Commander Di was impulsive, a little too firm a believer in his own edicts.

"I fear you will have to do some reorganizing and start from the beginning along some lines. The tupan have run wild. But a roundup should bring them under brand control again. And you will be permitted to recruit your own riders, as well as be given all possible assistance from Confederation officers."

"Promising quite a lot, are you not, Citizen?" Troy kept as tight a control over his emotions as he could. Every one of Dragur's words had been a whip laid on sensitive skin. He dared not believe that there was a fraction of truth in the offer, dared not for the sake of his own equilibrium of heart and mind.

"I am promising nothing that I cannot deliver, Range Master Horan." And in that moment Troy was forced to believe him.

"Korwar is a Council planet." Troy hedged, tried to test his assurance from another angle.

"Which again means nothing—to me." And once more his tone and the will behind it carried conviction.

"And in return for Norden what do you ask?"

"A small task successfully performed—by you, Range Master. It seems by some quirk of fate you alone now on this world are able to communicate with some runaway servants of mine. I want them back, and you can get them for me."

That was it: produce the animals—and get Norden. Norden and everything his father had held ten years ago! Simple and deadly as that.

"They must be very special, these servants of yours," Rerne cut in.

"Indeed, noble Hunter, as you already know. Their breeding is the result of many years of research and experimentation. They are the only ones of their species—"

"On Korwar." Rerne's words were not a question, but a statement that carried both force and meaning. Troy caught the inference. Yes, the five he had left in the Wild might be the only ones of their species on Korwar. And yet in other places, other solar systems, similar tools were being employed by Confederation agents.

Dragur shifted slightly in the weird chair. "What happens on other planets is none of my concern, noble Hunter, nor the Clans'. In fact I will assure you that once my servants are returned to me, there shall be no cause to fear any more activity of this type on Korwar. The experiment, due to the human element here, has been a failure. We shall admit defeat and withdraw."

And that, too, Troy believed.

"And the animals themselves?"

"Are now expendable. I do not think that you will hesitate for a moment to weigh the lives of five animals against your return to Norden, will you, Range Master?"

Troy's tongue tip wet his dry lips. He had to use all his will power to fight shivers running along arms and legs.

"You cannot be sure I can bring them in."

"No, but you are the only contact with them. And I think my crab will jump with all his energy for this tidbit, do you not agree?"

"Yes!" Troy's answer came in a harsh explosion of breath. "Yes, I do!" He saw, from the corner of his eye, Rerne's head turn in his direction, a flash of surprise deepen to bleak distaste on the ranger's face. But Rerne's opinion of him could not matter now. He must keep thinking of the future. Dragur was so right; this crab was willing to jump—very high!

"So!" The agent spoke to Rerne now. "You see how simply

matters can be arranged. There is no need for Clan interference—
or their hope to have a hand in this. I take it, Range Master,
that the animals still are in the Wild?"

"They left the flitter for the woods just before your men slapped
that pinner on me."

"How easy to understand once one knows the facts. Very well,
we need have no worries now. You, noble Hunter, shall be our
passport to the Wild. A happy chance brought you here in time.
One might almost begin to believe in the ancient superstitions
regarding a personified form of Fate that could favor or strike
adversely at a man. We shall be a hunting party, just Zul and
I, you, noble Hunter, Range Master Horan, and my Guildsman.
And if all goes well, we shall have this matter decided before
nightfall tomorrow. I am sure we are all sensible men here and
there will be no trouble." He raised the needler.

Troy was not sure Rerne noted that warning gesture. When
the ranger replied, his voice was remote. "There is no argument,
Citizen. I am at your service."

"But, of course, noble Hunter, did I not say you would be?
And now we shall go."

# EIGHTEEN

Troy had no idea how far into the Wild they had penetrated. As Dragur had foreseen, Rerne talked them safely through the Clan patrols. Dawn came and mellowed into day, the day sped west as they bore east. Troy put his head back against the cabin walls, closed his eyes, but not to sleep.

His right hand braceleted his left wrist, moving around and around on the smooth, cool surface of the band he had involuntarily worn out of Ruhkarv, until that movement fell into rhythm with his reaching thoughts.

The flitter moved at top speed, but surely thought could thrust farther and faster than any machine. He tried to call up a sharp picture of that tongue of woodland into which the animals had fled—was it hours, or days ago? Simba, if he could contact Simba! If he could persuade the cat, and through him the others, to come back to that meeting point, be waiting there—

Norden—No, he must not think of Norden now, of how it would be to ride free once more down the valley. With a wrench of thought that was close to physical pain, Troy crushed down memory and dreams born of that memory. He must concentrate with every part of him, mental and physical, on the job at hand.

There was only Dragur's word that none of them here could

communicate with the animals. But if that was not true, why did they want his help so badly?

His whole body was taut with effort. He was not aware that his face grew gaunt with strain or that dark finger-shaped bruises appeared under his eyes. He did not know that Rerne was watching him again with an intentness that approached his own concentration.

Slip, slip, right, left, his fingers on the bracelet—his silent call fanning out ahead of the ship. Troy aroused to chew a concentrate block passed to him, hardly conscious of the others in that cabin, so tired only his will flogged him into that fruitless searching.

And to undermine his labors there was a growing dismay. Perhaps the animals, having witnessed his capture, had pressed on past any hope of their being located now. Only Sahiba's injury could curtail such a flight.

Nightfall found the flitter well into the plains. Dragur heeded the protests of the Guildsman who alternated with Zul as pilot and agreed to camp for the night.

"Which," the agent remarked with courtesy exaggerated enough to approach a taunt, "provides us with a problem, noble Hunter. You, in this, your home territory, will have to be bodily restrained. I trust you will forgive the practical solution. Our young friend here needs no such limits on his freedom."

Rerne, hands and feet bound, made no protest as he was bedded down between Zul and the Guildsman. Troy, oblivious to his company and surroundings, fell asleep almost at once, his weariness like a vast weight grinding him into darkness. Yet in that dark there was no rest. He twisted, turned, raced breathlessly to finish some fantastic task under the spur of time. And he awoke gasping, sweat damp upon his body.

Stars were paling overhead. This was the dawn of the day in which they would come to the wood. For a fraction of one fast escaping moment he knew again that sensation of freedom and fresh life that had first come to him on the plateau, which would always signify for him the Wild. Then that was gone under the lash of memory. Troy did not stir, save that his hand unconsciously once more sought the band on his wrist, and from the touch of that strange metal a quickening of spirit reached into body and mind. His thoughts quested feverishly, picturing the fringe of saplings and trees as he had seen it last. Simba crouched beneath a bush—waiting—

"Found!"

Troy flung up his arm, the cool band of Ruhkarv pressed tight to his forehead above his closed eyes. And under that touch his mental picture leaped into instant sharp detail.

"You come?"

"I come," Troy affirmed silently. "Be ready—when I come." He tried to marshal the necessary arguments and promises that would draw them to the place where Dragur would land.

"So—you have made contact at last, Range Master?"

Troy's arm fell away from his forehead. He frowned up at the Confederation agent. But there was no reason to deny the truth. What he had had to do he had done, to the best of his ability.

"Yes. They will be waiting."

"Excellent. I must compliment you, Horan, on your commendable speed in seeking to fulfill your part of the bargain. We shall eat and then get on to the netting."

Troy ate slowly. So much depended now on Simba's response to his appeal, on the cat's dominance over his fellow mutants. If the slight bond between man and animals was not stout enough to lead them to trust him now—then he had failed completely.

Back in the flitter he made no further attempt to keep in touch with the fugitives. He had done all he could during that early morning contact. Either they would be waiting—or they would not. The future must be governed by one or the other of those facts—which one he would not know until the flyer landed.

In midmorning, bright and clear, the flitter touched with an expert's jarless landing at the edge of the wood. Dragur ordered them out, the barrel of his needler as much on Troy as on Rerne.

"And now"—the agent faced the woodland—"where are they, Horan?"

"In there." Troy nodded to the cover. Yes, they were all there, waiting in hiding. Whether they would show themselves was again another matter.

The Guildsman drew his blaster, thumbed the butt dial to spray beam. Troy gathered himself for a quick leap if the other touched the button. But the agent spoke first. "No beaming," he snapped. "We have to be sure we get them all and in one attack." Then he turned to Troy. "Bring them out."

"I have no summoner, and they will not obey me to that point. I cannot bring them against their wills. I can only hold them where they are."

For a second or two he was afraid that Dragur would refuse to enter the shadow of the trees. Then Troy's statement apparently made sense to the agent.

"March!" Dragur's tone sheared away the urbanity of earlier hours. Troy obeyed, the agent close behind him, needler ready.

Horan rounded a bush, stooped under a hanging branch. "Here! Here! Here!"

Simba, Sargon, Sheba—

Troy threw himself face down into the leaf mold, rolled—Dragur shrieked. Troy came to his knees again and faced the man now plunging empty-handed toward him.

Simba clung with three taloned feet to the agent's shoulder, as with a fourth he clawed viciously at the man's face and eyes, while both foxes made a concentrated attack with sharp fangs upon the agent's ankles.

Troy caught up the needler the other had dropped when Simba had sprung to his present perch from a low-hanging tree limb. Horan was still on one knee, but he had the weapon up to cover Zul as the small man burst through the bushes to them.

"Stand—and drop that!"

Zul's eyes widened. Reluctantly his fingers loosened their hold upon the blaster. The weapon thudded to the ground.

"You, too!"

The Guildsman who had prodded Rerne on into this pocket clearing obeyed Troy's order. A furred shadow with a long tail crooked above its back flitted out of cover, mouthed Zul's blaster and brought it to Troy, then went back for the guard's weapon. Dragur staggered around, his arms flailing about his head where the blood dripped from ripped flesh on his face and neck. Simba no longer rode his shoulders, but was now assisting the foxes to drive the man, with sudden rushes and slashes at his feet and legs.

Blinded, crying in pain, completely demoralized by the surprise and the unexpected nature of that attack, the agent tripped and fell, sprawling at Rerne's feet, while Simba snarled and made a last claw swipe at his face. The ranger stared in complete amazement from the team of animal warriors to Troy.

"You planned this?" he asked in a voice loud enough to carry over Dragur's moaning.

"*We* planned this," Troy corrected. He thrust the two blasters into his belt, but he kept the needler aimed at the others.

"Now"—he motioned to the Guildsman—"you gather up Citizen Dragur and we will go back to the flitter."

There was no argument against the needler. Half carrying the moaning agent, the Guildsman tramped sullenly back to the flyer, Zul and Rerne in his wake, Troy bringing up the rear. He knew the animals were active as flanking scouts though he no longer saw them.

"You"—Troy nodded to Rerne—"unload water, the emergency supplies."

"You are staying here then?" The ranger showed no surprise.

"*We* are staying," Troy corrected once again, watching as the other dumped from the flitter the things he might need for survival in the Wild. Then the Guildsman, under Koran's orders, gave Dragur rough first aid, tied him up and stowed him away, afterwards doing the same for Zul, before he, himself, submitted to binding at Rerne's hands.

"And how do you propose to deal with me?" the ranger asked as he boosted the last of the invaders from Tikil into the flitter.

"You can go—with them." Troy hesitated for a moment and then, almost against his will, he added roughly, "I ask your pardon for that tap on the head at Ruhkarv."

Rerne gazed at him levelly. The mask he had worn in the city was back, to make his features unreadable, though there was a spark of some emotion deep in his eyes.

"You were within your rights—an oath breaker deserves little consideration." But behind those flat words was something Troy thought he could read a different meaning into.

"Those waiting were not your men but patrollers?" He demanded confirmation of what he had come to suspect.

Simba appeared out of the grass, by his presence urging an end to this time-wasting talk.

"So you saw that much." The flicker in Rerne's eyes glowed stronger.

"I saw, and I have had time to think." It was an apology, one Troy longed for the other to accept, though that acceptance could lead to nothing between them now save a level balancing of the old scales.

"I will come back—you understand that?" Rerne stated a fact.

Troy smiled. The headiness of his victory bubbled in him. Release from the strain of the past hours, or past days, was an intoxicant he found hard to combat.

"If you wish, Rerne. I may not be your equal in the lore of the Wild, but together we shall give you a good run—"

"We?" Rerne's head swung. If he was looking for the other animals, he would not see them. But they were all there, even to Sahiba crouched under the low branches of a bush.

"Still *we*?"

"And Norden?"

Troy's smile faded. That was a wicked backstroke he had not expected from Rerne. His braceleted hand went to the belt where the studs were no longer burnished bright.

"The crab did not jump," he replied evenly.

"Perhaps it was not offered the right bait." Rerne shook his head. "This is the Wild and you are no trained ranger. By our laws I cannot help you unless you ask for it, and that would mean surrender." He waited a long moment, as if he actually hoped for some affirmative sign from Troy.

The other nodded. "I know. From now on it will be you and yours against us. Only do not be too sure of the ending, Rerne."

He watched the flitter rise in the vertical climb of a master pilot. Then the carrying strap of the needler across his shoulder, he made a compact bundle of the supplies.

Sunset, sunrise, another nightfall—morning again—though here the sun made a pale greenish shimmer in the forest depths. Troy only knew that they were still pointed east. At least under such cover he could not be tracked by air patrols. Those hunting him would have to go afoot and so be subject to discovery by the keener senses of the animals. Shang took to the treetops, Simba and the foxes ranged wide on the ground, able to scout about Troy as he marched, carrying Sahiba.

Once Simba had been stalked in turn by a forest creature, and Troy had blasted it into a charred mass as it leaped for the cat. But otherwise they saw few living things as they pushed forward.

To Troy the Wild did not threaten. About him it closed like a vast envelope of content. And the memory of Norden was a whisper of mist torn away by the wind rustling through the boughs over his head. With the animals he had moved into a new world, and Tikil too was a forgotten dream—a nightmare—small, far-off, cramped and dusty, well lost. The only thing to trouble him was a vague longing now and then for one of his own kind to share the jubilation of some discovery, the exultation when he awoke here feeling a measure of his birthright returned to him.

On the fifth day the ground began to rise, and once or twice through a break in the trees Troy located peaks in the sky ahead. Perhaps in those heights he could find a cave to shelter them—something they would need soon if the now threatening clouds meant a storm. "Men!"

Troy froze. The sobering shock made him recoil against a tree. He had half forgotten the chase behind. Now he heard Simba squall in fear and rage, the fear thrusting into Troy's brain in turn as a spearhead. A pinner! The same force that had gripped him at the time of Zul's pursuit glued them all to the earth once again. Yet there was no flitter in sight, no sign of a tracker.

"How far away?" he appealed to the scouts.

"Up slope—they are coming closer now." From three sides he had his replies as noses caught scents he could not detect. "They have set a trap."

Troy tried to subdue the rising panic of the animals. Yes, a good trap. But how had they known that Troy and his companions would emerge from the wood at that point? Or had they laid down a long barrier of pinner beams just in case?

There was no chance for him to use the needler; he could not raise his hand to the blasters at his belt. All of them would remain where they were to await the leisure of the unseen enemy. And the bitterness of that soured in his mouth, cramped his now useless muscles.

Sahiba whimpered in his hold. The others were quiet now, understanding his trap explanation. He knew that each small mind was busy with the problem—one that they could not solve. Not singly—but together?

Why had he thought that? Swiftly Troy touched each mind in turn—Simba, Sargon, Sheba, Shang, Sahiba. Simba must be their choice for the experiment. The black cat whose whole battle technique depended upon quiet stalking, instant, lightning-swift attack. If they could free Simba—!

This was a last fantastic attempt, but the only one left to them. Troy focused the full force of his mind on a picture of Simba free, Simba moving one padded paw skillfully before the other as he crept up the slope before them to locate the pinner broadcaster. The others took up that picture, fed into it their combined will and mind force. The thread became a beam, a beam of such strength as to amaze one part of Troy's brain, even as he labored to build it deeper, wider, tougher.

A trickle of moisture zigzagged down his cheek. It was crazy to hope that mind could triumph over a body pinned. Perhaps only because of the freedom of the past few days could their desperate need nourish such a hope. Troy was weak, drained. Yet, as he had fought to reach the animals from the flitter, so now he labored to unleash Simba. And in that moment he knew that it could be done!

Troy did not see that small streak of black bounding up the hillside. And the man operating the pinner could not have seen it coming. There was a howl of pain from above, and Troy was free. He leaped out of the brush and went to one knee, the needler ready to sweep the whole territory ahead.

Rerne arose from behind a rock well up the slope, his hands up and empty. Out of the grass sped Sargon, Sheba, Shang, and, descending in a series of bounds, Simba. Once more Troy was one in their half circle of defense and offense.

"You broke pinner power!" Rerne came down at an even pace, his eyes never leaving Troy's face.

"And you found us." In spite of his overwhelming victory against the machine, Troy tasted the ultimate defeat. The Wild no longer remained their coveted escape.

"We found you." Rerne jerked one hand in a signal. Two more men started to move along the hillside, their hands conspicuously up and empty. One was Rogarkil; the other wore the uniform of a Council attache.

Rerne spoke to them over his shoulder. "So—now have you seen for yourselves?"

"You underestimated the danger!" The Council attache's voice was harsh and rough, he was breathing fast through his nose, and it was plain he did not find his present position one that he relished.

"Danger," Rerne observed, "is relative. Belt knives have been shifted from the sheath of one wearer to that of another without losing their cutting edge. You might consider the facts in this case before you commit those you represent to any hasty course of action."

Clansman spoke to Council as an equal, and, though the attache did not like it, here in the Wild he must accept that. His mouth was now a tight slit of disapproval. In another place and company those lips would be shaping orders to make men jump.

"I protest your arguments, Hunter!"

Rogarkil answered in a mild tone. "Your privilege, Gentle Homo. Rerne does not ask that you agree; he merely requires that you report, and that the matter be taken under sober consideration. I will say also that one does not throw away a new thing merely because it is strange—until one explores its usefulness. This is the Wild."

"And you rule here? The Council shall remember that also!"

Rogarkil shrugged. "That is also your privilege."

With a last glare at Troy and the animals, the officer strode back up the hill, joined, when he was at the crest, by an escort of patrollers who gathered in from the rocks. Then he was gone, as the wind brought the first gust of the storm down upon them all.

"Truce?" asked Rerne, his shoulders hunched against the elements. Then he smiled a little.

Troy hesitated only for a moment before his own hand went up in answer and he slung the needler. He ran toward the shelter the ranger had indicated, a space between two leaning rocks. The area so sheltered was small, and they were still two companies, Troy and the animals on one side, the Clansmen on the other.

"That one will do some straighter thinking on the way back to Tikil," Rerne remarked.

Rogarkil nodded. "Time to think is often enough. When and if they do move, we shall be ready."

"Why are you doing this?" Troy demanded, guessing from the crosscurrents of their speech that, incredibly, the Clans seemed to be choosing his side.

"Because," Rerne replied, "we do believe what I said just now to Hawthol—a knife changing sheaths remains a knife. And it can be used even to counter a blow from its first owner. Kyger died because of a personal feud. But for that chance this attack against the Council, and against Korwar, would have succeeded. And because this espionage conspiracy was in a manner aimed against Korwar, it concerns us. Our guests here, the Great Ones of the galaxy, must be protected. As we told you that night in Tikil, the continuance of our way of life here depends in turn upon their comfort and safety. Anything that undermines that is a threat to the Clans.

"Now if the Confederation tries this weapon on another planet, well, that is the Council's affair. But such an attack is finished here. And I do not believe that Kyger, or Dragur, or any of those behind them ever realized or cared about the other potentials of the tools they developed to further their plan. It could be very illuminating to see what might happen when two or three species long associated in one fashion move into equality with each other, to work as companions, not as servants and masters—"

"And who is better fitted to make such a study than the Clans?" asked Rogarkil.

Troy stiffened. They were taking too much for granted. Both men and animals must have some voice in their future.

"Will the crab jump to his bait, Horan?" Rerne leaned forward a little, raising his voice above the gathering fury of the storm. "Rangers' rights in the Wild for you and your company here— granting us in return the right to know them better? This may not rank with being a Range Master on Norden—"

He paused nearly in mid-word at Troy's involuntary wince. But that hurt was fading fast. Troy's thought touched circle with the other five. He did not urge, tried in no way to influence them. This was their decision more than his. And if they did not wish to accept—well, he still had the needler.

The answer came. Troy raised his chin, looked to the rangers with a cool measurement such as he could not have used a week earlier, but which was now part of him.

"If you make that a trial agreement—"

Rerne smiled. "Caution is good in a man—and his friends. Very well, rangers, this shall be a trial run as long as you wish it so. I will admit that I am eager to have a catseye view of life—if you will allow me into this hitherto closed company of yours."

Troy's eyes met Rerne's and the younger man drew an uneven breath. Norden's plains were gone now. Instead he had a flash of another memory. A rock-walled room on a cliff above a lake and Rerne's voice talking of this world and its fascinating concerns.

"Why?" He did not stop to think that perhaps his question, which seemed so clear to him, might not be as intelligible to the other. But—as if Rerne's thought could touch his like the animals'—the other answered him: "We are of one kind, plains rider." Then Rerne looked beyond the man to the animals. "So shall we all be in the end."

"So be it." Troy agreed, knowing now he spoke the truth.

# Night of Masks

*The author wishes to express appreciation
to Charles F. Kelly, who supplied
the information leading to the
development of Dis*

# ONE

Outside, the day was as gray as the wall behind Nik Kolherne, where he hunched under the arch of roof well above his head. The steady drizzle of rain was as depressing as those thoughts he could not push out of his mind, even by the most determined effort. His thin-fingered hands moved restlessly, smoothing the front of the worn and colorless jump coat that hung in folds about his thin chest and shoulders. The damp had him shivering, but he made no move to seek shelter through the door immediately behind him.

There was shelter inside but nothing else in the big barracks of the Dipple. Those without family ties held no more rights than the tentative possession of a bunk, and that only as long as they could defend it, should one of their fellows in misfortune take a liking to it.

Nik's right hand came up in a gesture now so much a part of him that he was no longer aware when he made it. Without actually touching his face, his palm covered chin and nose, masking all that lay below his large, penetratingly brilliant blue-green eyes. He hugged the wall of the entranceway, giving good room to two men splashing in from the yard. Neither noticed him as they pushed into the barracks.

Moke Yarn and Brin Peake. In the world of the Dipple, they

were solid citizens of a sort. Or should one correct that? Nik, his hand mask still upheld, searched for a proper term to cover the activities and standing of Moke Varn and Brin Peake.

Maybe not solid citizens in the sense used by the free world beyond the Dipple gates. But at least they had power, and their standing within these walls was firmly based. And since it was undoubtedly true that the Dipple would continue to be Nik's complete world, its terms of reference must be the ones used in evaluating his fellow unfortunates—not that either Moke or Brin considered himself unfortunate.

Once there had been no Dipple; once there had been no war. Once—once a little boy had been someone different, very different. His blue-green eyes held a shadow as Nik stared dully into the slanting lines of rain. But there *had* been the war, and all the dispossessed flotsam had been swept up and thrown into the refuse heaps of the Dipples on many planets—to rot forgotten, as if they were not people at all but statistics and footnotes in some little-read history book of a time the free worlds were now working hard to forget. The war had ended in an exhausted tie, but hate lingered, smoldering under the surface of the here and now, a hate that—

This time Nik's fingers closed tight against his face. His stomach heaved in a retching spasm. The furrows of scarred skin were harsh under his touch. He had a mask all right, one out of nightmares and one he could never put aside. Ten years ago a freighter spacer had been temporarily turned into an escape ship for a small colony on a frontier world lying within enemy-patrolled territory. That freighter had been pursued by the enemy and had crashed on a barren moon.

How in the name of the Spirit had Nik survived that disaster anyway? Why had a child with a torn and burned face continued to live when all those about him had mercifully died? Then—out of nowhere—had come rescue, men in space armor tramping into the small area of the ship where Nik had cowered almost witless. After their coming, there was a jumble of impressions cloaked with delirium and pain, the terror of the unknown. Finally, there had been the hospital here at the Dipple on Korwar. Then—just the Dipple in which he was always alone.

He dreamed—yes, sometimes he dreamed of a country under another sky with a different tint and a warmer sun. But was that a real memory or just a dream? He could remember only such small bits after the crash. His sole link with that other world was the identity disk they had found on him—Nik Kolherne, a name combined with symbols that had not made sense to any authority here. At first, he had asked questions of his fellow internees until their reactions to his gargoyle face had driven him into a solitary life and to the reading tapes.

To a tape, it did not matter that Nik was only human-seeming from eye level to the top of his head with its tight curls of wiry hair the color of burnished jet. So he had fled into the world of the mind, soaking up materials upon which his imagination fed, so that he *was* able to lead another life—one he could summon up at need, perhaps as vivid as that a haluce drinker knew.

Sometimes nowadays Nik was more aware of that other life than he was of the Dipple, though a ripple of disquiet came like a half-heard warning now and then to disturb his dreaming. But he pressed that down, strove to rout it utterly. He had his dream world, and in it he was free! He clung to it passionately.

The need to return to his fantasy now drove him forth into the rain, and he scuttled from the barracks to the next building, the supply warehouse. The bored guard at the door did not see Nik flit by—he was an expert at finding hiding places. Seconds later he reached his latest one, a tiny opening through which he could squeeze, to wriggle up on some crates and lie on a ragged bit of blanket.

Nik stretched out. The layer of stuff beneath his sharp shoulder blades was not thick, but he was oblivious to the discomfort. The drum of rain on the roof not too far above him was soothing, and he closed his eyes, ready to plunge into his dream.

"—has to be right—all a one-time blast-off—"

Those words had no part in the fantasy Nik was creating. In themselves, they were only a minor disturbance, but something in the voice brought Nik's eyes open, made him listen.

"No move until we are sure—"

"And while we're sittin' on our fins waitin' for a take-off, the whole deal can turn sour—into a real bad burn-off—"

Nik hitched around on his pad and began a worm's progress to the end of the box from which he should be able to view the speakers. There was no light in the gloom below. The meeting had all the aspects of a private one. Of course, there were a good many undercurrents in the Dipple. This was not the first time Nik had been on the fringe of secrets or learned what could prove dangerous should his knowledge be discovered by others.

"I repeat—in this there can be *no* chances—not in the ground-work. It's too big to allow any off-course work. Do you understand that?"

Stowar! Nik could see the two figures below only as shadows among other shadows, but that one voice he knew. Stowar was big here in the Dipple—a king shark to such small predators as Moke and Brin. If a man could raise the price to buy into the Thieves' Guild and so open a door out of this rat hole, Stowar was the negotiator who carried out the deal. Stowar had things to sell, too—haluce and other drugs. He had contacts, they said clear up the Veeps of the half world on Korwar and even off-world, too.

Nik shivered. To eavesdrop on one of Stowar's little deals could be very dangerous. He dug his nails into the surface of the box on which he lay and tried to still his breathing, not daring to withdraw for fear they could hear his movements.

"All right—so no chances." The other sounded impatient and not a bit overawed by Stowar. "But that course's been plotted twice—an' each time it cost us a fistful. If we have to go to Margan again, he'll up the price on us. He's no fool, and he'll do a little thinking on his own."

"There are ways of dealing with Margan—"

"Yeah, and those wouldn't be healthy either. Meddle with Margan and you'll have the Brethren down with blasters out, ready to do some cookin'! Don't you planet crawlers ever forget that Margan is our man, and we'll cut in for him. We *need* Margan; he's the best course man in the business. This trick of yours is just one trip as far as the Brethren see it."

The Brethren! Nik's mind was wholly freed of the mist of fantasy now. Stowar could well have contacts with the Brethren—the space-borne section of the Thieves' Guild who sought their prey on loosely held frontier worlds. That meant this deal could be very big. Though Stowar might head the lawless element in the Dipple, to the Guild itself he was a small operator to whom the real Veeps threw the small crumbs.

"Commendable comment. But our friend here is right on one point. This is no time to come in for a two-fin landing, Bouvay—"

A third man down there! Nik tried to pick out his shadow, but he must be standing, out of sight, in the crack between the crate on which Nik himself perched and its fellow.

Stowar had been easy for Nik to identify because, seemingly indifferent to Nik's disfigurement, he had, from time to time, given the boy small tasks, Nik's only means of earning a credit or two to finance the purchase of new tapes.

"All right. But a third run with Margan will be suspicious—maybe make real trouble."

"We are duly warned," agreed the unknown in the crack. "You say we have five more days?"

"Five more days for this course. Then you wait three planet months before you can try again."

"So be it. We'll just have to wait it out."

"But—" Stowar began an instant protest.

"Five days—to find our man, to set up the whole plan? It can't be done. I've tried some so-called impossible things in my time, orbited in on one or two of them, too. But short of going into stass and taking all of Korwar with us, we're going to have to pass on this run and wait out those three months."

"And in the meantime"—Stowar's voice soared—"we can see i'Inad make some change to spoil everything. I say—much better make it a straight snatch—"

"Which is completely impossible," came a chill retort. "They have the ultimate in security. The pattern can't be broken by us except by the setup Heriharz has worked out. You yourself were urging caution just a moment ago, friend."

"Caution, reasonable caution, certainly. But every delay gives i'Inad a chance to counter us—"

There was a soft laugh from the dark alley. "Seems an impasse, doesn't it? But I have faith in the stars, Stowar. We'll either turn up our key or—"

"Or have to write it all off. Some tricks you can't pull ever. This is a dead rocket if I ever saw one."

"Your commander doesn't agree with you, Bouvay, but it's your privilege to cry off if you want."

Only a mutter replied to that. Nik tensed. That voice out of the dark carried a note of confidence rarely heard here. The diction was smooth, the tone authoritative. This was no Dipple dweller. Everyone knew that the Guild had their undercover men in the Planet Guard, among the port authorities, with the spacer crews. This man could well be one of them.

"Three months—" That was Stowar, but this time there was a resigned note in his voice. "And at the end of three months—if we have not found the right man?"

"Then we make some other decision. But FC says we will."

Some one of his listeners snorted. "Then why'n green blazes don't that tame machine tell us *where* to find him? Maybe he ain't on Korwar. Ever think of that?"

"The probabilities, according to FC, are that he is. Look about you, man—what's in a Dipple?"

"A bunch of dim beats as has had it!" returned Bouvay promptly.

"According to your estimation, yes. But on the other hand, right between these walls we have a big cross section of galactic races and types. When they swept up refugees and deportees and dropped them down here, there wasn't any sorting. We have inhabitants from forty worlds, survivors of ship disasters, a mixture such as you won't find anyplace else."

"Except in another Dipple," cut in Stowar.

"Just so. And where is the nearest other Dipple? On Kali, a good six-month flight from here. How long have we been sifting the stock right in front of us? About one month. FC says the probabilities are he *is* here; we just have to find him. And because you haven't turned up the proper combination yet, Stowar, is no reason that such a person does not exist."

"I know." The Dipple man sounded more confident. "You're right. If there's such a man, we ought to have him here. There's a mix as will turn up about anything. The only thing they've in common is that they all look human."

"That's the only factor he has to have," commented the unknown. "Our man *has* to register human or he can't get by the spy line. So, we practice patience and—"

Nik was startled. The speaker had stopped, almost in mid word. All Nik caught thereafter was a sharp hiss. The shadows that were Stowar and Bouvay had frozen. Nik listened. His mouth was dry, his heart beginning to sharpen its beat. Somehow he could sense a wariness, an alerting. Had they discovered him? But how could they—?

He cried out, tried to jerk free, kicking out with one foot, but the hold on his right ankle remained firm. It was as if his whole right leg was glued to the top of the crate. Then the power in the left suddenly failed. That leg lay beside the right, both now immovable. Thoroughly frightened, Nik tried to lever his half-dead body up by using his arms, only to have them fail him in turn. He was pinned to the surface under him as if he had never had any power to move.

Then he did move, but not by his own will. Stiff in his invisible bonds, his whole body rose from the crate and slid out over the open space where the men he had spied upon stood waiting for him. Shaking with a fear he could only control to the point of not screaming his terror aloud, Nik sank down, helpless to defend himself against any action they chose to take.

"Stack rat!"

Nik was still descending when that fist snapped out of the general gloom and connected against his cheekbone with force enough to scramble his senses. He was aware dazedly of another blow. And then there was only darkness until light beat into him, and he tried to raise his hands to shield his eyes, blinded by the full glare of a torch.

"—you're away off orbit—"

"I don't think so. Look, man; just use your eyes for once!"

A painful grip on Nik's hair jerked his head closer to the light. He closed his eyes.

"Who is he, Stowar?"

"Just what Bouvay called him—a stack rat. Gives most of the people horrors, so he keeps out of sight."

"Sure—look at his face! Enough to turn your insides straight out of you! What do you mean about his being any good to us? Give him a blast and let it go at that. Put him outta his misery. He can't enjoy life lookin' like that."

"His face—" The voice from behind the torch sounded speculative. "That doesn't matter too much. What is important is that he's about the right size and age—or looks it anyway. It's just possible we have what we want. If he goes, there'll be no one to ask questions—he won't be missed."

"I don't believe you can use *him*!" Bouvay was emphatic.

"You don't have to. But I believe in luck, Bouvay, and it may be that Lady Luck is pushing comets across the board to us right now! Gyna can do wonders with raw material."

"Anyway, we'll have to do something with him." That was Stowar once more. "Stow him in the box there, and I'll send a couple of the boys to take him to my place. How long does this tie of yours last?"

"Not much longer, unless I want to burn out the unit."

"Fair enough. I'll just take care of that problem."

The last words Nik heard were those from Bouvay. For the second time he was struck and sagged back into the dark from which the torchlight had momentarily dragged him.

He was lying on a hard surface—the blanket must have been dragged from under him on the crate. And this was the first time he had come out of a dream with a badly aching head. Dream? But this had not been one of his visits to his secret world at all! Nik found thinking a shaky process, and the feeling of nausea, which, oddly enough, seemed located more in his painful head than his middle, swooped down into the proper section of his anatomy as he tried to move.

The patchwork of recent memories began to fit into a real pattern. He lay with closed eyes and forced himself to make those memories whole. The warehouse—and the three who met there—Stowar! Nik's suddenly tensing muscles hurt. He had been caught listening to some private plan of Stowar's!

Now he tried to make his ears serve to inform him on his present surroundings. He was lying on a hard surface—that much he already knew—but before he opened his eyes and so perhaps gave away his return to consciousness, he wanted to learn everything else he could.

There was a sound—a murmur that might be the rise and fall of voices from a distance. Now that he had himself in hand, Nik could use his nose, too. The faintly sweet smell—that was only one thing, Canbia wine. Just one inhabitant of the Dipple could afford Canbia—Stowar—so he was now in Stowar's quarters.

Nik dared to open his eyes and looked up into complete darkness. With great effort, he lifted a limp hand. A fraction of an inch from his side, it struck against a solid surface. The left hand discovered a similar obstruction on the other side.

He could see light now—a faint outline over him, enough to tell him he was in a box. In a moment of raw panic, he struggled to sit up, only to discover the effort beyond his powers. Then all the patience and self-control he had so painfully learned went into action. So—he was in a box. But he was still alive, and if they had wanted to erase him, they would not have gone to the trouble of carting him here. Stowar wanted no trouble in his own quarters.

Nik puzzled over his fragmentary memories of those last moments when he had been so strangely lifted out of hiding and delivered, helpless, into the hands of the enemy. The method of attack did not concern him now; the reason for his being here did. What had the stranger said—that he was the right age and size and that his face was not important. Not important.

The sound of boot heels on the floor outside his prison made Nik strive once more to move. His hands—he could pull them up a little. The rest of him seemed frozen still.

Then the cover over him banged back, and he was looking up into the face of a stranger. The skin was browned in the deep coloring of a spaceman, so that the single topknot of hair above the almost totally shaven skull looked like a white plume in contrasting fairness. The regular features were handsome, though the eyes were so heavily droop-lidded that Nik had no idea of their coloring.

And now there was a quirk of a smile about the stranger's lips, giving a certain relaxation to his expression. Nik found himself losing the first sharp edge of his apprehension.

A bronze hand swooped down and caught at the front of Nik's jacket. He was drawn up in that hold as if his own weight were feather-light as far as the other was concerned. Then an arm about his shoulders steadied him on his feet, and he was standing.

"Don't worry. You'll be able to blast in a minute."

Under the stranger's guidance, Nik regained enough power to step out of the box and take a stumbling step or two. He was lowered onto a stool, his back against the wall of the room. The other sat down, facing him.

The stranger wore space leather and ship boots. The triple star of a captain winked from the throat latch of his tunic. He leaned forward, his fists on his knees, to survey Nik. For the first time in years, Nik Kolherne made no attempt to mask his ruined face with his hand. There was a kind of defiance in his desire for the other to see every scar.

"I was right!" The white-hair plume rippled as the stranger nodded briskly. "You *are* our probability."

# TWO

Nik's head and shoulders were propped against the wall, and as the stranger leaned forward, their eyes were much on a level. He matched the searching stare. And now he said, "I don't know what you mean."

"Not needful that you do—yet. How long have you had that face?"

"Ten years, more or less. I was fished out of a wreck during the war."

"Nobody tried to patch it up for you?"

Nik willed his hand to remain on his knee, willed himself to face that frank appraisal without an outward tremor. There was no disgust, no shrinking, only real bewilderment in the other's expression. And seeing that, Nik replied with the truth.

"Why didn't they fix my face? Well, they tried. But it seemed I couldn't adapt to growth flesh—it sloughed off after some months. And other experiments, they cost too much. No one had the credits to spend on Dipple trash."

That had been the worst of his burden in the years behind him, knowing that right here in Korwar were cosmetic surgeons who might have been able to give him a human face again. Yet the costly experimentation needed by a patient who could not provide natural rooting for growth flesh was far out of his reach.

"Something could be done even now."

Nik refused to rise to the bait. "I'm not the son of a First Circle family," he replied evenly. "And if growth flesh fails, there's little they can do, anyway."

"Don't be so sure." The stranger got to his feet. "Don't discount luck."

"Luck?" queried Nik.

"Yes, luck! Listen, boy. I'm on a winning streak now. The comets are all hitting stars on my table! And you're a part of it. What would you do for a new face—the face you should have had?"

Nik's stare was set. Plainly this was meant in all seriousness. Well, what would he give, do, for a face—a real face again? He didn't have to hesitate over that answer.

"Anything!" It would be worth it, any pain or sacrifice on his part, any effort, no matter how severe or prolonged.

"All right. We'll see. Stowar—!" At the space officer's call, the Dipple man came to the door of the room. "I'm standing for Kolherne."

Stowar's flat, emotionless eyes slid over the boy. He was frowning a little. "The choice is yours—now," he returned, but not as if he agreed. "When do you take him, Leeds?"

"Right away. Now, Kolherne"—the other swung to face Nik once more—"it's up to you. If you want that face, you have to be prepared to earn it, understand?"

Nik nodded. Sure he understood. Anything you wanted you had to earn, or take—if you were strong enough and well armed enough to make the grab practical. He did not doubt that Leeds was either one of the Guild or the Brethren, operating well on the cold side of any planetary or space law. But that did not bother him. Within the Dipple, one learned that the warmth of the law was for the free, not for the dispossessed and helpless. He was willing to walk the outlaw's road; that was no choice at all with the promised award ahead.

"This is the story—you're the son of a spaceman, my former first officer. I found you here, will sign bond for you. That will release you from the Dipple. The guard won't do much checking. They're glad to get anyone off the roster legally. Got anything you want to collect from a lock box, Nik?"

What did he have to call his own? A tape reader and a packet of tapes. Nothing he really needed. And those belonged to the Kolherne who had no hope at all—save through their temporary means of escape. Now something as wild as anger or fear was boiling inside Nik; he could hardly keep it bottled down. He did not recognize it as hope.

"No—" His voice seemed so little under his control that he did not say more than that one word.

"Then, let's go!" Again that strong grasp bringing him up to his feet, steadying him. He stumbled across the room, out into Stowar's business quarters, hardly noting Moke Yarn there. Moke was of no importance any more. This was one of Nik's dreams taking on the solid reality of flesh in the hand guiding him ahead, in the surprised expression on Moke's flat face, in the bubbling and churning in Nik's middle. He was drunk with hope and the excitement Leeds had fired in him.

"Now pay attention." Leeds' tone sharpened as they emerged into a mist that had followed the rain. "My name is Strode Leeds. I'm master of the Free Trader Serpent. Got that?"

Nik nodded.

"Your father was my first officer in the Day Star when the war broke out. He was killed when we were jumped by the Afradies on Jigoku. I've been searching the Dipples for you for the past three years. Luck, O Luck, you are riding my fins today! I couldn't have set this up better if I'd known you were going to come down out of the roof back in that warehouse. You stick with me, boy, and that luck has just naturally got to rub off a little on you!"

Leeds was smiling, the wide satisfied smile of a gambler ready to scoop up from the table more than his hoped-for share of the counters.

Nik, still a little wobbly on his legs, tried to match his stride to the captain's, willing to go where Leeds wished, holding to him the promise the other had made, the promise that still seemed part of a dream. He listened to Leeds' glib explanation at the Dipple Registration and nodded when the supervisor perfunctorily congratulated him on his luck. There it was—luck again. He who had never remembered seeing the fair face of

fortune was beginning to believe in it with some of the fervor
Leeds exhibited.

Then they were out of the Dipple. Nik dragged a little behind his
companion, savoring that small wonder that was part of the larger.
In all his existence on Korwar, he had been out of the Dipple's
gray hush no more times than he could reckon on the fingers of
one hand. Once to the hospital in a vain attempt to have them
try skin growth on him again, to return defeated and aching with
the pain of the medical verdict that it was useless. And the rest
on hurried trips to the nearest tape shop to buy the third-hand,
scratchy records that had been all the life he cared for. But now he
was out—really out!

Leeds punched the code of a flitter at the nearest call box. It
was beginning to rain again, and the captain jerked the shoulder
hood of his tunic up over his head. Nik licked the moisture from
that scar tissue that should have been lips. Even rain was different
beyond the Dipple walls; it tasted sweet and clean here.

As they seated themselves in the cab and Leeds set the controls, he glanced at the boy. The captain was no longer smiling.
There was a sharp set to his mouth and jaw.

"This is only the first step," he said. "Gyna and Iskhag, they
have the final decision."

Nik snapped back into tense rigidity. One part of him was
apprehensive. So—there was a flaw in this "luck" after all? This
was only what all his life had led him to expect.

"But," Leeds was continuing, "since the main play is mine, I've
the right to say who's going to lift into this orbit—"

Nik's first seething glow had faded; his old-time control was
back. All right, so Leeds had talked him out of the Dipple.
He'd have to go right back if the captain's plan failed. Nowhere
on Korwar could he show this face and hope for a chance for
freedom—unless it was freedom to starve.

Korwar was a pleasure planet. Its whole economy was based
on providing luxury and entertainment for the great ones of
half the galaxy. There was no place in any of its establishments
for Nik Kolherne. On another world, he might have tried heavy
labor. But here they would not even accept him for the off-world
labor draft once they took a good look at him.

The flitter broke away from the traffic lanes of the city and slanted out on a course that would take it to the outer circle of villas and mansions. Nik gazed down at a portion of the life he had never seen, the wealth of vegetation culled from half a hundred different worlds and re-rooted here in a mingled tapestry of growing and glowing color to delight the eyes. They lifted over a barrier of gray thorn, where the pointed branches and twigs were beaded with crystalline droplets—or were those flowers or leaflets? Then the craft came down on the flat roof of a gray-green house, part of its structure seeming to run back into the rise of a small hill behind it.

The rain splashed about them and poured off in runlets to vanish at the eaves of the building. Nik followed Leeds out of the flier, saw it rise and return to the city. Then he shivered and wiped his sleeve across his face.

"Move!" That was Leeds, giving his charge little or no time to look about him. The captain had his boots planted on a square block in the roof. He reached out a long arm and caught at Nik, pulling him close. There was a shimmer about the edges of the block on which they stood. Abruptly the rain ceased to drive against them. Then the shimmer became solid, a silver wall, and Nik was conscious of a whine that was half vibration.

The silver became a shimmer again, vanished. They were no longer on the roof under the dull gray of the sky but in a small alcove with a corridor running from right to left before them.

"This way." Leeds' pace was faster; Nik stumbled in his wake.

The walls about them were sleekly smooth and the same cool gray-green as the outer part of the house. But Nik had the feeling that they were not in that structure but beneath it, somewhere in the soil and rock upon which it stood.

Just before the captain reached what appeared to be a solid wall at the end of the corridor, that surface rolled smoothly back to the left, allowing them to enter a room.

The carpet under Nik's worn shoepacs was springy, a dark red in color. He blinked, trying to take in the room and its inhabitants as quickly as possible, with all the wariness he could summon. There were two eazi-rests, their adaptable contours providing seating for a man and a woman. Nik's hand flashed up to his face, and then he wondered. She must have seen him clearly; yet there was none of that distaste, the growing horror he had expected to see mirrored in her eyes. She had regarded him for a long moment as if he were no different from other men.

She was older than he had first judged, and she wore none of the fashionable gold or silver cheek leaf. Her hair was very fair and hung in a simple, unjeweled net bag. Nor did her robe have any of the highly decorative patterns now preferred. It was a blue-green, in contrast to the red cushions supporting her angular body, restful to the eye. Between the fingers of her right hand rested a flat plate of milky semiprecious stone, and from that she licked, with small, neat movements of her tongue, portions of pink paste, never ceasing to regard Nik the while.

In the other eazi-rest was a man whose ornate clothing was in direct contrast to the simplicity of the woman's. His gem-embroidered, full-sleeved shirt was open to the belt about his paunch, showing chest and belly skin of a bluish shade. His craggy features were as alien in their way to the ancestral Terran stock of the others as that blue-tinted skin. His face was narrow, seeming to ridge on the nose and chin line, with both those features oversized and jutting sharply. And there were two points of teeth showing against the darker blue of his lips even when his mouth was closed, points that glistened in the light with small jewel winks. His head was covered with a close-fitting metal helmet boasting whirled circles where human ears would be set.

There were non-Terran, even non-humanoid, intelligent species in the galaxy, and Korwar pulled many of their ruling castes into tasting its amusements, but Nik had never faced a true alien before.

Both woman and alien made no move to greet Leeds, nor did they speak for a long moment. Then the woman put down her plate and arose, coming straight across the room to stand facing Nik. She was as tall as he, and when suddenly her hand struck out, catching his wrist, she bore down his masking hand with a strength he could not have countered without an actual struggle.

Grave-eyed, she continued to study his wrecked face with a

penetrating concentration as if he presented an absorbing problem that was not a matter of blood, bones, and flesh but something removed from the human factor entirely.

"Well?" Leeds spoke first.

"There are possibilities—" she replied.

"To what degree?" That was the alien. His voice was high-pitched, without noticeable tone changes, and it had an unpleasant grating quality as far as Nik was concerned.

"To the seventieth degree, perhaps more," the woman replied. "Wait—"

She left Nik and went to the table by the eazi-rests. She spun a black box around to face a blank wall. And the alien pressed a button on his seat so that it swung about to face the wall also. There was a click from the box, and a picture appeared on the blank surface.

A life-size figure stood there, real enough to step forward into the room—a man, a very young man, of Nik's height. But Nik's attention was for the unmarred, sun-browned face whose eyes were now level with his own. The features were regular. He was a good-looking boy; yet there was an oddly mature strength and determination in his expression, the set of his mouth, and the angle of jaw.

The woman had stepped to one side. Now she glanced from the tri-dee cast to Nik and back again.

"He says growth flesh did not take on transplant," Leeds commented.

"So? Well, there are ways—" Her reply was almost absent. "But look, Iskhag—the hair! Almost, Strode, I can believe in this luck fetish you swear by. That hair—"

Nik looked from those features to the hair above them. The wiry curls on the pictured head were as tight as his and just as black.

"It would seem," shrilled Iskhag, "that the FC was right. The probabilities of success at this point outweigh those of failure. If, Gyna, you think you have a chance of performing your own magic—?"

She shrugged and snapped off the tri-dee cast. "I will do what I can. The results I cannot insure. And—it may be only temporary if the growth fails again—"

"You know the newest techniques, Gentle Fem," Leeds interrupted, "and those are far more successful than the older methods. We can promise you unlimited resources for this." He looked to Iskhag, and the blue alien nodded.

"Does he understand?" The high chitter of Iskhag's speech came as he looked at Nik.

Leeds took out a small box and flipped a pellet he took from it into his mouth. "He understands we promise him a face again, but that it has to be earned. Also, I signed him out of the Dipple and will guarantee his Guild fee—"

The woman came back to Nik, her long skirt rustling across the carpet. "So you will earn your face, boy?"

Before he could avoid it, her hand made another of those quick moves, and her fingers closed on his misshapen chin, holding it firmly.

"You are entirely right," she continued as if the two of them were alone in the room. "Everything must be earned. Even those to whom birth gives much make payment in return, in one form or another. Yes, I shall strive to give you a face, for our price."

For the first time, Nik summoned up enough courage to take a part in this conversation about him and his affairs.

"What's the price?"

The woman loosened her hold on him. "Fair enough." She nodded as if that question had, in some obscure way, pleased her. "Tell him, Leeds." That was no request but an order.

"So"—Iskhag swung his eazi-rest back to its former position—"take him to his quarters, tell him—make all ready. We have been too long about this matter now!"

Leeds smiled. "In a matter of this kind, haste makes for mistakes. Do you wish for mistakes, Gentle Homo?"

"I wish for nothing but to set a good plan to work, Captain." Was there a shadow of withdrawal in Iskhag's reply?

The woman had picked up her plate of pink paste. Once more her tongue licked, in small, tip-touch movements, at its contents, but she watched Nik as Leeds caught him by the shoulder and gave him an encouraging shove toward the door.

Down the corridor, past the alcove where they had entered, then through a second sliding doorway they went, and they were in another luxurious room. Leeds motioned Nik to a seat on a wide divan.

"Hungry?" the captain asked. Without waiting for an answer, he went to a dial server on the wall and spun a combination. A table slid out, drawer fashion, the closed dishes on its surface numbering at least six. Nik watched as it moved into place before the divan, and Leeds sat down beside him to snap up the heat covers.

"Tuck in!" the captain urged, sampling the contents of the nearest dish himself.

Nik ate. The food was so different from the mess-hall fare of the Dipple that he could hardly believe it could be called by the same name. He did not know, could not even guess, at the basic contents of some of those heated platters, but it was a banquet out of his dreams.

When an unaccustomed sense of fullness put an end to his explorations, Nik came to himself again, to the uneasy realization that in accepting this bounty he had taken one more step along a trail that would lead him into very unfamiliar territory and that had its own dangers, perhaps the more formidable because they were unknown.

"Now"—Leeds pressed the return button and the table rolled away from them—"now, Nik, we talk."

# THREE

**B**ut the captain did not begin. He was watching Nik with that same searching scrutiny the woman had turned on him earlier. And under that regard, as always, Nik squirmed, inwardly if not visibly. The boy had to call on strong will power to keep his hand away from his face.

"It's amazing!" Leeds might have been talking to himself. "Amazing!" he repeated. Then he came briskly to the point. "You must have gathered this is a Guild project?"

"Yes." Nik kept his answer short.

"That does not bother you?"

"In the Dipple you don't live by the law." Nik had never really tried to reason out his stand before, but that statement was true. Those in the Dipple had a brooding resentment of the in-powers who had long since condemned them to that forgotten refuse heap because they could neither protest nor fight back. There were three ways a man could escape the Dipple, and two of those had been closed to Nik from the beginning.

He could not possibly hope to hire out to any businessman on Korwar, and he could not ship in deep sleep to be sold as a laborer on another world. But the fact that he was now allied with the Thieves' Guild did not bother him at all. In a world—or a life—turned permanently against Nik Kolherne, any ally was to be welcomed.

"You have the proper attitude," Leeds conceded. "Gyna thinks she can give you a new face. And if she thinks so, you can just about count on it."

"Gyna?"

"The Gentle Fem you just met. She's a cosmetic surgeon of the first rank."

"That tri-dee cast—I'm to look like that?" Nik ventured.

He had heard of the cosmetic surgeons and the wonders they were able to perform for fees impossible for an ordinary man to calculate. That one was tied to the Guild was perfectly in keeping with all else rumored about that shadowy empire. But it still remained something not to be believed that he could ever resemble that picture. Now Nik added a second question before Leeds had replied to the first.

"Who is he—that man in the tri-dee?"

"Someone who has life but no body," Leeds replied cryptically. He had a drowsy, satisfied look, as if he were content, satisfied in a way that had no relation to the food he had just eaten. "Yes, life—and we hope you'll provide the body."

Nik's imagination leaped. "Parasite!" He tensed again. There *were* some things worse than his face, and his fantasybred thoughts could supply a list of them.

Leeds laughed. "Give you the horrors, Nik? No, this is no monster rally. You're not being set up to provide a carcass for some other life type to move in. You're just going to be a dream, a hero out of a dream."

Completely baffled, Nik waited. Better let Leeds tell it his own way. If the captain did carry out his promise, Nik would owe him more than his life.

"Don't suppose at your age you pay much attention to politics." Leeds settled back on the divan. He took out his box again and began to suck one of the pellets from it. He did not wait for the boy to reply.

"The late war ended more or less as a draw—the fighting, that is. Then a real struggle started around the peace table when terms were offered, bargained for, schemed over. No one got as much as he wanted and most of them enough less to leave sores on their hides as tender as blaster burns. We're still at war in a way, though it's behind-the-scenes action now—not sending in ships and men and burning off a world here and there. And the Guild's for hire in some tricks for either side."

That made sense to Nik. On the lower levels, the Thieves' Guild might deal in ways that had given it its title, but in the upper strata, there were services such a band of outlaws could offer the heads of governments, sector lords, who would pay very well indeed.

"We've such a ploy on now, but it's been hanging fire because we needed a front for the first move."

"That's me?" Nik asked.

"That may be you," Leeds corrected. "And this is the truth." He still wore the half smile, but his eyes held no humor at all. "There will be no out once you begin."

"I guessed that."

"All right—then here's the full course. A year ago a warlord of one of the Nebula worlds sent his only son here to Korwar, just so pressure couldn't be brought on him through the boy. He picked one of the High Security villas, and that was that."

An HS villa was one that no unauthorized person could enter and that held its inhabitants safe as if they had been sealed in a double-illumi plate.

"Two months ago," Leeds continued, "the warlord ceased to be of any concern."

"Dead?" Nik was not surprised at Leeds' nod.

"Now the boy is no longer important as a hostage, but he is important for what he controls. Locked in his mind is the answer to a time-secure device that only he and his father knew. And behind the device are tapes that have information—of no value to the boy but of vast importance to two different parties. The one in power at present chooses to keep him under wraps—maybe for life. The other—"

"Wants him out," Nik finished.

"Yes. But they can't get him except by coming to us."

"And the Guild can crack an HS?"

"They could have cracked it any time within the past year. That doesn't mean they could get the boy out. His father took every precaution. He has been blocked against any stranger, even one altered physically into a copy of a friend. He also has a circuit set in his brain. Force him or frighten him, and the information we need is totally wiped out."

"Then how?—" Nik was intrigued.

A small tri-dee scene, vividly real in spite of its size, glowed there. The landscape of the background was none that Nik had ever seen before. Rugged black heights were stark against a yellowish sky, and black sand lay level at their foot. Milky liquid flowed there in a crooked course. At the edge of that flood, the same dark-haired figure Nik had been shown by Gyna was down on one knee, engaged in skinning some reptilian creature.

The yellow light made a dazzling sparkle of parts of his clothing where metal overlays were fastened to a form of space uniform, but his head was bare and noticeable. Standing watching him was a much younger boy wearing a similar uniform. His hair was also black, and his hands grasped a weapon, a small edition of a blaster. His attitude was of one standing guard in dangerous territory. Leeds switched off the beam, and Nik waited for an explanation.

"Children cut off from normal friendships and lonely," the captain observed, "have a habit of imagining companions. Vandy Naudhin i'Akrama is no exception."

"Imagined companions," Nik repeated. "But that tri-dee showed two people—"

"What you saw was the fantasy Vandy has built up in his mind. He and his imagined companion-hero are not in the garden of the HS at all. They are on another world—I believe Vandy calls it Veever. Over a period of two years, he has been building up an elaborate fantasy existence that is most real to him now. And he lives in it for hours at a time."

"But how—?"

"How do we know this? How did we get this tape?"

Leeds shrugged. "Don't expect an explanation of the mechanics from me. The Guild has its resources. There are certain snooper-machines that have never been marketed, that are unknown to the public. None of the secrets men have sought to keep remain undiscovered. The Guild has the power to bid for such discoveries or take them. It remains that there *is* such a device, one that has snooped on Vandy's dream world for months and built up a complete file on his activities in that fantasy for our use."

"How?" Nik accepted Vandy's fantasy easily enough because of his own, but he still could not quite see how Leeds or the Guild proposed to use such a discovery for their purposes.

"Vandy has been blocked against all contact except through five people, two of whom are now dead," Leeds explained. "As far those who prepared him for this exile-protection know, there is no one now who dares to approach him without triggering the circuit that will erase instantly the knowledge we need. However, suppose Vandy *was* to meet, say in that particular portion of the HS garden where he feels most free from interruption, Hacon—"

"And Hacon is—?"

"You have just seen him, skinning a monster Vandy recognizes as an enemy on Veever. You will see him again as soon as possible, we all hope, in any mirror you care to glance into."

"So I meet Vandy as Hacon, and he tells me—" Nik began. The impossible was beginning to seem merely improbable.

But Leeds shook his head. "No, you meet Vandy and suggest an expedition—"

"Outside? Where?"

Leeds smiled lazily. "As to that, I can't give you any information. Since you are not an astro-navigator, anything I would tell you would make no sense. But you'll have an LB locked on a certain course. Once aboard, you and Vandy will go into stass. When you come out of that, you'll be where we want you."

"Off-world?"

"Off-world. In a place where we won't have to fear any chase. There you'll have time to consolidate your position with Vandy and get the information we need."

"And afterwards?"

"Afterwards, Vandy will be sent back here. You'll be a member in good standing in the Guild, with a face and a future. Nobody gets hurt except some politicos who've tried to gobble up more than they can safely swallow. In fact, Vandy will also have the satisfaction of tripping up a couple of those who helped to erase his father."

"But why off-world?"

"Because we *can* crack the HS, yes, but we can't preserve that crack for any length of time. You wouldn't have a chance to talk Vandy into any more than going with you. And we'll get you both off-world in a shielded LB because Vandy can be trailed by com-cast anywhere on Korwar. I told you his father took every precaution when he planted him here."

It made sense, and it could work, providing Gyna was able to turn Nik into Hacon. He thought of that smooth brown face, of Leeds' promise that that was what he might see in any mirror he cared to use. The price was a small one, and the reward—Nik drew a deep breath of wonder—the reward was out of one of his own cherished dreams.

"When do we start?" he asked eagerly.

Leeds hoisted his body off the divan and tucked his box of pills into his tunic. "Right now, Nik, right now."

Part of what followed Nik was to remember in sections that were hazier than his cherished fantasies. Most he was never to recall at all. And time had no meaning during this metamorphosis of Nik Kolherne into Hacon.

But there came an hour when he stood staring with incredulous wonder at a figure not on the wall this time but in a mirror, as Leeds had promised. And he was Hacon! A wild exhilaration filled him, and he found himself laughing with a laughter that was close to chest-tearing sobs.

Leeds, who had brought him this miracle, stood there laughing, too, but more gently, before he nodded to Gyna.

"Well done, Gentle Fem." Leeds found words; Nik had none at all. But when he turned away from the mirror to face her, a little of his ecstasy was dampened by a vague apprehension because he could read no satisfaction in her expression.

She did not meet his gaze but glanced at Leeds, her soberness somehow a warning. And then she turned abruptly and left the room. Nik, puzzled, looked to the captain for enlightenment.

"What—?" And this time it was the other who would not meet Nik eye to eye.

He went back to the mirror, drew one hand down its glistening surface, and saw those fingertips meet the ones in the mirror reflection. So, that *was* he—no trickery there. But still something was wrong. His hand sought his face, not to mask it this time but to reassure himself by touch as well as by sight that there was firm brown skin there, flesh unscarred, bone no longer missing. He could see, he could feel—

"What is wrong?" Nik turned to stand before Leeds, making that demand with a fear all the keener because of his exhilaration of moments earlier.

"We had months to do a job that might have taken more than a year," Leeds said slowly, "three months lacking a few days. Gyna is not sure it will last unless"—now he did meet Nik's gaze—"unless you can get back into her hands within another two months, Korwar-planet time."

"But, you mean it will be the old story—no growth flesh—?" Nik dared not face his reflection again. That first blasting failure had occurred years ago, and he had been too young then to grasp the horror of what was happening. But now—now he would know!

"No," Leeds replied quickly, "this was done by another technique altogether. Gyna is sure it would have succeeded with the right time element; now she cannot be sure. You may need a tightening process to recover any slip. But it will hold long enough for you to do the job. Then you'll come back here for the checkup."

"You'll swear to that?" Nik's rising fear was like a shaking sickness.

Leeds' hands held onto his shoulders. He stood tense and taut in that grip. "Nik, I'll swear by anything you want to name that we'll keep this promise, providing you deliver. The Guild takes care of its own."

There was enough truth in that to allay the icy fear a little. Nik knew the reputation of the organization—it was loyal to its own.

"All right. But in two months—"

"You'll have plenty of time. You start today, and you have all that you need right here." The captain lifted one hand from Nik's shoulder and tapped him in the middle of his forehead.

That was true. During the time he was being turned into Hacon outwardly, all the information gathered by snoopers had been fed into his mind by hypo-induction. Everything Vandy had created in Hacon and about Hacon was in Nik's mind, including the approach that would best entice Vandy into the needed adventure.

"When?"

"Right now," Leeds answered.

Nik had not been out of the suite of rooms for days, probably weeks, but the captain took him now with a sense of hurry that Nik's own need built. How long would Hacon last? Would he fail in his task and so lose everything? Yet the meeting with Vandy could not be too hurried; the boy's suspicions must not be aroused. Nik knew everything about Vandy that the snooper tapes could tell, but that did not mean he knew Vandy.

"You have all any induction can give you." Leeds did not sound in the least worried as they went down one of the long corridors that Nik knew were underground. "It's been so well planted in your mind that you can't make a wrong move, even if you wanted to. Just get him into the LB—"

"But when we get there—on that other planet?"

"No need to worry about that. The setup on Dis has been in order for months. You'll have all the help you need there."

They came out not on the roof of the gray-green house this time but on a hillside, where a cluster of rocks and a fringe of bushes had concealed the opening. There was a small glade in which a flitter waited, another man already aboard. That flier had an odd shimmer about its outline, a light that made Nik's eyes smart and forced him to look away quickly. Some other trick device for its concealment, he decided. Leeds climbed in and took the controls, proving that the flier was not on a set flight pattern.

"Set?" Leeds asked of the other passenger.

The man consulted the timekeeper on his wrist. His lips moved as if he counted; then he snapped his fingers, and on that signal the flitter bounced into the air under a full spurt of power. They were out of the masking greenery and flying into the wilderness beyond the fringe of the city.

"Correct course and speed," the man behind Leeds ordered. "Two—four—hold it!"

The flier bore on. They lifted over the first range of hills, and Nik looked down into the tangled mass of vegetation. Then he caught a glimpse of red stone walls surrounding a solid-looking building.

The flitter came about in order to approach the building from another direction.

"What about the LB?" Nik dared to ask. How could they have planted any craft as large as a space lifeboat undetected by the guards below?

"It's ready." Leeds appeared to have full confidence in that. "When, Jaj?"

"Now!"

The flitter gave a forward leap like the spring of a stalking beast upon its prey, coming down between trees. Leeds signaled Nik out through the hatch Jaj held open. He landed with a roll on thick and cushioning turf. As he scrambled to his feet, he looked up.

There was no sign of the flitter at all, nor could he hear a motor hum. So far Leeds was right. Nik was past the safeguards of the HS villa, only a few yards from the very point where the snooper had been planted in the beginning. Well, the captain had also said that the Guild Forecast Com had given 73 per cent odds on the success of this part of the plan.

Nik brushed down the fantastic spacer's uniform Vandy had created for Hacon and walked quietly forward. He stood between two drooping limbed bushes to look into a small hidden glade.

Someone was there before him, sitting down with knees hunched against his chest, his attention all for a hopping creature making erratic progress across the sod.

Nik came into the open. "Vandy?" he called.

# FOUR

Nik was crawling down a tunnel of cold dark, but ahead was an encouraging spark of light, a promise of warmth. The light closed in about him as he lay looking up at a rounding curve of blue, which held the hard, sleek sheen of metal. He blinked and tried to think clearly.

There was a chime ringing in his ears, growing more strident. He raised himself on one elbow, and the wink of a flashing light dazzled his eyes. This—this was the LB! And he was coming out of stass.

The chime—that meant they were nearing the end of the voyage. *They!* Nik sat up abruptly to look at the other bunk. Vandy lay there, still curled in sleep, his dark lashes shadows on his cheeks, the netting of take-off straps holding him in safety.

Nik's own straps were taut across his thighs. And the wink, the chime, were warning enough to stay where he was. He wriggled down and fastened the second belt. Coming in for a landing—but where?

Korwar was one of a six-planet system and the only inhabitable world in that system. And Leeds, while being evasive over their destination, had insisted that they need not fear pursuit. Probably their voyage had removed them not only from Korwar but from its sun as well. And to Nik, ignorant as he was of galactic courses, they could be anywhere, even on Vandy's Veever.

Vandy's Veever, Vandy's Hacon, Vandy's dream—Nik lay flat, waiting for the landing controls to take over, and thought about how right Leeds had been so far. From that moment when Vandy had looked up in the garden to see Nik standing in the open sunlight, he had accepted Nik unquestioningly. Nik squirmed now on the plasta-foam filled bunk. Too easy—this whole operation had begun. His hand twitched, but the straps prevented his raising it to his face, to feel tangible evidence of the change he accepted as a small part of truth, the one thing he clung to fiercely. And how long could he continue to cling? Leeds had said perhaps two months—

LB's were fashioned to rove wide courses in space. The very nature of those escape craft meant that they had to be almost equal to the fastest cruisers as they took the "jumps" in and out of hyper-space to carry out their rescue missions. But how much time had passed now? Nik had no idea of how long it had been since they had taken off from Korwar. Any minute the change in him might start—

His smooth lips twisted on a sound that was close to a moan. Leeds—surely Leeds would be waiting for their landing. Nik believed that Leeds was the leader in this Guild operation. But what if he wasn't there or if he did not have power enough to make good on his promise? And how long would it take to learn from Vandy the information they wanted? Even if the boy had accepted Nik easily as an adventure companion, would he share something he had been taught to keep secret? The holes in the future became bigger and blacker all the time!

With a final clang, the chime stilled, and Nik was aware of the increasing discomfort of landfall. His past traveling on ships had been long ago, and now he was conscious of the strain on his body, though an LB, which might be transporting injured, was rigged with every possible protection against pressure.

"Hacon!" The cry shrilled with a sharp undertone of fear and made Nik force his head to one side on the bunk. Across the narrow space between them, he saw Vandy's eyes wide open, the fear in them.

"All—right—" Nik got out the words of assurance. "We're setting down—"

Then he felt the surge of the deter-rockets, and the weight of
change brought him close to the edge of a complete blackout.

They were down, a smooth three-fin landing he judged, though
his knowledge of such was very meager. Wriggling one arm loose
from the straps, Nik pushed the button on the side wall and
looked up expectantly at the visa-plate for the first glimpse of
the new world. And in spite of all the worries nibbling at him,
there was a small thrill of excitement in waiting to see what lay
outside the skin of the LB.

Dark—darker than the blackest night on Korwar—with a faint
glimmer in the distance. But such dark!

"Hacon—where—where are we?" Vandy's voice was thin, shaken.

"On Dis." At least Leeds had supplied him with a name. But
where Dis was remained another matter.

"Dis—" the boy repeated. "Hacon—what are we going to do
here?"

Nik unbuckled his straps, sat up, and reached across to do the
same for Vandy. "We"—he tried to make his voice express the
proper authority—"are going to have an adventure."

"The Miccs—they're hunting again?"

The Miccs—those were Vandy's ever-present, ever-to-be-battled
enemies. But no use in Nik's building what he might not be able
to deliver, well-versed as he was in Vandy's fantasy world.

"This is just a scouting trip," he replied. "I don't know whether
they are here or not."

"Hacon—look! Something's coming!"

Nik glanced at the visa-plate. There was movement there, the
on-and-off flash of what might be a torch, and it was advancing
toward the LB. He helped Vandy from the bunk and drew the
boy with him to the escape lock at the end of the small compartment, but he made no move to open that until he heard the
tapping from without.

Air poured in—humid, hot, with a sweetish, almost gagging
odor, as if it had blown across a stretch of rotting vegetation. It
was cloying, clogging in the nostrils. Vandy coughed.

"That smells bad," he commented rather than complained.

"All right?" The inquiry came from without. The light from the LB port showed a man, his face, raised to view them, half masked with large goggles. "Here." A hand reached to Nik, and obediently he took the ends of two lines, both made fast to the welcomer's belt. "Tie those on," he was ordered. "This is no place to be lost!"

The humidity of the dark beyond was so oppressive that Nik was already bathed in perspiration, and he breathed shallowly, as if a weight rested above his laboring lungs. He knotted one cord to his own belt, one to Vandy's, and then dropped from the lock hatch, lifting down the boy.

"This way—" Their guide had already melted into the all-enveloping dark, towing them behind him. Luckily, he did not walk fast, and the ground under their feet appeared reasonably smooth. Vandy pressed against Nik, and the latter kept hold of the smaller boy's shoulder.

As they moved away from the lights of the LB, more features of the dark landscape became clearer. Here and there were faint halos of misty radiance outlining a large rock, a weird-seeming bush—or at least a growth that had the general appearance of a bush. But for the rest, it was all thick black, and when Nik turned his eyes to the sky, not a single gleam of a star broke the brooding blackness. Always the rotten stench was in their nostrils, and the humidity brought drops of moisture rolling in oily beads across their skin.

"Hacon—" Vandy was only a small body moving under Nik's hand, not to be seen in this night-held steambath. "Why doesn't that man use his torch?"

For the first time, Nik's attention was drawn from their weird surroundings to the guide. Vandy was right; they had seen the flicker of a torch when the stranger had approached the LB, but since they had left the ship, he had not used it. Yet he moved through the soupy blackness with the confidence of one who could see perfectly. Those goggles? But why link his two companions to him by towlines? Why not simply use a torch and show them the way?

The lines became for Nik not a matter of convenience but a symbol of dependence, which was disquieting. He stepped up, bringing Vandy with him and closing the gap between them and their guide.

"How about using your torch? This is a dark night."

To Nik's amazement, the answer was a laugh and then the words, "Night? This is the middle of the day!"

If that was meant to confuse him, Nik thought, it did.

"First day I ever saw that was a complete blackout," he retorted sharply.

"Under an infrared sun," the other replied, "this is all you'll ever see."

Nik was puzzled. His education had been a hit-or-miss—mostly miss—proposition, so the guide's explanation was meaningless. But Vandy apparently understood.

"That's why you're wearing cin-goggles then," he stated rather than questioned.

"Right," the stranger began, and then his voice arose in a shouted order. "Down! Get down!"

Nik flung himself forward, taking Vandy with him, so that they rolled across a hard surface on which evil-smelling, slimy things smeared to pulp under their weight. Their guide was using the torch now, sending its beam in a spear shaft of light to impale in the glare a winged thing of which they could see only nightmare portions. Then the beam of a blaster cut up and out, and there was a curdling scream of pain and fury as the blackened mass of the attacker whirled on, already charred and dead, to fall heavily some distance away.

Again their guide laughed. "Just one of the local hunters," he told them. "But you see that planet-side walks are not to be recommended. Now, let's get going. There're going to be some more arrivals soon; they don't get a chance to dine on flapper very often." Jerking at the towlines, he hurried them along.

They were going on a downslope, Nik knew, and walls of stone were rising higher on either side. But whether those were purposeful erections or native cliffs, he had no idea. He did see at one backward glance that, where their boots had crushed the ground growths, there were small ghostly splotches of phosphorescence with an evil greenish glow marking their back trail.

But even if he and Vandy could regain the LB, the ship would not lift. The controls had been locked in a pattern to bring them here, and Nik had neither the knowledge of a course to take them home or the ability to reset the controls. Home? Korwar—the Dipple—His hand went to his face. What lay behind him was *not* home! And why did he wish to backtrack? The action, as Leeds had outlined it, was simple enough. Vandy accepted him without question, and to the boy this would be only a very real adventure straight out of his fantasy world. He would be induced to share with Hacon the information Leeds or his superiors wanted. Then Vandy would go home, and he, Nik, would have earned his pay. He knew from his briefing what Vandy had made of Hacon and what he would have to do to sustain his role. Only, in these surroundings, with their total and frightening alienness, could Nik Kolherne be Hacon long? Already he was baffled by information Vandy knew and he did not, and he would be a prisoner wherever they were going until he gained some manner of sight. He was sure that this was a planet on which Terran stock were total aliens and where every danger was to be fronted without much preparation on his part.

But once he saw Leeds—Nik held tightly to that thought. Leeds was the stable base in this whole affair and meant security.

Without warning, there gaped before them a slit of light, which grew wider as they approached it. Then they passed through and into a rock-hewn chamber, for that was what it was, not a natural cave. A click behind them signaled the closing of the door.

The humid, sickly air of the outside was thinned by a cooler, fresher current, and their guide shed his goggles. He was a stocky, thick-set man, with the deep browning of a space crewman, like any to be seen portside at Korwar. Now he stepped into an alcove in the wall and stood while a mist curled out and wreathed about him. In a moment he came out and waved Nik and Vandy to take his place.

"What for?" Vandy wanted to know.

"So you don't take them inside." A crook of thumb indicated the floor.

There were the smears from their boots, and in those smears tiny lumps were rising. One branched in three—waving arms? Branches? Tentacles? A quick-growing thing from smears. Nik shivered. That flying creature their guide had killed he could accept, but these were different. He took firm hold of Vandy and shoved the boy in before him so that they huddled together in the alcove, sniffing a bracing air that carried a spicy, aromatic odor, the very antithesis of the humid reek outside this chamber.

Beyond the entrance, they found themselves in a barracks-like series of corridors and rooms, all hollowed in rock, mostly empty of either people or furnishings. They passed only two other men, both wearing space uniforms, both as nondescript as their guide.

Nik sensed a growing restlessness in Vandy. None of this resembled the dream adventures he and Hacon had shared in the past. Nor, Nik realized, was his own passive part akin to the figure Vandy had built up in his imagination. Nik had promised him an adventure, and this was far from the boy's conception of that.

"In here!" A jerk of the head sent the two of them past their guide into another room. This was manifestly designed as living quarters, with a bunk against the far wall, a fold-up table, and a couple of stools. The air current sighed overhead at intervals, coming through a slit no wider than the edge of Nik's hand. When he turned quickly, the door had closed, and he did not have to be told that they were prisoners. He pressed against the slide panel just to make sure of that point, but the barrier held.

"Hacon!" Vandy stood in the middle of the room, his fists on his hips, his small face sober with a frown. "This—this is real!"

"It's real." Nik could understand the other's momentary bewilderment. He had fashioned fantasies, too. And when he had fallen captive to Leeds' weapon in the warehouse, been freed from the Dipple, and gained what he had wanted most—why, at times all of that had seemed just part of a dream. But there had been moments of awareness, of doubt—and those were more than fleeting moments now. If Leeds had been here, if Nik had been told more of what to expect—

"Hacon, I want to go home!" That was a demand. Vandy's scowl was dark. "If you don't take me home, I'll—"

Nik sat down on the nearest stool. "You'll what?" he asked wearily.

"I'll call Umar." Vandy fumbled with the mid-seal fastening that covered a carry pocket in the breast of his tunic. He brought out a glistening object, which he held on the flat of his palm and studied with concentration. A moment later he looked up. "It doesn't work!" The scowl of impatience was fading. "But Father will find me; he'll bring the guard—"

Hadn't they told Vandy his father was dead? Nik's fingers picked at the broad belt with its fringe of weapons and tools that Vandy had thought up for his created hero. There were plenty of those. It was a pity they didn't have the powers Vandy had endowed them with—or would some one of them provide him with a weapon, a tool, so that he would not have to wait passively for trouble?

Why did he expect trouble, one part of Nik's brain demanded even as he began to pull that collection of show armament out for examination? Because he had been set down on a world where he was blinded among sighted men? Because he was limited by lack of information and driven by a feeling that there was little time?

"This is real, Vandy," he said slowly. "But it's an adventure, one we'll take together." If only Vandy hadn't build Hacon up as invincible! How was he going to keep Vandy believing in him? And if Vandy learned the truth, then the chances of getting what Leeds wanted sank past the vanishing point. And if he, Nik, could not deliver—

He was holding a small rod in his hand, one that was tipped with a disk of shining metal. In Vandy's imagination, it could generate a heat ray to cut through stone or metal. Now it served Nik as a mirror to reflect the smooth face he still did not dare to accept. If Nik Kolherne did not, and speedily, keep his part of the bargain, could he hope to keep that? He had to get Vandy's knowledge, and he could do it only by preserving Vandy's image of him—or rather of Hacon. Which meant that his own doubts must be stifled, that he must make a game of all this.

"Why are we here?" To Nik's ears, that held a note of suspicion.

"They think that they have us." Nik improvised hurriedly. "But really we came because your father is going to follow us—he can trace you, you know. And then at the right moment, we'll get him in. Then the Miccs will be taken—"

"No!" Vandy's shake of the head was decisive. "These aren't Miccs—are they, Hacon? It's Lik Iskhag's doing! And how are we going to help anyone if they keep us shut up? If Umar tells Father and they come to get us—maybe it's all a trap and Father and Umar will be taken, too! We have to get out of here! You get us out quick, Hacon!"

None of this was promising. Nik shoved the "heat ray" back in its belt loop. With Vandy in his present mood, Nik would never be able to talk him into telling what Leeds wanted. And Iskhag—that was the blue-skinned alien on Korwar. But Vandy wasn't of the same race. How did Iskhag fit into the picture or into the story Leeds had detailed for Nik?

"Listen, Vandy. I can't work blind, you know. Remember when we went hunting for the jewels of Caraska? We had to have information such as those map tapes we found in the derelict ship, and we had to learn the Seven Words of Sard." Feverishly, Nik delved into past Hacon adventures. "Now I have to know other things."

"What things?" There was a note of hostility in that, Nik believed.

"You're helping your father, aren't you, Vandy? Keeping some information for him?"

When the boy shook his head, Nik was not too surprised. Whatever had been left in Vandy's brain under the drastic safeguards Leeds had described was not going to be extracted easily.

"Why else would Iskhag want you?" He tried a slightly different approach.

"Bait—to get my father!" Vandy replied promptly.

"Why? What does Iskhag have against your father?"

"Because Warlord Naudhin i'Akrama"—there was a vast pride in Vandy's answer—"is going to hold Glamsgog until the end. And Lik Iskhag wants the Inner Places—"

The reply had no meaning for Nik at all. And why didn't Vandy know his father was dead? Had that been kept a secret from him for pity or for policy?

"If Father comes here and Iskhag gets him," Vandy continued, "then—then Glamsgog will be gone and every one of the Guardians will be killed! We have to get away before that happens—we have to!"

Vandy pushed past Nik and set his palms against the sliding surface of the door. His small shoulders grew stiff with the effort he was making to force it open. "We have to!" he panted, and his fear was plain to hear.

# FIVE

"Vandy!" Nik made that sharp enough to attract the boy's attention. "When did pounding on walls ever open a door?" He was working by instinct now. Hypotapes had made him part of Vandy's fantasy world; he knew that to the smallest detail. But with Vandy himself, beyond that imagination, rich and creative as it was, he trod unknown territory. How much dared he appeal to the boy's good sense?

He did not even know Vandy's real age. Various branches of once Terran stock had mutated and adapted so that a life span might vary from seventy to three hundred years. Vandy could be a boy of ten or twelve; also he might be twice that and still be a child. And Nik realized that the perilous gaps in his own information concerning his companion were dangerous. Surely Leeds could not have intended this companionship to endure for any length of time.

Vandy had come away from the door to face Nik. There was a shadow on his small face, but his jaw was set determinedly.

"We have to get out."

"Yes." Nik could echo that. "But not without a plan—" He grabbed at the one delaying suggestion that might not only give him time to think a little but might also produce information from Vandy. To his vast relief, the boy nodded and sat down on the other stool.

"Once we're out of this room"—Nik took the first difficulty that came to mind—"we can't manage without goggles."

"That man had them," Vandy pointed out. "We'll need blasters, too. That flying thing—there may be more of those."

"All right. But even with goggles and blasters, we can't go back to the LB—that was set on a locked course." Nik was listing the problems. "But just what we can do—"

Nik, sensitive without being conscious of it to some change in the atmosphere, glanced at Vandy. His eyes were normally golden, but now there seemed to be sparks of red fire in their depths. His small face was expressionless.

"You aren't—" he began when Nik made a sudden warning gesture.

Behind Vandy, the door panel was opening. Nik arose to face it.

The same crewman who had brought them here tossed some ration containers in the general direction of the flap table. One missed and rolled to Vandy's feet. He stooped to pick it up.

"I want to see Captain Leeds," Nik said quickly.

"He ain't here."

"When will he come?"

"When he's sent for, unless he gets some big ideas and makes the jump on his own."

"Then who's in charge?" Nik persisted. If Leeds was not, what did that mean for him, for Vandy, for the whole plan?

"Orkhad. And he wants to see you now. No—the kid stays here," he added as Nik motioned to Vandy.

"I'll be back," Nik promised, but Vandy's level gaze, still holding that ruddy spark, did not change. He said nothing as Nik hesitated irresolutely.

"Come on. Orkhad's not a Veep as takes kindly to waiting," the crewman said.

Nik went, but his first uneasiness was now a definite dislike of both his surroundings and the situation here. As they went down the corridor, he surveyed the physical features of the place. The walls were rock, hollowed out, not built up by blocks. Though the current of air was fresh, there were slimy trickles of moisture marking their surfaces. Who had fashioned this place Nik did not know, but he was convinced it was not the present inhabitants.

There were several chambers opening off that hall, all fitted with metal doors far newer than the walls on which they were installed. From quick glances, Nik learned those other rooms were living quarters, all like the one where he had been with Vandy.

They passed a larger room with a rack of blasters on the wall and various storage boxes piled within. Then the hall ended in large space dimly lighted. They threaded their way along a narrow balcony hanging above a wide space in which at least a dozen passages met in star formation, as if this were a grand terminal of some vast transportation system. But there was nothing to be seen in the half gloom save all those tunnel mouths evenly spaced about the expanse of the chamber.

The balcony brought them into another corridor, and Nik sniffed a new scent on the air. He had known that on Korwar. Someone not too far away was or had lately been smoking suequ weed.

Holding some of the same sickliness that seemed to be a part of the natural air of this world, the aroma grew stronger as they neared the end of the second corridor. And with every breath Nik drew, his fear grew. Suequ weed was one of the many drugs mankind had discovered to rot body and mind, and its side effects made for real trouble. The smoker lost all sense of fear or prudence, any sane balance of judgment. And the drug fostered recklessness that could involve not only the user but also his companions, were he in any position to give orders. If this Orkhad was the suequ smoker—

The room at the end of the corridor was different, in that an attempt had been made to lend it a measure of comfort. There was a strip of matting across the floor and a cover of black feathers fluffing from the bunk. Fastened to the wall above that was a picture—not tri-dee but rather a round of crystal in which were suspended a number of brightly hued creatures, either insects or birds.

Oddly enough, the smell of suequ was not so strong in the room, though the empty pipe lay on the table to the right of the man sitting there, turning around in his fingers a cup that was a barbaric art of precious metal and roughly cut gems.

He was plainly of Iskhag's race, though his present dress was far removed from the other's foppish splendor. His tunic was well cut but bare of ornament, and there was not so much as a jeweled buckle on his belt. His boots were those of any spaceman, though new, and the over-all color of his clothing was a russet brown. He was not armed, though the hooks of a blaster hold were riveted to his belt.

Nik's guide sketched a casual salute and took his place against the wall, leaving his charge in the open to face Orkhad. The alien did not break the silence, and Nik, wondering if the other were trying to needle him into some impatient mood, held to the same quiet.

Then Orkhad suddenly brought his cup down on the table top, the metal against metal producing a ringing note.

"You"—the thin notes of his high voice had a monotonous sound—"what do you do?"

To Nik, the question made very little sense. His job had been clearly defined back on Korwar. He was to bring Vandy here—wherever in the galaxy "here" was—and wheedle out of the boy the information Leeds needed.

"More of Leeds' work!" Without waiting for any reply, Orkhad spat out that name, making it sound like an obscene oath. "Why did you come? To put the boy in the ship was all that was necessary. We are not so well-supplied that we can feed extra mouths. You are not needed here."

"That isn't what Captain Leeds said. I do not have the information yet—"

Orkhad only stared at Nik. The eyes in that blue face slitted instead of widened, as if the alien narrowed vision to see the better.

"Information?" he repeated. "What is this information?"

"Captain Leeds gave me my orders."

"And Captain Leeds"—Orkhad made mockery of the name and title with the first real inflection Nik had heard in his voice—"is not here. He may not be here for some time. Here I am Veep—do you understand? And it is for me to determine the orders given—and obeyed. You have brought us Warlord Naudhin i'Akrama's son. That is well. For him we have a use. And this is a world that is all your enemy. Do you understand that?

"It has a sun in the sky right enough—a red dwarf sun whose rays you cannot see, not with *your* eyes. I can see a little, but your breed can see nothing unless you wear cins. And it is a world to which things have happened—for it is close to its dark sun. Sometime—who knows how long ago—there was a flare that crisped out to make of this planet a scorched thing. Its seas were steamed into vapor, which still clouds overhead, though a measure of this comes earthward in rainstorms such as you cannot conceive of.

"There was life here before that flare. This"—one of those blue hands indicated the walls about them—"was perhaps a refuge wrought in despair by some intelligent life form long before Captain Leeds' friends homed in here to discover a base to serve us well. Yes, intelligence burrowed and squirmed, hoping to preserve life, only to be burned away. So now we have some life, but none we cannot master with a blaster. Only to venture out into that murk without cin-goggles, without weapons—that is death as certain as its sun once gave this planet. Do you understand that?"

Nik nodded.

"So, we are agreed. This base, it is life; out there is death. And in this base it is by my will that life continues. Since the boy knows you, will be quiet with you, you shall continue to be with him until we are ready to deal with him. That small purpose you may serve. Fabic, take him away."

Nik went, adding up small items. Fabic was matching him step for step, and when they reached the balcony above the terminal, the crewman spoke.

"I never saw you with the captain."

"I wasn't one of his crew."

Fabic grinned. "So you wasn't of his crew. That figures—you'd have to be some older to make that claim. But you are his man now, and so I'll pass on a warning. Don't know when the captain will fin in here, but until he does, Orkhad gives the orders. You remember that, and there'll be no flamer to push you out of orbit."

"I have orders from Captain Leeds about the boy."

Fabic shrugged. "All right then, stall—and you'd better be smart about it, too. Let Orkhad get another pipe into him, and he's liable to try his luck at taking over. Then it wouldn't matter much what orders you had from the captain."

"You're a Leeds man?" Nik couldn't help that one question that might mean so much.

Fabic still grinned. "Me, I'm playing it safe—all the way safe! This is no planet to go exploring on. And I don't aim to be set outside without cin-goggles and a blaster and told to start walking! That has happened before. Sure, I'll back the captain—*if* he's here and ready to speak up. But I'm not stripping myself bare for him regardless. If you want to spit in Orkhad's eye, you'll do it on your own and take what he'll give you then all by yourself. Walk slow and soft and forget you know how to speak until the captain does show—"

"Which will be when?"

"When it suits him. Here's your hole. Crawl right in and remember to be invisible when trouble comes—"

Still trying to make something coherent out of those hints, Nik re-entered the cell-like chamber and heard Fabic click the door behind him. Vandy still sat on his stool, staring at an unopened tin of emergency space rations.

That gave Nik an idea for putting off explanations for a while.

"Let's eat!" He set the button for heating and, opening the nearest container, handed it to the boy.

When it popped open and the steam arose from its interior, Nik realized that he too was hungry. Vandy looked mulishly stubborn for a second or two, but it seemed that he could not resist that aroma either. They ate in silence, savoring the food. Nik counted the pile of containers Fabic had brought—enough for three days, maybe more. Did that mean they would be imprisoned here for that length of time or merely that Fabic did not want to make too many trips to supply them?

Leeds was coming, but, meanwhile, with Orkhad in command and hostile—What if the alien Veep moved against Vandy and incidentally against Nik?

How big were these underground diggings? That terminal with its radiating star of tunnels suggested size. Was Orkhad right? Were all these corridors, rooms, tunnels, part of a refuge system developed by a native race in a despairing attempt to survive the flare from their sun, an attempt that had failed? Did Orkhad have any large force here, enough to occupy an extensive section? If Nik only knew more!

Supplies for three days—and those tunnels. Nik's thoughts kept juggling those two facts, trying to add them as if he could make a satisfactory sum. As long as Leeds was not here, Orkhad was in control. Their safety rested on the very shaky foundation of the whims of a suequ smoker.

"I want to go home—" Vandy put down the empty ration tin. There was no panic now as he had shown earlier. But Nik, occupied though he was with his thoughts, read the determination in the boy's tone.

"We can't go." He was startled into a bald statement of truth.

"I will go!" Vandy sped across the room before Nik could move. He fitted his small fingers into the door slit, and the panel gave!

Nik launched himself at the boy to drag him back, while Vandy fought like a cornered dra-cat. Holding him on the bunk by the sheer weight of his own body, Nik strove to reason with his captive.

"All right, all right," he repeated. "Only we can't just walk out of here."

Why was the door left unfastened? Had Fabic overlooked that precaution on purpose or in carelessness? Did the crewman's weak allegiance to Leeds take that way out, giving Nik and Vandy an offer of escape? Or was it intended to be a method of getting rid of them both, organized by Orkhad?

Vandy lay quiet now, the red sparks blazing in his eyes.

Supplies, arms, cin-goggles—the tunnels—a chance to hide out until Leeds did arrive? It was wild, so wild that Nik could only consider such a plan because the fear that had been rising in him since their landing on Dis was now an icy and constant companion. He was sure that whatever plan Leeds had made had gone wholly awry, and the next move might be his alone.

"Listen!" Still keeping the tight grip pinning Vandy to the bunk, Nik spoke hurriedly. "We can't use the LB, but they must have other ships or a ship here. And Captain Leeds is coming. If we can hide out until he arrives, then everything will be all right. There are some tunnels—" Quickly, he outlined what he had seen during the trip to Orkhad's quarters.

"We need cin-goggles." Vandy's face was no longer closed and hard.

"We won't go outside!" Nik was determined on that.

"The goggles will be better to use than a torch in the dark," Vandy returned. "And if there is a ship, then we'll have to go out to reach it."

Back in the Dipple, Nik had spun his own adventures, neat pieces of dreamed action wherein all the major advantages had been his. But to start out blindly in the real thing was very different. He wondered fleetingly if Vandy found this true also. Superficially, this was not so different from the fantasies the boy had woven about Hacon and himself in that Korwarian garden, but Nik was not Hacon and this was no dream adventure.

"Blankets—" He might as well start off practically. Nik swept the supply tins from the table, bundled the coverings on the bunk around them, and secured everything into an awkward package with his belt. He was tempted to discard that fringe of mock weapons and tools but finally decided against that with the faint hope that some one of those might prove valuable after all.

Just how they were to obtain cin-goggles he had no idea, but blasters were racked in that room down the corridor. And with a blaster, he would feel less like a naked cor worm exposed to the day when the cover rock of its sleep chamber was torn away.

Inch by inch, Nik worked open the door. There was no change in the light of the walls. As far as Nik could see, the doors of the other chambers ahead were just as he had viewed them last, one or two half open, the rest closed. He signaled Vandy to silence and tried to hear any small noise that might herald waiting trouble. There was no sound, and he motioned Vandy out into the corridor and silently eased the door shut.

The bundle he carried by the belt fastening provided a weapon of sorts, always supposing he was the one to surprise a newcomer. At least, it was the only protection they had. With his fingers locked in that strap hold, Nik edged out into the corridor, Vandy between him and the wall.

They reached the first of those half-open doors. Vandy jerked at the edge of Nik's tunic and pointed. They could both see the strap, the round lenses. A set of goggles lay on the tip table in there. But most of the room, the bunk itself, was hidden. Suppose it was occupied? To get those goggles meant taking three, four steps in—

Before Nik could stop him, Vandy was on his way. Just inside, he stiffened, and Nik raised the bundle. The room *was* occupied! He dared not move to pull the boy back for fear of alerting the occupant. But Vandy—surely Vandy had sense enough to withdraw.

Nik bit his lips. Vandy was not retreating as his companion so fiercely willed him to. Instead, he squatted close to floor level, his attention all for something well to Nik's left and completely out of his range of vision. Then Vandy began to crawl on hands and knees, his body as close to the floor as he could manage. Helpless, Nik was forced to watch.

Now Vandy was directly below the table, his hand rising to the strap. Nik's heart pounded, so that the blood in his ears was a heavy beat. He had heard that snuffling, the rustle of bunk coverings as if the occupant stirred. Vandy's hand was motionless, his head turned. Nik could see one eye, very watchful. Then his hand moved down, and his fingers closed in triumph on the strap.

# SIX

Seconds stretched into nerve-racking minutes. Vandy hitched his way out of the room, the goggles clasped tight to his chest. He was at the door, getting to his feet again. Nik set aside the bundle, and his hands closed on the boy, jerking him back and out of what could have been a trap.

He looked down into Vandy's face. The boy's eyes were alight, his lips curved in a wide smile, but Nik did not respond. He pulled Vandy away from the door.

"Don't ever try anything like that again!" He thinned his whisper to the merest thread of sound, his lips close to Vandy's ear.

Vandy was still grinning. "Got 'em!" He dangled the goggles.

"And whoever was in there could have gotten you!" Nik retorted. "No more chances—"

Teaming with Vandy was trouble. Nik had been transformed into Hacon outwardly, but for a human being to resemble the imagined hero of a small boy was almost impossible. In the fantasy adventures of Hacon and Vandy, Vandy had always had equality of action. If Nik tried to impose the need for caution on the boy now, it might end in a clash of wills that would imperil their escape. Feverishly Nik searched his Hacon memory for some precedent that would render Vandy more amenable to his orders in the immediate future.

"This is a Silcon job." He brought out the best argument he could muster. "A slip will mean failure, Vandy."

"All right. But I did get the goggles! And we'll have to get another pair, won't we?"

"If we can." Privately Nik thought that their picking up the first pair had been such a piece of good luck that it was unlikely that such an opportunity would occur again. He recalled Leeds' belief in luck but was not moved to accept that belief for his own. To acquire one pair of goggles without mishap was perhaps all they dared hope to do.

The soft whish-whish of the air current over their heads was the only sound in the corridor. Nik counted doors to locate the room where he had seen the arms rack. Once both of them paused as a mutter from another sleeping chamber suggested the occupant was awake or waking. Nik was somewhat appeased by Vandy's present sober expression and his quiet.

At the arms room, they were faced by a closed door, which did not yield to Nik's efforts to slide it back. But the thoughts of the blasters kept him busy past the first sharp disappointment. To venture out into the unknown dangers of the tunnels without weapons was too perilous. He had too good a memory of that winged thing that had attacked outside the refuge. Perhaps other native creatives had found their way underground. Neither did he want to face any pursuit of Orkhad's forces with empty hands.

Nik's fingers traced the crack of the door. It did not give in the slightest to his urging. He turned the supply bundle around in his hands, examining those glittering "weapons" still in the belt loops. They could not deliver the power Vandy had imagined for them, but in their shapes and sizes, there might be one to answer his purpose now.

He chose the mirror ray and worked its curved edge into the door crack at the position of the locking mechanism. It was not a finger-heat seal, for which Nik was thankful, and his probing did meet obstruction. Carefully he began to pry, levering the mirror edge back and forth, so that it moved more freely.

Nik applied more pressure. His position was awkward, and he could not bring much weight to bear. But at last there was a click, and the door moved. A locked door should mean an empty room, and it was dark. Swiftly, Nik grasped the goggles, not sure they would work.

But they did, and he was able to see in an odd fashion, enough to make sure that the room was empty of all except its stark furnishing and the arms rack. He motioned Vandy in with him.

Four blasters stood in the rack slots. Nik took the first and saw that the dial butt indicated a full charge. At least Orkhad's men kept their arms in order. He thrust the weapon into the front of his tunic. Vandy reached for the second in the rack. Nik was about to protest and then kept silent. Whether Vandy could use the arm or not, a second one would be worth taking. Nik slipped the two remaining out of the rack, set their beams on full, and laid them on the floor. With any luck, they would lie there undiscovered until their charges were completely exhausted. It would take time to recharge them.

Luck again—he was beginning to think as Leeds did. And why was he so sure that the men here in the refuge were his enemies? Nik returned to the present problem, that of getting away from the quarters of Orkhad's force.

Vandy was staring, fascinated, at the wall beginning to glow red from the force beams. What effect that disintegration might have Nik did not know, but he shouldered the pack and pushed the boy back to the corridor. Outside, he shut the door once again and inserted in the crack another of the belt "tools," twisting the narrow strip of metal well into the slot and then melting it with his new weapon to make sure. That was a new door lock that would take them some time to break.

They came out on the balcony above the terminal of the tunnels. What if there was no way down? The expanse above that star-shaped convergence was big and shadowed. Nik could make out a matching balcony on the opposite side as he came to the edge to look over. There was nothing moving below, no sign that Orkhad's people had any use for that series of rock-hewn ways. Nik measured the drop with his eyes and then went to work.

The contents of the bundle were spread out and two of the covers knotted together. Yes, that ought to reach.

"We climb down?" Vandy whispered.

"No, I'll lower you, then drop—" Nik tested the knots with

hard jerks, listening all the while for any intimation that their escape had been discovered. Was the scent of suequ stronger? Had Orkhad gone back to the pipe? Nik fastened one blanket end to Vandy and helped the boy clamber over the rail.

He played out the improvised line and saw the pale face turned up to him as Vandy signaled safe arrival. Now up with the rope again. A bag was made of it to lower the supply containers. The whole thing dropped. Not too far away there was a rise in the surface of the tunnel level, close to Orkhad's quarters. Nik measured that distance by eye. To approach that end of the balcony was an added risk, but it was his best chance. He waved to Vandy and saw the boy nod vigorously.

Nik sped for that end of the balcony, Vandy matching him. Below the boy dropped the blankets in a heap as Nik climbed over the balustrade. As he had hoped, that tangle cushioned his fall. Jarred but unhurt, he got to his feet.

"Which way do we go now?"

Vandy's question was apt. Nik could see no difference in the radiating tunnels, no difference save direction. In that way, they should reach toward the outer world and the place where the LB had set down, which meant toward the spot where Leeds should come, in turn. But wouldn't Orkhad reason the same way? Nik hesitated as he faced the dark mouths in what seemed the right direction—left, middle, right—If the Veep did hunt in that direction, he would have to split his force in three. Success might depend upon how many men he commanded. Nik made his decision and took the tunnel to the right.

"That way!"

Blaster in hand, he started down the track to discover that, once into the passage, they did not need the goggles after all. At well-spaced intervals, there were plates set in the walls that glowed dully. Nik thought that those who had built these ways had certainly not shared his type of eyesight—perhaps to that forgotten and doomed race, those plates had presented a maximum of light. Had Dis always been a night world for Terran stock or had the sun flare altered more than its surface?

"Where are we going now?" Vandy asked.

"Wherever we can hide until Captain Leeds comes."

"Who is he, Hacon, a Patrolman?"

Nik grinned wryly. Strode Leeds was probably far from a Patrolman, but he was certainly their only hope of surviving this venture.

"No—he's just the man who'll take us away from here." And Nik hoped that was the truth.

"When is he coming?"

When—that was the question! For the first in what might have been hours, Nik's left hand sought his face. Time—time to keep him what he now was or just to keep him and Vandy alive. The conflicting stories concerning the boy returned to plague Nik as they walked on along what seemed endless miles of tunnel, with no change in the walls, no sign there was any end to this burrow hollowed for an unknown purpose long before either of them had been born.

"I don't know." Nik roused to answer that last question.

"If we hide, how can we tell when he does come?" Vandy was practical.

"We'll have to find a hiding place from which we can see the landing apron," Nik replied. "Only near there is where they will hunt us, too."

"Go outside?" Vandy sounded doubtful, and Nik did not blame him.

Stay in the burrows where Orkhad could eventually track them down—go outside into a nightmare world where only a pair of goggles would give them freedom of movement, perhaps mean the difference between life and death? But also—to go outside was the only way to be sure of Leeds' arrival. Nik had no assurance of the wisdom of his own decisions. He could only make them by choosing the lesser of two evils. And he clung stubbornly to the idea that in Leeds lay their only safety now.

"Yes." His reply was curt. And then he began to wonder if they *could* reach the outside world—if this tunnel had any opening onto the surface of Dis.

"Look!" Vandy's outheld hand was a vague blur in the gloom. What he indicated lay mid-point between two of the dim lights. It was a greenish glow, stronger toward the roof, tapering as it descended. Nik pulled up the goggles, startled by the sharp focus that leaped at him.

Plants—or rather fleshy growths against the bare rock. They had no leaves Nik could identify but innumerable thin arms or branches that matted together, intertwining and twisting until they made a thick mass. And they grew through a break in the wall only a little below the room. A way outside?

Nik could not bring himself to touch that mat of weird vegetation with his bare hands. The stuff had such an unhealthy, even evil, look that he thought of poison or fungoid contamination. Yet the chance of an unexpected bolt hole could not be missed.

"What is it?" Vandy demanded, and Nik realized that to the boy's unaided eyes the growth was a hazy mystery.

"Maybe a side door if we can open it." Nik dialed the low beam on the blaster and turned it on that twisted mass.

There was a burst of flame licking across the whole growth in one consuming puff. The stench of that burning blew back at them, forcing a retreat. Then it was gone, and only stained rock remained. But the crack the plants had masked was open, and there was light from it, light well visible to Nik's goggled eyes. Since the cleared space was big enough to scramble through, he leaped and caught at the sides, pulling himself up for a look.

Around him the concentrated stench made him gasp, and there was a whirl of thick and heavy smoke. It would seem that the fire started in the tunnel had ignited the vegetation here also.

Nik, coughing, held to his vantage point long enough to discover that the break was at the bottom of a wedgelike cut, the lips of which were far above. The fire puffed now up the walls of the cut, running with lightning speed along the trails of plants that must have originally choked most of that space.

The walls looked climbable, and Nik thought they had found their way out. He dropped back to wait for the fire to clear the cut, taking advantage of that interval to share a tin of rations with Vandy. They had food; now they must find a place to hole up for rest. Vandy had made no complaint, but Nik judged by his own growing fatigue that to climb out of the cut might be all the youngster could do.

He was right, Nik discovered, when they did climb. Vandy

was slow, fumbling, and Nik used his belt as a safety device to link them. Vandy was not just tired; he was climbing that grade blind, making it necessary for Nik to guide his hands and feet. When they at last pulled out on top, Vandy sat panting, his head bowed on his knees.

"I—I don't think I can go on, Hacon—" he said in a small voice. "My legs—they're too shaky—"

Nik stood surveying the landscape about them with concentrated study. The ground was rough with many outcrops of rock among which grew lumpy plants, some inches high, others branching into the height of normal trees, but none of them wholesome-looking. The dank humidity of the outer world was a stifling blanket, weighing down their bodies almost as heavily as the fatigue. No, neither of them could go far now, and the rocks offered the best hope of shelter.

The nearest was a cluster of squared blocks where patches of growth made lumpy excrescences. Whether those rises also contained any protecting crevices or niches he could not be sure, but he was certain Vandy could not go much farther. Somehow, Nik got the boy to his feet and half led, half supported him to the rocks. The cloying scents in the air made them both gasp. And once or twice during that journey Nik gagged at a smell alien enough to human nostrils to arouse nausea.

A creature humped of spine, which moved by hops, broke from hiding almost under Nik's feet and took a soaring leap to the top of one of the blocks. There it slewed around. A tongue issued from a wide, gaping mouth to lash across a patch of fungi-encrusted stone and transfer a burden of harvested vegetation to that lipless stretch of warty skin.

Nik sighted the shadowy space beneath that hopping thing's perch. A moment later he supported Vandy to the edge of a dark pocket, pausing only to use the blaster to clear its interior. Then they were in a slit passage running on between the blocks. Nik pushed Vandy along that narrow way. It was not a cave. The continued regularity of the walls made him sure that this was the remains of a structure.

A rattle underfoot drew Nik's attention from the wall to the floor. He had kicked a grayish object. About as long as his

forearm, it was formed of a series of rounded knobs linked
together until his foot had disturbed them and several had
rolled apart. Bones? Remains of what—and how recent the
death that had left them there? Was this the lair of one of
the killers of Dis?

Still, the way before them was open, and Nik had the blaster.
Now he saw light ahead—further proof that this was a passage
rather than a cave. Three or four more strides and he was fronted
by an opening well above the surface of the way, a window to
look out upon an eerie landscape so dark that even the goggles
did not help much in his inspection.

Ruins—that was surely true. The block piles were regular in
pattern. And they extended all along a shelf to his right. On the
left was an abrupt drop, and then another, as if he were on the
edge of a flight of steps intended for the use of giants.

No use trying to go on now, stumbling into the ruins. The
window opening was well above the surface of the pavement,
and if they bedded down immediately beneath it, they would
be well protected. Nik was shaking with fatigue, and Vandy had
slid out of his hold to lie still, his eyes closed, his panting breath
coming in a more even pattern. Vandy was finished for now, and
Nik had no strength to carry him. This had to be their refuge.
He managed to spread the blankets and roll the boy on them.
Then he sat down, his back against the wall, the blaster resting
on his knee, wondering how long he could hold out against the
sleep his body demanded.

# SEVEN

Nik awoke to darkness, a black so thick it was a match for the humid air about him. He was choking, gasping, blinded. For those few seconds, panic held him, and then he remembered where he was. But before he could move, there was an awesome roll of sound, and he thought he could detect an answer of vibration through the stone pavement on which he crouched.

"Hacon—Hacon!" The appeal was half scream.

Nik flung out an arm, but Vandy was not there. He pawed at his chest, hunting the goggles that had rested there when he had nodded off into slumber. They too were missing! Vandy and the goggles. Had the boy tried to return to the LB?

"Hacon!" The call came from not too far away. Nik clawed up to the window facing the ruins. A thunderous roll shook the air and the earth under him. As it dwindled into silence, Nik heard other sounds, a growl, then a high-pitched scream. He clung to the edge of the window and tried to force sight where his eyes stubbornly refused to grant it.

"Vandy!" He put all his power into that shout. "Vandy!"

If there was an answer, the third peal of giant thunder swallowed it. A flash of dim radiance around the bowl of the horizon followed, while wind battered the scattered blocks. A storm was coming, and such a storm as was possible only on this nightmare world!

Nik tried to remember how the stretch beyond had looked when he had worn the goggles. There had been a relatively open space—he was sure of that—before the next ruined structure.

"Vandy!" Against hope, he bellowed again.

Then there was a flare, blinding in intensity, that started a column of flame Nik could use as a beacon. Vandy must have fired his blaster at some of the highly combustible native vegetation. With that as his guide, Nik began to run.

The wind caught at the ragged banners of the flames, tearing them into long, tattered ribbons, which ignited other growth beyond. Vandy—caught in that! A roar that was not thunder, but from some animal, sounded. Nik raced around broken column, a section of wall, and came into an arena where the fire lighted a wild scene.

Vandy was there, standing on a block of masonry, his back to a pillar or stele. And he held the blaster at ready, though he was not firing at what moved below.

Nik saw them clearly in the light of the fire, but how could you describe them? Each world having life on its surface had grotesques, things of beauty, things of horror, and how one classified them all depended upon one's own native range of comparison. These had beauty of a sort. Their elongated, furred bodies moved fluidly, wound in and out as if they were engaged in some formal dance. And their heads, with the double fur-fringed ears and the glowing eyes were raised and lowered in a kind of rhythm.

"Vandy," Nik shouted from instinct alone. "Don't watch them!"

Weaving patterns were produced by those lustrous fur bodies to draw the eyes and focus the attention. Nik looked above and behind the boy. His own blaster came up, its sights centered on twin pinpricks of light over Vandy's right shoulder. Nik fired. He had dialed the ray to needle beam, but even then he had had to aim high for fear of touching Vandy. That ray must have missed the attacker or attackers leading the sortie from above, but the eye gleams vanished, and the weaving pattern on the pavement ceased abruptly. The heads swung in Nik's direction as they stood still, eyeing him.

Here in the hollow among the ruins, the wind did not reach,

but the fire had already eaten away at the growth and was now dying, so that Nik's sight of the hunters was curtailed. Several of the flankers dropped low, their belly fur brushing the ground as they glided toward him, pausing at once when he looked directly at them. They were not large animals. The biggest in the pack was as long as Nik's arm, but size did not mean too much if they hunted as a unit, and Nik thought that they did.

He began his circling, moving with his face toward the enemy, hoping to reach the point directly beneath Vandy's present perch. It was apparent that the creatures were cautious hunters. Perhaps somehow they had made a quick appraisal of the intruders' weapons in Vandy's use of the blaster.

Thunder was answered by a wide flash of the semi-invisible lightning. Neither sound nor light appeared to make any impression on the hunters. Nik had reached the edge of the stele; two more short steps would bring him below Vandy.

"Vandy!" He dared to hail the boy, and oddly enough his voice stopped the forward glide of the flankers and brought their heads up, swinging slightly from side to side as if the human mouthed word was far more disturbing than the approaching fury of the storm. "The goggles—" Nik held up his left hand without daring to see if the boy would obey him. "Give them here!"

A moment later the strap holding those precious windows into the dark was in his grasp. Then he heard Vandy.

"I'm covering—"

With that assurance, Nik dared to put the cin strap about his head and take the chance of looking away from the hunters. He gave a half whistle of relief. To have sight again—that was better than a glimpse or two with the aid of the almost dead fire. His confidence rose.

"Vandy"—he gave his orders slowly—"I'm going to move out from this block. You slide down behind me and take a grip on my tunic—now!"

Whatever influence his voice had had in the beginning on the pack was now wearing off. They had made a half circle about him, but so far they had not advanced beyond an invisible line of their own choosing.

He could not hear the sounds of Vandy's descent, for the

thunder rolled deafeningly. A jerk on his tunic told him the boy had followed orders. Nik began to edge sideways, pulling Vandy with him, his body between the hunters and the boy, his blaster ready for the first sign of attack. Why the Disian creatures had not already pulled him down, Nik could not imagine. He reached the end of the block, and the full force of the storm-driven wind struck at him, bringing with it torrential rain.

Instantly the hunting pack vanished, leaving Nik to blink unbelievingly as he threw out his left arm and clawed for anchorage against the buffeting of wind and rain. It was as if they had simply disappeared into the slanting lines of the falling water itself!

Shelter—Nik did not think they could make it back to the window corridor across the open space where the storm hit with hammering strength. A flash—and through the cin-goggles the brilliance of the dark world's lightning was blinding. That must have hit close by.

Nik was aware of Vandy's pulling at him, urging him to the right. He looked over his shoulder. The boy had kept his hold on Nik with one hand; the fingers of the other had fastened in the edge of an opening between two blocks.

To venture into such a hideout might be walking into one of the hunters' dens, but they could not remain in the open. Already the force of the wind was driving through the air pieces of vegetation and other debris. There was one precaution he could take. Nik threw an arm about Vandy, holding him well anchored against his own body as he beamed the blaster into the opening. Then he stooped to enter.

Here even the cin-goggles were not much use. The pavement sloped down and inward from the door, and small rivers of rain poured about their boots. Nik halted. No use going on to a basin where the storm waters might gather. He could see walls faintly, near to hand at his right, farther away on his left. And there was a ledge or projection on the right.

"Ledge here." He guided Vandy's hand to that and swept the boy's palm back and forth across the slimed stone. "We'll stay there; too much water running down here."

Nik boosted the boy onto the projection and then settled beside him. The water was now flooding down the ramp. It was hard to believe it was merely storm overflow and not some stream diverted into this path. How far down did it run?

Even though sounds were muffled here, the fury of wind and rain and the assaults of thunder and lightning made a grumble that vibrated through the wall against which they huddled. Vandy's body pressed closer to Nik's with every boom from the outer world, and Nik kept his arm about the small shoulders, feeling the shudders that racked the boy's frame.

"Just a storm, Vandy." Nik sought to reassure the other.

But on Dis a storm might well be catastrophe of the worst kind. If he only knew more about this black world, about the Guild refuge and those in it, about Leeds—

For that matter, about Vandy, too. Why had the boy taken the goggles and gone into the ruins on his own? If he tried that trick again, it could well lead to disaster for both of them. Nik must make Vandy understand that.

"Why did you take the cins and go out?" Nik raised his voice above the gurgle of the rushing water, the more distant wind and rain, to ask.

Vandy squirmed in his hold. "I wanted to see if I could find the ship." His voice had a sullen note.

So, he had been heading for the LB.

"Vandy, I'm telling you the truth." Nik spoke slowly, trying to throw into his words every accent of conviction. "Even if we were right in the LB now, we couldn't rise off-world. It's locked on a homing device to this port, and I can't reset that."

There was no answer from the other save that his body stiffened in Nik's hold as if he would pull away. Nik kept his grip tight.

Vandy was still stiff in his hold when he spoke. His lips were so close to Nik's ear that the puffs of his breath touched the other's now smooth cheek.

"There's something—something on the ledge—over there!"

Nik turned his head slowly. It was almost totally dark for him even with the goggles. How *could* Vandy see anything? A ruse to distract him? It *was* there, and to Nik's eyes it showed with frightening plainness. Where had it come from—out of the watery depths below or down the wall from above? Its hunched body had some of the greenish glow of the crushed

slime plants, but Nik could not be sure of more than a phosphorescent lump.

Between them and it dangled a glowing spark that danced
and fluttered. It took a full moment for Nik to trace that spark
back to the humped body to which it was attached by a slender,
whip-supple antenna. Now another of those antennae snapped
up into action, and a second spark glistened at its tip, flickering
about. Save for that play, the thing made no move to advance
toward them.

But before that display of twin dancing lights, there was other
movement on the ledge. Whether the second creature had been
there all the time or whether the action of the antenna fisher
had drawn it, Nik was never to know. But a four-legged furred
shape, like one of the hunters, arose from a flattened position
and began to pace hesitatingly toward the fisher.

The antennae with their flashing tips slowly withdrew, luring
the other after them. The pacer showed no excitement nor wariness; it followed the lures unresistingly.

"What—what is happening?" whispered Vandy, and Nik realized that the goggles gave him a view of the hunt that the boy
lacked.

"Something is hunting." He described what he saw.

The drama ended suddenly. As the antennae vanished into
the owner's bulk, the prey appeared to awake to its danger. But
already the fisher had launched itself from the stone with a flying leap into the air that brought it down on the unfortunate
it had lured into striking distance. There was a shrill humming
either from fisher or prey, and Vandy cried out, his hands catching Nik's tunic.

Continuing to crouch on its captive, the fisher was still. Nik
could not yet sight a separate head—nothing save a bulk with
that unhealthy, decaying sheen about it.

"Hacon, it wants—it wants us!" Vandy did not whisper now.
His voice was shrill. Whether that was a guess on his part or
whether some sense of malice was transmitted to the boy, Nik did
not know. But when those twin twinkling, dangling lights once
more erupted from the black bulk and whipped through the air
in their direction, he chose prudence and used the blaster.

As the ray lanced into the bulk, Nik caught his breath. He was not sure that he actually heard anything. It was more like a pain thrusting into his head than any cry his ears reported. But the thing and its prey twisted up and fell down into the rush of waters, to be carried on into whatever depths the ancient ruins covered.

"It's gone!" he assured Vandy. "I rayed it—it's gone!"

Vandy's shivers were almost convulsive, and Nik's alarm grew. He must get the boy under control, arouse him from the fear that made his body starkly rigid in Nik's hold—that had frozen him.

"It's gone!" he repeated helplessly. But he knew what might lie at the base of Vandy's terror. To be blind in this hole could feed any fear, could drive even a grown man to panic. If they only had two sets of goggles! And what if something happened to the one pair they did possess? What if both of them were left wandering blind on the outer shell of Dis, prey for the creatures of the dark? Their flight from the refuge had been a wild mistake. He was armed now. Better go back and take his chances with Orkhad than remain in this wilderness of horror.

Just let the storm die and they would do that. Nik could find the trail back from this point to the break in the tunnel, and from the tunnel he could scout the living quarters of the refuge, find a safe hiding place until Leeds came—

"Vandy!" He strove to make his words penetrate the locked terror he could feel in the body he held. "We're going back to the tunnel just as soon as the rain is over. We'll be safe there. And until then—well, we both have blasters. You used yours, remember, when the animals had you cornered in the ruins. Used it well, too. I couldn't have found you if you hadn't set fire to the plants. We hold this ledge. Nothing can come at us here as long as we're armed."

"But—I can't *see*!"

"Are you sure, Vandy? You told me that thing was there before I saw it, and I have the goggles. How *did* you know?"

Vandy's body was not quite so rigid and his voice, when he replied, was alive again and not dehumanized with terror. "I guess I saw something—a sort of pale light—like those plants we squashed with our boots."

"Yes. Some of the living things here appear to have a light of their own. And maybe you could see that better than I could just because you did *not* have goggles on, Vandy. Perhaps we'll need both kinds of sight to watch here." How true that guess might be Nik did not know, but its effect on the boy was good.

"Yes." Vandy loosed one hand hold. "And I do have the other blaster."

"Don't use it unless you have to," Nik was quick to warn. "I don't know how long a charge will last."

"I know that much!" Vandy had recovered to the point of being irritated. "Hacon, this was all part of a city once, wasn't it? It's scary though—like the Haperdi Deeps—"

If Vandy could return to one of his fantasy adventures for a comparison, Nik decided, he was coming out of his fright.

"Yes, it was a city, I think. And it does seem like the Haperdi Deeps, though I don't recall that we ran into any fishers with light for bait there." He hoped Vandy's confidence would not soar again to the point of confusing reality with fantasy, regaining a belief in their own invincibility. Hacon, the hero, could wade through battles with horrific beasts and aliens untouched, but Nik Kolherne was very human and perishable, as was Vandy, and the hope of survival must move them both. He said as much, ending with a warning as to what might happen if the cin-goggles suffered any damage before they regained the refuge. To his satisfaction, Vandy was impressed.

Now that he had made his decision to return, Nik was impatient to be on his way, but the water still rushed down beyond the ledge. And now and then the roll of thunder, the cry of the storm, carried to them. How long would this fury of Disian weather last? A day—or longer? And could they remain on their present perch for any length of time? Nik had no fear that they could not defend it against attack, but fatigue and hunger could be worse enemies. The supply containers they had brought with them had been left with the blankets back in the window passage. Already Nik was hungry and knew that Vandy must be also.

Time dragged on. Vandy went to sleep, his head resting on Nik's knees. Now and then he gave a little whimper or said a word or two in a tongue that was not the basic speech of the galaxy. Nik had plenty of opportunity to plan ahead, to examine all that had happened. He would, he decided, have done the same again—given his word to Leeds and the Guild for a new face. And the payment was bringing Vandy to Dis. Bringing Vandy—

Leeds' story of what was wanted from the boy and Orkhad's counter story—Vandy believed his father still alive. *Did* Vandy have information the Guild wanted, or was the boy himself the goods they were prepared to deal in?

Nik's fingers slipped back and forth across smooth cheek and chin, across flesh that felt firm and healthy, bone that was hard and well-shaped. How long would he continue to feel that? How long before his fingertips detected new, yet well-remembered, roughness there to signal his own defeat? There was no possible answer except to wait for Leeds.

And to tamp that thought and the uneasiness behind it well back into his mind, Nik tried to assess his immediate surroundings. They had not come too far from the tunnel opening. They could get back, and most of the way was under cover. His ears gave him hope. The rush of water below had slackened, and he did not hear the wild sounds of the storm any more. Even a lull would allow them to regain the window passage and the food there. He shook Vandy gently.

"Time to go—"

# EIGHT

Nik tested the current of the flood on the downward slope by lowering himself to stand with it washing about his boots while he held to the ledge. The water was glassy; its dark surface rippled now and then. Sometimes those ripples ran against the current as if life fought a passage upward. But the wash came no higher than Nik's ankles, and the force of it was not enough to impede wading.

At his assurance, Vandy dropped down, keeping a hold on Nik as he had when they had faced the hunters. Then they splashed toward the outside.

There it was still raining steadily, but the wildness of the wind had abated. The rain flowed by every depression to the edge of the drop the ruins lined, cascading over in countless small falls. There was something about that abrupt drop—could this city once have been a port on a long-vanished river or sea? But the mystery of the ruins was not their problem. To get back to the tunnel was.

"Keep hold," Nik ordered Vandy as he pushed into the open under the pelt of the rain.

Now—that *was* the window through which he had climbed! He boosted Vandy up and scrambled after. They were in the dry again, and Nik looked for the supplies. He triggered the heat-and-open button on one of the containers, holding it with care lest some of the precious contents spill. When the lid sprang up and the steam made his mouth water, he gave it to Vandy.

"Eat it all, but slowly," Nik ordered and took up another tin for himself. Rationing might be more sensible, but it had been a long time since their last meal. Nik felt they needed full stomachs for the job ahead. Once back in the refuge, there would be chances to get more supplies.

The humidity, which had been so choking before the storm, seemed even worse in the narrow passage. The smallest effort left Nik gasping. His clothes, soaked in the rain, had no chance of drying, but he made Vandy strip and wipe down with one of the blankets, doing the same himself, before huddling into their soggy clothes once more.

"My boots—they're shining," Vandy observed suddenly.

Nik glanced down. There was an odd luminescence outlining the boy's footgear—his own, too. He examined them more closely. A furred substance was there. Nik had a dislike of investigating by finger touch. With a blanket edge he wiped Vandy's boot toe. There was a slimy feel to the smear, and the blanket came away phosphorescent as had their tracks upon first entrance to the refuge. Their boots were growing some form of vegetation!

Quickly Nik surveyed the rest of their clothing. His belt—yes, that had the same warning glow, and so had parts of the ornamental harness Vandy had dreamed up for Hacon's uniform. But, save for the boots, Vandy appeared free. Neither of them dared to discard those boots and venture bare-skinned across Disian earth. Whether they were now carrying some deadly danger with them, Nik did not know. He could only hope that the weird growth would not root on their skins.

There had been vegetation in the tunnel, but where the roof break had admitted it, and it had not spread far from that point. Perhaps the cool current of air always flowing through the refuge was a discouraging factor. All the more reason for getting back there.

With their remaining supplies repacked, Nik steered Vandy down the passage. They had reached the other door of that way

and were near to the cut where the tunnel entrance lay when
Vandy cried out. But Nik saw it, too, and there was no mistaking
that kind of fire. A small ship was riding tail flames down for
a landing, probably on the same field where the LB had finned
in. That must be Leeds!

"There's another!" Vandy cried. "And—"

Two ships—a third! Leeds couldn't be leading a fleet! Was
Vandy right? Were those his father's ships, a father who was not
dead but lured here with Vandy for the bait? But if that was true,
where did Leeds stand? Nik halted the run that had brought him
to the edge of the cut.

The rain was pouring into the bottom of that hollow. It must be
curling in turn into the tunnel. Their back door might not even
be practical—if they still wanted to use it. That *if* was important,
and its answer could only come by learning the identity of the
planeting ships.

There was noise—not one of the great thunderclaps of the
Disian storm, but a shock through the ground under them. Vandy
screamed and tumbled forward into the cut. Nik tried to grasp
him. One hand caught a hold, and then the two of them were
sliding down. Nik brought up against a rock with painful force,
but that anchored them against a farther tumble. There was a
second shock in the ground, and out of the tunnel break air
exploded, carrying with it bits of rock and soil.

Down in the refuge, there had been an explosion. Had Orkhad
taken some drug-twisted way out of trouble by blowing up his
own stronghold? Or had the refuge been forced from without
and was it now under attack? At any rate, to drop into those
depths at present was asking for worse trouble than they had
faced so far.

"Got—to—get—away—" Nik panted. "Whole thing might collapse under us here—"

One of his arms and one side were pinned to the ground by
Vandy's weight and the boy had neither spoken nor moved since
they had landed there.

"Vandy!" Nik edged his head around.

Closed eyes, a trickle of blood across the forehead—Vandy
must be unconscious. Nik strove to wriggle free. His movements

brought an answering throb of pain. That slam against the rock had not been the easiest landing in the world. But Vandy, the boy might be seriously injured—

Their anchoring rock had seemed to give a little when Nik moved. He began to claw at the soil under him, loosening enough so that he could squirm around and put his head and shoulders upslope. The trails of rain were still flooding down. Splashes from one struck them. Vandy moaned and tried to move, but Nik was quick to pin him down. Another wriggle and they both might be on their way to the bottom. Luckily, there had been no more quakes or explosions or whatever had stirred up the earth hereabouts.

With Vandy a dead weight, Nik was defeated when it came to climbing, and he feared to descend. That explosion of air and rock must have blown a larger hole in the tunnel. To fall into whatever might be in progress down there was more danger than he cared to face.

A sidewise progress upslope—yes, he could make that—but not carrying Vandy. Could he leave the boy there, wedged in behind the rock, while he went to the top and devised some method of raising Vandy in turn? The boy was half conscious now but not alert enough to understand their predicament and cooperate by remaining quiet. Left, he could well fall into the tunnel hole.

The wet slope was a slippery way at best, but Nik still had the small pack of blankets and supplies. The blankets themselves? Nik tried to think coherently and purposefully.

He moved with infinite caution, dragging Vandy across his thighs so that the boy lay face up behind the rock. Then Nik unfastened the blanket roll and pulled it around.

Somehow, he managed the next move. One of the blankets was wrapped around Vandy, confining his arms and legs, the belt made fast, and the other blanket used again as a rope. From this point, the climb seemed mountain high, but Nik knew from their first journey out of the cut that it was not. If he could make the effort, they would win.

He chose to tackle the slope between two water streams where the earth was relatively dry, if any stretch of ground on this bedeviled world could be deemed that. Now he straightened cautiously and drove two of the supply containers into the yielding surface with all the strength he could muster, hanging his weight on each as a test.

Anchorage for a gain, now use the last two above those! Nik crawled face down against the slimed earth. It was time to loosen the lower containers—but only one would come free as he leaned at an almost impossible angle to struggle with it. Well, that one would have to serve. Drive it in above—crawl—

Then his clawing hand was over the edge where a portion of the cut wall had earlier collapsed. Nik strained with the effort to rise and rolled over into a puddle of rain.

He heard a moan from below and edged around. His arms were like heavy weights. Nik was not really certain that his overtaxed muscles would obey his demand for more effort. His breathing came in snorts, which did not supply enough air to his laboring lungs, but he grasped the end of the blanket rope and began to pull.

The package that was Vandy slipped around, and for once the slick ground surface served rather than thwarted. Nik pulled with a desperate need for getting this over and brought Vandy upslope into the same puddle where he knelt.

Now, only a few feet and they would be at the top. Nik did not have enough energy left to lift Vandy. Pushing the boy before him, he crept up the incline and lay there, the humid air thick in his nostrils, seeping with difficulty into his lungs.

It was then that the third and last shock came. For one desperate instant, Nik thought they would slide back. He flung out an arm to roll Vandy on and kicked himself away from the slipping earth. So they were saved from being carried down once more.

As soon as that upheaval ended, Nik began to crawl, pulling Vandy, determined to get away from the danger point, not really caring in which direction, so long as it was not down. They were in the open among the ruins, and the sheets of rain continued to sweep over and about them.

Nik headed for the passage from which they had emerged only a short time earlier, desiring nothing now but to be out of that torrent. He was almost under that cover when he heard, above the rain, a sharp crack that he could not believe was part of the natural noise of the storm. He hunched around, his hand to his blaster.

Out and up from somewhere near the landing field it soared, not one of the winged Disian creatures but a flier—and a planet atmosphere craft, not a spacer.

It skimmed through the rain like a black shadow, seeking no great altitude, rising only far enough to clear the heights that roofed the refuge. Then it headed out across the ruins of the ancient city.

Tracers of fire followed that flight, shooting angry lashings into the storm. Nik was not familiar with the tricks of evasive action, but he sensed that the unknown pilot was making a masterly escape from whatever fate had overtaken one party or the other in the storming of the refuge. That the fleeing man or men in the flitter were of the Guild he had little doubt which meant that the invaders were in control below and on the landing strip.

But who were the invaders? Forces of Vandy's people? Leeds' men forcing a showdown with Orkhad—though Nik hardly believed that. Could Leeds have mustered three ships, which he estimated had been used to break into the refuge? Law in the persons of the Patrol?

He crouched there, watching the shadow of the flitter weaving back and forth, flying low in the rain. At least the invaders were firing only ground-based missiles, not making chase by air.

There was a splash of fire to the right. One of the missiles had fouled with a fire ray and exploded with a clap of sound. Then one of those fire spears touched a fin wing on the flitter. The craft whirled, fluttering back and forth. Nik tensed, imagining the frantic fight of the pilot to keep the machine aloft or sufficiently under control to land it safely.

The flitter sideslipped to Nik's left. It was falling rather than landing under control. But before it was quite out of sight, it steadied. If it did make a landing, it would be down in the gulf of the drop below the ruined city, perhaps on the bed of what seemed a one-time sea.

And those who had aimed the lucky shot that finished it—they would be moving out to hunt the wreckage, which meant they would come in this direction! Nik chewed on that unhappy reflection. If he remained where he was, he would be detected. If this was the Patrol or any official expedition hunting Vandy, they would be equipped with any number of devices to locate another human on Dis. He had heard a lot of stories about such mechanical man-hunters. And to be scooped up now by either party would mean his own death warrant, as he well knew. The squadron that had used such force to break into the refuge would not be tempted to argue out a surrender. Nor could he be sure they were on the law's side.

Orkhad had hinted at two parties in the Guild. This could be a jack job. If he only knew!

What Nik did know, however, was that this was not a good place to stay.

"Hacon—" Vandy wriggled in the blanket roll, striving to throw off his bindings. "What—what happened?"

"A lot." Nik knew a small surge of relief. If Vandy was conscious and able to go on his own two feet, their flight would be easier.

And flight it was going to have to be! There was a smoldering, sputtering patch of fire on the heights where a ray had ignited vegetation. The highly inflammable stuff seemed able to burn even in the rain, and the smog of that burning carried through the thick air as a stifling gas.

Nik pulled the wrappings from Vandy as they both choked and coughed. To return to the ruins would do no good. Not only were there the things that lived in the shadows there, but also the gas of the burning settled thickest in that direction. They should get down to a lower level. And that would take them in the general direction of the vanished flitter, along the very path pursuit would come, but they were cut off on the other three sides.

Nik leaned over Vandy. "Can you walk?" He asked the immediate question.

"I think so—"

He hoped that was the truth. But when he helped the boy to his feet, Nik kept his arm about those small shoulders. Then, half guiding, half supporting Vandy, he started on through the ruins to hunt some way down the cliff the city edged. And, with Vandy lacking cin-goggles, Nik's sight had to do for them both.

Their first break of better fortune came when the rain actually began to slacken. That needling force of water was now a drizzle, and the streams finding their ways across the broken and earth-drifted pavement were thinning visibly. By the cin-fostered sight, it was now as light as cloud-gloomed Korwarian day, and Nik was thankful for that.

They threaded a path along the verge of the cliff, and Nik sighted piles of tumbled blocks that might once have been wharfs for the convenience of surface shipping. One of those they used as a stairway down to the first level below the city surface, where the oily vapors of the burning had not reached.

Nik's throat was raw with coughing, and Vandy was sobbing as they came to the end of that tough scramble. There was a large pool there filling a depression but already draining through a channel toward the outer reaches of the onetime sea. Nik went down on one knee beside it and put his hand into the liquid.

So far they had managed on the supplies from the refuge, but those were gone. Now they would have to chance the water and what food they could find on Dis, and that chance would be only one more danger in the many they faced.

Nik scooped up a palmful of the water. It had no scent he could detect. And they had inadvertently swallowed some of it in the form of rain on their lips and faces ever since they had been caught in the first gusts of the storm. He licked up some of the moisture greedily, and it relieved the parching of his mouth and throat.

"Water, Vandy!" Nik cupped his hands and filled them, lifting the trickling burden to the boy's lips and supplying more a second and third time.

How long this water would last, Nik could not tell, but it was now a wealth all about them. And their path at present would take them along the foot of the old shoreline cliff, away from the refuge. What their goal was, Nik could not have said, except shelter of some kind until he might gain some idea of the forces now ranged against them. How he was going to make that identification without walking directly into the enemies' hands, he had no knowledge, either.

The same fungoid vegetation that grew thickly above straggled here, but not in such profusion or size. Nik avoided the patches whenever he could, remembering how their boots had left trails of shining prints before. The rain was coming to an end, and the measure of daylight increased. It was hard for him to recall that this was still black night for Vandy. He kept reminding himself of that fact, keeping his hand on the boy's shoulder as a guide.

Vandy was not going to be able to keep up this travel for very much longer. Nik could carry him for a while, and he would, but there would be a limit to that also. They must hole up somewhere for a rest, and yet, for all their efforts, they were still so close to the refuge, so easily tracked by any pursuers.

The ruins of the old wharves were well behind. When Nik looked up at the one-time shore, he saw that there had been an increase of height there, as if the ancient city had been walled on this side by small mountains. And the cliff to his right soared higher and higher. Its surface was broken by the dark, ragged patches of cave mouths. This once must have been a wild place when the sea battered along those walls. Ahead and not too far away, an arm of the cliff stretched out to bar their present path with a wall of rock, which must mark an old cape dwindling to a reef. And that was a barrier they could not pass in their present fatigue. Somewhere along the broken length of that Nik must find them a temporary refuge which he could turn into a fortress against pursuit.

# NINE

Nik raised his head from his forearm. It was full day, and the steaming heat brought visible curls of vapor from the recently drenched soil until there was a mist lacing the rocks. Back in the shallow cave hole he guarded, Vandy was sleeping in a small measure of coolness. But how long could either of them continue to take the surface atmosphere of Dis?

Both their boots were covered with a red fur of growth, which appeared in patches also on Nik's belt and the ornamental tabs of his tunic. Even though they had washed in pools of rock-held rain water, they could not free their skins from a greasy feel, which carried the sensation of perpetual filthiness. And there was never any chance to be really dry! Clothing continued soggy and almost pulpy to the touch.

The mist was nearly as hindering to the vision as the loss of the cins might be, Nik thought dully. Anything or anyone might be creeping upon them now within its twisting, curling envelope. And he believed that his powers of hearing were also distorted.

So far, their occupancy of the barrier crevice had been challenged by only one creature—a thing of long, jointed legs, the first pair of which had been armed with claws of assorted sizes. Stalked eyes had sighted them and brought the thing scuttling in their direction, but a blaster beam had curled it up wriggling, to kick away its life at the foot of a nearby rock. And since its floppings had subsided, smaller things had cautiously ventured forth to sample a feast they had never expected to enjoy so opportunely.

Its attack had taught Nik the need for wariness. Only there was a limit to endurance, and he had reached it, nodding now into unquiet dozes from which he roused with a start of warning. He would soon have to wake Vandy, to trust the boy not only with a blaster but also with the cin-goggles when he went on sentry duty. And dared Nik do that? What had happened back in the ruins when Vandy had taken off on his own was still in Nik's mind. Had he made plain to the boy the danger of trying such a run? Luckily, Vandy had not shown any interest in the nature of the pursuit Nik expected. But suppose Vandy did believe that those were his father's men back at the refuge. Would he try to return?

Did he believe Nik's explanation of a fight among the men there—a rift in the Guild forces? Vandy had witnessed the landing of the spacers, which could have been the enemy. To place the boy on sentry-go was the same, or could be the same, as inviting him to desert.

However, if Nik waited until he went under from sheer exhaustion, then Vandy would have an easy opportunity to leave, which he might not be so inclined to do if his companion shared some of the responsibility with him. It all depended now on how much of the Hacon influence remained. Vandy had shown signs of breaking with his fantasy several times lately. On the other hand, he also clung to Nik, appealing for help and comfort. Would Nik remain Hacon if Vandy faced in their pursuers someone he knew or would he turn on Nik for what he was now, a kidnaper and an outlaw.

There were two choices, and his brain was too tired to make a clear-headed selection. Either way, Nik might be choosing his own end. But wearily he turned and reached to touch the sleeping boy's leg.

Moments later, blind in the eerie dark of non-goggle sight, Nik stretched out in the hollow between the rocks. He could not even be sure that Vandy was in the lookout, ready to obey orders and arouse Nik at the first sign of any native creature or off-world searchers. He sighed, unable to raise again his weighted eyelids. His last awareness was of the blaster, about the butt of which his fingers tightened.

Muddled dreams haunted him, of which he could remember only a sense of frustration and terror. He came out of them groggily at some urging he was not able to understand at once.

"Hacon!"

Nik sat up, obeying the pull at his shoulder, blinking into a dark broken here and there with feeble touches of a pallid luminescence. Vandy leaned above him.

"Over there!"

But "over there" was still a mystery in the dark for Nik, trying to assemble some measure of wits.

"I can't see—" he protested dully.

"Here!" The goggles came into his hand. He put them on and faced in the direction Vandy indicated.

It was disturbing to have sight return instantly with the aid of those lenses. The reef was clear, sharp as it would be under normal sunlight. Nik looked for what had excited the boy.

"Where—?" he began, and then he saw it! Or rather—them!

Issuing from a rock-bordered crevice well along the reef, fronting what must once have been the waters of the vanished sea, was a trio of creatures. They stood very still, heads aloft, as if facing into the wind and spray of the past. Nik brought up the blaster and sighted on the nearest of that trio, before he noted that there was no stir in their position, that no pull of breath moved their monstrous sides, that the wind did not disturb the thick manes that lay about their massive shoulders.

The watchers were not alive; yet the long-forgotten artist who had created them had given such a semblance of reality to their fashioning as to make deception easy.

In form, they were not unlike the creatures that had surrounded Vandy in the ruins save that they were much larger, majestic in their stance. The black of their bodies was stark against the lighter gray and red of the rocks, and Nik caught a glisten of eye in the one he had originally marked as a target, as if some glittering gem gave it the necessary touch of realism.

Guardians of the coast, symbolically erected to warn off invaders in times past, he wondered? Monument to some ancient feat or victory.

Then Nik started. There—there was something—someone behind the watchers!

A shadow of rock overhung that spot, so that his line of vision was obscured. But, he knew after a moment of study, he had been right—there was something behind the statues. And to see it clearly, he would have to leave their crevice refuge and work his way farther along the reef. He said as much to Vandy.

"But the animals—" the boy protested.

"They look alive, but they are just statues. It's what's behind them counts now—"

"I'm going, too," Vandy declared.

These rocks were nothing to cross without cins, but Nik could not order him to remain. He gave the goggles back for a time, made Vandy survey the stretch they must negotiate, and then resettled them over his own eyes. With Vandy linked by a hold on his belt, Nik began a creeping advance along the weathered reef.

Now, he should be able to see from here—unless the lurker had moved in turn. With caution, Nik braced one arm against a spire of stone and leaned well back to look up at the watchers.

He jerked up his blaster and then hesitated. Again the supreme art of the sculptor or sculptors had deceived his off-world eyes. There was something standing behind the watchers, yes, but it, too, was stone.

Nik blinked, almost gasped. Just seconds earlier there had been no head there! Now there was a black furred one, gazing from that point straight out over the drained sea bottom with much the same fixity of stare as the three giant watchers. But the static pose of that head did not remain. It changed position, turned on the green shoulders, and Nik knew that what he saw was one of the hunters from the ruins mounted on the broken figure as if on lookout duty.

A scout for the hunting pack? If so, this might be the most

dangerous perch he and Vandy could have. To be caught among the broken rocks by those hunters could be disastrous. Did the creature hunt by sight or scent? And how many of its kind would follow it?

Nik flattened himself against the rock spire, whispered a warning to Vandy, and stared about him. Every shadowed crevice was now suspect. But, if they went out into the open sea bottom where there was no cover for the enemy, then he was sure he could hold off any rush by blaster fire. He remembered how the ambush had been set up in the ruins—those eyes that had betrayed the hunter creeping on Vandy from above. Yes, get out—get away from the rocks, which could cover an attack.

But to strike out into the sea bottom itself—As long as they kept the shoreline for a guide, they would not be lost to the general neighborhood of the refuge. Their supplies were gone. The rain pools could provide water, but they had to have food—and Nik had clung to the faint hope that there might be some chance of getting that from some dump at the Guild base. Yes, they could take to the open of the sea bottom but not out so far as to lose contact with the shore as a point of reference.

He glanced again at the figure behind the watchers. Once more the green shoulders were headless. And that fact drove him into action. With Vandy holding to his belt, guided by his instructions, they climbed over the reef and headed out toward the open, where the low growing vegetation could provide no cover for an attack.

Once off the skirts of the reef, the walking was easier, and they moved faster. Nik kept looking back to check their trail. A good view of the watchers and their headless companion could be had from this point, and he had been right about the eyes of the former—they flashed now and then as if they were lighted within. But the shoulders of the green man were bare; the furred scout had not returned.

Luckily, much of the mist and steam that had drifted from the ground earlier had been diffused, and Nik judged the extent of visibility gave him a present advantage over any trailers—from Dis or from the refuge—always providing the latter were not airborne. He set a course that kept to the bottom land just a little to shoreward of that second sharp drop to another one-time sea level.

Below, the runnels of water had fed a lake of some size, though the streamlets themselves were dwindling fast, many leaving only cuts as reminders of their flood courses. And on that lower level the vegetation was even scantier. Hillocks of rock sprouted from the lake's surface, one such rising to a respectable height, and Nik guessed that its crown had once been a true island.

He did not stop his inspection of their back trail. And it was on the third such pause for careful survey that he thought he detected a hint of movement at the base of the reef, as if what lurked there was taking care not to be sighted. The pack on the hunt? Or even an off-world scout of his own species?

"Hacon, is there something to eat?" Vandy waited quietly, not losing his hold on Nik's belt. "I'm hungry."

Nik licked his own lips. The supply tins were back in the tunnel cut. What dared they use of Dis to answer the demands of their bodies for sustaining fuel? He gagged at the thought of attempting to mouth any of the growing stuff about them. Meat—one of those thin-legged, clawed creatures such as had stalked them on the reef? Or one of the furred hunters that might be trailing them? Or something such as that fisher in the dark of the ruins? When it was a choice between life and starvation, a man could stamp down repugnance born of appearance.

"We'll find something." He tried to make that reassuring and knew that he would have to fulfill that promise soon.

There was a screech torturing to his off-world ears. Vandy cried out, his eyes straining to pierce the dim, but Nik saw clearly. Not so far ahead there was a commotion on the verge of the rain lake below. Winged things flapped and fought over a surface that was ruffled and dimpled in turn, as if some life form wallowed and swam. One of the fliers made a dive into the center of the disturbance and arose, uttering harsh squawks of what might have been triumph, since it carried in its claws writhing, scaled prey.

Two of the flier's fellows followed it aloft, harassing it as if to make it drop its capture, rather than trying a catch on their own. The successful hunter dodged, screamed, and skimmed just above the surface of the higher level, while its tormentors harried it with determination.

One soared and then made a sudden swoop, deadly intention in every beat of its sustaining leathery wings. The attacked made a futile effort to evade and crashed into the companion pursuer. There was a squawking, screeching whirl of fighting fliers falling fast to the ground. The prey the first had raped from the lake was loosed.

The airborne battle had swept close to the place where Nik and Vandy stood. And the twisting, turning captive fell only a little away. That third combatant, which had delivered the attack from above, avoided the struggling fighters that had also struck the ground and were still clawing at each other. It swooped above Nik as if some of its fury had been transferred to the man.

Almost in reflex action, he fired the blaster, catching the flier full on. The force of the ray blast carried the creature back so that it fell, already dead, over the cliff to the lake level. Then weapon still in hand, Nik strode forward to inspect the cause of battle.

It was still flopping feebly, but even as he came up, it straightened out and was still. Though its body was weirdly elongated, it bore some resemblance to a fish, enough so that Nik picked it up.

One of the battlers had left the other and came scuttling across the ground screeching, its long neck outstretched, its narrow head darting back and forth with a jerky vehemence. One wing was held at a queer angle, and there was blood smearing its torn body.

Nik jumped to the left, and the creature sped on, seemingly unable to change course—to plunge over the cliff like the flier before it.

"Hacon! Hacon, what was it? What are those things? What are they doing?" Vandy's voice was shrill. To him, the struggle must have been frightening, carried on in the dark.

Swiftly Nik explained. He was still holding the fish, and now he let Vandy examine it by touch.

"Is it good to eat, Hacon?"

"It could be." Nik hesitated. Anything put in their mouths on

Dis might be rank poison, but they had to start somewhere, and perhaps that was here and now.

"How do we cook it?" Vandy continued.

"We don't," Nik replied shortly.

"Eat it—like this?" Vandy faltered. He almost dropped the limp body.

"If we have to, yes. But not here and now." Nik was hungry, and even the thought of eating a Disian fish raw did not diminish that hunger. But he had no intention of consuming it here, when they could be the focus of attack from other predators. He took the fish from Vandy and hooked it into one of his belt attachments, one that was free of any phosphorescence.

As they skirted the cliff, they saw other turmoil in the lake and witnessed the fishing of other fliers. The winged creatures appeared reluctant to touch water in taking their prey. Only a few dared that, as if the lake held some menace they feared.

The lake itself stretched along the second cliff edge, lapping the outcroppings of the irregular ground. The surface on which Vandy and Nik traveled was sloping down with indications of eventually merging with the lower level, while the cliffs of the one-time shore were rising.

Nik made another cast behind. And this time the pursuers were not so careful to keep concealed. A furred hunter stood over the flier killed in combat by its fellow. It nosed the body and then began to eat.

"Hurry—!" Nik caught at Vandy, pulling the boy along. Ahead he could see one of the island hillocks, though this must have been a mere dot of island in the days when the sea washed this land. The light was less than it had been when they had left the reef. Nik did not doubt that the day's end was coming. And at night that hillock might mean safety. Perched up there, they would have defense against anything that would climb to attack.

Another glance showed him that a second hunter had joined the first at the feast. Unlike the fliers, the first did not attempt to drive off or attack his fellow but moved a little to one side, allowing the newcomer a chance at the food. This was odd enough to make Nik wonder. Cooperation in feeding, as well as hunting, suggested a higher form of consciousness than the fliers, who tore each other for the prey. The hunters were smaller editions of those three magnificent watchers on the headland. They had been esteemed by the original natives of Dis to the point that infinite care had been taken to establish highly artistic representations of their species on a prominent place before the city. Animals that had been sacred to the one-time rulers of this world? Pets—protection?

"I can't go—so—fast—" Vandy stammered. He stumbled and nearly fell.

Nik, eaten by the need for some form of shelter before the coming of what was a double dark, caught him up and kept on. They were directly below the island hill. He struggled up and on, finally pulling out on an expanse of rock ledge below a sharp crest. He pushed Vandy back against that crest and looked back.

There were the furred hunters, still eating, and still only the two of them in sight. If they were scouts for a pack, the rest had not yet caught up. Now, Nik got to his feet and turned slowly to get a good look at what lay about them. To his right was the rain lake, to his left a dip and then the cliff of the old shore.

Anything trying to reach their present perch must either swim the lake and then wind up an almost sheer drop or come up the same way he and Vandy had used, to be met by blaster fire. They had their refuge for the night, as safe a one as he could devise.

Nik sat down and unhooked the fish from his belt. Methodically, he cleaned it and cut the whole into portions. They would now try the provender of Dis.

# TEN

"Vandy! Vandy!"

Nik held the boy, wondering whether that violent retching would ever stop, whether the convulsions that shook the small body could be endured for long, his feeling of guilt rising like an answering sickness within him. He had never witnessed such a terrible attack of nausea before. It was as if the few bites of fish Vandy had taken had been virulent poison; yet they had had no similar effect on Nik.

Vandy lay limp now, moaning a little, and Nik hesitated. Should he try to get him to drink some water or would that bring on another attack? He feared another such violent upheaval might be truly dangerous. There was nothing he *could* do for Vandy—no medicine he could offer. Back at the refuge—

Back at the refuge—to return there—If Vandy's people had led the attack, or the Patrol—But suppose the other possibility was the truth, that the struggle had been some inter-Guild dispute? Or was Nik clinging to that merely because it was what he wanted to believe for his own safety? Vandy's head rolled on Nik's shoulder; the boy's breathing was heavy, labored.

In spite of the night, with the cin-goggles, he could start now, carry Vandy, retrace their journey, and find the hunters waiting out there while he was too burdened with the boy to make a fighting stand. Nik bit his lip and tried to think clearly. This could be only a passing illness for Vandy; the boy could have an allergy to the strange food. And to be caught by the hunters—

Perhaps to wait right here until any trailers from the refuge came would be the wise move. Nik could remain with Vandy until he saw them coming, then leave the boy to be found, always providing those trackers were friendly to Vandy. And he honestly doubted he could get far carrying the boy.

How long had that sound been reaching his ears without his being conscious of it? Nik shifted Vandy's body to free his right hand for the blaster. It came from the down side of their island hill where the rain lake washed—a splashing, not just the normal rippling of wind-ruffled water lapping the shoreline.

Nik inched along the ledge, hoping to see what lay below. And it was not too difficult to make out a bulk floundering there, not swimming, but wading through shallows, staggering now and then, once going to its knees and rising with an exclamation.

A man!

Nik stiffened, watched. By all he could discover, the wader was alone. Coming in that direction, he could well be from the flitter that had fled the refuge in the last moments of battle.

The man reached the shore of the rain lake and steadied himself with one outflung hand against a rock. He looked up as if searching the island hill for hand holds. Cin-goggles made a mask to conceal his face, but this was not Orkhad or any of his race.

Plainly, the stranger decided the rise before him unclimbable. He began to move along it, still supporting himself with one hand against the rock wall. Now that he was free of the water, Nik saw he was limping, pausing now and again as if the effort to keep moving was a heavy one.

He neared the place where Nik and Vandy had climbed. Would that tempt him also? Vandy was quiet. Carefully, Nik laid him down against the crest that crowned the hill. He waited in silence for the stranger's next move.

"Hacon?"

Startled, Nik glanced, at Vandy, but that had not come from the boy. The low hail sounded from below! And only one person other than Vandy would have called him by that name. Eagerly Nik leaned over the edge of the ledge and stared down at that goggle-masked, upturned face.

"Captain Leeds!"

"In person. But not quite undamaged. In fact, I don't believe I can make that perch of yours without a hand up—and we may all need a perch soon!"

"They're after you?"

"Oh, not the Patrol, if that's what you mean. No, this mismade hell world has its own hunters, and a couple of them have been sniffing up my trail for longer than I care to remember."

Nik scrambled down the slope. The captain's hand fell on his arm, and he gave support to the other's weight.

"You're hurt badly?"

"Wrenched my leg when I took a tumble some distance back there. Couldn't favor it much after I fought off that night lizard. Knew the rest of its clutch would be coming. And they were—at least two of them! You have any arms at all?"

"Two blasters. Don't know how much charge they have left."

"Two blasters—that's about the most comforting news I've had since I lifted off Korwar. Talk about luck—we've got a lot of it now—mostly all bad.

"First, that Patrol snoop ray picked me up on the big orbit in; then they were able to slam three ships after me before my rocket tubes had cooled. Feel as if I've been doing nothing but running for days now. Give us a hand *up*—"

Somehow, they made it up, but Nik sensed that Leeds must be close to the end of his strength. The captain gave a grunt as Nik settled him on their perch, but a moment later he crawled back to the edge and examined the terrain below.

"Couldn't have picked it better myself, boy. Any crawler trying to claw us out of here can only come up this way, and we'll burn out his engine before he gets within clawing distance. What's wrong with the boy here?" He looked back at Vandy.

Nik explained about the disastrous meal of Disian fish.

"No off-world supplies, eh?" Leeds asked.

"No. I left the containers I had back at the tunnel break." Hurriedly, Nik outlined the main points of their flight for Leeds.

"That's going to complicate matters," the captain said. "Vandy's conditioned—"

"Conditioned?" Nik repeated uncomprehendingly.

"I told you, he is conditioned all the way—against going with strangers, against everything that would make it easy to lift him out of HS."

"But he ate what was in those rations without trouble."

"Those are LB supplies—emergency food. No one of Terran ancestry can be conditioned against those. It's an elementary precaution rigidly kept. Suppose Vandy's spacer had been wrecked on the way to Korwar—there would be a chance of escape by LB. So he could eat LB rations. Now, he can't eat anything else—on this world."

"But—" Nik realized the futility of his protest. Without LB rations, Vandy would starve. And the LB rations, the cans he had driven into the wall of that cut to serve as a stairway and then abandoned thoughtlessly, were far behind. Those containers meant Vandy's life—unless there were other supplies he could tap.

"Yes"—Leeds pushed back from the rim of the ledge to set his shoulders against the crest rise—"it presents a problem, doesn't it? But there is a solution. Vandy's our way out of here."

"How?" Nik demanded.

"The Patrol—they've taken the refuge. Probably some scout squad is out there now hunting down my flitter. They'll track me here, and then—then we'll have our bargaining point, Vandy for our freedom. Boy, you gave both of us about the best break in this whole bungled job when you lit out with Vandy. Him for us—my spacer, free air out of here—Yes, I thought you were a gift from Lady Luck; now I know that's the truth! We have the boy—so all our comets slid over their stars on the table. You ever play star and comet, Nik?"

"No."

"Well, it's a game of chance they tell you—sure, it is. But there's skill to it—real skill—and most of that lies in selecting the right opponents and knowing just how far they're ready to plunge in answer to any bet you're reckless enough to make. I know how far the Patrol will go to get Vandy back—and it's pretty near all the way. He's about the most important pawn in a big-system game going on right now, so much so that the orders from our top were to erase him—"

"Erase him?" Nik echoed.

"Sure, the Guild deal was to take him out of the game permanently. These Gallardi—they're very family and bloodline conscious. The boy's father is the warlord who's holding the key stronghold on Ebo. To wipe out his family line would mean he would then make some suicide play—"

"But Vandy's father is dead—" Nik said bewildered. His hand was at his chin, cupping the firm bone and smooth flesh he needed for reassurance. Leeds' story, which had bought him that face—

"On the contrary, Jerrel Naudhin i'Arkrama was very much alive the last I heard. At least, he was to Lik Iskhag, which was the important point as far as the Guild was concerned. Iskhag paid to have the Naudhin i'Akrama line finished—"

"Then the story you told me—"

Leeds shrugged impatiently. "Was a story, a good one. I didn't know I had it in me to do a regular tape-type tale. Only now it's all worked out for the best, anyway. We can use Vandy to get out of here. And—believe me, Nik—I had my own ideas about the boy and this erase order all the time. Of course, his being conditioned meant trouble, but he could have been kept under wraps until Iskhag got what he paid for—the surrender of the garrison on Ebo. Then Vandy could have been turned loose. I don't hold with erasing children any more than you do. Orkhad's being here wasn't part of the plan as I was told it, either. But maybe it was good that he was—he made you take to the hills, and that certainly saved Vandy. Now, all we have to do is wait for the Patrol to get a direction on us and argue it out—"

"And if they do come," Nik asked, "do you plan to turn the boy over to them on their word to carry out their bargain?"

Leeds laughed. "No—I'm no fool, and neither do I think you're one, Nik. We get the spacer and free air, Vandy going with us. Outside, we put him in a suit with a beeper and space him. They can easily pick him up on a directional signal. And by the time they've retrieved him, we're in the clear and long gone. The plan isn't completely free of a misfire, but it's the best chance we have now."

"And if they don't find us, Vandy has to have food." Nik stated the immediate problem. Leeds had talked a lot, and he wanted to think it over.

The captain moved his shoulders against the rock support.

"Yes, let me think about that. I took a jump from the flitter, and she fire-smashed out there. The emergency rations on board must have gone up with the machine. Those you left back in the cut seem our best chance now. Of course, the Patrol might already have prowled that area and found your trail. But it's still the quickest way—"

"You mean—I go after them?"

"Seeing as how I can probably not even make it down from this ledge again for a while, I'd say you are Vandy's only chance of getting some food in the immediate future. If you are picked up by the Patrol, you still have your chance, and a good one. I'll be here with the boy, and I'll swear by anything you want that any bargain I'll make is for the both of us! That's the truth. I wouldn't be in any position to bargain if I didn't have Vandy. And who gave him to me—you did! We get out together. And if you are netted, you tell the truth—that you know where Vandy is and that he will be delivered safe and sound on our terms. Anyway, we're small fry in this as far as the Patrol is concerned. They want Iskhag, those behind *him*, the man who made the bargain in the first place. You can say I'll give some help in that direction—I don't like the erase plan enough to cover up for those who gave such an order.

"But you may be really lucky and get in and out of there without getting caught, or least only picking up a tracker, and if you do that, it will be just what we want, anyhow."

Leeds leaned over to touch Vandy's forehead.

"Guess he's asleep now, but you can tell them if they pick you up, that he's none too happy. Could just hurry the whole matter along, and that would suit us all."

Nik sat quietly. Again everything Leeds said made good sense, good sense if you accepted his new story and its logic. But to do so meant leaving Vandy here with Leeds—the two of them alone—and going straight back into trouble himself. And how could he be sure that this story was any more the truth than that other this same man had told him back on Korwar? Perhaps Leeds had followed that same thought, for now the captain said:

"Nik, you're rubbing that face of yours. Still smooth and real, isn't it? Mightn't be for long—remember? Of course, maybe Gyna did a lasting job, but she said the odds were against that. You want to go back to the Dipple and no face?"

"But if we get out of here, the Guild won't do anything for someone who has helped to spoil a job." Nik had found the flaw in that argument.

For a moment, he thought he had Leeds, but the silence did not last long enough to suggest that the captain did not have a ready reply.

"This was a job split—don't you think that an erase on a child has blast backs at the top? I had *my* backers, too—and you did just what you promised, brought Vandy here. The minute you landed on Dis, you'd done your part. Most of this mix-up was Orkhad's doing, and he was being watched already from above. You played straight, and that makes it a Guild promise for you. Just let us get off-world, and you'll keep your face. But if we sit this out too long or fail—" He shook his head slowly. "So, you see you have a big stake in this, too. You kept your part of the bargain; the Guild will keep theirs."

In the end, it all added up to just one sum, Nik saw, and that was his job. Vandy could not live without food; the nearest available food was back at the refuge. Leeds was too injured to make the trip, so Nik had to go. He looked out at the back trail.

Even with the goggles, the Disian night was too dark for him to see much, and there were hunters in that dark. He was tired from the long day's travel, and a tired man makes errors of judgment, is duller of sight and hearing. It was not going to be easy, and he wanted every possible advantage on his side.

"I'll go—in the morning."

"Fair enough!" Leeds moved against his back support. "No use going it blind. Maybe we'll be lucky and they'll reach us by then."

Vandy rolled over. "Hacon—" His voice was a husky whisper.

"Here," Nik answered quickly.

"I'm thirsty—"

Leeds pulled a canteen from his belt. "Filled this down there at the lake. Give him a pull."

Nik supported the boy with one arm and held the canteen to his lips whale Vandy drank in gulps. Then he pushed the container away.

"I hurt," he said, "right here." His hand moved across his midsection. "Guess I was pretty sick."

"Yes," Nik agreed. "You try to get some sleep now, Vandy."

But the boy had struggled up a little. "There's someone else here." His head swung around toward Leeds, and his eyes were wide and staring. "There is, isn't there!" That was more demand than question.

"Yes," Nik told him. "Captain Leeds' flitter crashed out there. He just got here."

"Captain Leeds," Vandy repeated. "He's one of them, one of the men back in that tunnel place—"

"Not one of those who were there, Vandy. He's the one we've been waiting for."

Vandy pawed at Nik's arm and strove to raise himself higher.

"He's one of them!" That was accusation rather than recognition.

"No." Nik thought fast. If Vandy looked upon the captain as his enemy, he would not be willing to remain here while Nik backtracked in the morning. "No." He repeated that denial with all the firmness he could summon. "Captain Leeds was trying to find us, to get us out of here. He *is* a friend, Vandy."

"But he's one of them back there—"

"He only pretended to be, Vandy." Nik sought wildly for a plausible explanation. "He was coming here to help us; that's why we were hiding out here. Remember? We were waiting for Captain Leeds. And he was driven out by them, too. He's been hurt and can't walk far—"

"Hacon." Vandy turned in Nik's hold, his eyes now striving to the other's face above him. "You swear that—by the Three Words?"

All that past Vandy had created for his chosen companion tightened around Nik. Vandy's faith was not that of Nik Kolherne nor of the Dipple, but it was a firm bastion for him, and he had made it a part of the world he had imagined for Hacon. Now Nik found his indoctrination in that fantasy had brought a measure of belief to him. He dared not hesitate, but as he answered, he knew the bitterness of his lie.

"I swear it—by the Three Words!" His left hand at his face pressed tight enough against the rebuilt flesh to bring pain. Hacon's face—and to Vandy he was Hacon.

"Believe him now, Vandy?" Leeds asked, his voice holding the same light, cheerful note that Nik had heard in it at their earlier meetings. "It's true. I came here to help the two of you. But I ran into more trouble than I expected, so now I'm tied to this perch of yours for a while. We'll have to hold this garrison together for Hacon—"

"Hacon!" Vandy's fingers were a tight grasp on him. "Where are you going?"

"As soon as day comes, I'm scouting." Nik had no idea whether or not Vandy was aware of his conditioning. At least, the boy had not mentioned it when Nik had urged the fish on him. And if he did not know, there was no good reason to frighten him when off-world supplies were still out of reach.

"But why?" Vandy was protesting, his tight clutch on Nik continuing.

"Because Captain Leeds may have been trailed. We need to know just how much trouble to expect." That was thin but the best Nik could concoct at that moment.

"Yes, just to scout and to pick up some supplies I cached when my leg gave out," Leeds added with his usual facility for invention.

"Oh." A little of that desperate grip lessened, and Vandy's head fell back on Nik's arm. "In the morning—not now?"

"In the morning," Nik agreed, "not now."

# ELEVEN

Nik fought a desire to turn and look back at the island hillock. The humid air was thick about him, though the storm streams had drained away, leaving only the cuts of their passage in the old sea bed. There was no sunrise visible on this cloud-shrouded planet, but the steam mists of the day before were not so thick, most of them confined to the yet lower level where the rain lake lay. He could see ahead and around enough to mark any lizard such as Leeds had fled from or the furred things out of the ruins.

As he went, Nik tried to imagine what Dis had been like before the sun flare had steamed up the seas and rivers and wracked the very bones of the planet with quakes and eruptions. It had always, of course, been a dim world by the standards of his own species. But to its natives, the infrared sun must have been as clear as the yellow-white stars were normal to Nik's kind. And it had been a civilized world, judging by the ruins. The high quality of art shown in the statues of the watchers and their humanoid companion testified to the height of that civilization.

Disians had tried to escape the wrath of their heavens by retreat to the refuge. Had any survivors lingered on in those prepared depths to waver forth again into a ruined outer world?

Did any still exist anywhere on Dis? Nik had tried to pry out of Leeds during the early hours of the night some information concerning this planet, knowing that any scrap might mean, by force of circumstances, life or death for him. But the captain had said, "I don't know," to most of his questions.

Dis's first discovery had one of those by-chance things. A Free Trader before the war, threatened by a power leakage, had streaked for the nearest planet recorded on their instruments and set down here. And because it was a Free Trader and not a Survey ship that had made the discovery, there had been no official report, the Traders seeing a profit in their knowledge. Traders formerly dealt with the Guild on occasion when that organization had a quasi-legal standing or when there was no chance of being drawn into trouble by such contact. Thus Dis had become an article of trade.

Leeds' own exploration had brought him knowledge of the refuge and had given the Guild an excellent base hideout—a hideout, Nik gathered, although Leeds was evasive on that point, within cruising distance of several systems in which the Guild had extensive dealings. But once the refuge had been stocked and was in use, the rest of Dis's outer shell was of little or no interest to the outlaws. In fact, they had a kind of horror of it built up by several accidents and encounters with its native fauna, which led them to use it to discipline any rebels. Being set loose on the surface without cin-goggles or weapons was an ultimate punishment.

So—only a small portion of Dis was known to those who used it. Were it not that Vandy was conditioned, they could have taken to the outlands and been safe. Safe from whom, another part of Nik questioned. The Patrol was here to get Vandy, to return him to his people. No, Vandy did not need to hide out in the wilds. That was Nik's portion and Leeds'. Yet the captain was so sure they could strike a bargain for their own benefit.

Nik had been seeing it for several moments before he realized that a bush to his left and ahead was not quite right. Right? Why did he think that? He paused and surveyed the growth closely for a moment or two until he understood what made the difference. It was the color! All the fungoid vegetation he had seen was, to some degree, phosphorescent, with a wan gleam of green or red. This bush had a warmer, yellow tinge.

And—

The color moved!

The yellow had been close to the ground on the left side at first, but it was now halfway up and in the middle, while the first portion had faded to wan glow. Now, the yellow was on the right!

It was not a question of a change in color—Nik was certain of that. But something behind the bush or within its fleshy branches had moved from one position of concealment to another, always keeping well under cover.

Nik tried an experiment. He circled back a little to the left, heading in a direction to take him to the back of the bush. Would the lurker move to face him? Yes! The glow turned with him almost at ground level, keeping pace with him.

Why the presence of that color should be so disturbing, Nik could not have explained. Was it because the source never came into view? Was that thing in ambush aware Nik was able to see it? Perhaps it did now guess because of his own movements.

He looked from the bush in question to others of its kind ahead and saw what he feared and expected. Three of those growths had the betraying glow. To avoid them, he would have to advance to the very edge of the drop to the next level. He could not bring himself to approach any closer to what might be a trap.

There was the blaster. He could here and now burn that nearest bush and its inhabitant into charred powder, but to attack heedlessly was no answer either. He held the weapon ready as he started along the cliff rim.

It was then that Nik heard the whistle, a piping call that was like a throb of pain beginning in his head and running along his nerves to make his flesh tingle. Three times that shattering call came. Now the lights in the bushes were steady; all faced him. Nik knew the menace of a before-attack. Were these the furred hunters? He did not believe so. But what?

To keep on along the edge of the drop now was to expose himself to a rush. But how else dared he advance?

It was coming—now! How Nik knew that, he could not have told. But he leaped into an open space where any attackers would be exposed to blaster fire.

The bushes shook, spilling the lurkers into sight. They came scuttling, at first on hands and knees. Then, from a crouch, they launched themselves at him—or two of them did, while three remained in reserve. Nik had expected animals, but these—these were men!

"No!" He heard his own involuntary cry, but the others ran mute.

And he saw that he was not confronting new refugees from the Guild base or Patrol scouts. These were naked, thin ghostly creatures. The foremost carried a club in the head of which had been set a row of ugly projections. His companion held a stone as big as his own head.

They sped toward the off-worlder, their eyes agleam with a terrible insanity. Nik fired, almost without consciously willing that push of the finger. The club carrier went down, and at the same time that throb of a whistle beat in Nik's brain and made his hands quiver and shake.

The second attacker stopped short when his companion fell. He retreated a step or two to stand over his body. His head swung from side to side, his nostrils expanding visibly as if to soak up some necessary scent.

On his bare body the glowing skin was stretched over a rack of bones. And there was no trace of hair on face, head, or body. The features on the face now swinging back toward Nik were roughly human, though the nose was very wide and flat, the nostrils large pits. The mouth was also wide; the lips were thin, rolled back in a snarl to display large, sharp teeth, while the eyes were sunk back into the skull, difficult to see in their twin caverns.

The stranger dropped his stone weapon, tossing it carelessly aside, where it was speedily pounced upon by one of the smaller lurkers. He wrested the club from the flaccid fingers of the dead one and swung it once or twice, as if testing its balance.

Nik tensed, waiting for a second rush, but the other made no move to renew hostilities. He backed away toward the bushes, keeping a wary eye on Nik, his three companions going to ground more quickly. Then as suddenly as they had appeared, they were gone, leaving the dead behind.

Who—or what? Nik knew of the prisoners who had been driven out of the refuge. But surely, humanoid though these creatures appeared, they were not of off-world stock! He marked their going in the bush glow, but they did not retreat far. Those betraying patches of light squatted, each in a hiding place, along the path he must take. Whatever the purpose of that attack, it had not been abandoned as far as the Disians were concerned. But they would not try a second rush into blaster fire.

Should he detour down to the second level of the sea bottom and climb again when he reached the old seaport? There was no reason to fear the outcome, even if all four rushed him; yet Nik shrank from a second battle. Whatever or whoever the strangers were, they were human enough to seem remotely of his kind. And to meet a club and a stone with a blaster was sheer butchery in Nik's mind. At the same time, he did not doubt that the Disians had no parallel qualms. Did they know that a body light revealed them to him, or were they unaware of that disadvantage?

Nik studied the ground ahead. The growth of vegetation that favored the concealment of the strangers did not extend too far. If he could keep on along the cliff edge and so come in to the open, he might avoid another encounter.

He broke into a trot, covering that area of inherent peril with what speed he could. Such exertion in this humidity left him gasping, staggering a little, as he burst into the welcome open. With one hand pressed against his laboring chest, he looked behind. The lights—they were moving again, not directly after him but for the cliff face of the old shoreline. He stood watching those now distant figures break from the brush cover and begin to climb the wall with the agility of those who had performed that particular maneuver before. Had they abandoned the chase?

No goggles on their faces—they *must* be native to this world! Were they degenerate remnants of the race that had fashioned the refuge, survivors of the catastrophe that had wrecked Dis? Goggles—Nik's hand went up to touch the ones he wore. Those were a very fragile hold on life. Just suppose he were to break or lose the cins—he would be easy prey for even a club man then. He drew a ragged breath and tried to quiet the pounding of his labored heart.

There ahead was where the winged fighters had battled over their prey, and that far the furred hunters had come. Nik examined the ground carefully. There was no cover he could detect large enough to screen one of the furred beasts, but he kept the blaster in his hand. As he turned to set out, he caught a last glimpse of the Disians. The club man was near the top of the cliff, and he, in turn, was looking down at Nik, watching the off-worlder with intent interest. Then his glowing body was up and over that last rise, and he was gone. But Nik had a strong feeling he was not abandoning the chase.

A pile of well-cleaned bones marked the place where the furred hunters had feasted, but there was no other sign of them. Nik forged ahead. He was in comparatively clear territory here, and his next landmark was the reef, though that was yet a good journey beyond. From there the climb into the city ruins—The city ruins! If there ever was a perfect place to lay an ambush, it was there—right there.

Nik tried to remember what he had seen of the ruins, to think whether there was some other way around them to reach the tunnel break of the refuge. But he was afraid that if he avoided the obvious landmarks, he might become hopelessly lost. There was something frightening about launching out into the open sea bottom away from the old shoreline. With those cliffs at hand, the reef ahead, he had a sense of security, of knowing in part what he could expect. He decided that he would retrace the path he and Vandy had taken earlier.

The coarse, gravelly soil slipped and slid under his boots as it had not earlier. He guessed that the moisture had drained out of it, leaving it the texture of sand, making walking just that much harder. His lungs still labored to separate air from the dankness, and he cut his pace.

There was no more commotion in the rain lake below. There were no winged fishers, no signs of turmoil in the waters, which had receded a goodly distance from where they had been at the end of the storm. In the midst of one such dry part, a glint caught Nik's attention, and he wavered to a stop. This was tangled wreckage, not a rock outcrop. It was something fashioned long ago by intelligence—a ship, surface or air transportation of some kind. Metal had gone into its making and gave back now that sullen glint of light.

It was still in sight when Nik knocked over a small creature with a thrown stone. He found himself holding a limp body with rudimentary leather wing flaps stretching between its front and rear legs, and that body was scaled. Trying not to think of its alien form, he skinned and cleaned it. Then he choked down mouthfuls of the rank-tasting flesh. Food was fuel, and fuel his body needed; he could not be dainty in his eating.

On again—the reef was ahead, and in the reef he would shelter by nightfall, preferring it to the ruins. He could not do without sleep forever. It was getting harder to think clearly. Nik halted, his hand going to his head. That throb! It was like something—the whistle call of the Disians!

Slowly, staggering a little, he turned about to view the cliff top to his left. Rock—that was all, just rock. No club wielder was climbing down again. But the muddle in his head—that throb which was more pain than sound—

The reef—he would get to the reef and hole up there. It was darkening; it must be close to the day's end. He could see the reef, a black streak across the dull sea bottom. Nik wavered on, the gritty soil slipping under his feet so that once he fell to one knee and found it difficult to scramble up again.

He feared a return of that throb in his head, shrinking from the very thought of it. His hand shook so that he had to belt hook the blaster. Was he sick from that food he had forced into him as Vandy had been sick the night before? There was something wrong—very wrong—

Once Nik swung around to go back, back to the island hill and Leeds and Vandy. But then he knew that he could not make it. It would be better to reach the reef and rest there. The crevice in which he and Vandy had sheltered beckoned him. Just get there and rest—rest—His hand wiped back and forth across his face. Once that movement pushed aside the goggles, and he cried out in fear as his sight was distorted. He was no longer truly conscious of what was happening to him, only that apprehension was clouding his mind and that the thought of the hiding hole in the reef kept him moving.

The rest of that day was a haze for Nik. But he roused when he lurched up against a rock and looked a little stupidly at a wall of them. He had reached the reef, he thought foggily. The reef—safety—rest—If he could only crawl a little farther!

There were bright glints of light—or eyes, eyes watching—waiting—assessing his fatigue, his bemused mind? Was it that additional prick of fear that pulled Nik farther out of the fog? Something gave him power enough to drag himself up, along the rocks, heading for the pocket he remembered.

He kicked away something that rattled against the stone and saw a claw-tipped bone flip up and away from his stumbling feet—the remains of the crawler he had blasted before their crevice camp. So, he was almost there now.

The glint of eyes—they were still at a distance. His sobbing breaths beat in his own ears, so that he could not hear anything that might be creeping up for the kill.

Just a little farther. Now—hold on to this rock, pull up to the next, an irregular stairway to the crevice. He reeled back against the very boulder where he had kept sentry two days earlier.

Once more he drew blaster fumblingly and laid it on the rock. His hands still shook, but he could use both of them to bring that weapon into play against the eyes—

A small part of Nik's mind was aroused enough now to wonder at his present half collapse. There was no real reason for him to be so exhausted, so dazed. Ever since that whistling when he had encountered the Disians—Nik rubbed his hand across his forehead, pressing the goggles painfully against his skin. No, he must not disturb those! He jerked his fingers away.

He was so tired that he could not keep his feet—yet those waiting eyes—Sobbing a little, Nik wedged himself erect, dimly thinking that any attack would be limited to a narrow front he could defend. But how long could he continue to keep watch?

His head fell forward; he was floating—floating on a shifting mist that enfolded, engulfed him, spun him out and out—

Pain throbbed from his head down into his back and arms.

Nik's head snapped up and back and struck against stone with shock enough to bring him out of that mist. The throb—but he was alert enough to see the thing working its way among the rocks, a shadow advancing from deeper shadows. He clutched the blaster and tried to press the firing button.

The ray shot across the top of the barrier dock. It missed the creeper but sent it into retreat. Nik dragged himself forward. He had to meet what was coming in the open. He had to!

His forward effort succeeded. Eyes—yes, there were the eyes again—one pair, two, more—He could not count them now—they spun, danced, jerked about in a crazy pattern when he tried to watch.

Nik cried out as another throb burst in his head. All those eyes—they were uniting into one! No! He was wrong—not eyes but a light! An honest light—not of Dis—He had only to follow that to safety.

He pushed away from the rock and crept around, angry that his body obeyed his will so sluggishly. He must hurry, must run to the light that meant an end to nightmares—only let him reach the light!

# TWELVE

The light was receding!

"Wait!" Nik got that out in a cry close to a scream.

And it appeared that the light did steady. He was far past wondering about its source. He believed only that it spelled safety. But his feet would not obey his will. He fell heavily, then tried to force his body up again, his attention all for the light.

Shouting—Through the fog in his head, he thought he could hear words, understandable words—yet they were too far away, too confused to count as did the light. Nik began to crawl.

He was close, too close, when the enchantment of the light failed, when he fronted the horror behind that mask. A Disian! Nik had a momentary glimpse of a naked body rising from behind another form, a dense, hairy blot from which wavered and sparkled the light. A memory, so vague that Nik could not hold it, came and went in a second—a fisher that used light for bait? When and where?

Then he was overborne by the attack, smelled the reek of alien body scent, and was pinned flat to the ground under the full weight of the other's spring. Nik struggled feebly against that hold, but there was no escape. And always the throb in his head and body grew stronger until he shook and quivered with its beat.

The weight on his back and shoulders was suddenly still, so still that one of Nik's squirms detached its hold. He made a greater effort and tried to pull free. The Disian collapsed in a limp tangle of limbs, still half pinning Nik, but from under which he was able to crawl. He sat up and strove to find the blaster, but his groping hand encountered only empty hooks. Had he had it when he left the rocks? He could not remember.

He jerked his feet from under the flaccid sprawl of the Disian. Why the other had gone down was beyond Nik's reasoning now. But that he had another chance, small as it might be, penetrated enough to send him scrabbling, still on hands and knees, back from that spot.

Things flowed up from the reef rocks, seeming to grow out of the ground about—creatures that could not have life, that were out of off-world nightmares or of Vandy's fantasies with which they had clogged his brain! Nik was the focus of a weird, menacing ring, and the ring was drawing in.

Nik gave a shriek of pure terror, pushed for a second almost over the border of sanity. He screamed again, but he also threw himself at the nearest of those monsters, driven to meet it rather than to wait for its spring. Raking claws in his face—pain—

How far can one retreat from horror into oneself? Was it exhausted sleep that held Nik or a kind of withdrawal from what he could not face? He came out of that suspension little by little, with a reluctance of which he was quite aware.

And because of that reluctance, he did not dare to move, to try to use his mind or his senses, lest he find himself back again in that circle of monstrous life.

How soon did that first small hint of reason awake? When did he note that the air he was drawing into his lungs was not water-soaked so that he must labor to get a full breath? How long had it been since he had breathed so effortlessly—and felt this cool and dry?

Or was this all part of some dream that would make the waking that much the worse for him? But perhaps it was the air that was clearing his mind as well as his lungs.

Fresh air—the refuge! He was back in the refuge, and with that guess he unlocked memory. But, the refuge was in the hands of the enemy—which meant he was now a prisoner.

For the first time, Nik willed his hand to move, only to panic when no muscle obeyed. This was not like the sapped exhaustion of his last confused recollection—this was a new helplessness. And once before he had been so frozen—when Leeds had taken him captive in the Dipple! He was a prisoner all right!

Now, as at that previous time, Nik tried to make his ears serve to give him some idea of his surroundings. The swish-swish of the air was easy to identify. But there were other sounds, too, some close, some distant, He heard a clicking in regular pattern, and he thought it marked the action of some machine or installation. Then there was another sound, followed by the snap of space boot plate soles hitting the floor. Someone was walking, not toward him, however. That snapping drew farther away. Was he alone now or were there others in the room? The swish of air covered any sound of breathing.

So, he was a prisoner in stass—which meant his body was pinned here helplessly—but his mind was no longer blanked out. How much of the immediate past was illusion and how much truth? He had certainly reached the reef and then been drawn out of that poor safety by the light. And the Disians had done that.

Then—what had happened? The blackout of his Disian attacker—did Nik owe that to his present captors? Had they witnessed that battle and saved him for their own purposes? There was logic in that.

So the Patrol had him. But they wanted Vandy, and there was a time limit on Vandy, giving Nik a talking point—unless they had already backtracked on him and made their own deal with Leeds—

Nik's mouth was very dry; he tried to flex his lips, to move his tongue, without success. This stass was complete.

There—more footfalls, and now the murmur of voices, voices speaking Basic, one with an accent.

This time the steps came up to where he lay—two people, Nik was sure.

There was silence for a long moment. They must be studying him—trying to learn if he had aroused to consciousness yet.

"Amazing—" That was the accented voice. "The one thing we did not foresee."

There was a sharp answering sound, which might have been an exclamation of anger or even a laugh without much humor.

"We long ago discovered, Commander, that there is so often something unforeseen. Perfection is an ending very far in the future, if we ever reach that state. No, this was hardly to be foreseen, but it worked—very well, if we are to judge by the results we have had to face so far. You've seen the tape we discovered. And that was probably only one of many; it would have to be under the circumstances. You can't cut off a small boy from all companionship on his own age level. If you don't provide a friend, he will have one, even in his own mind. So, we have Hacon here—"

"Yes, we have *him!*"

Nik's bonds would not allow any physical reaction to the menace in that voice, the promise of ill to come in the emphasis on *him.*

"Remember, Commander, he's our route to your young charge. He took the boy out of here before our attack, some time before it. You recall the testimony?"

"But you found him out there alone!"

"We found him coming back."

"Which means?"

"Probably that he was returning to set up a deal. There may have been more than one of these rats who took to the open before the end. If any of them were on Veep level or even had brains enough to do some moderate thinking, they'd want a deal. And they have only one thing to bargain with—the boy. So to send this bait of theirs back would be the logical move in opening negotiations."

"To bargain with such filth!"

"Commander, this is a big planet and an unknown one as far as we are concerned. You say the boy was fully conditioned, which means he'll need off-world food. They can't have too much of it out there. And they can be hiding anywhere. We have one radiation tracker, and that won't work—you saw it fail. This Dis is too far off our norm. Adjustments to the machine can be made, but that all takes time. With a conditioned boy held by desperate men, how much time do we have?"

"Then you say to bargain?"

"I say that the first consideration is the boy's safety. If that can be obtained by a bargain—we had better bargain."

"And afterwards?"

"Afterwards—we shall keep to the strict letter of any bargain, Commander, but the strict letter will not deter future action against those responsible for this. After all, this prisoner here was only a tool. Do you want just the hands? Is it not better to wait and take the brain behind them?"

"To bargain—" The disgust was plain. "But you are right, of course. How soon do we get to it—this bargaining?"

"At once!"

The stiff shell that had encased Nik was gone. They had loosed the stass. He opened his eyes and lay staring up at the two men.

One wore the black tunic of the Patrol, the diamond double star of a squadron leader on his collar. The other was brown of skin, and his hair was as dark as Vandy's. He was plainly of the same race as the boy. He too wore a uniform, more colorful than the Patrol officer's, and there was the glitter of decoration links on the breast of his dark red tunic. He stared back at Nik with a hatred and contempt that was hot and bitter, expressed in his eyes and the twist of his lips. The Patrolman had a calm detach-ment about the prisoner that was in a way just as forbidding. Nik was very glad he had had those moments to think ahead. The man in red spoke first.

"Where is the boy?"

Nik wet his dry lips with his tongue. His mouth felt cottony, so dry that he was not sure he could answer audibly. But matters were moving just as Leeds had foreseen. Vandy was their bargaining point, and both these men were ready to accept that. He swallowed and found a whisper of voice.

"Safe—so far—"

"I asked—where?"

Nik was too close yet to stass stiffness to avoid that blow. It cracked against his face, almost battering him back into dizzy half consciousness. When he was able to focus again, he saw that the Patrolman had a grip on that red clothed arm and had pinned it to the other's side.

"That won't do—any—good—" Nik was battling for more than Leeds' bargain now. He had no doubt that this commander, whoever he was, would try to beat the information out of him. He had to appeal to logic on the part of the Patrolman. "I'm not the one giving the orders—out there—"

"But you do know where he is? You were sent here to bargain—" said the Patrolman.

"No, came for food." Nik rubbed a trickle of blood from the corner of his mouth. "Vandy has to have food—"

"You—!" The commander lunged at him, and the Patrol officer twisted between them.

"i'Inad! Calm down, man. So you have no off-world supplies?"

"Not enough—and the boy can't eat native food."

"Then, by the Three Names," the commander exploded, "bring him back!"

He would like nothing better, Nik wanted to say. But there was the bargain—Vandy for a ship, a clear start—safety for Leeds and for Nik Kolherne.

"Why did you run with the boy in the first place?"

That question was so unexpected that Nik answered the Patrolman with the truth.

"They wanted to kill him—"

"Who did?"

There was no point in not telling the rest of it.

"A Veep called Orkhad. He was in command here."

"What did you expect to accomplish by running? There was no place to run to—or was there?" The Patrolman made that a question. "Another nest waiting?"

"Not that I know of," Nik returned promptly. To tell all the truth that did not apply to Leeds and their present precarious position was, he believed, his best move. For all he knew, they could have him, probably did have him, under a scanner now. If he supplied the truth in most things, they would be more likely to listen to him.

"So you just went out on the surface with the boy to hide out. What did you hope to gain?"

"I was expecting someone to come, someone who could over-rule Orkhad." Again the full truth.

"A division in their ranks, eh?" The Patrolman did not question that.

"I don't know." Nik chose his words with care. "But Orkhad was not following the orders I had been given."

"Which were?"

The truth—if they did have a scanner on him, they would know he spoke the truth. And he was sure they had him under such observation.

"To keep Vandy safe—for the information he had—"

Commander i'Inad moved closer. "Vandy—information?" he repeated. "But the boy has no information they couldn't have learned by other sources. That's a lie!"

The Patrolman had turned his head, and Nik followed that line of sight. The machine that had been clicking away so steadily—he had never seen a scanner, but he was sure that was one. And now the Patrolman proved Nik correct.

"No, that is the truth as far as this one knows. What kind of information?"

Again Nik told them the truth. He put Leeds' first story to him into a few terse sentences. It sounded thin, retold like this, but the scanner would bear him out. He was developing an affection for that machine—so far.

"And you believed that?" The commander was highly incredu-lous.

Nik pulled himself up on the bunk where he had been lying.

"I believed it," he returned flatly. There was no use adding that he had wanted to believe it, that he was eager to, considering what acceptance of the story meant to him.

"But when you got here, Orkhad had a different tale?"

"Yes." Nik told them that also.

"So you took the boy and ran for it? Why?"

"It was the only thing to do. I thought we could hide out until the captain came—"

"This captain—Strode Leeds?"

Nik was not surprised when the Patrolman named Leeds. He must have picked up a lot from prisoners taken here in the refuge.

"Yes—Captain Leeds."

"Leeds has the boy now?"

"Yes."

"Where?"

This was the hard part. Could he defeat the scanner by thought? Nik was not sure it could be done, but it was his only chance.

"I can't tell you where; there's no map. But I can take you there." Two full truths—one hedging. Would the whole come out on the truth side in the report?

The commander, as well as the Patrolman, was watching the machine for some confirmation or denial Nik could not read.

"Well?" i'Inad demanded, not of Nik but of the Patrolman.

"True—"

For the first time, Nik's tension eased somewhat. He had beaten the scanner by that much. Heartened by that victory, he ventured to prod a little on his own.

"I need food for Vandy—soon—"

"Let's go now!" That was i'Inad.

"Leeds will have the boy where you left him?" The Patrolman was not so quick to pick that suggestion up.

Of that Nik had no doubts. His injury was enough to pin the captain to the island hill. He could not get away and take Vandy with him in the boy's present weak condition, and he would not abandon the one chance he had of buying his freedom. Nik nodded.

"Let's go!" i'Inad repeated. He grabbed at Nik, dragging him off the bunk with a rough jerk.

The Patrolman had crossed the room. Now he returned carrying a container of liquid, which he held out to Nik.

"Drink it!"

Nik surveyed the contents of the cup warily. There were a lot of rumors about the Patrol methods. He had no desire to go out of here drugged, obedient to orders in spite of his will. The green liquid had no odor, but he hesitated even as he held the cup to his lips.

The Patrol officer frowned. "It's no drug—not the kind you fear." He must have read Nik's thoughts or else the scanner reported that, too. "That's Patrol iron rations. You'll need it to keep going."

Nik had to believe him. His own weakness of body when he tried to move warned him that he could not make any such trip on his own. He drank, and the stuff was warm in his mouth, even more heated in his throat, and hot in his stomach as he swallowed.

"We have to have cin-goggles out there," he said. That was his worst remaining fear, that they might refuse to provide him with those. Suppose they would allow him use of goggles from time to time in order to point out landmarks, would keep him blind most of the journey as a prisoner without bonds?

"All right. We have those."

They went through the passage of the refuge, collecting an escort of Patrolmen on the way—six of them. But when they trod a path through rubble to the outside, Nik, in spite of the cins, was totally at a loss.

"Well, which way?" i'Inad wanted to know. "Are you trying to say you can't tell?"

"I can't—from here." Nik told of their escape through the tunnel cut. When he had finished, the Patrol officer nodded.

"All right, we'll go back through that."

"He's stalling!" rapped out the commander.

"No, he couldn't just have walked out with the boy. Such a bolt hole is far more probable. We'll try that tunnel."

Back into the refuge they went, to the terminal of the ancient ways. But in the tunnel no break showed. Instead, they were faced with an effective stopper of earth and rocks.

"Those explosions when you broke in—" Nik found the answer. "They must have plugged this—"

"Clear it," the Patrol officer ordered.

Something more powerful than a blaster ray snapped on, and the barrier melted at its touch. But only more rock and soil poured in.

"That's not going to do it," the officer said a moment later.

"Take a bearing, Dagama. We'll try it over the surface with that as a guide."

Then they were back at the original refuge door, climbing up to the earth, guided by the small cube their advance scout held, which gave off a small beeping sound.

# THIRTEEN

They came into the city ruins by the emptied sea basin from a different angle. But once he sighted the shoreline, Nik was confident of his path. As they went through what must once have been streets, he eyed every shadowed rubble cave, every opening leading to darkness. What had truly happened to him back there by the reef, he did not know. That the city had its inhabitants still, he now believed, inhabitants of one kind or another—degenerate Disians or animals.

There was no blaster in his belt hooks, but the rest of the party were armed. And Nik noted that they were as much interested in possible ambush spots as he was. Finally he dared to ask a question.

"How did you find me?"

"Fighting off a hunting party," replied the officer crisply. "One of our scouts had sighted you from the cliff top. He followed along until all at once you came out from some rocks and walked straight at trouble. When they jumped you, Riswold beamed the one who had you down—"

"Then they did fish me out with that light!" Nik was remembering now. "Just as that thing did on the ramp way—"

The officer paid no attention to that, for he was continuing. "Our men picked you up by a reef in that direction."

"Yes, we go down to the sea bottom here and then head that way."

Nik rubbed his head. He had no idea whether this was morning or evening or of what day. The outward world, even when viewed through goggles, was darkening. And outside the refuge, the humidity again caught them in its soggy grip. Commander i'Inad was breathing in short gasps, and even one or two of the Patrol guard seemed similarly affected. The restorative drink had strengthened Nik, but still he felt as if he were walking thigh deep in water, pushing sluggishly against a strong current that might at any moment sweep him off his footing to be perilously carried away.

They descended to the first level of the sea bottom. Visibility was fading. And then Nik saw the telltale flash on the horizon. Storm! Such a deluge as he had seen before? He stopped to watch the play of lightning.

"What's the matter?"

"Get along with you!" i'Inad caught Nik's shoulder and shoved him on with a force that almost sent him sprawling before he could reply to the Patrol officer's question.

"Storm coming—" Nik got out. "And they're bad here. To be caught in the open—"

The water that had cascaded over the shore cliff, cutting hundreds of swift-flowing streams, to flood this portion of the sea bottom and to build up rain lakes below, how high did that water reach? And if one were caught in the open, could it be fatal? Nik did not know, and he was not eager to find out.

"We'll have to find cover," he told the Patrol officer, knowing he could not appeal to the hostile commander.

"What do you think, Barketh?" i'Inad asked the other. Maybe that play of lightning and the horrible pre-storm smother of humid air made some impression on the commander.

"Planet's weather is definitely unbalanced. Yes, a storm could be nasty. And there're signs this is a drain basin."

"We can't go back!" i'Inad protested. "The boy—we have to reach him soon—if we can believe this—this graxal here!"

"How far is the reef? Can we make that before the storm breaks?"

Nik had no idea, but he did know that this was a time for action and not just stopping to consider what action. He started on at a trot, the best pace he could keep under the weight of the humid air. Yes, the spine of the reef promised shelter of a sort. And, though he had very little experience with Dis's worst, Nik did believe that they needed some protection against the coming fury. How long *did* they have? None of them knew. But no one of that squad attempted to stop him; they only stepped up their own pace to join his flight.

The visibility was shrinking fast. Clouds always hung heavy over Dis, but now the blanket was night-thick, and splinters of lightning dazzled rather than helped their sight. A snarling screech—shadows fleeing across their path gave warning tongue. For several paces, Nik ran beside one of the black furred hunters, and then the Disian animal drew ahead.

Nik's apprehension was as much a weight on his laboring body as the exercise. Had they—or rather he—made the wrong choice? Should they have returned to the ruined city to wait out the storm? He was not even sure now if they were heading in the right direction for the reef.

Flashes that were not of the Disian world stretched paths before them. Nik had forgotten the torches the Patrol must carry. That white-yellow light picked out the creatures that bounded and scuttled-raced for shelter. Another time Nik might have been amazed at the amount of life that had broken out of hiding on the sea bottom. Now he was intent only upon what might lie ahead, on how soon one of those beams would pick up the reef.

The boom of thunder that had begun as a sullen muttering was now creeping closer with a beat that carried a vibration to fill the whole world and even their bodies. It was as confusing in its steady "pound-pound" as that whistling that had bewildered Nik when the Disians had hunted him.

As yet there was no rain, but he feared the buffeting of the torrents when they came. The frenzied flight of the animals about them underlined the danger he suspected.

Rocks stood out more frequently in the path of those flash beams. They must be drawing close to the reef. Then the lightning

struck ahead, and the first of the rain came like a blotting curtain
to swallow them. Nik saw the flashes of the torches, but he was
no longer aware of any of the men near him. A small squealing
thing shot between his feet, tripping him up. He fell heavily, to
lie gasping the thick air into his laboring lungs, too winded for
the moment to regain his feet. A Patrolman loomed out of the
murk, stopped and caught at him, tugged him up, and pulled
him along for a space.

Water poured down upon them. This was like drowning while
one walked on land. Nik flung his arm across his nose and mouth,
trying to make a sheltered pocket in which to breathe. He staggered
under the weight of water. At least the wind was not as great here
as it had been back in the city ruins. He brought up against a rock
and clung to it with the same frenzy as a man would embrace an
anchor when being borne along in a wild current.

Another Patrolman, or perhaps it was the same one who had
aided Nik, blundered up, and this time Nik put out a hand to
draw him to that anchorage. Water streamed over them, about
them; it gurgled calf high about their legs. There was nothing in
the world but the fury of the rain and thunder, the crash and
clash of lightning. It was weather gone wild with a force Nik
could not have imagined possible.

There was nothing to do but to cling to the rock. To venture
on in this was to invite disaster. The Patrolman held to the
other side of that anchor with the same grim determination.
Water rose about them. Had they come to a stop in the middle
of a rain river? It was flowing quickly, pulling at them knee
high now. Nik flattened his body against the rough surface of
the boulder and put his head on his arm, hoping to breathe
better. How much of this could one take? His hands were
growing numb. What if he could not keep that hold? Would
he be swept by the stream now rising to his thighs? Only a
short way on, that stream must plunge over the second cliff to
the lower level, doubtless going to feed one of the rain lakes.
Hold on—he had to!

Lightning—a flash that was blinding that deadened the senses.
Now the wind was coming, driving the rain lashes across the
rock and the men, limpet-fast to its sides, a wind that strove to

pry them free from those desperate holds, to snap them away in its grasp.

Air—he had to have air to breathe! Nik choked in panic; he fought for each gasp. This was drowning. The water tugged and washed at him now waist high. But to abandon his hold was death, and Nik knew that.

He held, his muscles aching and then going numb, his consciousness retreating into nightmare, and then, past nightmare, into a near blackout. Yet he held on.

A hissing—not steady but broken as if by gasps. Inch by inch, Nik crept back from the refuge into which his mind had retreated. There was still rain, but the wild tumult of the storm was less. He recognized the signs. That hissing—

There was the sharp pain of cramped neck and shoulder muscles as he lifted his head and looked up into a monster's glowing eyes. The thing, squatting on the top of the rock to which Nik clung, flexed its wings and darted its head toward the off-worlder. Nik fell back, his arms and legs too numb to respond naturally.

He splashed into the water. His body was pulled away, though he fought wildly for a handhold, some anchorage. There was a cry—sounding more human than any screech from the winged thing—and a moment later another body came whirling through the water, striking against Nik. Together they were borne helplessly onward until another rock loomed out of the dark and they struck against it, Nik on top.

What followed next was never clear. He was out of that flood, and so was the other—the Patrolman who had shared his refuge. But the latter lay very still, his body responding a little to the tug of the water. Nik crawled on his hands and knees to what might relatively be termed land. Now without knowing just why, he turned to tug weakly at the other, winning him out of the flood by small pulls.

The rain shrank to a drizzle, but it shadowed the world about them so that Nik could only be sure of what lay within reach. He looked down at the Patrolman who lay face up, the rain glistening on his skin, on his face—!

This was Barketh, and his goggles were gone! Nik's hand

flew to his own eyes, just to make sure, though he should have known he would not be able to see this much had his own cins not been in place.

He could see; the Patrolman could not. It was as simple as that. The mishap the other had suffered gave Nik the advantage, and how could he best use it?

Swiftly he transferred the blaster from Barketh's belt to his own empty hooks, then the ration bag—He rolled the body over to free the pouch that had swung from a shoulder strap, terrified lest that also had been lost. No, it had been too securely latched. Each of the Patrol carried supplies, now Nik had this bag, enough to support Vandy for days.

Barketh had been so helpless in his grasp that Nik made a quick examination. The Patrolman was not dead, but a gash on his forehead supplied the reason for his present state. Now Nik had a choice. He could stay where he was and use a blaster to signal his position as soon as the rain subsided, or he could go on with the supplies in freedom.

"Wake up!" He shook Barketh. No need to pour water on the Patrolman; the rain was doing that. But Nik could not drag the other any farther, and neither could he go off and leave a blind and helpless man on the edge of a rain river.

Barketh moaned just as Nik was giving up hope of bringing him around. He opened his eyes, and his expression changed from vacancy to fear.

"Dark—" Nik had to lean close to hear that word. He spoke distinctly in return.

"Your goggles are gone."

"You—who are you?" Barketh struggled to lever himself up, digging his elbows into the muddy ground.

"I'm Hacon." Nik clung to the name Vandy had given him. "Now listen, the rain is slacking. I've your supply bag, and I'm going on with it. Here's your torch. When you can't feel the rain, shine it as a signal."

But, Nik wondered, would such a signal bring more than just Barketh's men? The furred hunters—the Disians? He felt for the blaster he had taken from the other. To leave a man without a weapon, without cins, alone here—

"You have goggles?" Barketh demanded.

"Yes. But I'm keeping them!"

Barketh felt for his blaster. "You took that, too?"

"Yes. I'm leaving you the torch. And wait—" Nik twisted out of the Patrolman's hold. They could not be too far from the reef. And there Barketh would have shelter. Hurriedly, he explained.

"You won't get far—" the other commented levelly.

"Maybe not, but I have the food, and Vandy needs it. How long would it take you now to get your squad rounded up again, for you to get going?"

"A point—small—but a point. All right, for the time being you give the orders. Stow me away and get going. I agree the boy has to have food."

He held out his hand, but Nik avoided that too easy contact. Reaching behind Barketh, he took hold of the Patrolman's belt and pulled him to his feet. Remaining at the other's back, Nik gave him a small push forward.

"Use your torch," he ordered, "and march."

He had slung the strap of the supply pouch over his own shoulder, where it swung loosely. The light cut a path through the dark, picking up more rock outcrops. Suddenly Nik heard a shout in the murk. He thought it came from above and to the right, as if they had been sighted by some scout who had made the reef. With that he loosed his hold on Barketh's belt, at the same time giving the Patrolman a swift shove, which he hoped would at least momentarily send him off balance and keep him from turning his light on Nik as a target.

As for his own path, he turned left and dodged in and out among rocks, keeping to the best cover he could and heading for the point he must pass. The supply pouch bumped his hip as he ran, and he had the blaster weighing down the carry hooks. By chance alone, he was coming out of this better than he had dared hope.

It was heavy going over the rain-sodden sea bottom. Pools from the drain streams linked here and there into lakes before they drained a second time to the lower level and the waiting "sea" there. Nik had to watch his footing to avoid both water and slick mud and stone. Once or twice a wind gust blew the drizzle so strongly against him that he experienced again the sensation of drowning in water-filled air.

Whether he could be marked by anyone now on the reef, Nik did not know. He went on with a curious tingling between his shoulder blades as if he expected to feel the ray of a blaster beam there. It seemed almost impossible that he would be able to get away without challenge. But he was certain it would not be without pursuit. Nik kept on doggedly, never once looking back, with the odd feeling that his refusal to look for danger in that direction gave him some form of protection.

The heat was rising as the rain slackened, following the pattern of the earlier storm when he and Vandy had seen the mists of steam curling from the ground. Now he smelled an unpleasant odor and moments later came out upon the edge of a great gouge extending from the shore straight across his track. Lightning had struck here and brought about a collapse of the first level of sea bottom. Between Nik and the road he must take to find the island hill was a slash of still-sliding earth and rock.

He went along its verge back to the cliff face, but there was no way to span it here. The rock was too sheer and slippery. Down the center of the gouge splashed a stream, which constantly ate at the stuff of its walls, bringing down more earth slips. He would have to follow it back to the second seaward shelf if he were to cross at all.

That was a nightmare journey, the worst Nik had attempted since he had climbed from the tunnel cut with the unconscious Vandy. Now he had only himself to worry about, but the loosened ground was as treacherous as a whirlpool, and every step started fresh movement.

Nik threw caution aside at last, determined that the only way was to choose his path and then go it with all the speed he could muster to keep ahead of a slide. The debris of the cut carried well out into the second level, and in the basin there the water collected, backing up to keep this disturbed earth fluid and shifting.

He took a deep breath and jumped from ground already moving under his boots to land on a relatively clear space, plunging into slimy soil halfway to his elbows, for he landed on hands and knees. Then he struggled up, rolled down to the verge of the lake, and splashed on with all the energy he could summon for a quick and powerful effort. There was no use trying to breast the other side of the cut. He had been unusually lucky in getting down, but to climb a constantly shifting surface was out of the question.

Nik dodged as a good section of wall gave way, thickening the stream water and sending up spray to fog his goggles. He clawed his way along in what he believed were the shallows, having to depend upon chance and unsure footing. Once he fell as a stone turned under his weight, but luckily the force of the stream was already slackening, and he was able to flounder out before he was carried into the depths of the lake.

Silvery streaks under the surface of the water converged on something floating not too far away. The surface roiled as those streaks fought and lashed. Where the fish had gathered from, Nik did not know, but their ferocious attack on the body of a dead furred hunter sent him splashing in turn as far and as fast from the dangerous proximity of the feast as he could get.

Rounding a point of the slide, he saw that the smaller pool into which the gash fed its water here joined the lake that had existed earlier, a lake that might, in years or centuries to come, form the sea the flare had steamed from Dis. To swim that, after seeing the carnivorous fish, was impossible. He would have to take the equally dangerous path along under the level rise, where there could be other slips to engulf the luckless.

The rain had almost ceased. The steam grew into a mist, which even the cin-goggles could not penetrate. Nik tightened the strap of the ration pouch and waded on. He had the cliff edge for his guide—and that he could not lose. Eventually, it was going to bring him back to the island hill.

With the waters ankle-high about his fungi-furred boots, he trudged along, wondering if he would ever feel dry again. The fresh dehumidified air of the refuge seemed a dream now. This had been going on for always—lifting a foot, setting it down into oozing sludge, trying to breathe through a water haze—this had been forever and ever, and to it there would be no end.

# FOURTEEN

The steam cloaked but did not completely hide the island hill. It was now more truly island than hill, for the lake water had risen to lap about its base. Nik gazed eagerly up at the ledge where he had left Leeds and Vandy. He could see nothing there—they must be lying flat.

Water arose about him as he sloshed to the hill. He moved slowly, worn out by the hours-long push he had made from the reef, suspicious of the footing here. There were signs of the fury of the storm other than just the water. The body of a Disian had been washed between two rocks and floated there face down, rising and falling with the movements of the lake.

A Disian!

Nik splashed on, trying to move faster. If the natives had attacked! He crawled up the slope.

"Leeds! Vandy!" There was no answer to his call.

He had never thought of their not being there, never faced the possibility of coming back to an empty camp. Where had they gone? And why? Had Leeds tried to follow him? But as the captain had pointed out, he could not have made that journey and taken Vandy, too, and certainly the boy could not walk.

"Leeds!" The name came out as a harsh croak as Nik made it over the edge of the ledge.

And the ledge was bare. Bare!

Nik huddled there, too numbed by that discovery to try to think. The storm—! On this exposed position, the storm must have broken with blasting force. Had those two been swept away by wind and water or had the captain somehow made an escape? With that very faint hope moving him, Nik sat back on his heels to look to the next rise of land. The shore cliffs were the only possibility, near enough so that with a determined effort Leeds might have reached them. But what chance had they offered for a semiconscious boy and a man with an injured leg? No, both must have been swept away.

Only stubborn clinging to unrealistic hope made Nik start for the cliffs. There had been plenty of warning about the impending storm, and Leeds knew Dis far better than Nik. The captain must have done *something*! If the cliffs were the only answer, then Leeds had tried the cliffs.

A flock of the leather-winged creatures wheeled over the rocks and screamed as they landed to shamble up and down, eyeing Nik. He gathered they were out to clean up the storm debris. Moving abruptly, Nik was answered by their taking off again with even louder screeches. There were several flocks of them along the cliffs ahead, and some were luckier in their finds, for they settled down to feed.

Had the rugged coast been pounded by the sea that had once filled that basin, Nik could not have made the journey, but the rain lake was waveless, unless purposely disturbed, and shallow, save for a deeper pool now and then. He still walked with caution, but he was trying to move faster.

A glint of light—to his right—from the face of the cliff! Nik waded to that spot. A mass of fungoid brush had been driven into a rock cul-de-sac, and it was from that the wink came. He tore aside the slimy stuff to be faced by a weak torch beam. Perhaps the battering of the storm had affected the charge, for this was only a wan echo of the usual light, but there was no denying that the rod had been carefully wedged into a crevice to provide a guide.

They had reached here alive and with confidence enough to leave a sign for anyone following! Nik had not known how greatly he doubted their safety until relief flooded in to lighten his fear.

And the torch would not have been so carefully set without purpose. He began to search the wall for some other clue, tearing away the matted flotsam with both hands. The last mass of that came free like a released plug, and he was looking into the dark mouth of a cave.

But why—why would Leeds take to such a hole? With the water rising outside, a break in the cliff could be a trap, but Nik was sure this was the road.

He had to stoop to get in, and the torch he had freed from the crevice was very feeble. The light was still strong enough to disclose that this was not a cave, or if it were, the dimensions extended well back into the rock wall.

"Leeds!" he shouted. The name echoed with a hollow, intimidating sound, but there was no other reply.

However, there was another trace of those who had passed this way before him, the shining growing prints of feet that had tracked in crushed plant stuff to the dried floor of the cave. Two sets of those tracks, neither running straight. So Vandy had been on his feet and walking when they entered here! Nik wondered at that minor miracle.

The footprints vanished as their burden of growing slime was shed little by little. But there was only one way they could have gone—straight ahead where the walls closed in to form a passage.

An upslope to the flooring formed a vent in the cliff, angling toward the surface of the shore above. Nik wondered at Leeds' luck in finding it—the perfect bolt hole out of the storm. But with his injured leg, how had the captain made this climb? There were places that were an effort for Nik. He stopped at each and called, certain each time he would be answered—only he never was.

He emerged suddenly into a space he sensed was large but the walls of which he could not see. And standing there, Nik was puzzled. Which way now? To find a wall and work his way around, he decided, was the best answer. The feeble glow of the torch showed him the wall to the right, and he began the journey.

Nik was several feet along before the nature of the wall itself attracted him. This was not rough stone, as were the walls of the cave passage, but smoothly finished with the same coating given to the chambers of the refuge. Here within the sea cliff was another hollowing of the Disians. Another refuge?

There was no cool current of air, just the general dankness of the outside atmosphere, but perhaps not as heavily humid as on the surface. Whatever the purpose of this room, he came across no fixtures, none of the pallid light that had been in the refuge—or had that been added by the Guild?

The size of the chamber was awe-inspiring. Nik was still walking along one wall, the expanse on his left echoing emptily to the sound of his boots on stone. Was this a gallery running within the length of the cliff?

Nik was shivering a little in spite of the humidity. This place did not welcome his kind. For whatever purpose it had been fashioned, those hollowing it had been aliens, and he was not at home here—no off-worlder would be.

"Leeds!" Once more he paused and called. This time the echo came back from all sides until it rang in his head almost as that throbbing whistle had done.

But there had been an answer! A cry that was not a real word but that echoed in turn, so that he was certain he had heard it, if not what it was.

"Vandy!" Nik faced outward into that unknown space to his left and put the full force of his lungs into that shout.

This time no answer came. He tried to think where the earlier sound had come from, but the echoes made that impossible. To strike out from the wall was dangerous. He could only keep on exploring with that as his guide. But there was a need for hurry, and Nik began to trot.

A few moments brought him to a corner and the angle of another wall to follow. This was broken by slits, which had been filled in, perhaps at a later time, with rough stones wedged and mortared together. Windows walled up? Exits closed against some peril?

His torch caught and held in one that was a dark gap, not sealed. Nik hesitated. A way out—or *the* way out?

He listened. Now that the faint echo of his own footfalls had died, was there anything to hear? Just as he had been alerted to the Disian ambush by those lights, so now he was uneasy because of the very silence about him. His imagination pictured only to readily something lurking there—waiting. For what? For Nik Kolherne to come within attacking distance?

The dim torch flashed within the wall cavity, giving him nothing save the assurance that it was more than a niche, an entrance to either a passage or another room. He could not stay here forever—he must either take that door or continue his wall-hugging advance. And something he could not define urged him into the passage. After all, he could always return—

There was an oppression here that he connected with the humid air but that carried with it a dampening to more than just the physical senses—an oppression of spirits as well as of body. Why had he suddenly thought of it that way? Men—or at least intelligent entities—had made this place for a purpose, the desperate purpose of a refuge? Or had this existed before the time when the Disians had foreseen their world's end and tried to last out catastrophe and chaos?

Nik went one step at a time, pausing to listen for that odd cry, for sounds of movement that might mean he was being stalked. His imagination could provide more than one answer, but still he crept on.

This was not another room but a lengthening passage, so narrow his shoulders brushed the walls. Nik began to count the paces, ten, twelve—Now the outline of another door was visible.

More than an outline, there was light ahead—the outer day? But Nik came out into another chamber where the alien quality of his surroundings reached a peak.

Reptilian life! He almost drew his blaster—until he saw that those rounded lengths were not legless bodies but roots—or branches—of plants. They stretched across the floor, tangled and intertwined, but they all reached for a crack in the middle through which flowed a stream of water. The roots were outsize, the plants they nourished relatively small, forming a line of white fleshy growths along the walls. And from them arose a musty odor, adding to the heaviness of the air.

"Welcome back!"

Nik started. He had been so intent upon that loathsome growth that he had not seen the man within the arch of roots until Leeds spoke.

"How—" Nik stepped over a hump of root, somehow shrinking from any contact with the growth. "Vandy?" he demanded before he completed his first question.

"All right. You're alone? You didn't get the rations?"

Leeds' eyes were deep in his head; his face was fined down until the bony ridges of cheekbones and chin were too clearly defined. He did not move as Nik came up.

Leeds' eyes—his goggles were gone! The light from the unearthly plants must give him a measure of sight, but what had happened to his cins? Nik bestrode another root tangle and was at Leeds' side.

The captain's injured leg was stretched stiffly out, tightly bound to a length of thick plant stem, the end of which protruded beyond his boot sole and was splintered and worn.

"I take it the storm's over," he said wearily.

"Yes." Nik looked for Vandy, but the boy was nowhere in sight.

He shifted the strap of the ration bag from his shoulder and dumped the pouch beside Leeds. "Here're the rations. Where's Vandy?"

Leeds grimaced. "An answer I wish I could give you—"

Nik stooped to catch the other's shoulder. "What do you mean?"

"Just that. No, you fool, I didn't leave him behind or knock him out or do any of those things you're thinking! Why should I? He's our only pass out of here. That's why you have to find him."

"Find him! But what happened?"

"I had a packet of Sustain tablets." Leeds' voice was very tired. "Thought about them later and gave them to him—they brought him around all right. Then, we saw the storm coming and knew we had to move. He didn't want to go—had a tussle with him—but without goggles he didn't want to stay alone either. We went along the cliffs and found this hole. But it was a long trip in this far with my leg bad. By the time we reached here, I was pretty tired. Then the boy took over."

"Took over—how?"

Leeds' mirthless grin was a wider stretch of tight skin and thin lips. "By knocking me out, taking the goggles, and going on his own. There's no way of telling how long he's had to set distance between us. But he's gone—somewhere. And you're the only one who can track him—unless you *did* bring the Patrol. And that wouldn't be good for us under the circumstances. He has both blasters, too—at least mine's gone!"

"But why—" Part of this Nik thought he could understand—the taking of Leeds' goggles, yes. To be eternally in the dark on this hostile world would have led an older man to make such an attempt much sooner, but to strike out alone—Vandy, though, had once before played just such a trick on him back in the ruined city.

"He's conditioned," Leeds said flatly. "He'd stay with you but not with me. I thought he would be easy to handle—as soon as he got energy enough, he made a run for it. And I needn't remind you, Kolherne, that if the Patrol does catch up with us and he isn't here—This bag—did you go all the way to the refuge?"

"No, they found me. I was with them coming here when the storm hit." Nik remembered Commander i'Inad. Yes, Leeds was entirely right. If the Patrol caught up with them now and Vandy was missing, they would suffer for it. There was no evidence that they ever had the boy at all. They *had* to find Vandy with the cins and maybe two blasters, urged by his conditioning to put as much distance between Leeds and himself as he could—where would he go?

"You were here when he jumped you?" he demanded.

"Yes. A good thing for me. These plant things give off some light. If he'd left me in the dark with this leg—"

"And you don't know how long ago?"

"All I know is that I sat down to ease my leg. The next thing I remember, I was lying on my back with a big ache behind my eyes. And I'm not even sure how long ago that was."

"You'd better eat." Nik took one of the ration containers out of the pouch and handed it to Leeds. "Any other way out of this place except that passage? And does he have a torch?"

"No, we left that as a signal—which I see you found."

No torch. Even with the cins on, to retreat along that passage and into the big chamber was a move Nik would not care to make. But had Vandy been driven hard enough by his conditioning to do just that? He'd have a look around here first.

Leeds pressed the button on the container. The hands with which he held the tin were shaking. Nik gazed about the root-matted room. At the opposite end of the room, there was one easily noticed exit, the way the water flowed, and that was large enough for a stooping man to enter. Vandy could have walked through there. Nik went to inspect that exit.

He noted that any touching of the roots left dark bruises on their surfaces—one way of tracing Vandy's passage. But those clustered at the mouth of the water tunnel were unmarked. Either they had recovered in that interval of time between Vandy's flight and now or he had not tried that path.

Nik began a circuit of the walls. The plants were more thickly massed to the left; to the right only a few smaller and more widely spaced ones grew. The entrance to this whole series of cavern rooms had been hidden behind a plug of vegetation. Could another such exist here behind the plants? He loathed going near them, but it had to be done.

Only, as far as he could see, there was no break in the wall behind them, and the light given off by their fleshy leaves, those twining reptilian roots, was enough to make the rock surfaces plainly visible. It began to appear that Vandy had gone back down the entrance passage. Nik said as much, but the captain shook his head.

"Without a torch—no. He hated that place when we came through, dragged back on me all the way. That's what made me so tired that I got careless when I hit here and he stopped whining about being in the dark. The cins wouldn't give him vision enough there. He went some other way. Through that water channel probably—"

Nik went back to the channel. He did not see how even one as slight as Vandy could have worked his way through the mass of roots directly before that opening without leaving some trace on the vegetation. The marks of his own passing were not only darkened, but now, a few moments after that bruising, the stuff seemed to be sloughing off as if his touch had killed it. Vandy's path had to be the other way—in spite of Leeds' report.

The captain had finished the contents of the container. "Think the Patrol will follow you?"

Remembering Commander i'Inad, Nik had no doubt of that. But whether the Patrol could trace him into this cave maze, he did not know.

Leeds had been fingering the pouch; now he looked up with a very grim twist of lips.

"Well, I do!" he said. "Look here."

He turned the pouch upside down, sending its contents spinning and displaying to Nik the inner part. There was a small bar set there.

"Caster!" Leeds identified. "They probably have had a fix on this all the time. Any supply pouch taken would lead them right to us. They obviously foresaw a jump try on your part."

"So, the Patrol could be on the way even now, coming up the passage, and with Vandy gone—"

The goggles must not have masked his face too much for Leeds to read his expression, for the captain nodded again.

"Just so—they will be coming. And our answer is Vandy. So we'd better find him—and quick!"

# FIFTEEN

Nik fingered the supply bag, staring down at the telltale rod. The Patrol would have a fix on that all right. Maybe Barketh had deliberately set him up this way, allowing an escape at the first opportunity so they could trace him and then claim the bargain off—but they were not here yet. Methodically, he began to twist and wad the pouch into as small a compass as possible. Now he and Leeds needed time. Finding this had changed his plan for trailing Vandy. He could not leave the captain here alone to be picked up by the Patrol with no Vandy. Commander i'Inad might just burn him out of hand.

"What are you doing?" Leeds wanted to know.

"Giving them something to follow." Nik went back to the stream exit from the root chamber. He was certain now Vandy had not gone that way, but something smaller and more dangerous to them could. Nik thrust the supply bag between two of the curling roots into the water, where the current of the stream, weak though it was, tugged the container out of sight. The Patrol fix was on the move again, and Nik thought that any tracker might have a rather difficult time following it along its present path.

"That makes sense." Leeds applauded his action. "But they'll come this far—" He pulled himself up a little as if to test his ability to get to his feet.

"Yes, so we'll be gone," Nik answered. "Only we have to pick the right road." He went back to his survey of the chamber walls. Vandy had left here, and Leeds seemed very sure the boy had not backtracked on the way in. Then there was another way out, and, taking it, he must have left some trace for Nik to find.

"I'm not exactly up to a clean lift out of here," the captain commented. He was standing, or rather leaning, braced among the roots. "You can't blast off at a good rate with me slowing the rockets, and back there I'm lost without goggles." He spoke levelly, not as if he were trying to ask for assistance but as one merely pointing out the disadvantages of some proposed plan. Neither did he offer any suggestions.

"Vandy got out of here some way!" Nik's frustration at not finding any trail was rising to something stronger than irritation. By all he could discover, Vandy had simply vanished into thin air—unless Leeds was wrong and Vandy *had* backtracked.

"He *must* have gone back!" he added, but the captain shook his head.

"You don't know how hard it was to get him through there the first time. I had to drag him. He kept saying there was something there waiting to get us—"

"He has the goggles now—" Nik was beginning, but the memory of that sensation he himself had felt, that there was something he could not see or hear lurking, ready and waiting for him to step beyond some intangible barrier of safety, came back to him.

"Even the goggles aren't much use without a torch there. I know they weren't for me. We were really lucky to get this far."

Nik moved on along the wall. There was another exit here then, somewhere. And it was the susceptibility of the roots to touch that finally revealed it. A blackened, withering length caught his eye, and he hurried to it. Vandy must have set foot there to climb to the opening above. Nik regarded the hole with a measuring eye. It was small but not too small, he thought, for both of them to squeeze through. Yet what if they found the going on the other side rough—with Leeds crippled. On the other hand, could he leave the captain behind now with the Patrol following the fix?

"So that's the way!" Leeds hobbled across to join Nik, his step

a sidewise lurch and recover, which drew lines about his mouth
and tightened his lips.

"Can you make it up there?"

"It's a matter of have to now, isn't it?" the captain returned.
"We never know just what we can do until we have to. Give us
a hand now—"

Somehow with Leeds' straining to lift himself and Nik's boost-
ing, the captain made it up to the hole. He clung there to look
down.

"Better get those supplies—". He nodded at the tins beside the
stream. "If we do catch up with that brat, we'll need them."

Nik shed his damp tunic, bundled the containers into it, and
so fashioned a pack. How long *could* Vandy keep going on the
Sustain pills? It might be that they would find him exhausted
not too far ahead. He scrambled up to join Leeds.

"You'll have to be eyes for both of us from now on." The captain hooked his fingers in Nik's belt. "And I'm not up to either
a fast run or an easy climb. But let's take off—"

Nik had to keep the dying torch for emergencies and depend
upon the goggles. But in this crack, as they drew away from the
ghostly glimmer of the root room, he was almost as blind as
Leeds. And they must go so slowly, a crippled fumbling, when
he was goaded by the need for haste.

Luckily, the footing here was even, so regular that Nik thought
it had been purposely smoothed. This was no natural fissure in
the rock but an established passage. Also, there was a distinct
current of air, not quite as humid as that of the outer surface.
Could they be heading into another refuge?

There were tenuous traces of Vandy here. The footprints where
he had left some vegetable deposits from the roots made faint
marks on the flooring, but these dwindled, to vanish entirely.

"Listen!"

Nik did not need that alert from Leeds. Far away or else
distorted by the walls of the winding passage—there was no
mistaking that whistle that hurt the ears and was a throb within
the skull. Nik took a longer stride forward, and Leeds went off
balance, stumbling into him and bringing them both up against
the supporting wall.

"Keep on course!" the captain snapped. "What is it?"

"The Disians! They hunted me on the way back; now they must be after Vandy!"

"What Disians?" Leeds demanded. When Nik told him, he whistled in turn, but not the throbbing call of the natives.

"We never saw any of them! Men here—natives?"

"Not much like men now." Nik corrected grimly. "They're hunters and they hunt for—food—"

Vandy in the dark, being hunted as Nik had been—watched, driven, finally lured into the open. There, at the last, in spite of Nik's off-world weapon and determination to stand up to danger, the primitives had brought him out as an easy kill. And if they could do that to him, forewarned and armed, what would they do to Vandy!

"We have to get to him!" Nik burst out. He caught at Leeds' arm, pulled the captain close enough to support him, and then pushed them both on. Leeds made no complaint, but Nik could hear the panting breaths the other drew and guessed that the captain was straining his powers to the limit. Yet they still kept to a short-paced shuffle.

Just that one whistle. They did not hear another, although Nik listened not only with his ears, it seemed, but also with every nerve in his tiring body. Had that been the signal to begin a hunt, not to urge attack? Suppose they came up from the rear and caught the Disians from behind? Vandy was armed. After his experience in the ruins and on the reef, the boy would be alert against dangers native to Dis and the dark. Whether that would give him a small measure of safety now, Nik did not know. He could not do more than hope.

"Light—" Leeds got the word out between two gasping breaths.

It was very faint, that light, but it was there. They headed for it and came out in another large chamber.

"Refuge!" Leeds cried.

The walls had a glow that did not extend far down the passage. It was as if some invisible curtain hung there.

"It's bright—"

"Not to me. That's what the goggles do for you," Leeds commented.

"But it is like refuge light all right. We stepped this up back at the base after we took over."

"But this can't be the same refuge," Nik protested. "We're a long way from there."

"Maybe it's not the same series of burrows but another system. Or it could be the same. We never did explore a lot of the tunnels—no reason to. We just closed off those we didn't need."

"You can see here." Nik took in the possibilities of that. He thought, observing Leeds, that the captain would not be able to keep on his feet much longer.

"Yes, I can see." Leeds' tone was colorless, neither adding to nor denying that fact. "All right—you go on. Let me follow at my own pace."

The decision was the only one that made good sense. If the Disians were hunting Vandy somewhere in this maze, Nik had to find him before they closed in. And Leeds was close to collapse.

"Give me a couple of the supply tins—and your blaster and the torch," the captain continued. He had reached the wall of a room and was lowering himself with it as a steadying brace.

The supplies—yes, Nik would leave some of those. And the torch. It was nearly exhausted now. But the blaster—with Vandy ahead in danger? Nik had to weigh one demand against the other. He opened the tunic bundle and took out two of the containers. Now as he tied up the roll again, he said flatly, "I can't give you the blaster. The Disians are hunting."

"And if they double back here?" Leeds asked just as tonelessly. "The boy has two weapons—and you have that." He pointed to the fringe of mock tools and fantastic arms that were part of Hacon's equipment.

"Those? You know they're fakes!"

"Fakes maybe for the uses Vandy dreamed for them, but they could have other uses—"

Leeds was not so far wrong, Nik thought. He had used one of those gadgets to force open the armory door back at the refuge. But that any of them could be a practical weapon against Disian attack, he doubted.

"That one—" The captain pointed at the one that in some manner resembled a blaster. In Vandy's fantasy, it shot a ray that turned its victims into stone. Nik only wished that the property with which Vandy had endowed that hunk of metal were a true one.

"Have you tried it?" Leeds continued.

"It doesn't work." Nik wondered if Leeds' mind was affected by his exertions.

"Maybe not the way Vandy intended. But we gave you some fireworks to use to impress, and that is one of them. Try it."

Nik drew the weapon. It was lighter than the blaster, of course, a small, bright toy. Now he aimed it at a midpoint of the chamber and pressed the firing button.

A second later he cried out, his hand sweeping up to cover his goggled eyes. The answering burst of light had been blinding!

"Take off your goggles now," Leeds ordered.

Nik obeyed. Blinking, he looked out into the chamber. There was light there, but not blinding any more.

"To infrared based sight, that burst is blinding," the captain told him. "And the effect lingers for some moments, long enough for you to make some attack. Creech thought that one up, and he's a com-tech with real brains."

"Why didn't you tell me about it before?" Nik wanted to know. Back there in the ruins when Vandy had been surrounded by the furred hunters or later—when he had fallen prey to the lure of the Disians—he could have used this.

Leeds met his accusing stare unruffled. "I told you that I believe in luck. I didn't expect you to have to take off here on Dis but to stay put in the refuge. And—it's well to have some insurance. There was a chance, of course, that you'd discover its use, but there was also a chance we might have been put in a position to need a new weapon, just as we are. Nobody but Creech and I knew that rayer was more than a prop for Hacon the hero. And it's always well to nurse a star in reserve while you're moving your comet on the broad swoop. Orkhad came in on this deal against my wishes. I had to foresee the possibility of a showdown—"

Nik understood. This all fitted with Leeds as he had learned to know him.

"And if we were disarmed, they wouldn't suspect this tinware?" Nik flipped a finger along the fake equipment.

"Just so. But you have a weapon now, and I need the blaster."

Nik drew the more conventional weapon and weighed them both in his hands as he considered the point. The rayer was a weapon, right enough. But on the other hand, he was sure of the effect of the blaster.

"Make up your mind!" That was sharp. "You haven't too long—for more than one reason—"

"Yes, the Patrol and the Disians." Nik rehooked the rayer, but he still turned the blaster over in hesitant fingers.

"And a third—you haven't looked in a mirror lately!"

"Mirror?" Nik repeated. Then his right hand went to his face fearfully. He was afraid to brush fingers across cheek and jaw.

"Without your goggles"—Leeds was matter of fact—"it's beginning to show. Gyna was right in her doubts of full success. I don't know the rate of slip, but if you don't catch up with Vandy soon, you may not be able to play Hacon when you do. And if you front him as Nik Kolherne, I don't think you'll have any influence over him."

Under those questing fingertips, the skin did feel rough! How long—hours? A day? Maybe two before it really began to break and return him to the horror from which a small boy would shrink.

Nik was cold, shaking. He had to brace himself to keep on his feet. The blaster—there was one way he could end the nightmare—with the blaster.

But Leeds now moved with a speed and precision that Nik thought he had lost. His arm shot out, the edge of his hand chopped Nik's wrist, and the blaster fell between them, with Leeds scooping it up.

"I would advise you to go—and fast!" All the crack of an order was in that. "We have to get Vandy out of here. And if you ever want a human face again, you'll get him! Just to make sure you'll hunt him, I'll keep this—".

He held the blaster on the knee of his good leg, looking up at Nik with such complete belief in himself that it was as strong as a blow. Because Nik had been Hacon for so long without thinking of the change that might come, to return now to that other would be worse than he dared to consider. Pulling the bundle of supplies up under his arm, he did not even look back at Leeds as he staggered across the chamber to the opening on the far side, his hand to his cheek.

As he went through that doorway, Nik forced his fingers away, his arm down to his side. He did not want to know—he did not dare to learn how bad it was. Leeds was right as always. Nik had to find Vandy before he ceased to be Hacon and so lost all control over the boy. He had to find Vandy to buy his own future, his chance to be a man in the company of his kind.

For a space, he trudged on mechanically, all his thoughts turned inward, the chill of fear still riding him. Then he forced both thoughts and fears back and centered his attention on the task at hand. There had been only one way into that back chamber, and Vandy had taken it. There was only one way out—along here.

Nik snapped his goggles back into place, trying hard not to touch his face too much in the process. Instantly the walls glowed with a light as bright as any in the Dipple rooms—but he wasn't going to think of the Dipple and Korwar!

There was no trace of footprints on the floor of the passage, no break in the glowing walls. But there was—Nik lifted his head and expanded his nostrils, striving to catch that elusive scent. Yes—the sickly odor of vegetation! Either this passage ran on to the outside or to another root room. The current of air was blowing straight into his face, and it carried the smell.

No sound. Nik longed to shout for Vandy. Whether the boy would either pause or listen, or whether the noise might bring the other lurkers out of the burrows to him, he could not tell, but both risks were too great. He was trotting now, the bundle of supplies swinging and bumping against his hip, intent on beating time itself.

The corridor made an angled turn, and Nik found his opening to the outside, a break in the wall there where part of the cliff face must long ago have given way. But it was no door; the drop from the cut was a sheer one, past any descending.

Nik edged past that point and caught his first sign of the

fugitive, a boot print in the soil the wind had drifted in the cut. Vandy had been this way, but how long ago? No other marks except that. If he had been the quarry in some chase, the pursuers had left no traces of their own passing.

It seemed to Nik that the walls were less bright, that their glow was fading. And then there was an abrupt change from light to dark, as if whatever principle kept up the age-old illumination of the refuge had here failed or shorted.

There—that sensation of watchful waiting just beyond! Nik paused. He was so very sure he was not alone that he wet his lips preparatory to calling Vandy.

What kept him silent was perhaps some instinct for preservation he was not aware of possessing.

Light again—about chest high in the middle of the passage— stationary. No off-world torch, nothing he could understand. It did not spread to illuminate the walls, the floor, the roof above it—it simply was a patch of light seemingly born of the air without power to throw its beam.

Nik studied it with growing uneasiness. For a long moment, it was there, a bright dot in the dark. Then it began to move, not toward him, not in retreat, but up and down, side to side, in a series of sharply defined swings.

A lure—a Disian lure!

He backed away toward the lighted part of the passage and the break in the wall. If they were going to rush him, he wanted light for the battle. But the lure did not follow. He stopped again.

If it was a trap, it was one he had to dare. Vandy had taken this road. In order to find Vandy, he would have to travel it, too. The trap and the lure—with a blaster he could have burned the road open, but Leeds had the blaster. The rayer—could light save him here?

Nik slipped up the goggles, bringing the world about him into deep dusk. Instantly he realized he had made the right choice. There was a second glow ahead beside the lure—which he saw now only as if it were a tiny spark at the end of a long tunnel. This was an aura outlining something that squatted low beneath the lure, supplying the bait and perhaps the trap in one.

Once more he began to advance with the rayer in his hand. He aimed. The lure danced in a wilder swing, and Nik fired.

# SIXTEEN

**W**hat must have been an eye-searing burst to goggled eyes was bearable to Nik's naked sight. There was a shrill, thin screeching, which hurt his ears and his head as had the throb whistles of the Disians. That blotch of creature on the floor reared, throwing up and out long jointed legs, to crack and contract, until it toppled over and lay on its back kicking.

The light lingered as if the ray had ignited particles in the air. And now by its aid, Nik saw the other—one of the naked humanoids crouched behind its hound, if the jointed thing could be so termed. The Disian writhed, hands over his eyes.

Nik ran forward. This was his only chance, and he had to take advantage of it. The wriggling thing on the ground had stopped kicking, one of its clawed feet remaining straight up in the air. But there was space to pass that recumbent form.

He made that passage in a leap. The upright leg swung and struck Nik across the upper arm with such force that he staggered, but forward and not against the wall. The thing was scrabbling wildly, striving to turn over on its feet once again, squealing loudly as it struggled, to be answered with one of those whistles from its humanoid companion.

Nik faced around. The fiery light was dying. While the kicker still lay supine, the Disian was on his feet, shading his eyes but fronting the off-worlder. He had the stance of one ready to carry on the fight.

For the second time, Nik fired the rayer and then turned and ran, his heart pounding, the bundle of supplies knocking painfully against him at every step. He snapped down the goggles again, and instantly the glare behind him was a warning of the force he had loosed to pin his enemies fast. He might have been able to blind, to immobilize them for a space, but he had not gagged them, and the din behind was now a torment in his head, a mingling of the squealing and the whistle. Nik had no doubt that help was being summoned and he might meet it on its way.

The dark walls continued, and he held to the hope that any Disians answering that summons would betray themselves by their body glow, as had those who had set up the ambush without. He had to slow his pace. He could not keep running in the thick air of this burrow. His breaths were sobs that raised and racked his ribs and set a knife thrust of pain in his side.

Behind him, a little of the glare still existed. Perhaps a second dose had effectively removed the clawed thing from the field. It had taken the full force of the first raying and had been unprotected at the second. At least its squeal sounded more faintly, and Nik believed it had not stirred from the place where it fell. The Disian was another matter—the whistling had quieted. Did that mean that whatever message the native had striven to give was at an end? Or had he fallen silent because he was stalking Nik?

Twice the off-worlder paused to look back. There was the glow, but against it he could sight no moving thing. Only he could not be sure on such slight evidence that he was *not* trailed.

Light ahead again, another section where the walls still held their radiance. The small portion of dark before that was a logical place for an ambush. Nik studied the walls, the floor—not a glimmer of body glow. He had a feeling that if he could reach the lighted portion, he would be safe for the present.

Once more he forced his body to a trot, his hand pressed tight against his side. The effort exhausted him so much that he was frightened. That booster drink Barketh had given him back at the refuge—were the effects of it now wearing off? Would the need for rest and nourishment lead to his defeat? There was no place here where he would dare to stop for either.

Nik was tottering when he came into the light and had to lean against the wall, his shoulders flat on its surface, as he looked up and down the passage. Far back in the dark, there was still a shimmer of glow, the residue of the ray. Ahead, not too far away, the corridor made another turn, masking its length beyond. Nik tired to control his gusty breathing and to listen. The squealing had stopped; there was no more whistling. He could hear nothing from behind or beyond.

He edged along the wall, watching both ways as best he could. Had Vandy fallen into just such a trap as had faced Nik—and was he now in the hands of the Disians?

Nik reached the turn in the corridor, got around it, and saw before him a wide space giving opening to a score of passages, another terminal such as they had seen in the refuge. He sagged back hopelessly against the wall. To explore every one of those was beyond his strength or ability now. Only a guess could guide him. Vandy, if he had reached this point, would have been moved only by chance.

He also knew that he was almost at the end of whatever strength the booster had supplied. How long had it been since he had left the refuge in the company of the Patrol squad? More than a full Disian day, Nik was sure—perhaps even two. He squatted down, his back to the wall, at a point from which he could view at a glance all those empty tunnel mouths, and tried to think. The bundle of supply containers was under his hand, and he ached with the need for food. Just one of those—He had to have its contents inside him or he might never be able to drag on past this halt.

Reluctantly Nik took out a container and triggered its heat and open button. He ate the contents slowly, making each mouthful last as long as he could. As with all emergency supplies, this had a portion of sustainer included. The warmth and savor of the concentrated food settled into him, and he relaxed in spite of the need for vigilance. Food—rest—he dared the former but not the latter!

Five doorways before him, five chances of finding Vandy, and he had hardly time to take one—one—one—

It was dark and he was running through the dark, while behind him padded a hunting pack, the furred creatures from the ruins, the bare-skinned Disians and their insectival hounds—after him—after him!

Nik gave a stifled cry and strove to throw himself forward, out from under the grasping hands, the claws, the bared fangs—

His head, it hurt—He opened his eyes—into dark!

Dark! His hands went to his goggles, but there were no goggles! Frantically he felt for the cord at his neck—he must have fallen asleep and scraped them off somehow. But they were not there, hanging on his chest! He felt about him in the dark—carefully at first and then more wildly—but they were totally gone.

"I have them!"

Nik stiffened. "Vandy?" he asked, though he had to wet his lips to make them frame that name. "Vandy?" he repeated with rising inflection when there came no answer. He had thought a measure of subdued light might linger here as it had in the chamber where he had left Leeds, but perhaps this glow was different, for without the goggles he was in a dusk so thick that he might as well have been blind. He thought he could hear hurried breathing to his right.

"Vandy!" That was a demand for an answer.

"You aren't Hacon. There never was a real Hacon—"

Nik tried to think clearly. Hacon—what had that to do with the here and now? No, this was not one of Vandy's heroic adventures; this was very real and dangerous.

"*You* aren't real," that voice out of the dark continued. "You're one of them!" That was accusation rather than identification.

It was so hard to think. Nik must have been asleep when Vandy found him and took the goggles. How was he going to argue with the boy? He still felt dazed from that sudden awakening.

What had Leeds said back there? That the change in his face had already begun. No wonder, when he had taken the goggles, that Vandy had decided Nik was not Hacon. Nik's hand went to his face in the old masking gesture.

"You're one of them," Vandy repeated. "I can just leave you here in the dark. Like that captain—he was one of them, too!"

"One of whom, Vandy?" Somehow Nik was able to ask that.

"One of those who want my father to give up the stronghold. I'm going now—"

"Vandy!" All Nik's panic was in that. He fought back to a measure of self-control and asked, "Where are you going?"

"Out. I know that the Patrol are here. They'll find me—I can call them. Now I have supplies and blasters and goggles—" His voice was growing fainter. Nik caught a scrape of boot on rock—to the left this time.

His control broke. "Vandy!" He threw himself after the sound of those withdrawing footsteps and crashed against a wall. There was the patter of running. Vandy must have entered one of the tunnels. Nik sucked in his breath, steadied himself, and fought a terrible battle with insane panic. He was alone, without goggles, and Vandy had taken the supply bundle also—

He had two choices—to go back, to try and reach the chamber where he had left Leeds, which meant passing through the section where the Disian had laid the trap, or to trace Vandy on through the maze where he was a blind man. Which?

Nik was certain that Vandy had taken the passage farthest to his left. Trying to recall the terminal as he had seen it last, he believed he could find that opening. And the boy could not run far in this humid air. Sooner or later he would have to rest. Nik must follow him. To return through the Disian trap was more than he could force himself to try. He stretched out his arms and began to feel his way along the wall against which he had crashed. Seconds later, his right hand went into open space, and he knew he had found his doorway.

The weapon against fear was concentration, concentration upon what he was doing, upon sounds. Nik's senses of hearing and touch had to serve him now in place of sight. Fingers running along the rock surface to his left were his guides, leaving his right hand free for the rayer. And he tried to make his own footfalls as quiet as possible, so that he could listen with all his might.

Footfalls, far less cautious than his own, were ahead! Nik knew a sudden rush of excitement, so that he had to will himself to keep his own cautious rate of advance. He had been right. The run that had taken Vandy away from him had slowed quickly to a walk, which was hardly faster than his own creep. But—the boy could *see*! Let Vandy turn his head and he would sight Nik, and he had the blasters! An alarm could make Vandy use one of those almost as a reflex action. So much depended upon chance now—the chance that Vandy would not look behind him—the greater chance that Nik must take in trying to reason with the scared boy.

Vandy had thrown aside Hacon and the fantasy that had let him accept Nik, and he was conditioned against strangers. This meant that conditioning would now act against Nik and any contact he might try to make.

But every inch Nik covered with those footfalls still steady before him strengthened his belief in himself, stilled his first panic. It almost sounded as if Vandy knew where he was going and had some clue as to what lay ahead—not that that could be true!

Then the footfalls ceased. Nik backed against the wall. He was a small target in that position but one that could not escape blaster fire. He waited as weakness flooded through his body. Not to be able to see—

No sound, no sound at all. Vandy must be watching him—getting ready to fire? Nik ached with the effort to make his ears serve him as eyes.

Perhaps it was that very intensity of effort that sharpened Nik's thinking. He had been wrong in his handling of Vandy back there; he was certain of that now. At least he could try to repair the damage.

"Vandy!" He made that into a demand for attention, not an appeal. "Have the Fannards taken you over?"

Again he strained to hear. Because he had known that he was not Hacon, he had tamely accepted Vandy's recognition of that fact. But he had been thinking then as himself, Nik Kolherne, and not as Vandy. To Vandy, the fantasy world that had been Hacon's had been so real that he had accepted the appearance of its major inhabitant in the flesh as a perfectly normal happening. He could doubt Hacon's identity now, but there should be some residue of belief to make him doubt that doubt in turn. And if Nik could push him back into the fantasy, even for a short space, he could reestablish contact.

"Have they, Vandy?" He raised his voice and heard the faint echo of it. His face—had it been the change in his face that had set Vandy off? Again his searching fingers advised him of a slight roughness, but not the spongy softness he had feared to touch—not yet.

"There're no Fannards here." The reply was sullen, suspicious.

"How do you know, Vandy?" Nik pressed that slight advantage. At least the boy had answered him. "They can't be seen, even with goggles—you know that."

The Fannards—those invisible entities Vandy had produced for menace in one of the Hacon adventures. In this place, one *could* believe in them. Nik could—

He heard the click of boot plates, not away this time but toward him. Once more that sound stopped, but he was sure Vandy stood not too far away watching him. Nik spoke again.

"There are hunters here." He kept his voice casual, as much what Hacon's should be as he could. Hacon was Vandy's super-man. Nik must reproduce a Hacon now or complete the boy's disillusionment and probably doom the both of them. "They set a trap back there, but I got through—"

"There aren't any Fannards!" Vandy proclaimed loudly. "You aren't Hacon either!"

"Are you sure, Vandy?" Nik made himself keep calm and held his voice level. *He* was sure of only one thing. Vandy had come closer; he had not withdrawn yet. "We are being hunted, Vandy. And I am Hacon!" In a way he was—perhaps not the superman Vandy had created, but he was a companion in danger, devoted now to bring the boy out of that same danger. And so he was Hacon, no matter what his ravaged face might argue.

"No Fannards—" Vandy repeated stubbornly. But again the boot plates tapped out an encouraging message for Nik's ears. "This isn't the Gorge of Tath either!"

"No these are the Burrows of Dis, but still we are hunted. Vandy, do you know the way out of here?"

There was a long moment of silence, and then the boy answered in a low voice.

"No."

"Neither do I," Nik told him. "But we have to find one—before we're found. And the hunt is up behind—"

"I know." But Vandy came no closer. Nik did not know how much acceptance he had won, but he plunged.

"Why did you take this passage?"

"It was the nearest. Two of the others just end in rooms—no way out."

"What about it—do we go together?"

"Here—" Something flipped through the dark, struck against Nik's chest, and was gone before he could raise his hand to grasp it.

"On the floor, by your right foot." Vandy's direction came with cool assurance.

It was difficult to remember that what was dark to him was light for the begoggled boy. Nik went down on one knee and groped until his fingers closed about a piece of stuff that could have been a dried root or vine.

"What—" he began when Vandy interrupted him.

"I say the Fannards have taken *you* over. You're Hacon, but it's my story—always *my* story—and we are in it."

Nik felt the cord tighten; Vandy held the other end. Should he give that tie a jerk, try to get the boy within reach? But such an aggression on his part would break the thin bond of trust. He was impressed by the shrewdness of Vandy's reasoning. If Nik had endeavored to push them back into the fantasy, then Vandy would play—by the original rules. The adventures of Hacon had been created by Vandy and would continue so. That the boy had made the switch was the surprising part. His flight from Leeds might have been triggered by his conditioning and suspicion, but his ability to get this far, to remain reasonably steady in the whole wild Disian adventure, would have been more believable had he continued to think himself in some Hacon-Vandy adventure. Instead, he knew this was real and yet had not yielded to fright or panic. This suggested he was tough-fibered and determined.

There was nothing to do now but to go ahead with the game on Vandy's terms and try to win back to the Hacon-leader pattern, which the boy had earlier allowed. Nik gave the cord a twist about his wrist and the slightest of tugs to make sure his guess was right—that Vandy intended to lead him now. The cord held.

"There is only one way to go," Nik remarked. "They must be ahead of us—perhaps waiting all through these burrows. We'll have to go back. The Patrol will come in that way." Nik hastened to pile up arguments that might influence the boy. "They were with me until we were caught in a storm, and I lost touch—"

He stared into the dark. Vandy was watching him—he must be! And Nik's tone of voice and his expression were the only ways he had to influence the other.

There was a small sound, not quite a laugh, but it held a note of derision. Again Nik was disconcerted. Vandy was a boy, a small boy, someone to be led, protected, guided. The Vandy he met here in the dark was far too mature and able.

"So we go back? I thought you said they had traps there?" The amusement in that was not childlike.

Nik kept to the exact truth. "They do—I broke through one. But you have two blasters—"

"No, I used one up."

Was that the truth? Nik swallowed and began again. "There is still one—and the Disians give themselves away."

"How?"

"With the lures." Nik explained about the swinging lights and the aura given off by Disian bodies.

"Then you don't mean the worm things?" For the first time, Vandy sounded less assured and really puzzled.

"Worm things?"

"They light up when you step near their holes. There were a lot of them in one of the passages. That's where I used up the blaster. But I never saw these other things. This is for true?"

Again he was separating the real from the fantasy, and at the risk of losing contact, Nik kept to the truth.

"This is for real—just as your worm things were for real."

"All right. But to go back there—"

"To go on," Nik pointed out patiently, "is maybe to tangle with something even a blaster can't handle, Vandy. And the Patrol are behind." He took a bigger chance. "This is your story, Vandy, but it has to work out to the right end, doesn't it? Give me my goggles—"

The rope suddenly went lax, and Nik knew he had erred.

"No!" Vandy's response was emphatic. "I keep the goggles. I keep this blaster. If you want to come along, all right—but this is my story, and we're going my way."

The cord tightened once again, pulling Nik forward. For the moment he had lost. He accepted that—but only for the moment.

# SEVENTEEN

It was one of the most difficult things Nik had ever done to allow Vandy to tow him along through the dark. As he followed the tugs of the cord linking them, he tried to plan, to think of some way of regaining Vandy's cooperation.

"Vandy, are you hungry?" Nik made his first attempt on the level he thought might be easiest.

"I ate—while you slept back there!" Again that oddly adult amusement in the reply.

"Good." Nik felt that he must keep talking, that words could unite them better than the cord. "Vandy, you have the goggles. What do you see now?"

The boy seemed to consider that deserving of an answer.

"Just walls lighted up a little—not as much as back there, though."

"No openings in them?" Nik persisted. The possibility of another ambush was always in his mind.

"No—" Vandy began and then corrected himself as the twitch on the cord became a jerk. "There's a door—up there. And—"

But Nik saw this, too. His eyes, so long accustomed to the dark, made out a faint glow. He stopped short, pulling back on the cord.

"No! Wait!"

"Why? What is it, Hacon?"

To his vast relief, Nik heard the compliance in that query. The pull on the cord loosed. Vandy must have halted.

"I don't know yet. What do you see, Vandy—tell me!" That was an order.

"Shine—but just at one place," the boy reported. "It isn't a lure, I think. More like something big and tall just standing there waiting—" With each word a little of the confidence in his tone ebbed.

Then Nik heard a half whisper closer at hand, as if Vandy were shrinking back to him. "Not a story—"

"No, this is not a story, Vandy." He answered that straight.

"It—it wants us to come—so—so it can get us!" Vandy's whisper was a rapid slur of words.

And Nik felt that, also. Just as he had known earlier that sensation of a lurking watcher, so now he was caught—or struck—for that contact was as tangible in its way as a physical blow. Was it hatred, blind, unreasoning malice—that emotion beating at him? He was not sure of what had reached him like a spear point probing into shrinking flesh. He only knew that they were now fronting some danger quite removed from the animal furred hunters, from the Disians and their clawed hounds. This was greater, stronger, and more to be feared than all three of those native perils combined.

The blaster Vandy carried? The rayer in his own belt? Nik watched that gleam. Now he could see that it was as the boy reported—not a twinkling, dancing lure light but an upright narrow bar, unmoving as yet. Did it merely stand there to bar their way or was it gathering force for attack?

"It's—it's calling—!"

Vandy's body pressed against Nik. Perhaps that contact enabled him to feel it also. His arm went about the boy, holding him tight, while with the other hand he stripped off the second pair of goggles Vandy had hung about his neck. To put those on meant freeing the boy now threshing in Nik's grip, crying out with weird high-pitched sounds, almost as if he were trying to mimic the whistles of the Disians.

"Must—go—" The words in Basic broke through those squeals. "It wants—"

Nik knew that already, the pull, the insistent, growing demand. He swung around, dragging the struggling Vandy with him so that his body was now a barrier for the boy. The goggles—he *had* to have sight again. He must get them on!

So, he took the chance of freeing his hold on Vandy. Struggling with fingers made awkward by haste, Nik slipped the straps over his head and adjusted the fastening. Vandy pushed against him, striking out madly with small fists to beat Nik out of his path.

Sight again. Nik blinked at that sudden transition and whirled about. Vandy was already well down the passage toward that pillar of cold light. *Cold* light? Nik wondered. Yet that was true. The cold radiating from that alien thing was eternal—alien as the rest of Dis, in spite of its weird life, was not. The hunters, the Disians, and their hounds were strange to off-world eyes, but this thing of the burrows did not share blood, bones, and flesh with any species remotely akin to life as Nik knew it.

Vandy was running, his head up, his eyes fastened on the thing. And once he reached it—!

The rayer! It might not act against that creature, but wearing goggles as he was, Vandy would be blinded by the ray, momentarily out of action. It was the only answer Nik could think of in those few seconds. He clawed his own goggles down as he fired.

Light flared above and ahead of Vandy as Nik had hoped. The boy cried out and reeled against the wall, his hands to his eyes. That swirling mist of light, strong as fire flames for Nik, must have been scorching for Vandy. Nik hurried forward, caught at the moaning boy, and pulled him back.

The attraction from the thing was shut off as if some knife had snipped a tug cord. They were free! Nik did not halt to put on his own goggles again. The light in the corridor made diamond-bright particles, giving him a start on the backward road. Vandy did not fight him now but lay, a heavy weight, on Nik's shoulder.

Then, it struck at him! Not with the drag to bring him back but with an invisible whip of cold rage so potent that Nik cried out as if a lash had truly been laid across his quivering skin. He had no experience with which to compare this torment, which was not of body at all. A curling thong of sensation first used to punish, then to wrap about him, to pull him in—

He fought that, holding Vandy's dead weight to him, fought the demand to turn, to march back, to deliver himself and the boy into deadly peril. Nik leaned, panting, against the wall. Vandy flung out an arm, his fist striking Nik's face, tangling in the dangling goggles. He was threshing for freedom again but more feebly. A last wriggle brought him out of Nik's weakening grasp—to fall to the pavement.

Nik turned slowly, his teeth set. How much of a charge did that rayer hold? Would it fail him this time? It took infinite effort to bring the weapon up and point it in the general direction of the sparkling mist that still marked his first shot.

Once more that burst of light, bearable, just bearable this time, to his ungoggled eyes. And once again the abrupt cessation of communication freed him. Vandy was on hands and knees, crawling, moaning. Nik caught him by the back of his tunic and pulled him to his feet. He could not carry the boy any farther, but perhaps he could support him along. Nik started them both at the best pace he could muster back toward the terminal chamber.

The second dose of raying must have reactivated some of the remaining sparks from the first, for the light behind them lingered, and Nik did not pause to reset his goggles. He waited for another sign that the thing would pressure them to its will. The blaster—could the blaster stop it more effectively? Vandy had a blaster—but even to stop to find it now might be greater risk than straightforward flight.

They reeled out of the passage into the terminal chamber. Here the glow was only the faintest of glimmers. Nik allowed Vandy to slip to the floor again as he fumbled for the goggles. He was aware of an increasing cold, not in the atmosphere about him but within himself, as if in those two brushes with the alien's will he had been chilled, frozen. He could not still the shaking of his hands.

"Vandy." Nik leaned over the boy. "Come on—" He could

not carry him. Vandy would have to help himself in part. Nik's hands brought him to his feet. But the boy's head hung down on his chest, and his body was racked with even greater shudders than shook Nik.

"This way—"

At least he kept on his feet and moving, as Nik steered him toward the passage that would retrace their journey. As they went, Vandy seemed to regain more conscious will, and the farther they moved from that weird battleground, the firmer his steps became. At last he looked up at Nik.

"What was—that?" His voice shook.

"I don't know."

"Will it—come after—us?"

"I don't know."

They were still in the lighted portion of the passage, but beyond was the dark strip in which the Disian ambush had been. Nik fingered the grip of the rayer. He had to save it for extreme emergencies.

"The blaster," he asked Vandy. "Where is it?"

"It's—it's not much use. I tried it after I used the other up on the worm things." Vandy pulled the off-world weapon from the front of his tunic. "It flickers some—"

Flickering, the sign of power exhaustion! They had not known how long the charges would last, and Vandy had exhausted one and nearly finished the other.

"But it still worked then?" Nik persisted.

"Yes."

A few moments of firing power must remain. That would have to be saved for most dire need—which left the rayer, and how close that was to extinction Nik did not know.

They had reached the end of the lighted sector. Ahead was the dark and all it might contain. Nik looked back. Nothing behind, no glimmer of greater light, none of that menacing wave of broadcast fear. Perhaps whatever they had fronted had been bested by the second use of the ray or was confined for some reason to that special territory in the burrows.

"No!" Vandy's sudden cry startled Nik. The boy was staring ahead as if he sighted some trouble.

"What is it?"

"I don't want to go—not back there!"

"We have to!" Nik's patience and control had worn very thin. He wanted to get back to where he had left Leeds. That desire was an ache throughout his shaking body. Somehow that was a small island of security in this threatening underground world.

"I don't want to!" Vandy repeated, his voice rising. "It may be waiting there—to get us!"

"We left it behind," Nik pointed out, though he was dismayed by the tone of certainty in the boy's voice.

"It's—it's all wrong." Vandy spoke more quietly now. "It's not like all the others—the animals, the worms, the men you told me about. This—this can do things they can't!"

Like slide through solid rock walls? Nik forced his imagination under bonds. He could believe that, but allowing the idea to stop them on the mere suggestion that such action was possible was the rankest stupidity. They could not stay here forever, and he held to the thought of the Patrol's pursuit. To see even Commander i'Inad would give Nik a feeling of relief just now.

"We can't stay here, Vandy." Nik schooled his tone to an evenness and once more took firm hold of his patience. "And we know what is along this corridor. You don't—don't feel the thing ahead right now, do you?"

"No—" The admission was reluctant, but it was the one Nik wanted.

Vandy started on slowly, Nik's hand on his shoulder to steady him. The dark swallowed them up. There was the sound of their own heavy breathing, the click of their boot plates on the rock under them, but Nik could hear nothing else. And there was no light ahead.

"Hurry!" His hold on Vandy tightened as he pushed the boy along.

"I can't!" Vandy's protest was half sob. Since their meeting with the thing, he had lost much of his self-assurance. "Hacon—the Patrol *is* coming?"

"Yes." Nik did not doubt that at all. He wanted to pick up Vandy and run—the feeling of urgency was a goading pain—but he knew he did not have the strength.

Then it came with a jolt—the throbbing whistle—and he could not tell if it broke from ahead or behind them. Nik only knew that the hunt was up, that he and Vandy were the prey.

"Hacon—" That was a gasped whisper.

There was no need to keep the truth from the boy.

"The Disians," Nik said. But had that call been behind or ahead? They could only keep on going. "Watch—for—any—lights—" he told Vandy between panting breaths. "Especially any that move—"

But the way before them remained safely dark. Nik tried to remember how long that dark sector had been. Surely soon they would sight the shrine of the next lighted portion near where the break in the wall gave on the outside.

"Hacon!"

Just as the whistle had been one alert, so this was another, this stroke of fear as sharp as physical pain. Nik paused to look back. No glimmer yet, but he was certain the thing had left its station and was on the prowl behind them.

"Keep going!" he ordered between set teeth. "Keep going!" They must make it back to Leeds.

Vandy, Nik thought, was crying silently now, but he was going on, and they had not yet been trapped in the net of the thing's compelling will. Each glance behind told him the enemy had not yet appeared, not in person, but only in that black blanket of fear, which was one of its weapons.

The whistling began again, not in a single sharp throb but as a low, continuous bleat that filled the ears and became one with the blood of the listener. But, Nik realized, it did not become one with the fear projected by the thing. In fact, it warred with it so that the worst of that other depression lifted. Hunters who were natural enemies—who had *not* joined forces? Dared he hope that they might clash and so give their prey a fighting chance?

"Hacon, that noise—what's happening now?"

"That's the Disians' call. And I don't think the other thing is pleased—"

"Will they fight?"

"I don't know."

"There's a light—now!"

Vandy was right. There was a light ahead. But a second later Nik was filled with a vast relief. It was the end of the dark sector—not an attack signal. Once in the lighted passage, it was not too far back to Leeds.

"Just the passage light!" Relief made that almost a shout. "Keep going, Vandy, keep going!"

The whistling was louder, becoming a din, and under that lurked the fear. It was as if all the life that sulked in these burrows had been stirred into action. Could they, even if they reached Leeds, hold out against such a concentrated attack? But one thing at a time. Leeds knew more of Dis. He might have some answer to such danger. And there was the Patrol. Nik pinned his last hopes on the Patrol.

Vandy was weaving from side to side. Only Nik's grip kept him on his feet, but still he moved to that beacon of light. The pain had returned under Nik's ribs. It was sharp with every breath he drew. They must keep going—they must!

As suddenly as it had burst on their ears, the whistling stopped. Then the silence was worse than the din because Nik was sure it was prelude to action. And yet he did not know whether danger lay ahead or behind. He paused once again to look back and saw—

Lure lights! More than one, not only waving in the middle of the passage, but also from above and the sides, as if the Disian hounds clung to the walls and roof.

Nik and Vandy burst out of the dark and stumbled on. The boy looked back and gave a choked cry. Nik needed no alert against the nightmare boiling up there—the hounds coming at a scuttle.

"Vandy—give me the blaster!"

Nik jerked the weapon away from him. The charge might be almost gone, but perhaps enough remained to take care of the first attack wave. Only he must not use it until he was sure that no other party waited ahead to box them in.

Jointed clawed legs, round armored bodies—five—six—more coming through the dark. No sign of their Disian masters, if that was the relationship between the two so dissimilar species. They were slacking where the full light began. Nik thrust Vandy on with a powerful shove. The boy broke into a tottering run.

Nik was thankful that the creatures were not yet pressing the attack he feared. Then he wondered at that forbearance. Their rate of advance did not press the fugitives—why? He and Vandy were past the break in the wall. Just let them reach Leeds, and they would be able to hold off this pack with the second blaster the captain had.

Scuttle—click—but no more whistling.

"Keep going, Vandy!" Nik ordered. Then he saw their luck was beginning to fail; the creatures were drawing closer.

A throbbing whistle—

"Run, Vandy!" Nik got that out and swung around to face the pack. He pressed the firing button on the blaster.

A full beam answered! For an instant, he thought Vandy had been wrong about the weapon as that fan of fire crisped the first wave of crawlers. Then a warning flicker rippled down the ray.

But the first burst had had its effect. The second group hesitated at the cindered bodies of their fellows. Nik backed away. Did he have charge enough left for a second shot? He must save that. And afterwards—the rayer?

Every stride he took was that much gained. Now the first of the pursuers had scrambled over the dead and were tentatively following. Just let them collect in a body once more, and perhaps he could kill enough to discourage the rest thoroughly. Such a thin hope—but about the only one Nik had left.

# EIGHTEEN

The blast had taught the Disian creatures a measure of caution. Their advance slowed, and Nik hastened his own pace. He was sure Vandy was well ahead. And every moment he won, every stride he took, was a small victory.

But that breathing space was only temporary. Nik was warned by a new massing of the pursuers. And then he noted something that quickly revised his estimate of their intelligence. They were passing from one to another, over rounded shell backs, fragments of rock. Whether these were to be used as shields or weapons, Nik did not know, but he quickened his retreat.

A stone as big as his fist came at him, and he ducked. But his reactions were slow, and the missile grazed his head just above the goggle strap, so that he swayed back against the wall on his left. A blow on his shoulder before he had shaken free of the daze of that first hit numbed his left arm. He had not dropped the blaster, and for the second time he fired.

The beam was short, snapping out in a matter of seconds, but it curled up a row of the stone throwers and gave Nik time to lurch out of range. He had to make it—he had to!

At least he was coming out of the fog of pain that filled his head, and he had bought some more time. Time he could use—

"Hacon!"

The call sounded far away, but it pulled Nik together, and sent him scrambling ahead.

"Coming, Vandy." Had he answered that aloud?

An opening—the chamber where he had left Leeds! With a lung-emptying effort, Nik flung himself forward through that—and crashed into utter darkness.

"—easy—easy—easy—"

One word ringing in his aching head. What was easy? A faint stir of curiosity moved somewhere in the depths of Nik's darkened mind.

"—do as exactly as I say—say—say—" Echoes growing farther and farther away.

Do as who says—why? Again Nik was pushed into thought in spite of a desire not to be at all.

"—when they come, you will say this—this—this—"

Always the echo ringing in his ears as had the Disian whistles. Disian whistles! Memory awoke and prodded fiercely. Nik opened his eyes. There was a glimmer about him, a ghostly pallid counterfeit of true light. He was lying on his back, and his shoulder ached with a sullen, angry persistence.

"You understand it all now?" These were words with the crack of authority, a demand for obedience.

"Yes."

Vandy! There was no mistaking Vandy's voice. Vandy and— Leeds! Then they had reached the captain. But Leeds had to know about the hunters. They would be coming; they would erupt here! How long had he, Nik, been out? Another stone must have brought him down just as he came out of the passage—

"Captain?" That did not come out as a word. It was a rusty, croaking sound. Nik tired to turn his head, and a jab of pain followed, so intense as to make him sick. He retched dryly before he called again, "Captain?"

Movement through the gloom. Nik dared not move his head, but now he could see the shadow looming over him.

"Captain?" he asked for the third time.

"Right." But Leeds did not stoop. He remained a pillar hardly visible to Nik.

The dark! Nik made a vast effort and brought his hand up to his head. Before his fingers reached his eyes, he knew the answer. His goggles were gone. And he also guessed who wore them now. Just as that black and alien cloud of fear had closed on him back when he fronted the shining thing, so now he was uneasy. There was something wrong here—what?

"So, you're awake?" The cool voice rang in Nik's ears. In this half light, he could not read the expression on Leeds' face, but that tone—As if the captain were not standing there but had retreated to a far distance.

"The Disians—they are coming—" Nik gave his warning first. Again he tried to move, to see the opening through which they might rage. But the pain in his head and the answering agony in his shoulder kept him quiet.

"They haven't arrived yet." Again a certain cool disassociation with such concerns. "Vandy!" Leeds' head turned. "Get going!"

Going where, Nik wondered.

"Sorry." That was the captain. "You might have worked out—otherwise. Only I have to cut all losses now—"

Words that did not mean anything, or did they? Nik's wariness was acute. He made an effort, which left him sick and trembling, but he raised himself up on the elbow of his sound arm. Leeds stepped back.

"Where—are—you—going?" Nik got that out.

"To meet destiny—otherwise the Patrol."

"Back?"

"Back."

"Don't think I can—yet—"

"You won't be asked to try."

It took a long second for that to sink past the pain. Then Nik put a new fear into words.

"You mean—I stay here?"

Leeds was still retreating. "You stay. As you just said, you can't make it, and there's trouble coming. Hacon the hero is the proper rear guard, isn't he? Right in character to the end."

Nik still could not believe it. He pushed up to a sitting position and watched the dusky space about him twist sickeningly.

One determination held through that whirling punishment. He would not beg.

Click of boots on rock—Leeds *was* going! He had Vandy back, he would make his deal with the Patrol—and he was leaving Nik as a rear guard or rather as an offering to whatever Disian pursuit existed. Yes, Nik was the price the captain was willing to pay for his own clear escape!

And what that sorted itself out in Nik's mind, he felt such rising anger as he had never known before in his short life. All the frustration and hatred stored up during the years in the Dipple were fuel for that rage. There had been nothing then he could do to fight back. But here and now he could do something, if it were only to draw after Leeds the very trouble he feared. Nik might not be able to walk, but he could crawl.

He hunched together, gathering strength. Goggles were gone again. Once he left this chamber, he would be plunged into the dark. His right hand moved along his belt—the rayer was gone. Well, he could not have expected Leeds to overlook that, could he? Nothing but his bare hands and the determination not to be counted out armed him now.

Nik made himself wait, hoping that he presented to Leeds, should the captain glance back, the picture of dejected submission to fate. It was still hard to think clearly. Only rage gave him the strength to make a move.

He could no longer hear the irregular tapping marking the captain's limping progress. And there had been no sound from Vandy at all. Nik raised his head. As far as he could see, he was alone. He could not get to his feet, but there were still his hands and knees—

Nik had to fight with every scrap of will within him to enter the dark beyond. No sound of footfalls ahead. But he was listening, too, for what might be behind.

The way might have been shorter for a man able to walk it, but to Nik, creeping along, it seemed endless. He could put so little weight on his left arm that even his crawl was one-sided and slow.

Leeds and Vandy must have already reached the root room. Nik strove to hurry, but the greater effort brought back his giddiness.

At least there was no whistling and none of that invisible menace cast by the other thing.

Nik tried to piece together what had happened in the immediate past. He had been running from the hounds and had just reached the lighted chamber when—Had one of the stones struck him or could Leeds have deliberately knocked him out?

Since their meeting at the island hill, Leeds had needed Nik—first to get the supplies, then to help him regain control of Vandy. Yes, Leeds had needed Nik. But now—did he need him any longer? Nik had been the one who had actually removed Vandy from the HS villa back on Korwar. Now Leeds could say that he had nothing to do with the kidnaping. He could return Vandy and make a much better bargain without Nik than he could if he tried to cover him with the same immunity. Leeds' present action was good sense if the captain wanted to make the best deal. Nik's sustaining anger grew with his realization of his own stupidity. Leeds had used him from the start—with bait he knew that Nik could not resist, a new face. And that, too, had all been part of the deception. There had been no new techniques used on him, no way to keep the operation intact for long. He was a temporary tool, to be used and discarded. Leeds had probably never even bought him into the Guild!

Nik crawled on. He wanted Leeds' throat between his two hands—that was the burning desire filling every part of him. But Leeds had Vandy, all ready to bargain with the Patrol. If only that bargain could be marred! To fail now would be worse for Leeds than any other hurt Nik could deal him.

What had been the bargain as Leeds had outlined it? To get a ship and free passage off Dis—then to release Vandy in a suit to be picked up by the Patrol. Nik licked his lips. Vandy released in a suit? Now he did not believe that either. Vandy could either be such a threat that his death *must* ensue, or he could be used again in some game for Leeds' advantage.

What had been Leeds' parting shot? Hacon the hero—Well, there was no future for Nik Kolherne, even if he were able to reach his own kind again and not be pulled down by some nightmare of these burrows. But he might accomplish something against Leeds—he had to! And perhaps he could make sure that the trickery that started in that Korwarian garden would finish here—that Vandy would not continue to be bait or loot or whatever Leeds wanted him to be.

The sickly light of the root chamber was ahead, and Nik remembered the drop from the crevice to the floor below. Would Leeds be lingering there or would he already have herded his captive on into the dark ways? Nik clung to the thin, very weak hope that the two were still in the root chamber. His chances of doing something in the passages beyond that point were close to the vanishing point. He wriggled forward to look into the room.

The light was greater because he had come out of the dark. Nik surveyed the scene with a deliberation he forced on himself. Leeds and Vandy were both here. The captain sat in much the same position as Nik had seen him—was it hours or days before?—examining the ties that held the splint on his wounded leg. His movements were slow, and he winced once. Nik was certain his injury was a drag.

Vandy was within arm's distance of his captor. He wore goggles, but his arms were tied behind him. Nik longed for one of the stones the hounds had thrown, though whether he could have used it to any purpose, he did not know. If he came into sight through the crevice, Leeds could pick him off before he reached the floor of the chamber.

Apparently the captain was not planning to move on at once. He opened a ration container and held it first to Vandy's mouth and then his own, so they shared the contents. Nik's empty stomach was a new source of pain as he watched.

"We shall give your friends"—Leeds' voice was still cool and light—"some more time. They were probably misled by the zeal of your late champion when he sent the tracer bag downstream. But you have your own way of contacting them, haven't you, Vandy? And I would suggest you use that gadget now."

Little of the boy's face could be seen below the masking goggles, but Nik noted the fining down of cheek and chin, the hollows beneath the grimy skin.

"You'll blast anybody that tries to come—"

Once more Nik heard that new maturity in Vandy's voice.

"On the contrary, my boy, I will welcome them with open arms. There is certainly no future here. And to return you to your anxious friends is a good way to get out, whole skin and free. You saw what I did to the man who brought you here in the first place."

"Hacon said—"

Leeds laughed. "My poor boy, please understand the simplest of truths—there is no Hacon, except in the wonderland of your own imagination. That port rat who pulled you into this mess is Nik Kolherne from the Dipple. He is not even a member of the Guild."

"You are." Vandy held to his point.

"I am Guild when it suits me to be and no time else! There's a big reward waiting for the man who returns Vandy i'Akrama—I want that and my ship. We'll make a bargain, and that is the last you'll see of me, I assure you. After all, Vandy, you have only to tell the truth. I *am* bringing you back; I *have* disposed of the man who stole you from Korwar. There isn't any scanner on this world or any other that wouldn't pass me clean on those two questions."

"What'll happen to Hacon—to him back there?" Vandy asked slowly.

"He'll stay and nurse a sore head until the Patrol wants to pick him up."

"But there were those other—other things. What if they find him first?"

Leeds shrugged. "All right, what if they do? He's no friend of yours. Now I'm telling you, boy, get out that fancy little com of yours and give it a tinkle. I heard that Commander i'Inad is with the Patrol—"

"Staven?" Vandy's head came up. "Staven's here? You'll have to untie me or I can't use the mike, you know."

"Yes. One hand, Vandy, just one hand. You're a slippery little fish, and you're not wriggling off until we are all safe and sound again. Turn around—"

The boy, on his knees, twisted around so Leeds could get at the ties on his wrists. Nik measured the distance he must drop, the space before the roots could give him limited cover. In his weak state, he had to have more time—

Vandy's free hand was at the breast of his tunic and came out with something cupped in the palm. He put it close to his lips and appeared to be breathing on it. Leeds watched him closely, the drawn blaster resting on his outthrust splinted leg.

Not a chance, thought Nik, not one little chance unless Leeds moved. In this light the captain's face was a blue mask of goggles and shadowed flesh. Blue—!

Nik stared, alerted now to the odd change taking place in the misty light of the chamber. It was blue! Not only that, but there was also a distinct chill in the air. He levered himself up so that he now crouched in the crevice. As yet, neither of those below apparently noticed the alteration in the atmosphere.

Movement! Nik wrenched his attention from Leeds and the boy to focus on movement among the entwined roots of the weird growth. Something alike in size and shape to those worm roots was edging out into the open. More than one—from other directions—!

"Any contact yet?" Leeds demanded.

Vandy was quiet. Then he stiffened. His hand dropped from his mouth, and his lips shaped a cry. Leeds followed the boy's horrified gaze and went into action. Roots and that which moved from them crisped in an instant.

Only it was not the crawlers that were to be feared the most. Vandy was on his feet, backing away, not from Leeds or the remainder of the crawlers, but from a space below and to the left of Nik's perch. It was there, pulsating, growing, from nothingness into the totally alien shining thing.

Leeds fired again, this time directing his blaster at the growing core of light. And it absorbed the raw off-world energy of the weapon, seeming to suck the power away until Leeds looked down with terrified bewilderment at an empty tube. He began to back away as had Vandy.

The thing made no attack, no outward threat—it merely was. Nik wanted to draw back into the dark of the tunnel. Only one thing held him where he was—Vandy's face, upturned a little now to front the unknown.

Leeds had been right. Vandy was here only because of Nik Kolherne. And Nik Kolherne was finished any way you reckoned it. Better make it as good a finish as he had the chance to—

"Leeds!" Nik shouted. "The rayer—use the rayer!"

That blinding light had stopped the thing back in the tunnel and might be the only defense now.

Leeds' foot caught in a root tangle when he tried to move. Had Nik's call pierced through the wall of Vandy's terror? The boy flung himself on the captain, pawing at the other's belt as Leeds strove to throw him off. Something clattered, spun across the rock, and stopped at the very edge of the stream.

The pillar of light was growing closer to Nik. To reach that weapon, he would have to pass it, and every nerve shrank from any contact with that light. Vandy crept toward the rayer, but Leeds suddenly caught the boy by one foot and hurled him back and away. Had the captain gone mad?

Nik gathered his feet under him. He looked away determinedly from the pillar and concentrated on the rayer. Then he swung down from the crevice. The fringe of the light struck his left side. It was a cold so intense that he was numbed, and he tottered rather than leaped for the rayer.

A shout, and Leeds threw himself as if to intercept Nik. Sprawling forward, the younger man flung out his arm in a last desperate try, and his fingers touched the smooth metal. Somehow he turned over, aimed at the towering pillar of icy light, and pressed the button, praying that all its charge had not been exhausted.

There was a flash, blinding. And all the air was filled with a moaning—or did he feel rather than hear that? He saw Leeds crawling, his splinted leg trailing behind him, heading into the light.

"Leeds!" Had Nik shouted that warning aloud or was it swallowed up in the noise that was a part of the air, of him, of all this buried world?

At any rate, the captain did not heed. He crept on into the swirling light. And Nik knew that, wearing the goggles, the other had been blinded. Then he saw Vandy staggering forward, also being drawn on into the place where the pillar had stood.

Nik made a last effort, rolled his body across the boy's path, and threw up his good arm to prevent Vandy from merging with the chaos that had swallowed Leeds. He was still holding the weakly struggling boy, though he did not know it, when Vandy's call was answered.

The window was too high for Nik to see through, but outside was real sun. A bar of its light was warm across his hands and face. This was the first time he could remember rising from the bunk in the drab room and moving about. How long had he been here—and where was *here*?

Nik thought he *was* awake now, but for a long time he must have dreamed. Or could he call it dreaming just to remember every searing fact of his past, all the hurt from the moment he had been found in the wrecked ship up to that last sight of the burrows of Dis when he had concentrated on saving Vandy from the thing that walked there?

"Hacon!"

Nik continued to stare up at a cloud, which was the only moving thing the window allowed him to view. But he knew he heard that call in the here-and-now, not out of memory.

"There is no Hacon," he said harshly before he turned, his hand flying up in the old gesture to mask a face he had not dared to touch since his waking.

Vandy was there and a tall man in uniform—a man with Vandy's eyes.

"No need—" The tall man caught Nik's wrist and pulled his fingers down with a strength the other could not withstand. "Look!"

He was holding a mirror at the level of Nik's eyes, and the other could not defy that order.

"Not—not true!" Nik was shaken.

"What is not true? That you do not see correctly or that Leeds added another lie to all the rest?" asked the man with Vandy's eyes. "You see the truth—that face remains. Now, does the rest of it?"

"The rest of what?" Nik asked dazedly.

"Of Hacon?"

"But Hacon never existed—really."

"Did he not? My son created a man and then found him—"

Nik was still bewildered. But there was a smile on Vandy's face, and the man was continuing.

"My son dreamed of a hero, but he found the truth under the shell of that dream, masked by it. So, in creating a myth, he also brought forth new truth. We have in the past days learned what lay behind that mask, in the memory of Nik Kolherne—who is dead—"

So compelling was the emphasis in those words that Nik glanced at the bunk, half-expecting to see himself lying inertly there.

"For Hacon, Vandy and I have a certain responsibility. And we are deeply in his debt."

"But—I stole Vandy—took him to Dis—"

"And there you saved him, several times over, I would say. No—you are not Hacon, but neither are you any longer Nik Kolherne. Suppose you try being the man whose face you have earned. The price for a son comes high among our people. We will remember that when we meet with Hacon—"

Nik's hand went to his face again, but now he fingered smooth flesh. Only, more than his face had somehow been mended. He was not altogether sure he understood what the warlord meant, but he was willing to learn—to learn how to be someone who was not Hacon and a hero, or Nik Kolherne, who was nothing at all. There was no mask needed, and he had come out of the night indeed!